EXECUTIVE SUITE

EXECUTIVE

SUITE

by
Cameron
Hawley

HOUGHTON MIFFLIN COMPANY · BOSTON
The Riverside Press · Cambridge

TO
ELAINE

Friday
June 22

*"The king
is dead . . ."*

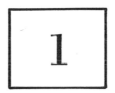

NEW YORK CITY
2.30 P.M. EDT

A minute or two before or after two-thirty on the afternoon of the twenty-second of June, Avery Bullard suffered what was subsequently diagnosed as a cerebral hemorrhage. After fifty-six years, somewhere deep within the convoluted recesses of his brain, a tiny artery finally yielded to the insistent pounding of his hard-driven bloodstream. In the instant of that infinitesimal failure, the form and pattern of a world within a world was changed. An industrial empire was suddenly without an emperor. The president of the Tredway Corporation was dead— and no vice-president had been designated for succession.

It was not a coincidence that Avery Bullard had been thinking, in the minutes immediately preceding his death, about who his new executive vice-president might be. It was a question that had been in his mind many times during these three months since John Fitzgerald had died. Today, he had thought of almost nothing else. This morning George Caswell had warned him again that the investment fund executives were asking why a second-in-command of the Tredway Corporation had not been designated. "You can't blame them," Caswell had said. "Continuity of management is an important consideration to anyone holding large blocks of an industrial security."

Caswell had been right, of course. Avery Bullard had willingly admitted that. If they were to float a debenture issue in the fall, they would need the support of the investment trusts. Those crew-cut boys who analyzed securities for them liked to see everything done just as their textbooks at Harvard Business had said it should be done. A big corporation was supposed to have an executive vice-president. The chart didn't look right if you didn't have one. All right, Bullard had told Caswell, there would be no more delay. An executive vice-president would be elected at the board meeting on Tuesday. Before midnight tonight he would decide who the man would be. The only reason he had delayed as long as he had was to give himself a chance to check some top prospects outside the corporation. He had wanted to be sure that there was no better man available than one of his own vice-presidents. He was down to the last name on the list—Bruce Pilcher. All the others had been crossed off. He was having lunch with Pilcher at noon. Caswell had agreed that Pilcher was worthy of some consideration. "Most people seem to think he's done quite a job since he stepped in as president of Odessa," Caswell had said. "Apparently he's a very clever operator."

Five minutes before his death, Avery Bullard had left the small private dining room on the fifth floor of the Chippendale Building where he had lunched with Pilcher and old Julius Steigel, chairman of the board of the Odessa Stores Corporation. Waiting for the elevator, he had had no premonitory hint of the disaster that lay ahead of him. He felt unusually well. The luncheon had been an unqualified success. He had proved that Bruce Pilcher was not the man for the job and, to his secret amusement, he had done it without giving either Pilcher or Steigel the slightest suspicion of the true motive behind his visit.

In the sheltering privacy of the deserted corridor, Avery Bullard permitted himself a guarded smile as he recalled what Caswell had said about Pilcher. A very clever operator? It had taken less than two minutes for Mr. Pilcher to trap himself. He

[4]

had asked Pilcher a casual question about the net worth of the holding company that owned the twenty-six Odessa furniture stores. That was all it had taken to bait the trap. Pilcher had leaped like a starved wolf. You could almost see his mind working behind his cold gray eyes . . . the money-man who had caught the blood scent of a multimillion-dollar deal.

The elevator door started to slide and Avery Bullard plunged through the opening. He was a big man, six-four and heavy-muscled, but he moved so quickly that he had turned and was facing the door before it was fully open.

Yes, Pilcher was a money-man. They were a type. It was easy to spot them. You could always tell one by that cold fire in his eyes. It was not the hot fire of the man who would never interrupt a dream to calculate the risk, but the cold fire of the man whose mind was geared to the rules of the money game. It was a game that was played with numbers on pieces of paper . . . common into preferred, preferred into debentures, debentures into dollars, dollars into long-term capital gains. It was the net dollars after tax that were important. They were the numbers on the scoreboard, the runs that crossed the plate, the touchdowns, the goals. Net dollars were the score markers of the money-man's game. Nothing else mattered. A factory wasn't a living, breathing organism. It was only a dollar sign and a row of numbers after the Plant & Equipment item on the balance sheet. Their guts didn't tighten when they heard a big Number Nine bandsaw sink its whining teeth into hard maple. Their nostrils didn't widen to the rich musk of walnut or the sharply pungent blast from the finishing room. When they saw a production line they looked with blind eyes, not feeling the counterpoint beat of their hearts or the pulsing flow of hot blood or the trigger-set tenseness of lungs that were poised to miss a breath with every lost beat on the line.

No, Pilcher wasn't the man . . . and Pilcher was the last name on the list. None of them had been right . . . not Clark, or Rutledge, or that fellow over at United, or any of the rest. There had been something wrong with all of them.

Caswell's voice echoed in his mind. "Do you think it's possible that you've set your standard a little too high? If you're looking for another Avery Bullard I can tell you right now that you'll never find him. He doesn't exist. They made only one and then they broke the mold."

He had denied it then and now he denied it to himself again. He wasn't looking for another Avery Bullard. Why should he? He was only fifty-six. There were nine full years ahead of him before he was sixty-five. They would be the best years of his life. He could move fast now. His hand was sure and steady. There would be none of the fumbling, none of the false starts, none of the mistakes of inexperience that had slowed him down during those first years of building Tredway. He could accomplish as much in the next nine years as he had in the last twenty. A man wasn't old at fifty-six. He was just in the prime of life!

"I hope you find someone who will let you take it a little easier yourself," Caswell had said. "You absorb a lot of punishment, Avery, the way you drive yourself."

Punishment? Avery Bullard smiled. George Caswell didn't understand. It wasn't punishment! It was what a man had to have to stay alive. When you lost it you were dead.

The elevator door opened and Avery Bullard broadshouldered his way through the lobby crowd, driving himself with the self-perpetuating fire of his enormous energy. As he passed, men and women looked up at him, not with recognition but because there was something in his face that commanded attention.

His decision was made. Now he would pick one of his own men as executive vice-president. He would select one of the five. He'd do it tonight. It would be cleared at the board meeting next week. But who would it be . . . which one of the five?

His quick-roving eye saw a Western Union sign at the far end of the lobby. An idea flashed. He would get them together tonight for one last look before he made his final decision. Yes, that was the way to do it. He'd put some kind of a proposition before them . . . anything . . . the possibility of building a new factory in North Carolina. It would hit them cold. No one knew that he had even been thinking about it. Yes, that would be a good test. He would toss out the idea and then sit back . . .

[6]

watching, listening, judging. Then he would pick the man who showed up best. Yes, that's what he *had* to do . . . pick one . . . only one. The others would probably be sore as hell . . . throw them off their pace for a few days . . . but they'd get over it. They were good men . . . all of them . . . had to be . . . wouldn't be his men if they weren't. They'd understand why only one of them could be executive vice-president . . . Wall Street wanted it that way. But it wouldn't mean anything . . . just a name on a chart. Nothing would really change . . . nothing at all . . . not for nine years. Nine years was a long time. Anything could happen in nine years. Who would have guessed, even a year ago, that Fitzgerald would die?

The girl lounging behind the counter of the Western Union office moved a pad of message blanks toward him.

"Telegram," he said in brusque command. "Miss Erica Martin, Tredway Tower, Millburgh, Pennsylvania. Taking next train. Call executive committee meeting six o'clock. Sign it Bullard."

The girl looked up, parting her lips for the standard protest that he must write out his own message, but in the same instant she found herself touching pencil to paper. She wrote rapidly, hurried by some unaccountable fear that she might displease him. When she looked up, ready to check the message, he was gone. A crumpled dollar bill lay before her on the counter.

Outside the revolving door there was a blaze of summer sun, suddenly bright against the shadowed lobby, and Avery Bullard glanced down to protect his eyes. He saw the glitter of a small coin and, before he thought, stooped to pick it up. It wasn't a coin, only a bus token, and he felt a moment of self-consciousness as he saw that the street crowd was watching him. He quickly palmed the token into his pocket and, narrowing his eyes protectively, searched the stream of traffic for an empty taxicab. A windshield mirrored the sun and for an instant he was strangely blinded, as if fire had washed over his eyeballs, but it was a sensation that passed almost as quickly as it came.

A cab pulled to the curb, splashing the flood of dirty water that was streaming down the gutter from an open hydrant at the corner. Unflinching at the spatter, Avery Bullard reached out to clamp a possessive hand on the opening door. The woman passenger offered the driver a bill that he rejected with a shrug. Hurriedly, Avery Bullard took out his wallet, made change and, as the woman stepped out, he pushed past her, leaning forward, reaching out with his right hand—

Then it happened. A whiplash of pain exploded behind his eyes. Instantly, a giant force was twisting his head to the right until it seemed that the cords of his neck were being torn from his shoulders, disembodying his brain, washing it through the whirlpool of a crimson flood and then on into the engulfing blackness of a silent cave.

2.32 P.M. EDT

Patrolman Ed Canady, idly watching the two men who were repairing the leaking fire hydrant, saw the quick-gathering crowd around the taxicab in front of the Chippendale Building. He walked toward it, professionally calm, long-arming his way through the rapidly growing semicircle.

The limp figure of a big man sprawled before him, half inside of the cab, face down, legs hanging grotesquely out through the open door.

Canady took a deep breath and leaned in over the body, half expecting the reek of liquor. There was no odor of alcohol.

"For crissake, why's everything gotta happen to me?" a voice whined and Canady looked up. The taxi driver, slack-lipped and morose, was staring myopically over the back of the seat.

Canady froze his face. "What happened, Mac?"

"Nothing, I'm telling you. Crissake, I don't know nothing. I'm counting the change on a fare, see? Then I hears something go bump and a dame on the sidewalk yells and this is it."

Canady cut him off with a grunt, backing, twisting his shoulders out through the door.

A radio patrol car had stopped across the street and Canady cupped his hand and soft-shouted, "Ambulance."

The sergeant in the patrol car nodded and Canady turned,

making a routine but futile effort to force back the close-pressing crowd. Then he leaned inside the cab again, bending over the body, his fingertips searching for the tell-tale bulge of a wallet that might help him establish identification. There was nothing in any of the pockets that could be reached without moving the body.

Canady looked up at the driver who was still staring sullenly over the back of the seat. "He give you an address?"

"Crissake, didn't I tell you? The guy don't even open his peeper. Before I know nothing he takes a dive."

The policeman's lips tightened and he reached for his notebook, flipping pages until he found a blank. With a stub pencil he wrote, "2.35 P.M. Unidentified man collapsed on street front of Chippendale Building."

His glance slipped past the edge of the notebook. For the first time he noticed that the right foot of the prostrate body was dangling in the swirl of dirty water that was flooding down the gutter. He reached down, cupping his hand under the ankle, starting to lift the leg, but his sense of touch transmitted the feeling of sodden resistance. He loosened his hold and let the foot drop back again. The water flooded and twisted around the shoe, wrapping a streamer of wet paper over the instep, and then another and another until the jam of debris had completely hidden the highly polished leather.

2.36 P.M. EDT

Bruce Pilcher leaned against the ornamentally carved window casing on the Madison Avenue side of Julius Steigel's private office, smoking a cigarette as if he were practicing an art of which he was a confident master.

"It is my professional opinion," he said slowly, stylizing his voice in an attempt at humor, "that we have just entertained a damned clever horse trader."

Steigel grinned, puffing his cheeks. He was a round little elf of a man with a pleasantly patriarchal face. "Don't I tell you? With

[9]

a man like Mr. Avery Bullard it is a pleasure to do business. You make a good deal with Mr. Avery Bullard, you are not taking candy from a baby."

Pilcher bowed theatrically. "Of course, my dear Mr. Steigel, precisely the same thing could be said of yourself."

The old man smiled, pleased but modest. He had begun life as an itinerant peddler of tinware along the backroads of eastern Pennsylvania. Now, at seventy, he was a multimillionaire, a financial status that he had achieved with remarkably little change in the exterior manifestations of character. He remained an openly simple man with the same incipient twinkle that had once charmed tight-pursed Pennsylvania Dutch housewives into buying his angel food cake tins at ten cents above the town price.

Pilcher's eyes followed a lazy drift of cigarette smoke. "You're quite sure that Bullard is interested?"

The old man nodded. "Naturally he don't say so. Mr. Avery Bullard is a very smart man. He don't say he's anxious to buy my stores like I don't say I'm anxious to sell. But the napkin tells. You see the napkin? When we are through eating he puts it on the table and it is all twisted like a rope."

Pilcher bowed again. "My compliments on your powers of observation."

"Some things, my boy, you learn when you are a peddler. The lady is twisting her apron, pretty soon she is handing you the money—just the way Mr. Avery Bullard is pretty soon handing us five million dollars—maybe six."

Bruce Pilcher rearranged his long legs, straightening his trouser seams with his thin fingers. "You're not thinking of cash are you, Julius?"

Steigel rolled his head. "Cash? Yes, cash. What else?"

Words waited behind Bruce Pilcher's lips until the split second when he felt the timing was right. "You may have forgotten my mentioning it when I originally suggested the possibility of this deal, but there are ten thousand shares of unissued common stock in the Tredway treasury."

"The cash is better," Steigel said uneasily.

"I wonder." There was an overtone of cunning in Pilcher's

voice. "Tredway stock is widely scattered. There are no big holdings. With a solid block of ten thousand shares you'd have representation on the board of directors—not too far from a practical working control of the company. You'd have Avery Bullard right under your thumb."

Steigel spread his hands, smiling. "Why do I want him under my thumb? My thumb is too old. This year I am seventy."

"It wouldn't be necessary to carry the load yourself," Pilcher said, elaborately casual. "I'd be quite willing to take over for you —sit on the board—represent your interests."

The old man hunched his shoulders and his neck seemed to disappear.

Pilcher, sensing resistance, pressed on. "A lot could be done with Tredway. Excellent production facilities but inadequate management. The real trouble, of course, is that Bullard's running a completely one-man show."

"That's bad?" the old man asked blandly.

"Of course. All you have to do is look at the ratio of net return to invested capital to realize that—"

A flutter of Steigel's pudgy hand cut him off. "My boy, you are a good lawyer—you know the law. Also you are a good financial man—you know stocks and bonds. I know something, too. I know companies. All my life I watch companies. I want to know why they are a success. Always it is the same answer. You hear, always the same answer—always one man. You remember that, Mr. Pilcher. Always when you find a good company it is what you call a one-man show."

"Perhaps during the early stages, the period of expansion and development, but when a corporation—"

"You have the right man, you have a good company. You don't have the right man, you have nothing."

Pilcher hesitated. The size of his salary prompted perpetual diplomacy, yet his ambition forced him on. "Perhaps the point I want to make, Julius, is that a company needs a different management technique during different stages in its development. While it's going through a period of major expansion, breaking into new ground, there's no doubt that it takes a two-fisted dictator with a whip in both hands to make things go—an Avery Bullard. However, when that period is over future success depends upon efficiency of operation and maintenance of position. Then you need a different kind of management."

A twinkle played around Julius Steigel's watery eyes. "Nice speech, Mr. Pilcher."

"It's true. Take any of the big corporations. The promoters who put them together weren't the men who stayed on to make them operate."

"Mr. Bullard don't do so bad. Last year, four million net after taxes."

"It should have been twice that on the volume of business they did."

The twinkle broadened to a grin. "Mr. Pilcher, if Tredway is such a bad company why do you say I should take stock instead of the cash? A bad company, it is a bad stock."

Pilcher shook his head. "It's an excellent company—potentially. All they need down there is some modern management—sound organization. Do you realize that Bullard doesn't even have a second in command? Fitzgerald, who was executive vice-president, died last March and Bullard still hasn't appointed anyone else to take his place. There are five vice-presidents, all with equal authority. Imagine!"

Steigel's grin broke again. "They have Mr. Bullard. Maybe that is enough."

Bruce Pilcher chose to disregard the obvious fact that Julius Steigel was having a bit of fun at his expense. "Suppose something would happen to Avery Bullard?"

"He is a young man."

"Fifty-six on the nineteenth of September," Pilcher flashed back, hoping to impress the old man with the meticulous accuracy of his information.

Steigel shrugged. "Fifty-six is a young man. When I am only fifty-six I am just getting started. You know how old I am, Mr. Pilcher? My next birthday, seventy-one."

Dutifully, Bruce Pilcher picked up the cue. "Not really, Mr. Steigel! No one would ever suspect it."

"Seventy-one," the old man repeated, his eyes glinting guardedly with the satisfaction of again having bested his new president in an argument. He disliked Pilcher but it was very necessary to keep from showing it. He needed him. Business had gotten so complicated these last few years that you had to have someone like Pilcher. It wasn't enough any more to know how to run stores and buy and sell furniture. Last year alone, Pilcher had saved almost two hundred thousand dollars in taxes.

A siren moaned to a stop on the avenue below the window and Pilcher turned, looking down, accepting the chance to avert his eyes. He was keenly disappointed at his failure to maneuver himself into a Tredway directorship. Odessa was only a rung on the way up. Tredway was the top of the ladder. If he could get on the Tredway board there was no telling where he might go. Avery Bullard would be no harder to handle than old Julius Steigel had been.

The ambulance had stopped and the thick crescent of the crowd opened and closed like gaping pincers, swallowing up the hurrying man in white. Pilcher sharpened his interest only enough to block the aggravating drone of old Julius' voice. The man in white was signaling and the driver was pulling out a stretcher, swinging it to force back the crowd, straightening it, bending down to lift the body.

Pilcher began to speak but his voice froze in his throat. The man they were putting on the stretcher was unmistakably Avery Bullard.

The old man was at his side now, puffing a little as he strained over the sill. "It looks maybe like—"

"It's Avery Bullard," Pilcher said, sharply grim.

A low moan escaped from Julius Steigel's lips.

A blanket blotted out the figure on the stretcher and Pilcher swung around, standing stiffly, his eyes narrowed. "He's dead."

Julius Steigel was an old man, at the moment a very old man, mystified and staring. "Only a minute ago you are saying, what if something should happen."

Pilcher brushed past him, snatching at the telephone on the desk. "This is Mr. Pilcher. Get me Caswell & Co.," he barked at the receiver. Then a warning flashed in his mind . . . George Caswell would be too inquisitive . . . he was a Tredway director.

"Wait!" he commanded. "Get me Slade & Finch. Mr. Wingate."

He covered the mouthpiece with his hand. "Might as well salvage what we can out of this."

He was talking to the old man's slumped shoulders, black against the light of the window. The sound of the siren faded away and finally lost itself in the overtone of street noises.

The call came through. "Wingate? This is Bruce Pilcher. Now make this fast!" He flicked a glance at his wrist watch. "There's only twenty-one minutes before the bell. Start selling Tredway common short. Feed out everything you can before the close. What? I said everything you can get rid of. Call me back at my office."

The receiver clattered down in the silence of the room. Steigel was facing him, gray-faced, wetting his thick lips. "You —you think—?"

"When the street finds out in the morning that Avery Bullard is dead, that stock will break ten points." He glanced at his watch again. "Damn it, only twenty minutes. We'll be lucky to get short of a couple of hundred shares."

Steigel looked at him, slack-lipped and staring. "There are some ways it don't seem right to make money."

A lip-twisting smile formed on Bruce Pilcher's face. "If you'd prefer, Julius, I'm quite willing to handle this on my own account."

Bruce Pilcher watched the door close, beating a fast tattoo on the desktop with the tips of his long-fingered right hand. He felt a tremendous surge of exhilarated pride in the speed and decisiveness with which he had acted. There had been too many times in his life when he had fumbled opportunity, tripped by caution and fear. Poor old Julius was showing his age. The slightest excitement now and the old boy had to go to the toilet.

Alex Oldham, manager of the New York branch office of the Tredway Corporation, was having the kind of an afternoon that he always had when he knew that Mr. Bullard was in the city. He might decide to drop in and he might not . . . you never knew. All you could do was sit on the griddle and fry, sweating it out, waiting, keeping an eye on the office to be sure no one started any horseplay. If you relaxed for one minute and let some fool thing happen, that was sure to be the very instant old Bullard would come busting in the front door. That's the way he was . . . you could have one undusted piece in the whole showroom and, by God, he'd walk right up to it!

Oldham poured a glass of water out of the silver carafe on his desk. The water was lukewarm and tasted like dust, gagging him. He spat it back in the glass and felt as if he were about to retch.

"Mr. Oldham, I—oh, I'm sorry."

It was his secretary, Mary Voskamp, backing embarrassedly through the door she had just opened.

"No, no! Come here!" he commanded. "Miss Voskamp, would you mind making certain that I have fresh water every morning?"

"But you almost never touch it. I—yes, sir. I'm sorry, Mr. Oldham."

"What is it?"

"Mr. Flannery called and wanted to know if he could bring Mr. Scott over at four-thirty. It's about that finish complaint on those tables. But if you're too busy—"

Oldham worked his lips nervously. "I don't know. Mr. Bullard's in town. He might stop in."

"Mr. Bullard? Isn't he going back to Millburgh on the three-five?"

"Three-five?"

"We got him a Pullman seat and sent it over to his hotel. He called in just before lunch."

"You might have told me!" he flared.

"I didn't know that you were—I'm sorry, Mr. Oldham."

"All right, all right," he said, straining against collapsing anger. "Not your fault, Miss Voskamp. Just—well, it's been one of those days."

"I'll tell Mr. Flannery that it would be better to wait until tomorrow. He said that would be all right if you were tied up."

Oldham nodded gratefully. "Yes, make it tomorrow."

He waited until he heard the door close and then slipped the palms of his hands over his face like a blanking curtain, shutting in the terror. Something's happened to me . . . never used to let things get me this way . . . maybe I'm cracking up . . . like Wally in Detroit. No! I've got to hang onto myself. If old Bullard ever gets an idea that I'm slipping . . . if he ever suspects . . .

"The bastard," he whispered aloud—and then he said it again. The syllables made burning little puffs of air in the damp palms of his hands. It's the waiting that raises hell with a man . . . how can you help having an ulcer . . . all this damned waiting . . . never knowing?

2.51 P.M. EDT

Anne Finnick opened the door of the women's washroom just wide enough to assure herself that there was no one else inside. Then she slipped through the door, snatched a paper towel, and with three quick steps shut herself inside a toilet compartment.

Swallowing hard, she opened her hand bag and lifted out a soggy, filth-stained man's wallet. Gingerly spreading the wet leather, she saw a thick sandwich of green bills. Her lips trembled through a moment of indecision and then she clutched the money into a crumpled wad and jabbed it inside the front of her blouse, holding herself against flinching as the shock of the wet cold struck the warm valley of her breasts.

Breathing heavily she sat down on the toilet, looking furtively about the narrow enclosure, trying to decide what to do with the wallet. It was full of little cards. She began peeling them off the wet pack that they made, reading the type and the water-blurred signatures. They were membership cards in clubs, credit cards for hotels, insurance identification . . . Avery Bullard . . . Avery Bullard, Millburgh, Pennsylvania . . . Avery Bullard, President, Tredway Corporation.

"No guy like that needs it like I do," she whispered silently, standing. One by one, she tore the cards into little bits. They made a swirl of multicolored confetti in the water of the toilet bowl, spinning like a kaleidoscope when she pulled the flush lever.

It was a shame to throw away the wallet. Those initial dinguses might be real gold. Maybe it would be all right when it was dried out and she could give it to somebody. But not to Eddie! She wasn't ever giving Eddie anything again . . . a cheap guy that would let a girl worry herself sick, saying every day that he was going to get the money for that doctor. Now she had the money herself. Eddie could go to hell!

Her eyes blinked back tears and she began to tremble violently. It almost hadn't happened. It had been so close to not happening. Today was the first time she'd gone out for a chocolate malted in a whole week. If she hadn't gone just when she did, she'd never have seen the wallet lying there in that muddy mess at the curb in front of the Chippendale Building. It almost made a person believe in something.

Someone was coming in the washroom.

Anne Finnick flushed the toilet again. The sound was a protection against the terror of silence.

"I'm not stealing it," she said to herself. "Sometime, when I get it, I'll pay it back. I won't forget his name—Avery Bullard." She looked at the gold initials . . . they would help her remember . . . A.B. for Avery Bullard.

2

MILLBURGH, PENNSYLVANIA

2.54 P.M. EDT

THE TELEGRAM that Avery Bullard sent from the Chippendale Building in New York was received at the Western Union office in Millburgh, Pennsylvania at 2.54 P.M. As the words TREDWAY TOWER spattered down on the uncoiling yellow tape, Mary Herr immediately swiveled her chair to face the keyboard on which she would retransmit the message to one of the battery of teletype printers in the Tredway Tower. As she turned she flicked her eyes toward the window through which she could see the sky-thrusting shaft of the Tower, dazzlingly white against the heat-faded blue of the sky.

Mary Herr's quick glance at the Tredway Tower had no direct relationship to the handling of the message. It was something that she, in common with almost everyone else in Millburgh, did a hundred times a day. There was no part of the city from which the Tower could not be seen, and there was no man or woman whose eyes could long escape its attraction. Most often they looked without seeing, as a sailor involuntarily glances at the sky, or an office worker at the clock, but there were other times when they stared in conscious awe. Early-rising men, on their way to work, frequently marveled at the way the warm sun would strike the top of the Tower while they still walked in the predawn chill. In the evening, after the sun had set for the rest of the city, they would sometimes see the upper reaches of the Tower still bathed in an unworldly glow of flame-colored light. On days when clouds came scudding in through the Alleghany passes and filled the whole river valley with gray mist, the top of the Tower would occasionally be lost in the sky. It was then that they looked upward most often, staring and uneasy, as if their minds were incapable of coping with their imaginations, as if some needed thing had been unfairly snatched away.

If the Tredway Tower had been built on the island of Manhattan, it would have been only a tree in a forest, possessing neither distinction nor magnificence. In Millburgh, it is the wonder of wonders. No other building is taller than six stories. The Tower rises an incredible twenty-four. Almost as impressive as its size is its whiteness, a white so startlingly clean that it almost seems as if some supernatural intervention protects it from the film of soot that smudges the low-lying clutter of old buildings that make up most of the downtown area.

There are only a very few people in Millburgh who do not regard the Tredway Tower as a thing of great beauty. W. Harrington Dodds is one of the few. Although two decades have passed since it was built, Mr. Dodds' criticism of its design has grown no less bitter. He still calls it "an architectural monstrosity inspired by an Italian wedding cake and designed by a pseudo architect who should have been a pastry cook." Such remarks by Mr. Dodds are usually accepted as the acid result of a bad case of sour grapes. At the time the Tower was built he had been the leading architect of Millburgh and a man of some standing in his profession, the former vice-president of the state chapter of the American Institute of Architects. Nevertheless, old Orrin Tredway had completely passed him by and had given the architectural commission to a New York firm. He had not even tossed W. Harrington Dodds the face-saving designation as "consulting architect."

Despite the circumstantial evidence against the validity of

Mr. Dodds' criticism, there is more than a little justification for some of his caustic oberservations. The Tredway Tower does bear more than a little resemblance to an enormous wedding cake. The first twelve stories are a frosted white block, fitted as squarely to the four streets as if they were the edges of the pan in which it had been baked.

On the foundation of the twelve-story block, off center, rises the constantly narrowing tower of the building. The higher it rises the more elaborate its ornamentation becomes. Around the setbacks at the sixteenth and twentieth stories there are garlands of intricately worked white-glazed terra cotta which, as Mr. Dodds is fond of saying, would be "highly appropriate for a Gothic Christmas cookie." They are reputed to be the finest work of a great sculptor, but their artistic merit can only be judged by an occasional high-flying pigeon, for they are completely invisible to the earth-bound observer.

The final thrust of the Tower, the lance of the shaft, is so highly embellished with a bristle of minarets that it appears from the street to be an area completely separate and distinct from the rest of the building. It is. Orrin Tredway had wanted it that way. He had planned it himself and the architects had not argued. On the twenty-third floor he had placed the offices of his vice-presidents. To the twenty-fourth he had transplanted three rooms that he had torn out by the roots from a sixteenth-century manor house that he had bought in England. The oak paneling had been disassembled by museum workers, marked piece by piece for re-erection, and the twenty-fourth floor of the Tower had been designed with no other consideration than to form a shell for the transplantation. What once had been a library for nine generations of the English peerage became the office of Orrin Tredway. The adjoining study, where at least three Prime Ministers had sat in conference, became the office for Orrin Tredway's secretary. The old main hall had become the directors' room and Orrin Tredway sat at the head of the same table, and in the same chair, that had been used by six lords of England. There were no other offices on the twenty-fourth floor. Orrin Tredway had wanted no other man to touch his feet to its hallowed parquetry without his personal invitation.

Eight months after he moved into his office, Orrin Tredway was dead. One night in January, Luigi Cassoni, the operator of the private elevator that served the Executive Suite, heard what was unmistakably a shot. When he finally got up enough nerve to break the rule that Mr. Tredway was never to be disturbed by opening the door of his office, he found that Mr. Tredway was beyond being disturbed.

The coroner obligingly reported that Orrin Tredway had been killed by the accidental discharge of a pistol that he had been cleaning. No one was fooled. Everyone suspected suicide. A month later they knew for sure. By then the motive for self-murder was clearly evident. Orrin Tredway was bankrupt. He had squandered his entire personal fortune and all but ruined the Tredway Furniture Company in order to build the Tower. It had been a colossal financial blunder, the senile floundering of an old man who, in the last years of his life, was trying desperately to fulfill the promise of his ancestry. There had been great men in his lineage, men who had left their mark on Pennsylvania since the days of William Penn, but the strong blood was gone before it came to Orrin Tredway's veins. He was the last of the line. There was no Tredway to succeed him as president of the company.

The people of Millburgh had bowed to the anticipated loss of the Tredway Furniture Company as another inevitable downward step in the slow disintegration of the city's industry. It had been going on for a long time. The days of Millburgh's greatest glory lay so far back in its history that there was no man still alive whose memory could span the years. There were those who could recite the facts, but their recitations came from legends preserved in the mice-smelling rooms behind the public library that served as the headquarters of the Millburgh Historical Society.

There were even people living in Millburgh—as horror-stricken members of the Historical Society were occasionally made to realize by papers at its first-Friday-after-the-first-Thursday meetings—who did not know that Millburgh had not been named for the mills that once lined the Susquehanna, but for John Mills of Liverpool, England, who had established the riverside settlement that eventually became Millburgh.

In either 1747 or 1748, the exact date being as unverifiable as it is unimportant, John Mills sailed up the Susquehanna with a party of British traders who were intent upon buying iron from the furnaces that had recently been established in the river hills. Along most of the river, the hills came down sharply to the water edge and there was little flatland, but the Mills' party discovered one place where prehistoric erosion had cut back the hills to leave a flat half-moon of lowland. It was almost three miles across the river face and, at the center point, there was over a mile between the water and the steep-cliffed palisade of the cutaway hills. It was here that the party stopped and began the building of a warehouse for the collection of iron until it could be loaded on the barges that were to float it down to Baltimore for shipment to England.

What scanty historical evidence still remains indicates that John Mills was more generously endowed with the spirit of private enterprise than with loyalty to his British employers. A year later he was in business for himself, contracting with furnace owners to supply the large quantities of charcoal that were used in the production of iron.

From the cutting of wood for charcoal to the cutting of wood for lumber was an easy step and by 1752 the sawmill that John Mills erected on Cutlass Creek was reputed to be one of the three largest in the colonies.

Much of the lumber was hauled overland to Philadelphia. Hauling required wagons and John Mills started to build them. It was a logical enterprise. The wood came from his own sawmills and the iron forges to make the necessary metal parts were close at hand. He had already acquired a controlling interest in one forge and was a partner in another.

The tide of emigration to the West had started to flow in earnest and the fame of the covered wagons that were built at Mills Landing spread through the taverns up and down the Eastern seaboard where men gathered to plan their treks to the lands beyond the Susquehanna. They came to Mills Landing to buy wagons and John Mills saw the chance to sell them other things as well. Great stone warehouses were built along the waterfront to house all manner of goods, but John Mills was a manufacturer at heart, not a trader, and soon there was a mill for the weaving of hempen canvas, a tannery and a harness factory, a pottery near the claybank on Cutlass Creek, and all manner of smaller shops. The wagon works suggested a natural expansion into agricultural implements and the Mills plow became as famous as the Mills wagon.

A letter written in 1761 by one W. Crayton to his waiting compatriots in Philadelphia, describes the Mills Landing of that year.

HONOURED SIRS:

This is to send you the intelligence that you should come with All Haste and it is in no ways necessary to burthen yourself for this part of the journey since all that is needed by us for our westward venture can be Purchased Here to good advantage from Mr. John Mills who is the Proprietor of such as I am sure will Amaze you. The shops are of a magnitude that is beyond belief and the sound of the smiths so great and constant that is as if a great Battle was being fought even into the night.

Our two waggons have been promised for the 9th instant but both taverns are crowded with those who wait before me and I do not view the date with Certainty. To hasten our departure I have ordered of Mr. Mills such articles as you will find on the list which I beg you to examine for your approval. The axes and scythes are of Superior Design and the chests are Iron Bound and most Nicely Made.

There is one matter in which I do not feel free to act without your counsel and it is about Horses. On his plantation, which is on the high level above the town, Mr. Mills raises a fine beast which is called the Conestoga Horse and there are teams of such which are yet for sale although I cannot perceive if all will not soon be boughten by others which is one cause why I implore you to Hasten here.

Do not Speak of this next matter to Mary but I have six jugs of Spirits made in Mr. Mills' distillery. It is of Uncommon fineness and I mention it to add to your Haste in coming.

It was in the same year as Crayton's letter was written, 1761, that the town was formally laid out and renamed Millburgh. Prior to that time everything at Mills Landing was owned personally by John Mills, including more than two hundred stone houses which he had built for his employees. The favored workers were the English wheelwrights and carpenters whose emigration from England had been arranged by John Mills, and he carefully managed the sales of houses and lots so that all of his countrymen lived in the northern half of the town. The south half, where the mills and shops fronted the river, thus became the home of the German and Swiss ironworkers and was soon called "Dutchtown." The two main east and west streets were named George and Frederick, recognizing the reigning kings of Great Britain and Germany.

George Street and everything north became the "best" section of Millburgh. Social standing began to be measured by distance from the river. The mansion houses of those who grew rich from John Mills' favor were built along North Front Street and they became known as "North Front families," the top of Millburgh's social scale.

South of Frederick Street, in Dutchtown, the houses that were built by the workers were of red brick instead of gray limestone, huddled closely together on small plots of land, many being built in the row fashion of Philadelphia and Baltimore with no division between them except a common wall.

John Mills held himself aloft from the rabble of the town. His plantation of over three thousand acres completely surrounded the cliff-edged bowl of Millburgh and, centrally on the rim, so that all of his domain could be seen from his veranda, he built the great mansion of Cliff House. It was started in the spring of 1760 but, according to a legend which the house still stands to verify, the elaborateness of the interior woodwork demanded nine years for its completion. John Mills was one of the richest men in the colonies and he lived on a scale to fit his purse. When he died in 1784, a contemporary account records that more than two hundred house servants and plantation workers followed the casket on foot.

James Mills, John's eldest son, carried on in his father's tradition and continued to expand the factories. Whether through wisdom or good fortune, his greatest expansion was in the lumber business and it was there that he laid the foundation for the high-water mark in Millburgh's economic history.

After the War of 1812, the British flooded the American market with ironwork and agricultural implements priced so low that the Millburgh forges and factories could not compete. The lumber business took up the slack. The local timber had long since been cut, most of it to make charcoal for the iron furnaces, but now great rafts of white pine came floating down the river from the upper reaches of the Susquehanna. The Millburgh sawmills were waiting and the town became the center of lumber supply for Philadelphia and all of southeastern Pennsylvania. It was a lusty, rip-roaring, money-coining period. Millburgh had been a boom town since its birth but there had never been anything to match this. On South Front Street, raftmen stood six deep at the tavern bars. On North Front Street, the militia guarded the mansion dwellers from the drunken roistering rivermen who recognized no limits in their quest for port excitement. Every month there were more mansions to guard. New fortunes were being made so fast that the old designation of a "North Front family" had already begun to lose some of its meaning.

The lumber boom lasted well into the eighteen-thirties. By then the upriver sawmills at Williamsport, Lock Haven, and Renovo began to take the business away and Millburgh's tide had turned. The iron and steel industry moved West and the farm implement business trailed the ironmasters. The old Mills Plow Company dwindled into insignificance. The tannery closed and the kilns at the brickyard crumbled into ruins.

The Civil War brought a respite in the city's declining fortune but, with the Reconstruction years, the downward course continued. Only three local industries of any importance survived the panic of 1873—the Mills Carriage Works, with which no descendant of John Mills was any longer associated, the Mills Iron Foundry, now owned by the Krautz family, and the Everett-English Cotton Mill, which was the lineal inheritor of the weave shed where John Mills had woven the flaxen canvas for his covered wagons.

The Tredway Furniture Company could not then be listed as an important Millburgh industry but its advertised claim-phrase, "Established 1788," can be historically justified. Josiah Tredway, a cabinetmaker by trade, came from England in 1766 to carve the decorations on the fireplace mantels of Cliff House and stayed on to make Millburgh his home. In 1788 he opened a shop on the alley behind Cromwell Street between George and Frederick, the present site of the Tredway Tower, for "the makeing of tables, chares, and cabinets in the style of England and of the best qualities." The shop was carried on by his son, George, and during the early years of the nineteenth century was one of dozens of little one-man furniture shops in Millburgh, a natural outgrowth of the fact that many of the men John Mills had brought from England for his wagon works were cabinetmakers. From 1788 forward, various Tredways were continuously listed as "cabinetmakers" on Millburgh assessment rolls. The designation of "factory owner" does not appear until after Oliver Tredway's name in 1874.

Aided by the depression of values brought on by the panic of 1873, Oliver Tredway managed to acquire one of the old stone warehouses that had been built more than a hundred years before by John Mills, equipped it with discarded machinery from one of the old sawmills, and gathered a complement of skilled woodworkers from the bread lines that formed daily on South Front Street. The company prospered and by 1910, when Orrin Tredway became its head, it was Millburgh's largest industry, a distinction that it had acquired not only through its own expansion but also from the default of its rivals. The panic of 1907 closed the Mills Carriage Works. Shortly afterward the cotton mill owners uprooted their machinery and transplanted it to North Carolina. Only the Krautz Steel Company—the former Mills Iron Foundry—remained and its days were numbered. In an attempt to compete with the Pittsburgh steelmakers, George Krautz had kept wages low and fought the unionization of his employees with the same unyielding independence that had kept him from selling out to one of the big steel combines. The eventual result was a strike that dragged on and on, frequently flaring into violence. One morning after a man had been killed in a picket-line brawl, old George Krautz climbed to the roof of the office building and shouted to the mob of men below that unless they went back to work that very day he would close the mills forever. The announcement was greeted with derisive catcalls. George Krautz was a man of his word. The mill never opened again. The machinery was moved away and the ghostly skeletons of the buildings, eaten away by the red cancer of rust, slowly dropped their sheet-iron skins into the weeds of the yard.

The Tredway Furniture Company that Orrin Tredway inherited from his father, Oliver, was a sound and substantial concern. In the 1910 edition of *Whittaker's Index* it was ranked eighteenth in size among the furniture factories of the nation. If there had been a listing based upon profits, its rank would have been higher. Oliver Tredway had something of a genius for extracting gold from wood. Few men have made fortunes from furniture manufacturing. Oliver Tredway was one of the few. Much of his success was attributable to his mechanical ingenuity. During most of the first quarter-century of the company's existence, furniture of the rococo Turkish and French styles was in vogue and Oliver Tredway invented machine after machine to reduce the cost of the elaborate carving, turning, and scrollwork. When the buying public finally revolted against overdecoration and turned to the severely plain Mission style, Oliver Tredway mechanized manufacture to an extent never before seen in the industry, reducing his labor costs so drastically that a number of other factories bought from him because, even after Oliver Tredway added a generous profit, his selling prices were still under their own production costs. In common with many of the industrialists of the period, Oliver Tredway's prime interests were centered in the factory. His office was seldom used. He spent most of his working day wandering through the factory, frequently removing his frock coat and yellow doeskin gloves to lend a hand at tinkering some new piece of machinery into production. The gloves were a concession, as all of his intimates knew, to the propriety that a big factory owner should not have grease on his hands. When Oliver Tredway wore his gloves, no one could see the unremovable stains.

Orrin Tredway inherited little from his father except his wealth and the control of the company. Father and son were almost as temperamentally dissimilar as it is possible for two human males to be. Millburgh explained it by saying Orrin "took after his mother," which was seldom spoken as a criticism, for Orrin's mother had been an Elwood and the Elwoods were one of the oldest and most distinguished of the North Front families. She had wanted Orrin to follow his maternal forebears into the law as a steppingstone to high governmental service, but his years at Harvard revealed that what talent young Orrin Tredway had was better suited to the life of a dilettante in the arts than to an attorney. After college he spent most of his time abroad, and the back draft of occasional bits of rumor linking his name with famous artists and writers made him something of a local celebrity. Afterward he deserted the arts and took up international society. He was the only resident of Millburgh who had ever been the house guest of an English duke. His return to Millburgh after his father's death was delayed, so it was said, because he had been asked by a member of the royal family to stay in England until after the coronation of George V.

There were some people who were surprised that Orrin Tredway returned to Millburgh at all, more who predicted that he would never take over the active management of the Tredway Furniture Company, and still more who prophesied catastrophe if he attempted it. The happenings of the first few years confounded the critics. Not only did Orrin Tredway step in as president of the company but he made an auspicious start at the job. While in England he had seen the decline of William Morris' Arts and Crafts movement and realized that the pendulum of public taste was due for another swing. He guessed that it would be toward colonial reproductions and, against the advice of his father's former associates, forced through a sample line that was strongly influenced by Sheraton and Hepplewhite. It was a great success. The next year he scored again with the introduction of new furniture woods, particularly with black walnut, which had hardly been used at all by American furniture makers since the end of Medieval and Gothic fashions in the eighteen-eighties.

Orrin Tredway proved as much a dilettante in business as in the arts. In a few years his interest flagged. In 1915, through the influence of his maternal uncle who was an ambassador, he was appointed to a governmental commission and from that year until well after the end of World War I, he spent less and less time in Millburgh. The affairs of the company drifted, but profits were still high until the depression of 1921. It was rumored that the company lost almost a quarter of a million dollars that year. Orrin Tredway came back to his desk. Half of the factory was closed, more than half of the men were laid off. He rose to the emergency, using his political connections to get furniture contracts for government buildings. Even more important to the future of the company was the employment of a young salesman named Avery Bullard who, having quit his job with the old Bellinger Furniture Company, had walked in with the order for all the furniture for a chain of hotels.

The men came back to work in the factory and Orrin Tredway drifted away in search of a new interest. He found it through his appointment as General Chairman of a committee to arrange for the celebration of the one hundred and seventy-fifth anniversary of the founding of Millburgh. The hero of the occasion, of course, was to be John Mills, and Orrin Tredway conceived the idea of restoring Cliff House, the old Mills mansion. It was hidden away in bramble-laced thicket of second-growth brush, untenanted for over fifty years, and in a very bad state of repair. The committee saw no hope of financing the restoration, so Orrin Tredway took over, bought the property, spent almost two hundred thousand dollars on it, and moved into Cliff House as his own home. Not only did he adopt John Mills' home, he also adopted his extravagant manner of life.

Business boomed as the years of the twenties went by. The Tredway Furniture Company's profits were large but not large enough to keep pace with Orrin Tredway's spending. He was an old man now, fog-brained with delusions of aristocratic grandeur, and it was then that he decided to build the Tredway Tower. No argument could stop him, as no argument could have stayed the finger that touched the trigger of the gun that ended his life.

In the month after Orrin Tredway's death, Avery Bullard quietly moved up from the twenty-third to the twenty-fourth floor of the Tower. His election to the presidency of the Tredway Furniture Company was not generally regarded as an event of any great importance. The Millburgh *Times* gave it only a one-column headline and a stick of type. It was the general attitude of the community that the company had been ruined beyond salvage and the only reason for the election of anyone as a new president was to provide a signature on a petition for bankruptcy.

Having accepted the death of the furniture company as an accomplished fact, the citizenry of Millburgh were slow to awaken to the miracle of its resurrection. It burst upon them with spectacular suddenness in the fall of 1935 when the Millburgh *Times* published the story, this time under a banner headline, that Avery Bullard had announced the merger of seven other furniture factories and the formation of the Tredway Corporation, that the local manufacturing operation would be expanded and four hundred new workers would be employed. The next morning every policeman in Millburgh was taken off his regular beat and rushed to the Tredway plant to quell the riot of hungry job-seekers that crushed down upon the Tredway employment office.

There was more news in the months that followed. An addition was started to the Tredway factory on Water Street, the first new industrial building that had been erected in Millburgh in over a quarter-century. Tredway securities were admitted to trading on the New York Stock Exchange. The Millburgh *Times* front-paged a photo of the "For Rent" sign being taken down from the Tredway Tower and a syndicated picture service spread it all over the country. A furniture-trade magazine published a cartoon in which Avery Bullard, in the armor of St. George, was slaying a dragon labeled "Depression" with a sword branded "Courage."

Somewhere along the way, at some unmarked moment, Avery Bullard became the first citizen of Millburgh. The Federal Club, established by John Mills in 1781, and still housed in the old Federal Tavern where Lafayette and four signers of the Declaration of Independence had been entertained, hastily amended its blue-blood tradition in order to escape the embarrassment of not having Avery Bullard as a member. He seldom entered the club's portals but a corner table in the grill was always reserved for his use. When he did come for lunch, there was no man in Millburgh, even the president of the Susquehanna National Bank, who could escape the temptation of bragging to his wife that he had lunched that day at the table next to Avery Bullard's. Arm-locked lovers, wandering along the dark streets, would look up in awe at the square pinpoints of light that burned into the darkness at the top of the Tower. "Sure, honey, that's old Bullard himself up there right now. They say he never goes home. Some nights he works right through. You know what? The other day I saw him getting out of his car. I swear to God I was so close to him I coulda reached out and touched him!"

When Florence Bullard divorced her husband in 1938, she generated only criticism, receiving little of the sympathy that she felt a neglected wife deserved. With only a rare exception, even her closest women friends regarded Florence Bullard as a fool. They thought that when a woman was lucky enough to be married to a great man like Avery Bullard, she ought to have the sense to realize that she couldn't live an entirely normal life, not the kind of a life that a woman would have if she were married to some ordinary man like the president of the Susquehanna National or the owner of Churchill's Department Store, or the rector of St. Martin's.

As the months went by, Avery Bullard gave little comfort to the few Millburgh citizens who guardedly whispered their secret prediction that his fall would be as rapid as his rise. The

Tredway Corporation kept on growing. The big new Pike Plant was started in 1945, just as the nation began its postwar clamor for furniture. In 1949 the sales of the Tredway Corporation passed fifty million dollars and the following year went even higher. By contrast with huge corporations like General Motors or United States Steel, Tredway was small, but in the furniture field it was a giant company. It was the backbone of Millburgh's economic life. One out of every three of Millburgh's families lived on Tredway pay checks. Many of the factory workers were now fourth- and fifth-generation Tredway men. In some families, like Mary Herr's, there were three generations working for the company now. Her grandfather, her father, and two of her brothers were all in the core-making shop. All four had been a little shocked when she had gone to work for Western Union. It seemed like something approaching disloyalty. The only explanation she could offer was that "someone had to be different." It didn't matter very much. Western Union was a good company, too, and practically all the messages she handled were for Tredway anyway. It was a good job. She was on the inside. She knew a lot of things that her father didn't know, even if he was night foreman of the core-making department at Water Street.

BULLARD. She typed the signature of the message in a flurry of movement, her fingers speeded by the countless times that they had repeated the same combination of seven letters. When she first started for Western Union she used to tangle the keys typing Bullard . . . it was just one of those quirk words for her . . . but now it was easy. She must have typed Bullard a million times in these last five years . . . and she'd probably type it a million more in the next five if Kenneth didn't ask her to marry him pretty soon.

TREDWAY TOWER
3.06 P.M. EDT

Luigi Cassoni stepped from his elevator cab and, as he did many times every day, carefully extracted his watch from the tight little pocket at the waistline of his trousers and compared its dial with that of the giant bronze clock suspended from the ceiling of the black marble lobby. Luigi had no special interest in the time but a great pride in his watch. It had been personally presented by Mr. Bullard himself on the occasion of Luigi's twenty-fifth anniversary with Tredway.

The watch, like so many of the other wonderful things that life had heaped upon him, represented a blessing far more generous than Luigi knew he could possibly deserve. He regarded himself as a very fortunate man, a state of mind that was partially responsible for his almost perpetual happiness.

A second factor in Luigi's happiness derived from his underestimation of his own mental capacity. He always thought of himself as being less intelligent than he actually was. Since he did not credit his mind with the ability to arrive at any worthwhile conclusions through conscious thought, he wasted little of his time in disturbing speculation and thereby achieved great serenity.

As the operator of the private elevator to the Executive Suite on the twenty-third and twenty-fourth floors of the Tower, Luigi occupied a position so completely gratifying that he regularly included his thanks in his prayers. That was no more than just. Divine Providence had unquestionably intervened in his behalf. Without supernatural beneficence it was totally incredible that he, little Luigi Cassoni who had been born with no right to expect anything from life but a peasant's work in the olive groves, should now be one of Mr. Avery Bullard's closest personal friends. That was true. No one could deny it. Mr. Bullard had said it himself on that never-to-be-forgotten night eleven years ago. "Luigi, sometimes I have a suspicion that you're the only real friend I have in this whole damned company."

Luigi knew that his intimate personal association with Mr. Bullard was recognized up and down the floors of the Tredway Tower. Even the vice-presidents on the twenty-third, riding up to twenty-four for a presidential audience, frequently said, "Luigi, what kind of a mood is the old man in today?"

His answers were always carefully guarded because he recognized the horrible danger that he might, by some inadvertent slip of the tongue, say something that would be disloyal to Mr. Bullard.

Despite the perpetual pleasure of his employment, Luigi was always conscious of a slight discount on his happiness when Mr. Bullard was out of town. When the president was not in the Executive Suite, the flash of the twenty-fourth floor signal light was different. Then it was only a pinpoint of red light, not the exciting crimson flare that sent him skyrocketing up the shaft.

Mr. Bullard had been out of town for two days now. He had been in New York since Wednesday. In this whole day, Luigi had made only seven runs to twenty-four . . . Miss Martin up this morning . . . Miss Martin down and up at noon . . . four trips with mail.

Now, unexpectedly, the yellow light blinked on the control board of his cab, signaling a special call from the mail room.

Luigi threw the control lever and the cab dropped to the sub-basement. As the door opened, the sliding panel revealed the spare and angular figure of Emily Gastings. She was waiting impatiently, her face frozen in her never-varying mask of icy criticism. For even longer than Luigi had been with Tredway, Emily had supervised the handling of all mail and telegrams. She was so clearly the frustrated spinster that she seemed an overdrawn caricature of the type. Through the years her mind had become something like a sour-soil plant that perpetuates its habitat by the self-generation of an acid atmosphere.

"Telegram for Miss Martin, and don't take all day getting it up there. It's from Mr. Bullard."

The perpetually lurking smile behind Luigi's eyes neither warmed nor cooled. He had long since learned that the easiest way to stay happy was to disregard unpleasantness.

He saw that Emily was perversely standing just far enough away to force him to step out of the cab to reach the envelope, but he took the step without resentment. "Mr. Bullard coming in tonight?"

She took a quick gasping breath as if his words had touched some inviolate spot. "None of your business. Telegrams are strictly confidential."

Luigi held his smile until the closing door screened his face.

Women were funny . . . if you asked them something and the answer was no, they'd say it right out . . . if the answer was yes, they'd shut up like a clam and not say a word. Mr. Bullard was coming home tonight.

He had thrown the control, express to twenty-four, and the cab was flying up the shaft, alive with silent flight, no sound except the soft swish of the air. Luigi nodded with satisfaction as he passed sixteen. That little clicking sound between fifteen and sixteen was gone. He had been right in forcing Building Maintenance to have it fixed immediately. George had tried to tell him that Mr. Bullard would never notice it, a sound that you could hardly hear even when you were listening for it. The trouble with George was that he didn't really know Mr. Bullard, not the way Luigi knew him. There wasn't a thing in the whole world that Mr. Bullard didn't notice, not one thing.

The cab leveled at twenty-four and the door ghosted open. Luigi locked the controls and stepped out. There was a slide that would have carried the telegram to Miss Martin's desk but he ignored it as he always did on days when Mr. Bullard was out of town. It was much more pleasant to walk around the corner and deliver the telegram to Miss Martin hand to hand.

He walked slowly, his eyes savoring the surroundings. Even after all of these years, and the thousands of times that he had experienced it, there was no diminution in the aesthetic pleasure that Luigi Cassoni derived from the twenty-fourth floor.

As a boy he had lived in a tiny Italian village at the foot of a hill that was crowned by a castle. Looking up at its impregnable walls, he had often engaged in boyish imaginings of the wonders that must be inside. There was an unbreakable link between those childhood dreams and the reality of the top floor of the Executive Suite, a linkage that persisted despite the incongruity of the castle having been in Italy and the fact that old Orrin Tredway had created the twenty-fourth floor by transplanting a sixteenth-century English manor house.

In the first months after the Tredway Tower had been built, Luigi had heard old Mr. Tredway recount the history of these rooms, stories filled with kings and queens and lords and ladies, but there had been too much to remember from the first telling and, before the stories could be retold, the teller was dead. It was Luigi who had found Orrin Tredway lying on the floor of his office, his red blood lost in the design of the Oriental rug, his outstretched hand white as chalk, the pistol glittering coldly under the blue desk-light. Strangely, for all its horror, that moment of gruesome discovery had not remained in Luigi's mind as a vivid association with the twenty-fourth floor. It had been quickly submerged by the overriding memory of that morning shortly afterward when he helped Mr. Bullard move up from twenty-three. An essential rightness was created then that gave validity to Luigi's mental association between the castle and the Executive Suite. There was a duke who had lived in the castle in Italy and there was much about Avery Bullard that reminded him of the duke.

Luigi recalled how all the children had stood in silent respect as the Duke rode past in his carriage, not because silence was demanded but because there was some aura about the Duke that made him unmistakably the man above all other men, the man who owned all that there was to own—the shining carriage and the black horses, the streets and the shops and houses, the fields beyond and even the smallest loose stones that lay upon the earth. One of Luigi's earliest memories was of his father's distress when a branch had been accidentally broken from an olive tree that stood near the hut that was their home. His mother had attempted to console him by saying that perhaps the Duke would not notice. Luigi's father knew better. There was nothing in the world that the Duke did not notice.

If it had not been for certain moral considerations which weighed heavily in his mind, Luigi could have fitted Miss Martin into the child-formed pattern of his thinking with no more effort and concern than he employed in transforming Mr. Bullard into the Duke who lived in the castle. Miss Martin even looked a little like his memories of the Duchess. There was that same up-carriage of her head, that same alert perception, that same ever-watchful anticipation of the Duke's desire. "Wine," the Duchess had ordered on the fiesta day when the Duke had made a speech in the hot sun of the piazza, and when the wine had been brought and the Duke had drunk thirstily, Luigi had stood staring at them and trying to understand how it was that the Duchess had known. His eyes had not left the Duke's lips in all of the time that they had been there and he knew that the Duke had not spoken to the Duchess. Yet she had known. There must be, he had reasoned, some mysterious manner of silent speech between them. Now he knew that there was that same gift of wordless communication between Mr. Bullard and Miss Martin. She, too, had some way of knowing what he wanted before he asked for it. He had seen it happen many times.

Luigi had never dared to pursue the parallel because he also knew that the Duchess was the Duke's wife and Miss Martin was only Mr. Bullard's secretary. If, in the case of the Duke and the Duchess there had been some connection between the love that made them man and wife, and their ability to talk without speaking, there had to be some other explanation for the case of Miss Martin and Mr. Bullard. Luigi never tried to find that explanation because he was certain that it would require a high order of thinking of which his mind was sure to be incapable. In any event it didn't matter. Miss Martin was, above any woman that he had ever known, beautiful and intelligent and kind, and a part of the pleasure he found in coming to the twenty-fourth floor were these moments when he stood in the doorway and spoke her name and she would look up pleasantly startled, speaking his.

"Hello, Luigi."

"Telegram, Miss Martin."

He waited while she opened the envelope, noting the quick-flashing instant of reaction as she read the message, following her eyes as she glanced at a time-table that seemed to have been waiting for this moment, then back at the time stamp on the telegram again.

"Mr. Bullard's coming in this afternoon. Probably on the five-four."

"You want me tell Eddie be there with the car?"

"Will you?"

"Sure, Miss Martin, I tell him."

"And, Luigi, please ask Eddie not to have the car sitting out in the sun. It gets so terribly hot and Mr. Bullard will be worn out after two hard days in New York."

Luigi nodded. "Mr. Bullard come back here from the train?"

"Yes. He's called an executive committee meeting for six o'clock."

"Then I tell Maria not to wait dinner."

"There's no reason why you have to wait, Luigi. There'll be a night man on who can take us down after the meeting."

"No, I wait!" he said quickly. "Waiting don't matter, not for him."

Unexpectedly, her eyes flashed up, searching his face as if she suspected some hidden meaning, giving him the uncomfortable feeling of having said some improper thing. Suddenly, his self-conscious concern seemed to be matched by hers and an instant later she was laughing.

"It's a hard life, isn't it, Luigi?" But the words had no meaning for they floated out on a wave of denying laughter. Then, as quickly as the laughter had come, she turned and was reaching for the telephone.

Walking back to the elevator cab, Luigi toyed with the temptation of trying to make himself understand what had happened —why Miss Martin had looked at him in that strange way and then so suddenly broken into laughter—but there was no explanation that came before he saw the first-floor signal glowing like a beckoning jewel from the control panel.

Going down the shaft, all that remained in his mind was the pleasantly echoing sound of Miss Martin's laughter. It was too bad that his wife did not laugh like that. But a man could not expect everything. He was very fortunate. There were men . . . even men who were very intelligent and had been to college . . . who did not have a wife.

3.11 P.M. EDT

Erica Martin hesitated, her fingertips playing nervously over the black arch of the telephone instrument. Here again was that annoying puzzle of organizational precedence. Which of the five vice-presidents should be called first about the executive committee meeting at six o'clock? It was one of those little things that should not matter but she knew that it would. If Mr. Alderson were to discover that she had called Mr. Grimm before she called him, he would be sure to give it some frightening supersignificance. It would be no better to start with Mr. Dudley or Mr. Shaw, or even with Mr. Walling. They were all vice-presidents, all equal in rank, all poised on the same knife edge of uncertainty. It wasn't their fault. You couldn't blame them. Avery Bullard should have settled the matter weeks ago by choosing one of them to be executive vice-president.

The nervous play of Erica Martin's fingers was a completely involuntary gesture of annoyance. If she had been conscious of it she would have stopped it at once, for she had long since schooled herself against any outward display of emotion, particularly where Avery Bullard was concerned and there was very little emotion in her life with which Avery Bullard was not concerned. She had been his private secretary for almost sixteen years.

At eighteen, Erica Martin had not been a pretty girl. At thirty-eight she was a handsome woman. As a girl she had been tall, heavy-boned and rather too strong-featured to match the current standards for sweet femininity. Now, at maturity, she had the compensation—inadequate and belated though it was— of inciting constant admiration. Men paid her the supreme business male's compliment by saying that she had a mind like a man's. Women, particularly those of her own age group, saw her as the strong, independent, and capable person that they might have been if they had not sacrificed themselves to the enervating demands of housekeeping, childbearing, and the constant catering to a husband's petty quirks and foibles.

The truth, which almost no one bothered to suspect, was that Erica Martin's life was not so very different from that of her long married compatriots. Her relationship with Avery Bullard, although completely platonic and totally devoid of any compensating display of even minor affection, did not differ greatly from the relationship between any intelligent and helpful wife and any dominant, driving, and brilliant husband. She was treated with slightly more respect than is usually typical in such a marriage, but that advantage was offset by the fact that there were no moments when a pleasant disrespect might be the prelude to an act of love.

As for a husband's quirks and foibles, no wife could have been subjected to more—and Erica Martin also had her moments when tolerance was difficult to summon. There were times when Avery could be a very annoying person. The silly thing about it was that it was almost always over some minor matter. Day after day, Avery would make decisions on big problems almost as fast as she could place them on his desk. She couldn't ask for better co-operation. Then, all of a sudden, some little thing would come along and, for no reason at all, he would decide to be stubborn about it, almost as if he were purposely trying to annoy her. Every week since Mr. Fitzgerald had died she had struggled to find adroit ways of nudging Avery into clearing the "executive vice-president" note from her personal reminder pad. Once she had even asked a direct question. Even then he had done nothing. That was as far as she could go. If Avery wanted to be stubborn he'd just have to be stubborn. "Elect executive vice-president" wasn't something that she could write at the top of his engagement calendar every Monday morning the way she wrote "Haircut." The disconcerting thing, of course, was that Avery never stopped to realize the unpleasant position in which she was placed as a result of his negligence. She was the one who had to call the vice-presidents. But, of course, he never thought of that.

She glanced down and the telegram in her hand was an urgent reminder that the minutes were slipping away. It was Friday afternoon. None of the vice-presidents knew that Mr. Bullard was coming back from New York. Any one of them might be planning to slip away for an early start on the weekend. She must catch them at once . . . all of them. Avery would throw a tantrum if anyone missed executive committee meeting and those tantrums weren't good for him . . . his blood pressure had been up two points last time.

Hurriedly she slipped through the door of her office and started down the winding, medieval oak staircase that joined the two floors of the Executive Suite. The foot of the staircase solved the problem of precedence. Directly opposite was the door lettered: Frederick W. Alderson, Vice-President and Treasurer. No one could possibly place any special significance on the fact that she opened that door first.

Frederick Alderson was sitting behind his desk, his body squarely in his chair, his head held plumb-bob straight, not a white hair out of place on the high dome above his wax-pink face. He sat as if his own presence were a part of the meticulously precise arrangement of everything in his office. His smile of welcome was in the same careful pattern.

"Come in, Miss Martin."

"I've just had word from Mr. Bullard that he's on his way home from New York. He's called a meeting for six o'clock."

There was an almost imperceptible fading of his smile, so slight and so quickly recovered that she all but missed it.

"I hope it isn't too inconvenient, Mr. Alderson."

"No." He made the one syllable say that there was nothing in his personal life that could ever overshadow the importance of a summons from Avery Bullard.

"I'm sure it must be something important," she said, "or he wouldn't have asked everyone to stay."

"Everyone?" Mr. Alderson asked in cautious inquiry.

"The executive committee."

"Oh, of course. Thank you, Miss Martin."

His voice stopped her at the door. "I don't suppose you have any idea how long a meeting it might be?"

"No. I'm sorry."

"Well, it really doesn't matter. Mrs. Alderson and I are going out to dinner at seven, but I'm sure our hosts will understand if we're a few minutes late."

As she was closing the door she saw him pick up a newly sharpened pencil and reach for his desk pad. Nothing ever happened in Mr. Alderson's life that did not seem to require a note to himself, written in a tight bookkeeper's script that looked like copperplate engraving.

Down the hall, Erica Martin wondered if Avery Bullard ever really stopped to appreciate the sacrificial loyalty of Frederick Alderson . . . a nice gesture if Avery were to make Mr. Alderson his executive vice-president . . . no reason why he shouldn't . . . every reason why he should. Mr. Alderson was the oldest of the vice-presidents. There would be no organizational complications and, since he was sixty-one, he would retire in four years anyway.

She passed the blank door waiting to be lettered with the name of the new executive vice-president and went on to open the door labeled: Jesse Grimm, Vice-President for Manufacturing.

Jesse Grimm was not in his office but the odor of his pipe hung heavily in the air. Erica Martin walked through to the door of his secretary's little cubicle. "Hello, Ruth. Mr. Grimm around?"

Ruth Elkins swallowed hard, sending another chocolate-topped cookie the way of all the thousands upon thousands of tidbits that had contributed to her puffball figure. "Gosh, Miss Martin, he left just a few minutes ago."

"You'll have to reach him, Ruth. Mr. Bullard's called an executive committee for six o'clock."

"Six o'clock? Gosh, Miss Martin, I don't know if I can or not. He's going down to his place in Maryland."

"How long ago did he leave here?"

"Maybe about ten minutes."

"Was he going home first?"

"I guess so."

"Then you still have a chance to reach him if you call immediately."

"Sure, only—gosh, it's a shame, Miss Martin. Mr. Grimm's been at the factory almost every night and this was the weekend—"

"If you don't reach him, let me know at once," Erica Martin said sharply, clipping off the subject. Ruth would blabber on endlessly if you gave her half a chance. How Mr. Grimm had managed to put up with Ruth Elkins all of these years was something almost beyond understanding. The only possible explanation was pure pity. That was like Mr. Grimm . . . his one weakness . . . demanding perfection from his machines but too quick to excuse the lack of it in his people. It was a fault

. . . Avery recognized it, too . . . but, as he had once said, if a man had to have a fault there were worse ones to have. Avery liked Jesse Grimm. That was plain. There was a special affection in his voice when he said, "Get old Jesse up here." The other vice-presidents were almost always referred to by their surnames . . . "Ask Mr. Alderson to come up for a minute."

The juxtaposition of the two names in her mind sparked a question. Was that why Avery was delaying? Perhaps he wanted to make Mr. Grimm executive vice-president but was waiting until he could find some way to do it without offending Mr. Alderson . . . no, she was wrong . . . Avery never shrank from facing anything that needed to be faced. Personal considerations had never stopped him before . . . he had the strength to override them . . . he couldn't hide behind that excuse. There *was* no excuse . . . he was just being stubborn!

J. Walter Dudley, Vice-President for Sales, and Don Walling, Vice-President for Design and Development, occupied offices that were joined by a connecting door. Dudley's office was empty but she heard his voice through the closed door and opened it. The two men were seated in front of a long side table over which a collection of furniture-design sketches was scattered.

Walt Dudley was on his feet instantly, a broad smile blooming. He was an impressive man—big, broad-shouldered, with prematurely white hair above a strong deep-tanned face—and he was a practiced master of the art of winning quick friendships. "Erica, my dear, you're just what we need—a neutral referee—but with a good eye for a fast-selling number. Don and I can't figure out which of these specials I should take along to the Chicago market tonight."

Erica Martin smiled in spite of herself. She knew that everything Walt Dudley said was a part of his own highly personal act—like the "Erica, my dear" that no other vice-president could possibly have said—yet he was able now, as he always was, to demand her smile.

"What you'd really like me to tell you," she said, letting the smile lighten her tone, "is which designs Mr. Bullard will like."

Dudley tossed his handsome head with an appreciative chuckle directed at Walling. "Don, haven't I always said she was a mind reader?"

Don Walling nodded in the demanded agreement but it was obviously tinged with an undertone of slight embarrassment. "I'm afraid that's putting Miss Martin on a spot—asking her to outguess Mr. Bullard."

"If I could outguess Mr. Bullard," she said lightly, "I'd be a vice-president myself."

Dudley's laughter was instantaneous. "That's not a qualification. If it were, there wouldn't be any vice-presidents."

She saw the conversation was fast reaching the forbidden ground of personal comment about Mr. Bullard and she cut it off with a quick announcement of the meeting.

For once Walt Dudley was caught off guard. His smile vanished. "But I'm taking the seven o'clock plane to Chicago. The furniture market opens Monday and we're to have a preview showing for the chain and mail order boys tomorrow." His last words weakened as if the hearing of what he had said destroyed its validity. "Well, I can probably get a later plane." The smile was back. "Dust off my chair, Erica, I'll be there."

Walling was facing her, frowning. "I don't see how I can possibly make it, Miss Martin. Everything's set to start our test run on the molding process as soon as the five o'clock shift comes off."

"Better hold it up," Dudley advised, the older man to the younger.

"We can't hold it up," Walling protested. "They've already started reacting the finish resin. It has to come off on schedule or not at all. We've spent a whole month getting things organized for this one weekend. If we miss now it will be a month before we can get things set again for another factory test."

"Couldn't they go ahead without you?" Erica Martin asked, framing the question so that it was a way of telling him that nothing must stop him from attending the meeting. Don Walling was a new vice-president . . . it had been less than two years since he had moved up to the Executive Suite . . . there were still things that he had to be taught.

"I don't see how. There'll be decisions to make as they go along," Walling said, "but under the circumstances, I don't suppose there's anything else that can be done except to hold up."

He was learning, Erica decided, but there was more to learn . . . he hadn't taught himself to hide his feelings.

"Cheer up, boy," Dudley broke in with a forced laugh, the good actor covering a fellow player's bad cue. "The meeting might turn out to be a quickie and then you could still get over to the factory in time."

Erica Martin was tempted. She knew how important the test run was. She had seen the preliminary estimates that had been attached to the appropriation request. If the new molding process worked out it might well become the most important development in years. A month's delay would be serious. If Avery were there he would almost certainly tell Walling to go ahead with the test run and not worry about the meeting. Yet she dared not yield to the temptation to speak for him. That was the frustrating prohibition that hemmed in her whole life. She knew, better than any living person, what Avery Bullard's reaction would be to any given situation, yet she never dared anticipate it. She could only repeat his words, relay his orders, echo his commands. That was all. Anything else was beyond the border line.

Outside the door, Erica Martin groped, as she had groped so many times before, to find some bench mark of reason that would make it easier to orient her thinking and find some justification for the unpleasant situation in which she constantly found herself. She was always in the bufferland between Avery Bullard and his vice-presidents. She had nothing to do with the orders that she relayed, yet she was forced to be the object of the resentment and anger that they aroused. The demand for a six o'clock executive committee meeting was an arbitrary act of dictatorship, issued without consideration of anyone else's plans or desires. She agreed. But it wasn't her fault. Why should they hate her . . . and they did hate her, all of them! Walling was the only one who had dared to show it, but that was only because he was new, because he hadn't learned yet that a mask was essential equipment for the vice-president's trade. They all had their masks, Dudley's was laughter, Alderson's was his impassivity, Grimm's was the thin blue veil of smoke that drifted up from his black pipe. Shaw's was . . .

The name was a prod and she hurried around the corner to the door that was lettered: Loren P. Shaw, Vice-President and Comptroller. There was a meeting in progress and she withdrew quickly, intending to leave the message with Shaw's secretary, but she was only a step away from his door when he popped out.

"Something, Miss Martin?"

"I'm sorry I disturbed you, Mr. Shaw."

"Not at all, Miss Martin. Nothing important, just a little gathering of our section heads. Getting our plans laid for the midyear closing, you know."

"Mr. Bullard is on his way home from New York. He's called an executive committee meeting for six o'clock."

Of all the masks, Loren Shaw's was the best. Her eyes were directly on his, yet she saw not the faintest flicker of reaction, nor was there the slightest hint of an unusual tone in his voice as he said, "Apparently there must have been some developments in New York today."

"Apparently," she said quickly. Did he know what Avery had been working on in New York . . . or was he making a guileful attempt to get her to tell him what the meeting was about? In either event there was nothing more to be said. "Thank you, Mr. Shaw."

"Not at all, Miss Martin. I'll be there."

She felt his eyes following her down the hall and it was not until she had turned the corner and was starting up the staircase that she heard his door close.

At the top of the staircase she suddenly realized why Shaw had been watching her. He was confirming the fact that he had been the last one that she had told. An unaccountable tremor of fear ran through her. She brushed it aside. Why should she be afraid of anything that Loren Shaw might think? He was only a vice-president. In less than three hours Avery would be here.

[46]

She walked through her own office and into Avery Bullard's. She had drawn the shades against the sun and now she closed the door, shutting out all of the light except the soft cathedral glow that came through the stained-glass ports between the heavy oak beams. She walked behind his desk, stopping when she could reach out to touch the back of his chair. Then, slowly, her hands dropped until her fingertips had passed over the hard roughness of the oak and found the soft yielding flesh-touch of the red leather. Her eyes did not follow her hands. She was looking straight ahead. There was no break in the mask of her face.

3

NEW YORK CITY
4.52 P.M. EDT

As is often the case with many another a public servant, Frank Gross was a harsh critic of the human shortcoming that accounted for the means of his livelihood. If, as he frequently suggested, every citizen were required by federal law to be indelibly tattooed with his name and Social Security number, the necessity for his employment would have been largely eliminated. That fact had no effect upon his caustic railing against all persons who were stupid enough to allow themselves to fall dead in a public place without suitable identification on their persons.

The eventual solution of the identification riddles that were placed on Frank Gross' desk gave him little satisfaction. From his viewpoint, he was wasting his effort and his ingenuity on something that should never have been necessary in the first place.

He opened the file that lay in front of him with particular distaste, recalling that MacIntosh had said when he brought it in, "Make this a special, Frankie. Looks like it might be someone important." Frank Gross had no love for important people.

If it weren't for his nineteen years of seniority . . . and that was something a guy with a wife and four kids couldn't forget . . . he would have told MacIntosh what he could do. MacIntosh was a pain in the tail. An ordinary guy drops dead, it's nothing but routine, but let a case turn up that looks maybe like it's got a couple of votes behind it and right away MacIntosh has got to make it "special" . . . yah, and at twenty to five just so it would make him miss his train.

Frank Gross replaced his glasses, blinked his eyes into focus, and examined the flimsy carbon of the report form. WALLET . . . no. PAPERS . . . none. LAUNDRY MARKS . . . none . . . there ought to be a federal law about laundry marks . . . initials A.B. on shirtsleeves. SUIT . . . medium brown with faint red overplaid . . . custom-tailored by D. Andruzzi, Palm Beach, Florida . . . no customer label. Coat . . . 44 long. Trousers . . . 40 waist, 35 inseam. HAT . . . Dobbs, 6⅞, initials A.B. CONTENTS OF POCKETS . . . small coins, total $1.57, bus token from Canton, Ohio, Camel cigarettes, Dunhill lighter with initials A.B.

Frank vented an impatient snort at the imbecile who had made out the report, mumbling aloud, "I know his initials are A.B. How many times you got to keep telling me?"

With a resigned sigh, he opened the upper right-hand drawer of his desk and took out a pad of message blanks. He wrote two telegrams. One was addressed to CHIEF POLICE, PALM BEACH, FLA., the other to CHIEF POLICE, CANTON, OHIO. On out-of-the-city cases, Frank never addressed a message to an individual of lesser status than Chief Police. If they didn't like it, so what? Served them right for allowing their citizens to make a nuisance of themselves to the City of New York.

The message written, Frank Gross walked to his locker, took out his hat, and started for home. MacIntosh had said to make it special . . . Okay, it was special. What more could he do?

5.02 P.M. EDT

George Caswell, breasting the five o'clock human tide that roared down Wall Street toward the subway entrance, finally managed to make the appointed corner. The traffic officer recognized him, grinned a polite salute and flipped his hand to indicate the Cadillac that was idling in the No Parking zone halfway up the block.

Neil Finch was already in the back seat and the chauffeur had the car moving the moment that Caswell was inside. The two men were friends of long standing, a relationship so secure that it had withstood both competition and proximity. They were the heads of two rival stock-brokerage houses—Caswell & Co. and Slade & Finch—and for the last nine years they had lived in adjoining Long Island estates. During the summer months they rode back and forth together, using their cars on alternate days.

"Hope it wasn't too inconvenient, Neil, my holding you up like this," Caswell said.

"No. Good thing. Gave me a chance to clear a few things off my desk."

They rode in silence until the car stopped, blocked by a traffic snarl.

"I hear your friend was in town today," Finch said.

"Who's that?"

"Avery Bullard. Wingate happened to see him coming out of your office."

"Oh. Yes, Bullard was in. As a matter of fact that's one thing that held me up, waiting for him to call me."

"Found himself an executive vice-president yet?"

"That's what he was to call me about.. He was having lunch with Bruce Pilcher."

"Bruce Pilcher?"

"You know him, don't you?"

"Of course." There was a pointed pause. "You say Pilcher had lunch with Avery Bullard?"

"Yes. Why?"

"Tredway in any kind of trouble, George?"

"Trouble? What do you mean?"

"Something must have happened at lunch that gave Pilcher an extremely unfavorable impression of the Tredway Corporation."

"I can't imagine what it could be."

"You're sure there's no bad news in the offing?"

"Positive."

"Well, you ought to know," Finch said. "You're still on the Tredway board, aren't you?"

"Yes. What do you mean about Pilcher getting an unfavorable impression?"

"This is confidential, of course?"

"Naturally."

"Could be only a coincidence, but it seems to fit together a little too well for that. What time was Bullard's luncheon date with Pilcher?"

"Twelve-forty-five at Julius Steigel's office in the Chippendale Building."

"Then the lunch would be over by two-thirty?"

"I imagine so. What are you getting at?"

Finch turned, half twisting his body so that he faced George Caswell across the wide back seat of the limousine. "A few minutes after two-thirty Bruce Pilcher called our office and gave us a wide-open order to sell Tredway common short."

Caswell jerked to attention. "So that's where all that stock came from."

"We got rid of two thousand shares in about twenty minutes."

"I know. I bought it."

"The hell you did! For your own account?"

"Yes."

"You must have a lot of faith in that outfit."

"I have a lot of faith in Avery Bullard," Caswell said, hesitating before he went on as if he were debating the propriety of an important revelation. "I've been building a block of Tredway for the past several years, picking it up whenever I could. It's not very actively traded, you know, most days not more than a few hundred shares. That's why I was so surprised when I got back to the office and found that the boys had bought me two thousand shares this afternoon. Frankly, that's considerably more that I'd expected to get when I told them to buy everything that turned up."

"When did you place that order, George—to buy everything you could get?"

Caswell turned, squinting, as if the question surprised him. "About noon."

"After you had talked to Bullard?"

"Yes."

"Then Pilcher must have wormed something out of Bullard at lunch that you didn't find out this morning."

"I don't see how that's possible."

"Pilcher is no fool. It's plain that he had a tip on some really bad news."

"There is no bad news. The company's in excellent shape."

Finch shook his head. "Bruce Pilcher wouldn't have gone short on that much stock if he didn't have a sure thing—if he weren't positive that there was something coming up that would really break the price."

"But what could it be?"

"Don't ask me. You're the specialist on Tredway. I'm simply telling you what happened. Cigar?"

"No thanks," Caswell said, preoccupied. "Is Bruce Pilcher a regular customer of yours?"

Finch glanced away from the match flame as if he were surprised by the apparent irrelevancy of the question. "Occasional —perhaps a half-dozen transactions a year."

"That's what I thought," George nodded grimly. "He has a very active account with us."

Finch got the point immediately. "You think he switched this order to us to keep you from knowing who was selling?"

"Obviously."

"Or else," Finch said with a taunting grin, "he'd just gotten tired of doing business with a second-string broker."

Caswell's smile was a weak attempt. "Unless I miss my guess, Mr. Pilcher has crawled out on a very long limb. He'll have a hard time covering a short sale of two thousand shares. The stock's too inactive and most of it's in very strong hands."

"I hope you're right, George. Hate to see an old war horse like you being put over the jumps by an upstart like Bruce Pilcher."

"Save your worry for your customers, Neil. Pilcher's the boy who's put himself on a spot."

"You still have no idea of what he might have gotten out of Bullard at lunch? He's a clever young fox, George. You know that as well as I do."

"Not clever enough to outsmart Avery Bullard."

"He must have found out something."

"I tell you there was nothing to find out," Caswell said, his voice sharpened with a quick-passing edge of irritation. "I spent two hours with Avery Bullard this morning. We went over the whole business from stem to stern. If there was any bad news in the wind he'd have told me about it."

"Sure? From some of the stories I've heard you tell about Mr. Avery Bullard I've gathered the impression that he can be a bit of a fox himself—if the occasion demands it."

Caswell shook his head vigorously. "If I've ever said anything to give you that impression of Avery Bullard it was completely unintentional. He's rough and tough and always swinging with both fists, but he's one of the most uncompromisingly honest men that I've ever known in my whole life. I think—yes, it's true—I have more respect for Avery Bullard than for any man I've ever done business with. If I were to lose my faith in him I'd lose my faith in everyone."

"I long since have," Finch said with a wry chuckle. "It's not as much of a handicap as you might think. Helps you keep your perspective."

George Caswell did not smile. He found no humor in Finch's cynicism.

"What's the matter, George, still worried?" Finch finally said, breaking the silence.

"Not worried," Caswell said slowly. "Just wondering why Avery Bullard didn't call me back this afternoon.

5.12 P.M. EDT

Bruce Pilcher, exercising his self-endowed prerogative as a third-generation member of the Greenback Club who had been proposed for membership on the day of his birth, ordered a

[53]

very dry Martini to be served in the reading room, a violation of the house rules.

Andrew, the oldest of the club's attendants, shuffled in with the cocktail and Bruce Pilcher flipped a dollar tip on the wet tray. The waiter sponged the bill dry, making no attempt to conceal the fact that his annoyance exceeded his gratitude.

Pilcher was completely unaware of Andrew's openly critical attitude but he would not have been disturbed even if he had noticed it. The perpetually sour mien of all of the club's employees was as much a part of the decorative scheme as the collection of gold-framed life-size nudes that sprawled lasciviously over the worthless stock certificates with which the walls were completely covered.

"Where are the late papers, Andrew?" Pilcher demanded.

The old waiter silently indicated the rack.

"I want the final editions. Is there any good reason why they shouldn't be here by now?"

Andrew shuffled out.

Pilcher lifted the cocktail, studying the tracery of lemon oil that marbled the surface. The tremor of his hand started tiny ringlet waves and, as if their consumption might banish his nervousness, he gulped deeply, half of the glass in a single draught.

There was no reason for nervousness, he told himself. It was perfectly understandable why there had been nothing in the Wall Street Closing editions about Avery Bullard . . . hadn't been time . . . might not be anything in the Final either. But that wouldn't matter. It would be there in the morning. No, that wasn't anything to be nervous about. Neither was the two thousand shares. Yes, he had been shocked when Wingate had called back to tell him that they had sold two thousand shares . . . hadn't expected anything like that in twenty minutes on an inactive issue . . . but still it was all right . . . better than all right . . . perfect! When you held the winning cards, the bigger the pot the better.

Wingate had told him that the reason he had been able to sell so much Tredway was that there was a rumor on the floor that some of the smart-money boys were expecting an unusually good semi-annual report on Tredway's first half.

Pilcher sipped his drink now. His hand was steady again. The smart-money boys wouldn't seem so smart when the *Times* and the *Herald Tribune* came out tomorrow morning with Avery Bullard's obituary. The *Times* might even use a picture. He smiled, remembering what Liebermann had said after the Congressional investigation. "About the only reward there's left for an industrialist in this country is a nice obituary in the *New York Times*."

The smart-money boys would have Avery Bullard's obituary served up to them with their breakfast. Then the fun would start. The sell orders would pile up before the opening. The first sale would probably be off a point or a point and a half. Then it would really start sliding. By the end of the first hour . . .

His mind braked to a dead stop. Tomorrow was Saturday . . . the market would be closed! He stood up, waiting for the pounding of his heart to subside, telling himself that he must hold his balance, keep his brain sharp and clear, stay cold and smart. Did it really matter? No. What didn't happen tomorrow would happen Monday morning. Monday would be even better. There would be the whole weekend of rumor and gossip about what the loss of Avery Bullard would mean to Tredway.

He marshaled more arguments but none was strong enough to counter the disconcerting knowledge that he had been guilty of an error of omission—there was a fact he had missed. The fact itself wasn't important but the missing was! What else had he overlooked?

Bruce Pilcher gulped the last of the cocktail and the glass chattered with his trembling hand as it touched the table. Where else had he slipped?

The sharp point of his mind reached back like an auditor's pencil, checkmarking the facts. Could he have been wrong about the man in the ambulance? No, it was unquestionably Avery Bullard. Was he dead? Yes, because the interne had covered his face. Wait! Did that mean for certain that he was dead? The checkmark hung suspended. The answer was vital. It was a key point. If Bullard weren't actually dead, the whole situation changed.

His eyes darted nervously about the room. The sight of a telephone instrument flashed a thought. He would call the hospital. Why hadn't he thought of that before? Roosevelt. He remembered the name on the ambulance. His hand touched the phone and then drew away. This line went through the switchboard. It would be safer to use a private booth.

Impulse urged him to run but he forced himself to walk with a carefully measured stride, out through the lobby, speaking casually to three entering members in a voice that betrayed nothing, on to the telephone booth. His fingertips left damp brands on the thin paper as he turned the pages, searching for the number. He found it and dialed.

"Please connect me with someone who can tell me about the condition of a patient."

"What is the name of the patient about whom you wish to inquire, sir?"

"Avery Bullard—Mr. Avery Bullard."

"One moment, please."

He waited, his lungs straining as if they had used up the last breath of air in the tiny cubicle.

"B as in Benjamin?" the voice finally came back.

"Yes," and he spelled Avery Bullard's full name.

"I'm sorry, sir, but we have no patient under that name."

"But you must. I saw—he was taken to the hospital in an ambulance this afternoon."

"There has been no one by that name admitted during the last twenty-four hours. Perhaps it was one of the other hospitals."

"No, it was Roosevelt! I'm sure that—"

There was a distant click and then silence.

5.15 P.M. EDT

"Miss Finnick," the girl at the desk in the waiting room said. "Down the hall. Second door on your right."

The doctor was looking at a card when she opened the door, the card that the girl at the desk had made out.

"I'm Doctor Marston. Won't you sit down."

Anne Finnick hesitated, knowing that if she sat down she might lose her nerve and not be able to go through with it. "I'm a friend of Mrs. Paul Sansom's."

"Oh, yes," the doctor said pleasantly, not seeming to notice that she was still standing. "What's the trouble, Miss Finnick?"

This was the moment . . . she had to do it. "I want to know if I'm pregnant."

She waited, watching his face. Viola had been right about him. He was a swell guy, not looking surprised or anything. She could say the rest of it. "I know if I am I got to go to somebody else to do something about it, but Viola said I would be crazy to get myself into a mess like that if I wasn't sure. I ain't asking you to do anything that ain't all right, am I, just telling me whether I'm pregnant or not?"

"No indeed," he said, softly positive. "And I hope you're not."

He really sounded like he meant it. Viola was sure right, this Dr. Marston was one awful nice guy. It didn't matter what he charged, it would be worth it, knowing for sure and being treated like a human being. She had all the money she needed. There had been five hundred and thirty-four dollars in the wallet.

5.21 P.M. EDT

The teletype bell rang, the machine buzzed, and then the type bars began to spatter black letters again: TAILOR D ANDRUZZI OUT OF BUSINESS RECORDS UNAVAILABLE WHEREABOUTS UNKNOWN POLICE PALM BEACH

5.27 P.M. EDT

Bruce Pilcher was in the strangling grip of total terror. He had known fear before but never anything like this. His mind had passed the point where panic was a stimulant. Now it was a poison, so paralyzing to the motor centers of his brain that it was all but impossible to form a coherent thought.

His call to Roosevelt Hospital had convinced him that he had been guilty of a staggering blunder. The man he had seen being put into the ambulance could not have been Avery Bullard. Through the fog of terror he could see the outline of the trap that was closing in on him. He was short two thousand shares. There was a strong demand for Tredway stock. The way his selling order had been snapped up proved that. If he had to go into the market on Monday morning and try to cover . . . $2000 . . . $4000 . . . $8000 . . . $16,000 . . . catastrophy multiplied in geometric proportion.

He had less than four thousand dollars in the bank. It seemed incredible but it was true. His divorce settlement had taken fifty thousand cash. The house in Westchester was mortgaged for every cent he could borrow on it. If the stock went up even a few dollars a share he was bankrupt. He would not be able to meet his obligations and that meant the end of his reputation and his career.

There was only one way he could save himself . . . get his hands on two thousand shares of Tredway stock before the market opened Monday morning. Where . . . where . . . where? The pounding of the word loosened a fragment from the hard shell of his memory . . . Shaw . . . Loren P. Shaw. Yes, that was it! Shaw was the comptroller of the Tredway Corporation now. Shaw could find some way to get that stock. He had Shaw under his thumb. Shaw wouldn't dare refuse him, not when he reminded him that he still remembered what had happened on that government contract for Alliance back in . . . No, good God, no! Was he insane? Shaw had more on him than he had on Shaw. He didn't have Shaw under his thumb. It was the other way around!

The fog was clearing. He could think again. Yes, that's what he had to do . . . think! It was the only way he could save himself . . . the way he had always saved himself before . . . with his mind. The thought of Shaw still ricocheted around in the dark labyrinths of his brain. Another fragment of memory was chipped loose. He had met a woman on Madison Avenue that evening after he'd had dinner with Shaw. Shaw had said she was the biggest stockholder in the company, the inheritor of the Tredway estate. What was her name? Tredway? No, she was married . . . lived in Millburgh . . . Julia? Yes, that was it . . . Julia . . . Julia . . . Julia? Suddenly the name flashed . . . Julia Tredway Prince!

Bruce Pilcher started across the library again, retracing his path to the telephone booth. He would find some way to get that stock. His mind was working again. That was the important thing. . . he had always been able to think his way out of tight spots before. He could do it again.

Everything was all right now. He had himself under control. He was walking the way a man walked when he was under perfect control, slow and steady and even-strided. Near the center of the lobby he passed Andrew coming toward the library with the Final editions flat on his outstretched arms. "Thank you, Andrew," he said pleasantly. Yes, he was all right now.

Inside the telephone booth he paused to make absolutely certain that the last trace of fog had left his mind. There was no doubt about it. It had been months since he had met Julia Tredway Prince, yet the moment he had asked his mind to supply her name, there it was. No, there was nothing wrong with his mind. It was functioning perfectly.

He dialed the operator. "I want to place a long-distance call to Millburgh, Pennsylvania—person to person—Mrs. Julia Tredway Prince."

5.40 P.M. EDT

"You're quite certain that it's been three months?" Dr. Marston asked.

"Three months last Saturday night," Anne Finnick said, dry-mouthed, not daring to take her eyes from his. "That was the only time."

"Then you're not pregnant."

"You're sure?"

"By the end of the third month we can determine pregnancy quite easily. If it's really been three months you have nothing to worry about."

[59]

A cry of ecstasy rose in her throat but all that escaped her lips was the low animal whimper of a frightened creature being released from the jaws of a trap.

Blindly, fighting tears, she groped for her purse.

"You can pay the young lady outside," he said softly, turning away so she was not forced to show him the tears that could not be fought back.

"That will be ten dollars," the girl at the desk said.

Anne Finnick opened her purse, shielding the opening with her hand, finding a bill from the center of the pack that was less water-stained than the others. She dropped it on the table, started for the door.

"Your paper," the girl called after her.

She turned, hurriedly retrieving the tight-rolled newspaper from the maple settee. It was a Final edition that she had bought half an hour ago. It seemed like half a lifetime.

MILLBURGH, PENNSYLVANIA
5.44 P.M. EDT

As Don Walling entered the black marble lobby of the Tredway Tower he glanced up at the great bronze clock and saw that he had wasted a quarter of an hour by his hurried departure from the Pike Street factory. He might have waited ten minutes longer, long enough to have seen at least the start of the first test-run, but he had not dared to gamble that the traffic on South Front Street would be as light as it had proved to be. Once he had gambled and lost. He had not forgotten the expression with which Avery Bullard had greeted him as he had walked into executive committee meeting six minutes late. That had been almost two years ago, soon after he had been made a vice-president, when pleasing Avery Bullard had seemed to be the very essence of living, but the memory still persisted.

Don Walling was certain that his presence at the meeting couldn't possibly be as important as staying at the factory to supervise the first test-run of the new molding process. Yet he had not dared to stay. Avery Bullard's command could not be denied. If there were a chance to talk to Avery Bullard before the meeting, he would be excused . . . but there would be no chance. The president would start the meeting the moment he entered the door of the directors' room, talking as he strode to his chair. There would be no way to interrupt, no chance for a pardon. Afterwards, when Avery Bullard found out he would demand, "Damn it, why didn't you tell me?" . . . and there would be no way to explain why he hadn't. There were some things you couldn't tell Avery Bullard . . . a great many things . . . more all the time. There had been a big change in Avery Bullard these last two years.

If Don Walling had been a highly introspective man—which he was not—he might have understood that at least a part of what he thought of as a change in Avery Bullard was actually a change in his own viewpoint and understanding. These last two years of intimate association had made him see Avery Bullard as something other than the faultless idol that he had once thought him to be. Inwardly, Don Walling had fought against that realization. Even now he hesitated to step across the thin and wavering line that marked the limit of his unswerving loyalty to Avery Bullard. It had been a long journey to that line, a journey that had taken all of his life, a journey over an up-and-down road, alternately high and low with peaks of idolatry and deep valleys of disillusion.

In the orphans' home, from the time he was old enough for remembered thought until he was seven, he had dreamed of a father and mother who would some day come and take him from the home. Then one day they had come, both a father and a mother, and they had lifted him to the first peak of his life—but the descent to the valley of disillusion was cruelly swift. A mother, he found, was not the warm source of solace for which his heart had ached, but a strange woman who cried most of the time and insisted that his name was no longer his own name, but that he was now someone else whose name was "MacDonald Walling, the Second." The man he was to call his father did not turn out to be the joyful companion about whom he dreamed, but a tired-eyed man who smelled of cigars and whiskey and spent the few evenings when he was home watching his wife over the top edge of a face-shielding newspaper.

Four years later, when he was eleven, after the horror of a night about which he remembered little except the startling redness of blood against the whiteness of the bathtub, and the after-gained knowledge that his foster mother had attempted to commit suicide, he had been taken to Rubble Hill Academy, a boarding school for boys. He never saw his foster parents again. But the next morning he met Mr. Andrews.

It was Mr. Andrews, the headmaster at Rubble Hill, who told him that he did not have to call himself MacDonald Walling, the Second. Mr. Andrews had proved it by telling him that his own name had been Bartholomew Meade Andrews but now it was simply Bart Andrews. The boy could be Mac Walling or Don Walling, whichever he preferred. He chose Don because Mac was what his foster mother had called his foster father.

That had been only the first step of the long journey on which Mr. Andrews had piloted young Don Walling. Bart Andrews led him into the world of books and art, of thinking and knowledge, and the excitement of learning. He became the boy's ideal, his unquestioned leader, the model against which he shaped his own development—until that day of disillusionment when Bart Andrews called him into his office and told him that his foster father had failed to pay his tuition for the next semester and, as an unfortunate but inescapable consequence, Don must leave Rubble Hill. Don Walling learned then that there was a price on friendship. He never saw Mr. Andrews again.

At Rubble Hill, Don was given five dollars, a railroad ticket, and told to report to a Mr. McIlhenny at the Orphans' Court in Pittsburgh. He never reported. Lost, wandering down Diamond Street, he saw a group of men loitering in front of an employment agency. He stopped to ask directions but, before his question could be answered, a man opened the door and shouted, "Twenty laborers on a construction job out in Schenley Hill. Anybody wants it, hold up their hand." Don held up his hand. He was only seventeen but he was big for his age and no questions were asked. The five dollars went for advance rent on a room. He had no money to buy meals until his first payday. Hungry, he picked a little restaurant near the job and asked for credit. That was how he met Mike Kovales. Mike needed a night dishwasher. Don took the job. For eight hours every day he shoved a wheelbarrow, for almost eight hours every night he washed dishes for Mike. That fall Mike promoted him to a counter man and talked him into going back to high school for his last year. The counter customers at night were mostly architectural students from Carnegie Tech and out of snatches of their overheard conversations, Don Walling built a new dream —he would go to college and become an architect.

Tech was a disappointment. Don had keyed himself to a high pitch of anticipation in preparation for what he expected to be an intellectual challenge. He did not find it. It was all too easy. The pace was too slow, the demands too light. Weeks were spent on textbooks that he found he could read and understand in a single night. Study problems seemed elementary and unrelated to the actual practice of architecture. He felt that he wasn't getting anywhere. He stayed on because he didn't want to be a quitter and because Mike had taken to bragging that "his boy" was going to be a college-graduated architect.

The second spring, when Don was a sophomore, Mike decided to remodel the restaurant. Because it was a chance to design something that was actually going to be built, Don drew the plan and made a perspective sketch. Mike was pleased and let him supervise the job. Twice a day Don went across the river to Trimmer's cabinet shop in Allegheny, ostensibly to check on the construction of the booths and counters, but actually to drink in the pleasure of seeing his drawings transformed into polished mahogany. It was an enormously stimulating experience, surpassing in emotional intensity anything he had ever known. He decided that he would specialize in the architectural design of store interiors and, by a quirk of fate, his decision was made on the same week that he met Karl Eric Kassel. According to the double-page advertisement of the Pittsburgh department store whose interior he had just designed, Karl Eric Kassel was "the undisputed leader of the great modern revolution that is sweeping the field of interior design."

Karl Eric Kassel came to Pittsburgh to lend his redbearded presence to the store's grand reopening. He was feted at Schenley Hall with a banquet that crammed the ballroom to its doors. Afterwards, the great man lectured to the Tech students and, to a second round of deafening applause, the chairman's awed thanks included the announcement of an annual competition for furniture designs in the modern manner. The first prize for each year's winner would be an opportunity to work as an apprentice in the New York studio of Karl Eric Kassel.

In his senior year Don Walling won the Karl Eric Kassel competition. After a parting with Mike Kovales that touched him more than he had imagined possible, he left for New York. It was the spring of 1931 and, although he was conscious of what people were beginning to call the "depression," he was not quite prepared for Karl Eric Kassel's contention that general business was so bad he would be unable to pay him more than ten dollars a week, plus the privilege of sleeping in the storeroom behind the "studio." Of course, as Mr. Kassel pointed out, there was the additional compensation of working with Karl Eric Kassel, a privilege that was something quite beyond mundane valuation, particularly since he was now pioneering a whole new field. Karl Eric Kassel was no longer a mere interior designer, he was now a "functional industrial stylist," prepared to add the selling power of aesthetics to any article "from a mousetrap to a locomotive." There was no reason, Karl Eric Kassel said, why Don Walling—given time, of course—could not find an "important niche" in this new field.

For several months Don did not suspect how short that "given time" was to be, nor how important his niche really was. Karl Eric Kassel did not enlighten him. He kept Don's drawing board heaped with "interesting little problems" and as fast as Don could reduce his problems to paper, Karl Eric Kassel took the drawings away with the uniform comment that they were "rather hopeful for a first attempt." Several months later, fanning a merchandising trade magazine, Don saw a picture of a newly announced electric range. It was his "solution" of one of Karl Eric Kassel's "interesting little problems," line for line without the change of a single detail. The accompanying article quoted the manufacturer as saying, "The $5000 fee which we paid Karl Eric Kassel for the exhaustive design analysis that led to this superlative creation has proved to be a splendid investment."

Don, white with anger, was packing when Karl Eric Kassel intercepted his intended flight. What happened then was something for which Don Walling spent most of the next year attempting to excuse himself. Somehow, as the result of a blend of verbal artifice to which he had never been exposed before, he allowed Karl Eric Kassel to talk him into staying. Afterwards, thinking about it and trying to prove to himself that his submission was not the result of a personal weakness, Don told himself that it most assuredly was not because Kassel had given him a hundred-dollar bonus and raised his salary to twenty-five dollars a week. Money didn't matter. What did influence him, according to the explanation in which he finally found some measure of self-justification, was Karl Eric Kassel's honest confession that he was a complete charlatan who couldn't draw a line himself, and that most of the work to which his name had been signed over the years had been done by the stream of talented young men who had been Don's predecessors.

The revelation was made all the more effective by Karl Eric Kassel's sudden dropping of the "Viennese" accent which Don had never suspected had been an actor's trick. He could not have been more surprised if Karl Eric Kassel had suddenly unhooked his red beard. "Listen, kid, it's time you learn something about the facts of life," Karl Eric Kassel had said, dropping not only the accent but all of the well-polished mannerisms with which he had veneered his personality. "You're a clever boy. You got imagination. You got brains. You got drive. You got guts. You got ambition. Where's it get you? Lemme tell you— nowhere—not unless you know the facts of life. That's what I'm trying to teach you. You stick with me and I'll hand you the front-door key to a gold mine. You think all the gold mines are in the hard rock of the big mountains? No. The biggest gold mine in the world is right inside the hard skulls of all these bigshot businessmen. Ask yourself this—how did they get what they got? How do they make all their dough? Simple. They found something that the public was a sucker for. Right? They make a sucker out of the public—so I turn around and make a sucker out of them. What's wrong with that? Turnabout's fair play, isn't it? Do I give them their money's worth? Sure—exactly the way they give a woman her money's worth when they sell her twenty cents worth of perfumed lanolin in a fancy jar for two dollars. Does she kick? No. She's satisfied. She likes it. All suckers like it. Makes them feel good. That's the whole secret, boy. These big shots are no different. They like it too. There's only one thing. They're big men. They know it. Everything around them's got to be big. They got to operate in a big way. If they're going to be a sucker they don't want to be no small sucker—they got to be a big sucker.

"You know Mr. A. W. Wilberson, president of C & W Housewares? A very big man. Big in all ways. Let us take a hypothetical situation—very hypothetical. You are not the associate of Karl Eric Kassel—you are only you. You go to see Mr. Wilberson—which is what I mean by hypothetical because when you go there he will not see you. So you write him a letter. You ask him to give you a job at a very large salary like thirty-five dollars a week and in two weeks you will design him a new percolator. What happens? He tears up the letter. Why? He is insulted. That way the new design would only cost him seventy dollars. You have treated him in a small way. That is wrong. You have treated him like a man who is smart enough to want to make a good deal. That is wrong. Also you have treated him with respect. That is wrong. You have made all those mistakes. Now Karl Eric Kassel steps in. I do not make those mistakes. I do not treat him like a smart man. I do not let him know that I have respect for him. I treat him like a sucker. That is what he wants. I give him the red beard. I give him the phony accent. I give him the big name—which is also a phony. I give him the big price. I do not insult him. I give him the chance to be the big sucker. That is what he wants. He likes it. He is willing to pay for it."

The appeal of Karl Eric Kassel's revelation was the appeal of an invitation to sophistication and Don Walling accepted it, somewhat as an adolescent toys with vice, but more as a student who steps over the barriers that separate him from a new field of learning without questioning either purpose or propriety.

Don Walling learned a great deal in the next ten months as Kassel allowed him to have more and more contact with prospects and clients. Some of what he learned followed the tenets of Karl Eric Kassel's teaching, some did not. He found some corporation executives of the type that Kassel had described, enough of them to keep a reasonably steady flow of commissions coming into the studio, but Don's reaction did not parallel Karl Eric Kassel's. Instead of generating cynicism, these men inspired pity. Most of them, despite their cultivated executive poise, lived with a terrible fear. They were trying desperately to find some way to counteract their own recognized shortcomings through buying talent and judgment to fill the void. What Karl Eric Kassel sold, even more than designs, was an escape from fear. Even if it was temporary, it was something. Even if it failed, it was a try. The "good try," Don learned was a merit badge in the world of business.

He had little chance to get to know the industrial executives who most incited his admiration. They seldom survived the prospect stage. They were too smart to fall for the pretentious antics of Karl Eric Kassel. One of those men was Avery Bullard.

Karl Eric Kassel had secured a commission to design a house to be exhibited at the Century of Progress Exposition in Chicago, and a second commission to create a new line of furniture to furnish the house. It turned out to be a one-man job for Don Walling. Kassel kept promising him assistants but, although there were unemployed draftsmen in every bread line, he somehow managed to avoid finding them. Don worked twenty hours a day for weeks on end. The final construction and furnishing, which he went to Chicago to supervise, was a nightmare seen through glazed and bloodshot eyes. On the night before the opening, completely exhausted, he had collapsed on a pile of furniture pads.

Sometime during the night the lights flashed on. Don awakened enough to be conscious that Karl Eric Kassel was giving some prospective client a preview showing as bait for his trap. Don heard the man's voice and there was something about its timbre that instantly completed his awakening. He listened and what he heard gave him a vindictive satisfaction. The man's words were slashing through the armor of Karl Eric Kassel's pretense. Finally there was a pause and then the heart thrust. "Kassel, who actually designed this furniture?"

Afterwards, over the years, when Don Walling was tempted to charge Karl Eric Kassel with all the bitterness and anger that he had felt during those two long years, there was always the book-balancing memory of the way the red-bearded charlatan had redeemed himself that night in the World's Fair house. Kassel had said, directly and simply, "This house and everything in it was designed by a very talented young man named Don Walling."

"I want to see him," the voice had demanded—and Don, more awakened than he had ever been in his life, unconscious of his grimy hands and his rumpled work clothes, unconscious of Karl Eric Kassel, unconscious of everything in the world except the necessity of obeying that command, walked out through the door to meet Avery Bullard.

Somehow, unnoticed, Karl Eric Kassel disappeared and left them alone. They wandered down to the lakefront, Bullard talking, questioning, gently probing. There was no sword edge in his voice now, but it had lost none of its exciting quality. It was the voice of strength and power, of integrity and purpose, of fearless imagination that leaped skyward with the same magic that the rising sun streaked the sky over Lake Michigan, setting even the water aflame.

Karl Eric Kassel was not surprised when Don told him that he was going to work for Avery Bullard. "I know," he said simply. "Good luck. He's a great man."

During those next two years, the years before the merger that created the Tredway Corporation, Don Walling worked closely with Avery Bullard. All his life he had been searching for a total challenge. Now he had found it. No matter how much energy and thought he poured into whatever they were working on, Avery Bullard could outwork him and outthink him. The range of the older man's ability was a constant goad. He would come rushing in, take one quick look at a design that Don had been working on for days and instantly put his finger on something which, the moment Don saw it, he recognized as a flaw that he should have caught and corrected himself. Even more exasperating was the way Avery Bullard could snatch up a pencil and redraw a line that Don, no matter how long he struggled, could seldom improve. Competence is a whip in the hands of a taskmaster, and the lash cuts all the deeper when the whip is held by a perfectionist. Avery Bullard was unrelenting. Once he made Don turn out twenty-six sketches for a little brass toe on a Duncan Phyfe table. When a sketch was finally selected and the first trial casting made, Avery Bullard took one look and literally threw it out of the window of his twenty-fourth floor office. Then they started all over again. Don agreed that the end result was worth all that it had cost in money and time. It was closer to perfection.

After the merger, which was the first major fulfillment of the dream picture that Avery Bullard had drawn in that pre-dawn hour on the shores of Lake Michigan, he had sent Don Walling to Pittsburgh to work with the Coglan Metal Furniture Company. "There are things we can do with metal that the furniture industry hasn't even thought about yet. Go out there and do them. Don't let anything stand in your way. Old man Coglan will tell you it can't be done, that they tried that before. Don't bother to tell him to go to hell, just disregard him. He doesn't count. I had to keep him for appearance' sake. He'll be out in a year. Work closely with the superintendent, a man named Jesse Grimm. I don't know him too well yet but he looks good. I think he's our kind. But don't rely on Grimm. Don't rely on anyone. Get out in that factory yourself. Learn how to work metal. Know what you can do with those machines and what you can't do—and when you want to do something that a machine won't do, design a machine that will do it. Get out in the trade. Talk to people. Go to the markets.

Find out what they want—even when they don't know yet that they want it—and then give it to them. One last thing, Walling. Don't wear out the seat of your pants on the drawing board stool. Hire a draftsman to get your ideas on paper. If you get enough ideas, hire two draftsmen—or three or four or five. Draftsmen are cheap. Ideas are what count."

Don Walling went to Pittsburgh fired not only with the incentive of a flaring opportunity but also with the chance to escape from the constant domination of Avery Bullard. Before the end of the first week the second motivation had lost its validity. He needed Avery Bullard and the recognition of that need revealed a weakness in himself that he set out to remedy. In the attempt, he began unconsciously to model himself in the Avery Bullard pattern. Trouble developed. The morale in the factory, stemming from a natural resentment of the forced merger, was none too good at best. Don Walling's aping of Bullard's tactics made it worse. Finally, in a midnight session on the back porch of Jesse Grimm's house, the superintendent said, "Somebody has to tell you off, Don, and I guess I'm elected. I don't know too much about Avery Bullard because I've only had two short talks with him, but I know something about the men in our plant. They won't swallow the idea that Avery Bullard sent you out here to be a twenty-six-year-old carbon copy—and I might as well tell you that it doesn't go down with me either."

Don's first reaction was one of angry resentment but, under the soft attrition of Grimm's reasonableness, it gradually dissolved into the reluctant acceptance of just punishment. He felt like a spanked child and it wasn't a pleasant feeling. He promised himself that no one would ever again call him a carbon copy of Avery Bullard. In time he became as good a friend of Jesse Grimm's as the older man's carefully impersonal attitude would permit.

Meetings with Avery Bullard were few and far between, much less frequent than Don would have liked. He said so once on one of his trips to Millburgh. Avery Bullard had grinned. "Hell's bells, boy, don't you know that leaving you alone is the

[71]

best compliment I can pay you? When I don't like what's happening you'll hear from me soon enough—more than you'll want to hear! By the way, we're boosting your salary to ten thousand."

It was then that he said, "I guess that ought to be enough to support a wife, Mr. Bullard."

"Who is she?"

He had hesitated, asking himself again the very secret question that he had asked himself so many times during the last two weeks. Then, more defiant than he had ever dared be with Avery Bullard before, he had said, "Her name is Mary Kovales. Her father used to run a little restaurant where I worked when I went to school. He's dead. She isn't in the social register and the first time she'll ever taste champagne will be at our wedding."

"How smart is she?" Avery Bullard had asked, and it was no idle question.

"Well—" Don hesitated, searching for some way to tell him. "She's a Ph.D. from the University of Pittsburgh and she has a job now as an assistant to an economist. She—"

"Good," Bullard broke in. "You'll need a smart wife. It's a hell of a handicap when you don't have one. Champagne? Well, that runs up the cost, doesn't it? In that case we'd better raise you to twelve instead of ten. Now get out of here and get back to Pittsburgh before Alderson finds out that I've wasted another two thousand of his precious dollars."

That next year Jesse went back to Millburgh as Vice-President for Production and Don was made General Manager of the Coglan plant. Then the rearmament program started and the Pittsburgh plant was converted to the manufacture of parts for aircraft and naval ships. There were four years when Mary said that she might as well have stayed single for all she saw of her husband. Don didn't agree and Avery Bullard didn't either. "I don't know whether you know it or not, Walling, but that girl's doing you a lot of good. You're beginning to get ripe."

Don wondered if there might be a hidden meaning in Avery Bullard's use of the word "ripe." The year after the war he found out. He was brought back to Millburgh to head the new

Design and Development department, responsible for styling and product development work for all nine factories.

Don Walling's return to Millburgh had not turned out to be the triumphal ascent that he expected. There had been a difficult period of personal adjustment. As general manager of the Pittsburgh plant, he had been at the top of the heap, with almost total authority. In Millburgh, he was only the junior member of the executive staff, hemmed in by the carefully guarded lines that marked the delegation of responsibility to a dozen other department heads. Even after he was given his vice-presidency, he still sat at the foot of the directors' table, outranked by all of the others. He had anticipated his return to designing with considerable pleasure, excited by the possibilities of centralized design control over nine factories, but Grimm and Dudley had thwarted most of his first efforts. Grimm had said that since the factories were all oversold as it was, there was no need to waste the money that putting out new models would entail, and Dudley had agreed that his sales department didn't want to extend the length of the line. Product development work had continually faced handicaps that grew out of the same situation. There was no laboratory building and experimental tests had to be made in the factories. The only way that new processes could be worked out was to stop production on a factory line and, as Shaw pointed out, and the others agreed, that would mean a cut in output and higher costs.

Until these last few months, Don Walling had felt no serious concern about the attitude of the other vice-presidents. It was Avery Bullard's attitude that really mattered and the president had always backed him up, ordering at least a few new patterns into the line every season, and a continuation of development work on the molding process as well as the experimentation that was underway on a new finishing method and a new dry-kiln design. Of late, however, Walling had sensed that Bullard's support was being given with greater and greater reluctance. It seemed that there had been a progressive weakening of the president's driving urge for constant improvement.

In the last month, Don Walling had been called to Avery

Bullard's office only twice and neither time had he felt the energizing stimulus that contact with the president had always given him before. The last conference had been the most unsatisfactory of all. He had gone up with a layout of the new finishing process and an armful of experimental samples showing what could be done with it. Avery Bullard had hardly looked at them. He had spent all of the time discussing a memorandum from Shaw which recommended that all development effort for the rest of the year be concentrated on projects that would have a direct effect on immediate profits. In the end, Don Walling won a partial victory—Bullard agreed that the work on the molding process should continue—but he had left the president's office with the disquieting feeling that, more and more, Avery Bullard's most admirable qualities were being destroyed by the comptroller's unrelenting drive to squeeze out the last penny of net profit from current operations. That had never been Avery Bullard's way of management. It was not the way he had built the Tredway Corporation.

Now, riding up in the elevator, Don Walling's thoughts were more of Shaw than of Avery Bullard, and the disappointment-born anger with which he had forced himself to leave the factory was transferred to the man who sat behind the closed door that he faced as he stepped off on the twenty-third floor.

"Meeting six o'clock, Mr. Walling," Luigi said importantly.

"I know, Luigi. Thank you."

5.53 P.M. EDT

During the minutes that had just passed, Loren P. Shaw had looked at his multi-dialed watch so frequently that an observer, if there had been one present, might easily have judged him to be afflicted with a severe nervous disorder. There was no observer. Shaw was alone in his office and acutely conscious of his solitude. The muffled sounds that came through the wall told him that the other vice-presidents were gathering in Alderson's office, as they frequently did before an executive committee meeting, to compare speculations on what Avery Bullard's next move might be.

Shaw knew that any attempt to outguess the unpredictable Mr. Bullard was a futile waste of time, yet he always found it difficult to restrain himself from joining his fellow vice-presidents' guessing circle. The fact that he had not once done so since Fitzgerald's death represented a triumph of reason over emotion. An executive's rank was measured by the offices he entered. If you went to another man's office instead of forcing him to come to yours, you openly acknowledged his superior status.

According to Loren Shaw's battle plan, the resistance of every such temptation was the winning of another skirmish that carried him one step closer to the executive vice-presidency. His eventual selection, of course, was inevitable—Bullard could not possibly pick anyone else as executive vice-president, it was obvious that none of the others were even remotely qualified —yet every day that it could be moved nearer meant the elimination of another twenty-four hours of tortured waiting.

Deeper in Loren Shaw's mind, too deep for completely conscious recognition, was the fear of what might happen in that moment after he opened the door of Alderson's office, when all eyes would be upon him, when he might be forced to recognize that there was no warmth in their greeting, no invitation to share their fellowship.

Even subconscious thought never passed that point because Loren Shaw had, as an instinctive measure of self-protection, solidly blocked his mind against the acknowledgment that he was not liked by other men. Since that day in high school when he had been defeated in an election for treasurer of the sophomore class, he had always avoided any situation where he might be demeaned by the worthless opinions of superficial fools.

Fighting against the tugging forces that held Loren Shaw in his own office was the full strength of a personal characteristic that was the dominating force in his life. He was an extremely inquisitive man. Curiosity is a normal human trait but in Loren Shaw it had been developed to abnormal proportions. When anyone else knew something that he did not know, particularly when that knowledge might have even an indirect bearing on his own personal future, he was driven to an emotional pitch that frequently pressed the limits of his endurance. Back in his high school days there had been several occasions when he had become physically ill while waiting for the announcement of examination results, despite the fact that he was always absolutely certain that he had made a top grade.

During this last hour and a half, Loren Shaw had endured the constantly mounting torture of not knowing why Avery Bullard had called a special meeting of the executive committee. Nervous perspiration had dampened the palms of his hands again and he opened his desk to take another fresh linen handkerchief from the supply that he kept in the carved teakwood box that fitted the bottom drawer. It was the tenth handkerchief that he had used that day, a necessary extravagance that he placed in the same category with his suits, all of which were made by the New York tailor who, according to *Fortune* magazine, confined his patronage to the nation's top industrial executives.

Loren Shaw closed the drawer on the slightly rumpled handkerchief, moving noiselessly to avoid the possibility of missing any sound that might come through the wall. There were no intelligible words but he could distinguish Walt Dudley's muffled voice and the low rumble of Jesse Grimm's answering laughter.

Shaw's thin lips curled in distaste. Dudley had told another of those moronic stories of his . . . still carrying on like a road salesman instead of a vice-president of the Tredway Corporation . . . blabbering fool! At least Jesse Grimm had the good sense to keep his mouth shut most of the time. But neither of them mattered . . . they were both out of the running . . . so was that old fuddy-duddy Alderson.

Once again, as it had a thousand times since Fitzgerald's death, the sharp needle of Shaw's mind found the same groove in the same record and he heard the same answer . . . Loren P. Shaw, Executive Vice-President. There *was* no other answer. There couldn't be! It was like a simple problem in mathematics. You could work it a dozen ways but the answer was always the same.

But now, in the same groove of the same record, came the unavoidable question and the equally unavoidable fear that always trailed it . . . why was Bullard delaying?

With every asking that question had squeezed out another drop of resentment, until now Loren Shaw's mind was brimming with the acid of long-distilled anger. He hated Avery Bullard with the special hatred of the tortured for the torturer. He hated him for the calculated cruelty that he had inflicted with these months of waiting, for his damnable secrecy, for going to New York without saying a word about what he was doing, for calling an executive meeting with no one knowing why.

No one? Shaw stiffened, apprehensively. Did they know in that office beyond the wall? Did Grimm know . . . or Alderson . . or Dudley or Walling? Walling? No, he hadn't heard Walling's voice. He must not be there. Wasn't this the night that Walling was running that factory test of the molding process? Yes, this was Friday. That meant Walling wouldn't be at the executive committee meeting. Of course not . . . Bullard would never insist on his fair-haired favorite inconveniencing himself!

Shaw reacted instantly. This was his chance! For two weeks he had been holding a special budget report showing that Walling had already overrun the first half budget for experimental work by $6254.18—and on top of that he had a special $6000 appropriation pending for some old press that he wanted rebuilt and set up at Pike Street. Shaw had not sent the report to the president's office because he knew that Avery Bullard would have brushed it aside. But reading the memorandum in executive committee meeting would give the matter an entirely different status. Once entered on the minutes it could not be disregarded . . . and tonight Walling wouldn't be there to soft-soap himself out of trouble. It was about time that somebody tripped him up . . . he had bilked Avery Bullard long enough. Of course they all did it . . . Alderson and Grimm and Dudley, too . . . slipping in to the president's office all the time for those secret little conferences of theirs . . . but Walling was the worst, the worst by far!

[77]

The sound of shuffling chairs came through the wall and Shaw glanced at his watch. Five-fifty-six . . . four minutes . . . the others were going up now. He could still wait one more minute. Then he could be sure that they would all be in the directors' room when he entered. Ever since Fitzgerald's death, Loren Shaw had made a point of timing his meeting entrances so that the others would be forced to look up at his entrance, demanding their acknowledgment that he was the acting executive vice-president, even though there had been a delay in the formality of his election.

His watch told him now that he dared not wait a second longer. Hurriedly snatching up a fresh handkerchief and the special budget report, he started out of the door and up the steps, setting his face in the same studied smile of quizzical inquiry that he had noted so often on the portraits of industrial leaders appearing on the covers of *Business Week* magazine.

As his eyes came level with the upper floor, Loren Shaw saw that his plan had doubly miscarried. The other vice-presidents were still standing outside the door of the directors' room, forming a half-circle with Miss Martin at its focus . . . and Walling was there! Their eyes were away from him, so he carefully folded the budget report and put it in his breast pocket. Timing was important . . . this wasn't the time.

Erica Martin's voice faded in as he reached the head of the staircase and walked toward the group. "—but I'm sure he'll be here on the six-thirteen. With the two trains so close together he could easily have missed one and taken the other. As a matter of fact, he didn't actually say that he was taking the five-fifty-four. I merely assumed that from the fact that he called the meeting for six."

Shaw stepped forward, his eyes on Erica Martin, avoiding the others. "Then Mr. Bullard isn't here yet?"

"No. Eddie called from the station. He's waiting now for the six-thirteen."

Shaw let his eyes circle the four vice-presidential faces, instantly recognizing the opportunity that their annoyance gave him for an effective countermeasure. Holding his smile, broadening it slightly to indicate that the extra half-hour of waiting should be a matter of no concern whatsoever, he unobtrusively took the single step that allowed him to put his hand on the knob of the door. Then with a gesture that was clearly that of a host opening the way for his guests, he pushed back the door. "Gentlemen, there's no reason why you shouldn't make yourselves comfortable."

He had a moment of elation as the group broke and moved past him through the door. No one held back . . . no one debated his position . . . no one even looked at him.

Carefully timing his movement, Loren Shaw turned from the door just as Erica Martin was about to disappear inside her office.

"Oh, Miss Martin?"

"Yes?"

He stood without moving, forcing her to take a step toward him. "It just occurred to me, Miss Martin, that there may be certain reports of one kind or another that Mr. Bullard might want at this meeting. Is there anything that you'd suggest I have ready for him?"

"I'm sorry, Mr. Shaw, but I can't tell you what the meeting is about. I don't know."

He felt the sharp tug of anger as he watched her turn and enter her office. It was a struggle to recapture the smile that was needed before he could step inside the directors' room.

Grimm and Walling were standing at the far side of the room with their backs to him. He circled the table, walking close enough to hear a smattering of their conversation. It was something about phenolformaldehyde resin. They didn't know what the meeting was about either.

He walked on toward Fred Alderson who had taken a notebook from his pocket and was jotting down something as Dudley talked. Before he could get within earshot, Alderson had closed the notebook and tucked it back in his vest pocket. Dudley stopped talking. It was a pointed silence that demanded breaking.

Shaw directed his eyes at Alderson. "Apparently things developed rather rapidly in New York, faster than we expected."

Alderson looked at him blankly. "I—well, I don't quite know what it's all about."

"You don't?" Shaw let his voice carry an unmistakable note of surprise, which he quickly changed to an adroitly embarrassed apology. "Sorry, Fred, I took it for granted that the old man had talked to you about it."

He held his eyes on Alderson only long enough to be sure that the shot had gone home. The silence in the room told him that no one else had missed it either. Their faces, seen as he turned slowly to pull out a chair from the table, confirmed the importance of the impression he had made. They were licked, every one of them . . . and they knew it! They didn't like it but that didn't matter . . . there was nothing they could do about it.

The palms of his hands were damp again and he reached for his handkerchief, opening its folds with a flip that was like the unfurling of a flag.

5.59 P.M. EDT

The telephone was ringing in Erica Martin's office. She answered it. The first sound of the caller's voice brought an instant reaction of annoyance to her face, but she was careful to screen it from her voice before she replied, "I'm sorry, Mrs. Prince, but Mr. Bullard hasn't arrived as yet." She waited, only half hearing the words that buzzed in her ear like the droning of a lazy fly. "Yes, Mrs. Prince, I'll ask him to call you as soon as it's possible for him to do so."

Erica Martin took a deep breath and then, as if she were practicing an exercise in self-control, let the trapped air escape slowly and evenly.

The droning buzz lingered in Erica Martin's ears after she had hung up, evoking memories of other times when Julia Tredway had called for Avery Bullard. Then, no matter how busy he was, Avery would drop everything and drive out to see her. The calls had always come late in the afternoon and he never returned to the office afterward. But that hadn't happened for several years now, not since Julia Tredway had married Dwight Prince. That should have ended it . . . apparently it hadn't . . . it was starting all over again.

The pencil lead snapped under the pressure of Erica Martin's fingers. A note wasn't necessary. She would remember . . . it would be impossible to forget . . . but a note would save her from the necessity of forcing her lips to repeat that creature's name.

6.00 P.M. EDT

The carillon in the lance-point of the Tredway Tower sounded an anticipatory phrase of bell tones and then struck the hour, six rolling resonant peals that vibrated the very walls of the directors' room. The architect of the Tower had failed to anticipate that the top floor of the building would prove to be a reverberation chamber that amplified the bell sound until it was all but unbearable to anyone anywhere in the Executive Suite. Orrin Tredway had endured it because the carillon had been his idea but Avery Bullard, as one of his first official acts after becoming president, had ordered that the carillon was never to be used while he was on the twenty-fourth floor. When Millburgh heard the bells, they knew that the president was not in the Tower.

Frederick Alderson, his liver-spotted fingers gripping the arm of the chair, felt the vibration so strongly that his whole body reacted to it, trembling as if he were caught up in some uncontrollable palsy. Bracing himself against the back of the chair seemed only to heighten the sensation.

The dead stillness that followed the fading of the sixth peal of the bells was something more than ordinary silence. Alderson shifted uneasily in his chair and the rustling crunch of the leather cushion made enough sound to attract the attention of the other four vice-presidents. Their anticipation forced him to say something that he had not intended.

"I hope this meeting doesn't stretch out too long. Mrs. Alderson and I have a dinner date."

"Me too, Fred," Walt Dudley said with a laugh that had no

point. "Got a date with a flying machine—seven at the airport."

"Chicago?"

"Yup. Preview for the chain and mail order boys tomorow. Monday we start sweating out the old market grind again."

Dudley's tone asked for sympathy but before Alderson could respond he saw Loren Shaw lean forward from his seat at the diagonally opposite corner of the table.

"If it isn't convenient, Fred," Shaw said casually, "I see no particular reason why you have to stay for this meeting tonight."

Alderson flinched inwardly, recognizing the trap. He knew that Shaw would like nothing better than to get him out of the way. Then, after Bullard came, Shaw would have another chance to drive a knife in his back. Yes, that was Shaw's game . . . the game he'd been playing ever since Fitzgerald had died.

"Better stick around, Fred," Jesse Grimm whispered from directly across the table, shielding his voice with the hand that was tamping his pipe.

The whisper was more than advice, it was moral support, and Alderson nodded in appreciation. Shaw wasn't fooling Jesse, not for one minute. Could Shaw be fooling the others? No . . . it was too obvious to miss . . . they all knew . . . they all had Shaw's number . . . everyone but Avery Bullard.

Alderson's glance around the table recalled the incident that rankled in his mind as the prime example of Shaw's total depravity. There were eight seats at the table, one at each end and three on each side. Avery Bullard had always sat at the west end and Fitzgerald, before his death, had sat at the east end. Alderson, as the vice-president with the greatest senority, had rightfully occupied the chair at Mr. Bullard's right and Jesse Grimm had sat at his left. In the week after Fitzgerald's death, Shaw had started his conniving. He had begun by managing to have the time of the regular executive committee meeting moved up from eleven to nine-thirty. That put the morning sun directly in Mr. Bullard's eyes and, as Shaw had undoubtedly planned in that snaky little mind of his, Bullard had shifted his seat to the opposite end of the table. That put Shaw at the president's right hand and he—Frederick Alderson, the senior vice-president—found himself sitting at what had suddenly become the foot of the table. He was struck then with an anger so deep-seated that it prohibited any possibility of forgiveness. Shaw had stolen the one most important thing in his life—the seat at Avery Bullard's right hand.

At sixty-one, Frederick Alderson had long since recognized that he had reached the peak of his career. It was clear that he could never be president of the Tredway Corporation. He was five years older than Avery Bullard and would be retired before him. That recognition had caused him no serious regret. He was satisfied with his status as the president's right-hand man. That was enough. He was content with what he had—but it was vitally important to his happiness that he never have less.

Frederick Alderson told himself that if Loren Shaw had been forgivable—which, of course, he wasn't—the one point that might be raised in his defense was the fact that Shaw didn't realize that if it hadn't been for what he had done for Avery Bullard back there in 1921, there never would have been a Tredway Corporation. That had been the start of everything, the beginning without which there could have been nothing.

Shaw wasn't the only one, of course . . . there were a lot of these younger men around the company now who didn't know that either . . . and some of the older men who did know sometimes forgot. There had even been times these last few years when it seemed that Avery Bullard had forgotten . . . but of course he hadn't. Avery Bullard was a great man. Great men did not forget. Sometimes they were too busy, or too distracted by someone else, to remember for the moment but in the end they always did remember. That was why they were great men.

There was no lack of remembering in Frederick Alderson's mind. Strangely, his memory seemed clearer now than it had ever been. Age, instead of dulling his recollection of those faraway days, seemed to have sharpened it. He could recall every thing that had happened all that year, every word that had been said, every action that had been taken. He could even see, as clearly as if he were staring at a perfectly preserved portrait, the exact expression on young Avery Bullard's face that morning he had come out of old Mr. Bellinger's office.

Alderson tipped his head back and, like the lifting of the lid of a music box, the inner voice of his mind began to repeat the words into which his frequent retelling of the story had crystallized the memory. "You probably never heard of the old Bellinger Furniture Company but it was quite a company in its day. Avery Bullard and I worked there together. I was a bookkeeper—that's what they called accountants in those days—and Avery Bullard was a young salesman who'd come with us after the war in eighteen. Well, sir, right from the start I could see that young Avery Bullard was no ordinary drummer so he and I got pretty close.

"In a lot of ways he was the same then as he still is—never liked being tied down to working with figures—so I used to help him with his estimates. The boys today don't know what estimates are—selling everything straight off the price list the way we do now—but back at Bellinger's everything had to be estimated—and right down to the last penny, too. That's where you could make or break yourself, especially on those big institutional orders, and that's what Bellinger went in for mostly —hotels, schools, hospitals and that sort of thing.

"Sometimes I'd stay up all night working out a big estimate for Avery Bullard. He wasn't much different then than he is now—he'd never stop having ideas. I'd no sooner get the figures worked up one way, than he'd think up a better idea and then I'd have to start all over again. But you didn't mind—not with Avery Bullard—because he always kept you sparked up. You always knew that you were getting somewhere. I guess you know what I mean.

"This was 1920 and we were having a terrific boom, prices sky-high and everybody scrambling to buy furniture—same thing we've had these last few years, history repeating itself— and old man Bellinger kept selling more and more case goods to the furniture stores instead of selling it on institutional contracts. You see, furniture being short, you could make a little

[84]

more profit that way. Well, along comes this big job—a chance to bid on all the furniture for a chain of seven new hotels. Avery Bullard went to work on it and when I say 'work' that's just what I mean—day and night, eighteen and twenty hours at a stretch and every day in the week. He designed a lot of special stuff himself. You didn't know Avery Bullard was a designer, did you? That's something a lot of people who haven't been as close to him as I've been don't know. When you get right down to it there isn't anything that man can't do if he puts his mind to it! Well, Mr. Bullard worked out a lot of special designs to submit with our bid and they were really good—not just good-looking, you understand, but good for the factory, too, the kind of stuff you can set up for and really turn out. That's another thing a lot of people don't appreciate about Mr. Bullard—the way he understands production.

"Well, sir, we finally got everything ready and Mr. Bullard went to New York to see these hotel people. He left on a Tuesday and got back on a Friday. I can remember it like it was yesterday. The minute he walked in the door I knew he had the order. You should have seen it—a half-million dollars worth of furniture! That would be a big order today, even for the Tredway Corporation, and you have to remember Bellinger was a small outfit. I guess you know how a young salesman like Avery Bullard would feel with an order like that—and I was feeling pretty much the same way, working along with him the way I had.

"The minute Mr. Bellinger got in that morning, Avery Bullard went right into his office—but it wasn't ten minutes until he was out again. That was the first time in my life I ever saw Avery Bullard really mad. Maybe you think you've seen him on the warpath but you've never seen anything like that! For a while he couldn't even talk . He just sat there as if he wasn't ever going to tell anybody what had happened. But I kept waiting because I knew sooner or later he'd tell me, he and I being as close as we always were.

"Finally it came out. Old man Bellinger had reneged and wouldn't accept the order. I'll never forget what Avery Bullard said. 'Fred,' he said to me, 'this is the end as far as I'm concerned. There's no future in any company with a coward for a president. It's the biggest order that old Bellinger has ever seen and he's lost his nerve.'

"Naturally I asked Avery Bullard what he was going to do. 'Fred,' he said to me, 'Bellinger told me he didn't want the order and I could do what I pleased with it—and that's just what I'm going to do. I'll find some factory that's smart enough to see what this order might mean. Business is getting jittery and store inventories are way up. Unless I miss my guess there's going to be a panic before long—anyway, a bad slump—and a noncancellable order for a half-million dollars worth of furniture at today's prices is going to be something worth having.' Then he asked my advice. 'Fred,' he said, 'where do you think I ought to go with this order?'

"Right then and there I told him he ought to go over and see Orrin Tredway at the old Tredway factory in Millburgh. That was how it all started. Yes sir, that was the beginning of everything.

"A couple of months afterward I got a letter from Avery Bullard saying Mr. Tredway had made him sales manager and if I ever wanted a job to come over and see him. Edith and I were packing almost before I got that letter back in the envelope. You see, it always has been that way between Avery Bullard and me—all he ever had to do to get me to do anything was just say the word. Oh, I'll admit he has his peculiarities—some people have trouble getting along with him—but not me. Avery Bullard and I have always been mighty close.

"You remember I said that was in 1920? Well, Avery Bullard was right. The 1921 depression hit and that big order of his was the only thing that kept Tredway going. If it hadn't been—"

The reverie was broken. Walt Dudley was tapping his arm and pointing to the door. Erica Martin was standing in the doorway and when he looked up she motioned him outside. Four pairs of eyes followed him to the door—and the sharpest of those eyes, the eyes that seemed to burn into his back like the focused rays of two sun-catching lenses, were the eyes of Loren P. Shaw.

"Mrs. Prince is on the line, Mr. Alderson. She's called twice in the last fifteen minutes trying to reach Mr. Bullard and now she's asked to talk to you."

"To me?" He was pleased to have been singled out as Mr. Bullard's alternate by Julia Tredway Prince. She was Orrin Tredway's daughter, the last surviving member of the family and, despite all the rumors about her, she was still a Tredway and still lived in the mansion house behind the high stone wall on North Front Street.

Alderson knew that she frequently called Avery Bullard for help in matters of business and that Mr. Bullard would sanction almost any effort in her behalf. Only last month, at Mr. Bullard's request, he had spent an entire afternoon working on an agreement covering a ground lease on some property that she owned.

"Yes, Mrs. Prince. This is Frederick Alderson speaking."

"Oh thank you for talking to me, Mr. Alderson. I've been attempting to reach Mr. Bullard but apparently he hasn't returned from New York?"

"No, we're expecting him but—"

"Something rather strange has happened. At least it's something that's never happened to me before, and I'm quite puzzled about it. Perhaps you can advise me what to do."

"I'll be glad to try, Mrs. Prince."

"It's possible that it may have some significance one way or another—something that Mr. Bullard should know about—and you, too, of course—although I'll admit that I'm completely at sea about it myself. I don't know whether it means anything or not."

"Yes?"

"You know Mr. Caswell of course?"

"Yes indeed."

"This afternoon Mr. Caswell called me to ask if I had sold any Tredway stock and I told him I hadn't. I didn't think anything more about it—and of course there may be no connection at all between the two calls—but about an hour ago I had a second call from some man in New York—a Mr. Pilcher. Bruce Pilcher. Do you know him?"

The name had some vague association in his mind but he could not immediately identify it. "That name does sound familiar. I—"

"He claims to have met me once with Mr. Shaw, but I can't remember him. He said he was with the Odessa Stores—or some such name."

"Oh yes, I remember now," Alderson said quickly, annoyed with himself for the lapse of memory. "Mr. Pilcher is president of Odessa Stores. They're one of our very large customers."

"Then he is someone who might have information about our company?"

His natural caution was heightened by the undertone of urgency in her voice. "That would depend, Mrs. Prince. Perhaps if you would tell me what he told you—I mean, if that's what you'd like to do."

"Of course. That's why I called you. He said that he had received some information that was highly unfavorable to the future prospects of the Tredway Corporation and—"

"What's that?"

"He said that he had—"

"Yes, I heard you, Mrs. Prince, but what was the nature of this information? I can't imagine—"

"I asked him that question but he said his information had come from a highly confidential source and that he wasn't free to tell me anything about it."

He paused, debating the propriety of revealing the approximate net profit that would be shown in the forthcoming semi-annual report, but deciding that he would not dare to do it, even for Mrs. Prince, without Avery Bullard's specific approval.

"I don't believe I'd be worried about any rumors like that if I were you, Mrs. Prince. When you see the semi-annual report I'm sure you'll be pleased with the showing we've made in the first half. We've just prepared our forecast for the fall months and—well, I wouldn't worry if I were you."

"I'm glad to hear that, Mr. Alderson. I really was rather concerned when this man was so insistent that I sell some of my stock."

"Sell your stock?"

"Yes, that was his whole point. He said that Tredway stock was sure to drop in price over the next few weeks and that even if I wanted to retain my holdings I could sell now and buy back a little later and have a very substantial profit."

"Well, I—well, it just doesn't make sense, Mrs. Prince."

"I know, it seemed strange to me, too. I asked him why he called me, and the only thing that I could get out of him was that he had a connection through which he could dispose of a block of two thousand shares—provided that I could give him an immediate decision—before six-thirty. Oh, yes, there was something else. He said that it ought to be a private sale—not go through the stock exchange—because that wouldn't depress the price so much. There was a lot more talk like that but it was all so financial and legal that it didn't make too much sense to me, but at least that was the general idea."

Frederick Alderson's mind, slow-starting, was speeding up under the impact of counterflashing fact and supposition. The manipulation of securities, with which he had been intimately involved during all of the years of the Tredway Corporation's expansion, had always been the most exciting part of his work. "Mrs. Prince, I can't be certain of what's happening, of course —never can be—but it looks to me as if someone is trying to pull a fast trick to get his hands on a block of Tredway stock."

"You think someone wants the stock?"

"Why else would he call you and suggest that you sell?"

"Yes, I see. I—you think then it was a trick?"

"Obviously."

"And you don't think I should sell?"

"No—at least not on the basis of any worry about the future of the Tredway Corporation."

"Thank you, Mr. Alderson. I'll take your advice, of course. It is strange though, isn't it—this man calling me up like that?"

"Yes, very."

"If it isn't too much trouble, perhaps you won't mind telling Mr. Bullard about it. It might possibly have some significance for him—the fact that someone seems to be trying to buy a block of stock."

"I'll tell him the moment I see him. I know that it's information he'll be happy to have and that he'll appreciate your calling us up about it, Mrs. Prince."

He hung up, pleased with himself for the way he had handled the situation, yet disturbed that it could not be matched to precedence. In all of his years of close association with the financial affairs of the corporation he had never heard of a similar circumstance.

Suddenly, as separate lightning flashes streak across the sky to join in a single blinding flash, he saw what was happening. It was Loren Shaw! She had said that Pilcher had mentioned Shaw . . . that checked . . . Pilcher was a friend of Shaw's . . . they had worked together for some company that Shaw had been with before he came to Tredway. Shaw had said that himself, the time the executive committee had discussed that price protection contract for Odessa.

But why was Shaw . . . ? The second answer flashed. Shaw only held 612 shares of stock. The figures were engraved on his mind as were the stockholdings of all the other officers of the company. His own holding of 1256 shares was, next to Avery Bullard's, the largest of any. If Shaw could manage to get his hands on two thousand more shares he would have a total of 2612—plus any more that he might have picked up on the open market that hadn't been transferred yet. The market had been active today . . . biggest turnover on Tredway in months . . . if Shaw had been buying . . .

Alderson short-circuited his alarm. He was getting unnecessarily excited. There was nothing to worry about. Shaw didn't have those two thousand shares of Mrs. Prince's . . . and now he wouldn't get them! He had been caught red-handed and tripped up. Wait until Avery Bullard heard about this one!

Peeping through the slit in the almost closed door of the president's office, he saw Erica Martin talking on the telephone. He waited until she hung up and then called her name.

She came to the door. "Yes, Mr. Alderson?"

"When Mr. Bullard comes I'd like to see him for a minute

before he comes into the meeting. I've just had some extremely important information and I know he'll want to have it at once. Will you call me out as soon as he gets here?"

"Yes, Mr. Alderson, but I'm afraid—"

Her voice had clipped off unaccountably.

"Is anything wrong, Miss Martin?"

"I don't know, I—" She stopped, momentarily searching his face as if she were debating a confession of fear. "While you were talking I had a call from Eddie at the station. Mr. Bullard wasn't on the six-thirteen."

"He wasn't?"

"No. There isn't another train until the seven-forty." She stopped again, weighing another revelation. "I knew you men would want to know whether there would be time enough to go for dinner, so I called the Waldorf-Astoria in New York to see what time Mr. Bullard had checked out. I thought that would give us an idea whether or not he'd be on the seven-forty."

"Yes?"

"He hasn't checked out."

"Well, in that case, Miss Martin—well, then he couldn't be on the seven-forty either, could he?"

"Mr. Alderson, do you think something might have happened to him?"

The urgent way her voice cut in on his made him look at her sharply. He had never heard that same quality in Erica Martin's voice before, yet it was a tone that was completely familiar to him. His wife used it constantly to express the concern for him that she never seemed able to escape. The association automatically influenced the timbre of his voice and what he said was an equally automatic response. "I'm sure there's nothing to worry about, nothing at all."

"But if he changed his plans, why didn't he wire?"

He could see now that she was truly alarmed, more so than he had suspected at first. "You know Mr. Bullard better than that, Miss Martin," he said with practiced reassurance. "When something comes up that gets him interested, he forgets everything else in the world."

"'I suppose something did come up," she admitted reluctantly. "At least we know he's still in New York."

"That's right," he said, changing his voice to open a new subject. "I might as well tell the others, don't you think? No use for any of us to wait any longer under the circumstances—and Mr. Dudley has a plane to catch."

She nodded, looking past him, preoccupied.

"You might give me a ring as soon as Mr. Bullard gets here in the morning, Miss Martin. This matter that I—oh, tomorrow's Saturday, isn't it? Well now, let me see—if you should hear anything from him, Miss Martin, I wonder if you'd be good enough to give me a ring at home?"

"Yes, of course," she said, suddenly over-crisp. "What shall I tell him that you want to see him about?"

He hesitated until he found a way to say it that would keep his secret and still avoid the danger of making Erica Martin feel that he did not trust her. "Tell Mr. Bullard that it concerns some information I've just received about certain manipulations that are going on in connection with the company's stock."

"Very well, Mr. Alderson."

He saw the quick dart of her eyes toward the telephone and, walking across the hall, his mind carried the impression that she might know more than she had let him think. It was possible that Mrs. Prince had told her what had happened. But it didn't matter . . . nothing mattered now except getting the facts into Avery Bullard's hands . . . that's all it would take, just the facts. That would be the end of Mr. Loren P. Shaw . . . just as the facts about taking a knockdown from the lumber brokers had ended the career of that fellow in the purchasing department back in thirty-four . . . Mr. Bullard had kicked him out.

Frederick Alderson smiled the smile of rewarded tolerance. He remembered something that Avery Bullard himself once said, "There aren't many real bastards in business, Fred, a lot fewer than most people think—and there's not much point in worrying about the few there are. All you have to do is sit back and wait. Give them enough rope and they'll put the noose around their own necks."

He opened the door of the directors' room and, for the first time in many months, his eyes made no effort to avoid Loren Shaw. Consciously, he looked directly at him. "I've had word that Mr. Bullard has been unavoidably detained in New York, so our meeting will have to be postponed. There's no point in any of us waiting any longer."

Shaw's eyes narrowed. "Did he call you? Was that Mr. Bullard on the phone?"

Alderson waited, savoring the moment. Then, without answering Shaw he turned away and spoke to the others. "Give anyone a lift? Have my car downstairs."

They were all looking at watches.

"I've got to get to the airport," Dudley said, "but that would be too far out of your way."

"I'll run you out, Walt," Shaw cut in before Alderson had a chance to reply, waving down Dudley's protest that he could catch a cab. "No, be glad to do it. Something I want to talk over with you anyway."

They went out together and, watching them, Alderson felt the strangeness of his new ability to restrain his anger.

"Want to stop by Pike Street with me and see how the rest is going?" Walling asked Grimm.

"Afraid I'll have to keep pushing if I'm going to get down to Maryland before dark," Grimm said.

Frederick Alderson followed them into the hall. He saw Erica Martin putting on her hat. "Mind if I use your phone?"

He dialed the number of his home and his wife answered almost immediately. "I'm starting now," he said.

"Fred, are you all right?" Edith Alderson asked anxiously. "You sounded so tired and worn out when you called before that I've just been sitting here worrying that—"

"There's nothing to worry about, nothing at all," he said. The words were bright and crisp, not tonelessly automatic as they usually were.

6.18 P.M. EDT

Julia Tredway Prince jabbed the sharp heel of her satin slipper into the white fur rug and spun herself around on the old

Victorian piano stool that she used as a dressing table seat. A second heel jab abruptly braked the turn so that she stopped facing the wide window through which she could see the distant white shaft of the Tredway Tower.

An errant thought suggested the possibility that Miss Martin might not have told her the truth about Avery's not being home from New York yet, but she quickly dismissed the suspicion. The woman was a bitch but she wouldn't have dared to go that far . . . unless, of course, Avery had asked her to do it. She would do anything he asked . . . and probably had!

"Stop it!" It was a command to herself, said aloud, a device that she had learned to use to keep her thoughts from straying into forbidden zones. Any thoughts of the relationship that might exist between Avery Bullard and Erica Martin was completely off limits. Even thinking of Avery Bullard alone was usually over the border line, but today the call from Pilcher had given it an eagerly grasped legitimacy. It was the first sustainable reason that she had had in a long time for calling him.

The recognized sharpness of her disappointment when she had found that she couldn't talk to him had made her enforce the self-discipline of asking Mr. Alderson to relay the story, but there still remained the thin thread of hope that Avery might call her back. It was such a remote possibility that she could risk the danger of thinking about it. She knew he wouldn't. There had been too many times before when he might have called but hadn't. At least he could say, "Thank you, Julia." Even that would be something, a pale echo of what he had once . . .

"Stop it!"

"What was that, dear?"

She was startled by the unexpectedness of her husband's voice, not having noticed that he had come into the adjoining bedroom.

"Just talking to myself," she said with a quick laugh, tossing the words over her shoulder as she spun the stool to face her dressing table again.

"Did you get Mr. Bullard?"

She could see him in the mirror, standing in the doorway like an unbidden guest, polite as he was always polite. "No, I talked to Mr. Alderson."

"Oh?"

"He advised me against selling."

"I suppose that's best then?"

"There's no reason why I should sell."

"No, I don't suppose there is." He hesitated and then, as if he were trying to make conversation, asked, "Have you called back the man in New York?"

"No," she said, starting to brush her hair.

The door in the mirror began to close.

"Oh, Dwight?" She turned now, pleasing him. "We're having strawberries for dinner and I told Nina that I might be able to persuade you to make the sauce."

His face lighted. "Of course, my dear."

"I should have asked you before."

"There's still time. I'll do it at once."

When she turned back he was gone from the mirror but the image of his smile still lingered in her mind. It was a smile of gratitude and she returned it. She, too, was grateful—most grateful that he was so easy to please.

At thirty-eight, Julia Tredway Prince was still filling in the blank pages of a lost life. At seventeen, in the month of her father's suicide, overwhelmed by the enormity of her loss, and almost as much by her mother's attitude that the disappearance of their fortune was even more of a tragedy than Orrin Tredway's death, Julia had been unable to hold her mind under a tight enough rein to prevent a headlong flight from the world of reason.

She had spent the next seven years in a sanitarium for the mentally ill. Those seven years had been lost in the mists of a clouded mind, so completely lost that she could trust none of her memories of those endless months. She could never be sure that some remembered thing had actually happened. There had been a long time when reality was undistinguishable from fantasy. She could not even be certain of when Avery Bullard had started coming to see her in the sanitarium because there had been a vast expanse of dayless months when he seemed to cross fade in and out of her vision, changing places with her father's image on the chair beside her bed.

Her trustworthy memories went back no farther than the day when she had finally come to the unshakable realization that Avery Bullard was not her father. His hand holding hers was too strong, his voice too uncompromising in its demand that she rise and walk and think and talk again.

Sometime near the end—she could not know exactly when because she had not progressed far enough yet to link the days with numbers on a calendar—she had talked to Avery Bullard about the payment of her bill at the sanitarium. Actually, what she said had begun only as the parroting of the overheard conversation of another patient, but he had been so pleased at this evidence of rational thinking that he had talked to her about her financial situation. Driven by a terrific urge to earn more approval, she had somehow forced her mind to understand. The old Tredway Furniture Company had grown into the Tredway Corporation. A part of her father's holdings, valueless when the company had been faced by the bankruptcy that had forced a pistol to his temple, had been salvaged for her and already had considerable value. Some day, he told her, she would probably be wealthy. The old house on North Front Street—the home that she had loved as a child, not the Cliff House mansion whose vast loneliness was a part of her terror—was ready and waiting for her. "You can go home any time that you can make yourself want to do it," Avery Bullard had said. A month later she had done it, walking out of the sanitarium alone and unaided, her body miraculously relieved of torture, her mind as clear as the rain-washed sky of that windy April day.

Julia Tredway was twenty-four years old when she returned to the normal world, but in many ways she was still seventeen. Seven years had gone by as a blank. Nature, in minor repayment for its major cruelty, had aged her mind to a maturity beyond seventeen—as it ages wine in a hidden and neglected cask—but she was still far from a normally developed person

[96]

of her age. She had not accumulated the myriad interlaced impressions that usually accompany the transition from adolescence to womanhood, so her mind was poorly stocked with the raw materials of thinking, but there was some compensating advantage in the lack of mental clutter and the added receptiveness and impressionability of a young mind. As a net result she was, in those first months after she left the sanitarium, like a precocious child with unusual maturity and a startling capacity for learning.

Her adjustment to society was difficult for she had neither anchorage nor reference points. Her mother's death—now only a formless cloud in those hazy lost years—had left her with no close relatives. The thin bonds of childhood friendship had long since been broken. There was only Avery Bullard.

During the first year she left the house and its grounds only to attend an occasional social affair, and always because he insisted. Except for pleasing him, she found little pleasure. The too bright smiles of the people she met, coupled with the way that everyone so pointedly avoided any mention of her years in the sanitarium, were barriers to comfortable friendship. She felt that way even about Avery Bullard's wife and he was understanding enough to realize it. After a few months he no longer asked her to his home, but then he came more often to hers.

The house was an important part of her first happiness. One of the strongest of her new impressions was of the day she came home from the sanitarium. Despite her remembered love for the old house, she had been terrorized that seeing it again might recall dangerous memories. But no fear of terror could stop her from responding to his demand that she walk through the gate in the white wall, up the bricked path, and into the house. Miraculously, there were no memories. She had been afraid to ask him how much the house had been changed for fear of betraying herself and disappointing him, so it was months before she learned that he had completely redecorated and refurnished the house. When she had finally been able to talk about it, he had brushed aside her thanks. "You've nothing

[97]

to thank me for, Julia. Everything was bought with your own money."

Nina had been there waiting that first day, a strange little woman with a sharp nose and a tight-drawn Psyche knot and a stiffly starched never-spotted apron, but with great black knowing eyes that always mirrored understanding. It was Nina who guided her to comfort and security and provided the constant flow of warm affection that she needed so much—and it was Avery Bullard who had given her Nina. No one else could have found her, no one else could have known that it was Nina she needed.

In the early days of her recovery, when she had not yet made the transition from thinking of herself as a child, Avery Bullard had seemed an elderly man. She had broken through the confusion that tended to identify him with the image of her father, but he still evoked something close to filial response. Later, when she finally awakened to the realization that she was a mature woman, the years that had been so quickly added to her age seemed to dissolve the span of years between them. By that time her affection for him had grown to such proportions that it was undeniably the love of a woman for a man, no longer the adoration of a child that loved without hunger for consummation. The hunger grew until it became such an overwhelming passion that she was afraid her mental balance might again be lost.

Looking back now, remembering, it seemed that there were times when her sanity had been lost. Only insanity could have driven her to do what she had done. A reasonable mind would have known that Avery Bullard, despite the momentary physical response that her guile produced, could never be trapped against his will. The year after his wife had divorced him, Julia had made the most insanely desperate try of all. There had been moments when she thought she would hold him forever—but years afterward she knew that what she had really done had only served to push him away from her.

Desperation had lingered on after he had stopped coming to see her except when some business affair demanded it. Even seeing him under those circumstances still carried a hope and she went to wild ends—shamefully remembered—to make him come to her house. When he made her a director of the company she suspected, with a suspicion born of frustration, that it was done only to force her to come to the office and to wipe out any excuse that she might ever have to ask him to come to her home. In consequence, she had never attended a directors' meeting.

It was out of a chance remark that she had discovered Avery Bullard's fear that the control of the company might be challenged if she ever sold her stock to someone else. Thus the threat to sell her stock became a new way to make him come to her and, in the last throes of her desperation, she had used it over and over again, hating herself for her shamelessness but unable to restrain her desire.

When she called him it was always Erica Martin who answered and her voice was a constantly harrowing reminder that it was she who was with him from morning until night—and it was an easy step to the suspicion that Erica Martin was with him in the nights as well.

In the end, Julia Tredway had won the victory of defeat. Avery Bullard had shocked her into it. One night when she had made him come to her with a ruse so transparent that she was forced to admit what she had done, he had said, "Julia, remember that you lost seven years of your life. If you keep on the way you are going, I'm afraid you'll lose the rest of it."

His demand for sanity was irresistible, as all of his demands had always been irresistible, and she had started a new life. Her marriage to Dwight Prince was the real beginning. She had not been in love with him nor, she suspected, he with her. Dwight's greatest asset was that there was nothing about him to remind her of Avery Bullard. He had neither strength, dominance, nor the ability to demand subjection. Furthermore, he needed her —needed her money to live the gracious but useless existence which was all that his inheritance and training had fitted him to live. He paid for it with an understanding and a gentle kindness that had given her more happiness than she had expected and there had grown up between them something that was not true love but was, at least, a relationship that she recognized as more desirable than what passed for love in many marriages.

Through the exercise of tight control she had kept herself from thinking of Avery Bullard and, as the years had gone by, it had become easier and easier to do—until today when Bruce Pilcher's call asking her to sell stock had been a too sharp parallel to the memory of other times when she had called Avery Bullard with that same threat.

She pivoted on the stool again, her eyes on the tip of the Tower. Yes, she had been right in giving the message to Alderson. Avery might remember . . . probably not . . . but he might.

5

NEW YORK CITY
6.22 P.M. EDT

BRUCE PILCHER, debating a third Martini, decided against it. Alcohol gave him false courage and that wasn't what he needed now. He had to *think*. Mrs. Prince had promised to call him back within an hour. It was almost an hour now and she hadn't called.

After he had telephoned the hospital and been told that Avery Bullard was not there, Bruce Pilcher had wasted no time in searching the Final editions of the newspapers that had been brought to the library at his request.

Now, more as an aftermath of an earlier desire than anything else, he absent-mindedly crossed to the table where Andrew had dropped the papers. His thoughts were occupied with the just made decision that he would wait another fifteen minutes for Mrs. Prince's call. If it had not been for his eyes' being caught by the name of the building in which he had his office, he would have missed the little item that was tucked in to fill the bottom of a first-page column.

UNIDENTIFIED MAN DROPS DEAD
IN FRONT OF
CHIPPENDALE BUILDING

An unidentified man collapsed at about 2:30 this afternoon while getting into a taxi in front of the Chippendale Building. He was pronounced dead upon arrival
at Roosevelt Hospital. The man was described by police as being well dressed, six feet three inches tall,
weighing about 220 lbs., dark hair, brown eyes, prob-
able age between fifty-five and sixty. The only clue
that police have to the man's identity is the initials
"A.B." which appeared on some of his personal effects.

The news struck Bruce Pilcher with stunning effect, creating
the sensation of being snatched from the deep black hole of
total terror and suddenly elevated to the brilliantly lighted
heights of complete self-justification. He'd been right all the
time. It had been Avery Bullard and Avery Bullard was dead!
The body's not being identified was a freak . . . accident . . .
not his fault . . . something that he could not possibly have
foreseen.

Self-confidence welled through Bruce Pilcher's mind, as
quick-acting as a powerful stimulant. He should never have lost
faith in himself . . . that was the only mistake he had made
. . . losing faith in himself.

Unnoticed, Andrew had entered the library and was standing across the table, waiting for him to look up.

"Yes, Andrew, what is it?"

"Telephone, sir."

Bruce Pilcher did not hesitate. "I haven't time to answer. Tell
her I've already left the club."

"It isn't a woman, sir. It's a Mr. Steigel."

"Oh!" So the old man had thought it over and now he
wanted his half of the profit on those two thousand shares? To
hell with that! Julius Steigel had had his chance and he'd lost his
nerve . . . there was no pay-off when you lost your nerve.
"The answer's still the same, Andrew. I've left the club."

He was not asking Andrew to lie. Before the old man could

get to the telephone, Bruce Pilcher had walked out the door and was striding up the street.

Walking was an aid to thinking, his footsteps tamping down the thoughts in his mind, fitting them back together into the solid pattern that he had interrupted with that hour of losing faith in himself. There was only one new fact to add . . . Avery Bullard's body was unidentified.

Unidentified? Was that good or bad? His thoughts fluttered for a moment like a sensitive scale-arm finding a balance point. He decided that the weight was a shade on the good side. The police would eventually make the identification but it would take time . . . several hours . . . maybe longer. That would give him time to do something else. Information was valuable. There were ways to use it. There were people who would pay . . . at least in gratitude . . . for an advance tip . . . people who had a special interest in Tredway stock. Caswell? No, not Caswell . . . that was too dangerous. Or was it? Caswell had a lot of connections . . . and Caswell was a gentleman. A gentleman wouldn't forget someone who had done him a favor. The scale arm fluttered again. Yes or no? Yes.

There was a drugstore on the corner and he went inside and found a telephone booth. As the coin dropped, his mind was working like a precision machine, selecting words, arranging and rearranging, polishing and punctuating. He wouldn't say too much over the telephone, only enough to arouse Caswell's curiosity. Caswell might invite him out to his house . . . that had never happened before . . . Caswell might even . . .

A busy signal sounded.

He hung up the receiver and the coin clattered down. He picked it up, surprised that his hand was trembling. He would wait until he got home to repeat the call . . . yes, that would be better . . . give him more time to think.

6.37 P.M. EDT

The way in which Anne Finnick happened to find the news item in the Final edition paralleled Bruce Pilcher's discovery. She, too, worked in the Chippendale Building and it was the name in the headline that caught her eye. However, it was not until she read the last line and learned that the dead man's initials were "A.B." that the news had any personal significance. She had not, until that moment, given any thought to how the wallet had happened to be lying in the gutter where she had found it. Now she knew that it had belonged to the dead man and, because she had found and taken it, the police were unable to identify him.

Her new knowledge complicated the already involved ethical problem with which she was faced. Until her visit to Dr. Marston, the desperate seriousness of her plight had seemed to justify keeping the money. Then the whole situation had changed. During this last hour, knowing now that she was not pregnant, she had been unable to find any argument with which she could convince herself that keeping the money was not a seriously criminal act. She could remember that a boy who had lived next door to her father's luggage store on Third Avenue had been sent to jail for stealing a ten-dollar bill. She had stolen five hundred and thirty-four dollars. The enormity of her crime was beyond the narrow limits of her comprehension, as was also the nature of the punishment that might befall her. Her fear had now become so great that it had completely destroyed the joy that she had found in the discovery that she was not pregnant.

In the same manner that a prisoner sees everything in terms of its potentiality as an instrument of escape, it was in that direction that Anne Finnick's mind had turned when she read the item in the newspaper. She finally concluded, through the transmutation of hope into reason, that since the man who had lost the pocketbook was now dead there was nothing wrong about keeping the money. She was helped in arriving at that conclusion by the memory of her Uncle Rudy who had died and "left" her father five hundred dollars. The similarity of the amounts added validity to the parallel. If her father had taken that five hundred dollars from Uncle Rudy before he had died, it would have been stealing. After his death it was all right. The money had been "left" for her father in the same way that this man whose initials were "A.B." had "left" the money for her by dropping his pocketbook in the gutter.

The solution of that problem only opened the way to another. Her sentimental affection for Uncle Rudy, regenerated by the recollection of his kindly wax-pink face as it looked up at her from the satin-lined casket, gave rise to an equally sentimental affection for the kindly but unknown gentleman who had bequeathed her so much money. She wished that she could go to his funeral and, as she considered the possibility, the wish became the slow-germinating seed which finally grew into the realization that there would be no flowers at the funeral. People would not know what name to put on the flower boxes. No one would come to the funeral because people did not go to funerals if they did not know whose funeral it was. Everyone who had been at Uncle Rudy's funeral had known that the man in the casket was Rudolph Finnick.

The solution, after she had thought about it for several more minutes, seemed quite simple. She would call the newspaper and tell them that the dead man's name was Mr. Avery Bullard and that he was the president of the Tredway Corporation. That's what it had said on all the little cards that she had flushed down the toilet bowl. Then they could put his name in the paper and everybody would read it and there would be a nice funeral.

Carrying out her intention was not quite as simple as it had seemed at first. The telephone was out in the dark hall, the electric light bulb had burned out, and she had to light matches to find the newspaper's telephone number. After she got the number she had a difficult time trying to make them understand what she was talking about, but the man who talked to her last was very nice. She spelled out the name just the way it had been on the little cards and hung up in a hurry.

After it was all over she felt better than she had felt in a long time. Now she could even think about how wonderful it was not to be pregnant.

6.44 P.M. EDT

As the wife of the manager of the New York office of the Tredway Corporation, Marian Oldham knew that she had certain responsibilities. She accepted them willingly enough but

[105]

their discharge was not always easy. There were times when she wondered if Alex really appreciated how difficult her position was. He was right, of course, in saying that they had to keep a cook in order to be able to entertain in the way that his position demanded, yet she doubted whether he understood how hard it was to hold a cook these days if you didn't keep your promises about meal hours.

Alex had plopped another ice cube into his glass and was reaching for the bourbon bottle again.

"Alex, dear," she asked softly. "Will you be ready to eat before long?"

His face, when he turned, had the pallor of extreme fatigue and she wished that she hadn't been forced into asking the question.

"I'm sorry, dear, but I promised Hilda that she could get away early. This is Friday and she has her club meeting."

"All right," he said, letting his hand fall away from the bottle.

"Oh, go ahead," she said, suddenly repentant. "It doesn't matter. I'll let Hilda leave and finish things up myself."

"No, I've had enough. Guess I drink too much of the stuff as it is."

"No, you don't." She stepped to his side, reaching out for his hand. "You need it—when the bad days come along."

"Getting to be too many bad days lately. They're all bad."

"At least, dear, you can forget it now until Monday."

"Yes." It was agreement in word only. "Get dinner on the table. I'll be there in a minute."

She watched him cross to the hall and go in the powder room, telling herself again that he was a good husband and rewishing that she might ease his troubles by sharing them. In the beginning, when they had been first married and Alex and been a salesman working out of the St. Louis office, there had been a perfect sharing. When he came home from a trip he would talk far into the night, telling her everything that had happened, every detail of every call. Her interest, sharpened by his enthusiasm, had caused her to memorize the names of all of his customers and the style numbers of every item in the Tredway catalogue. Gradually, as the years had gone by and Alex had risen in the company, her participation in his business life had become less and less. It had not happened, she knew, because of any conscious desire on his part to exclude her, but rather because it had become more and more necessary for him to find hours when he could escape from business.

There were times now when Marian Oldham felt that her husband would have found more escape through talking to her than by sitting in brooding silence, but she did not dare pick those times. Once in a while—though rarely now—he would tell her about something that had happened in the office. Even then there was a danger. If she tried, for his sake, to divert him and change the subject, there was the chance that he might think she wasn't interested. Yet if her interest was too evident there was always the inevitable ending when he would cut her off with the feeling that she had somehow harmed him by allowing his troubles to intrude within the haven of his escape.

Alex was right . . . there are getting to be too many bad days . . . too many nights when he came home as he came home tonight . . . no, not quite as bad as tonight . . . the days when Mr. Bullard was in New York were always the worst.

He came into the dining room, blinking his eyes as if they were smarting.

"I hope jellied consommé is all right, dear?" she asked.

He nodded, sitting down and starting to eat, staring silently past the rim of his cup.

She wanted to break the silence but it stretched on and on before she finally thought of something to say that had no business connection.

"I had a letter from Margie today."

"Oh?"

"She and Jeff are going through town the first week in August on their way to Maine. They're taking their vacation up there—Kennebunkport."

"Uh-huh."

"I wrote and told her that we'd love to see them but that

we'd probably be away on our own vacation about that same time."

He nodded, silent.

"Have you thought any more about where you'd like to go, Alex?"

"Not much."

His cup was less than half emptied but she saw that he had stopped eating. "Is there anything wrong with your consommé, dear?"

"No, it's fine. Not hungry, that's all. Too hot, I guess."

Hilda came in and they sat in silence until after she had served the lamb chops and the vegetables. There were always lamb chops on nights when Mr. Bullard had been in New York but it was one of the many things that she never called to his attention.

Suddenly, as if he were continuing a conversation that she hadn't heard, Alex said, "I've never thought much of the idea of taking a vacation with anyone else from the company, but with somebody like the Shaws it would probably be all right. His wife's folks have this place up on Cape Cod."

"The Loren Shaws?"

He looked up as if to accuse her of not having listened to what he had said before.

"They've invited us to come up there?"

"Didn't I tell you about it?"

She had no choice except to say, "I don't think you did, dear."

"Thought I had. He said something about it when he was up here last week. Nothing final—didn't actually invite us—but I think they're going to."

"Would you enjoy that, Alex?"

"Why not?"

"You aren't doing it because you think it's the thing to do, are you—because he's going to be the new executive vice-president?"

She thought for a moment that she had said the wrong thing, that he might either flare into anger or relapse into silence, but fortunately he did neither. "No, I wouldn't do anything for that reason. Life's too short. Anyway, there's nothing sure about his being the new executive V.P. It's just my guess, that's all."

She smiled her relief. "You like him, don't you?"

"Oh, I don't know. At least he has some consideration for the way other people think—your ideas mean something—not the way it is with the old man."

Marian almost asked a question about Avery Bullard's visit, but quickly decided against it. "You say the Shaws have a place up on—"

The telephone bell interrupted her. She pivoted off her chair and went to answer it.

"This the residence of a Mr. Alex Oldham?" a gruff masculine voice asked.

"Yes."

"He connected with the Tredway Corporation?"

"Yes. He's the manager of—"

"This is the police department. We'd like to talk to him. Is he there?"

Alex was watching her and a hundred wild thoughts spiraled through her mind in the time that it took him to reach her side. She handed him the receiver whispering, "It's the police."

She backed a step, watching her husband's face, hunting for clues in his short laconic answers.

"Yes—yes, that's right—yes—yes, I understand—yes— what!"

The last word was a startled exclamation and she saw the thin under-film of color drain from his face.

"But, it's—yes, the Chippendale Building—yes, I see—yes— no—yes, I'll come down—what?—all right—five minutes? Yes, I'll be ready."

He hung up, his hand staying on the instrument as if the brace of his arm were necessary to the support of his body.

"Alex, what is it?"

His head turned slowly, hesitating again before he spoke. "Avery Bullard is dead."

"Oh, no!"

"Collapsed on the street this afternoon in front of the Chippendale Building. The police have been trying ever since to identify him."

"Do you have to go down?"

"Squad car is picking me up in five minutes."

"Maybe it isn't Mr. Bullard. Maybe it's someone else?"

"No. Everything checks. Chippendale Building—he was there for lunch with Steigel and Pilcher, I know that. All the description fits. Can't be anyone else."

"Finish your dinner, dear," she said softly. "There's nothing you can do until the car gets here."

He seemed not to have heard her. "Have to call Millburgh right away." He started to lift the receiver and then put it down again. "But who the devil do I call?"

It was a question that did not ask for an answer but anxiety because of his tenseness made her say, "I should think you'd call Mr. Shaw if he's going to be—"

She had started to say, "the new executive vice-president," but she caught herself, realizing that everything was changed now.

"I suppose Walt Dudley," Alex said to himself. "He's the V.P. that I report to. No—forgot—Walt will have left for Chicago already. I talked to him on the phone this morning and he said he was taking an early plane. Alderson or Jesse Grimm, I guess—but which one?"

She didn't know what he had decided until she heard him say, "Operator, I want to talk to Don Walling in Millburgh, Pennsylvania. That's right—person to person—Mr. Don Walling."

He offered no explanation but she could understand what he had done. She had done the same thing herself once when a dinner party had presented an unsolvable problem in protocol. No one could object if the person served first was someone to whom first service could not possibly be considered as either an obeisance or an honor.

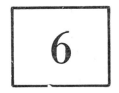

6

MILLBURGH, PENNSYLVANIA
6.56 P.M. EDT

THE ROUTE to Maryland was straight down South Water Street, but Jesse Grimm had taken the left fork and gone up Pike Street. He had told himself that the traffic wouldn't be as bad, a harmless bit of self-deception to excuse the waste of a mile of driving so that he could once again look down on the Pike Street factory from the high cliff edge at the corner of Ridge Road.

Beauty is measured in the beholder's eye and, to Jesse Grimm, the Pike Street factory was the most beautiful thing in the world. Avery Bullard had said, on that night when the news had come through that the A-bomb had been dropped on Hiroshima, "This is the end of it, Jesse, so let's get rolling. Take that plot of land up on Pike Street and build yourself the finest damned case-goods factory in the industry."

Jesse Grimm had done just that. He knew that he had succeeded. Architects and engineers from all over the country had come to visit and admire and pirate ideas. He had carefully accepted their extravagant praise, never allowing it to produce the slightest break in his sheltering shield of modesty, yet storing the words away as a miser hoards a precious treasure.

As much as he secretly valued the praise, Jesse Grimm's greatest satisfaction had come from something that he held even more secret—the way he had managed to keep Don Walling from having any part whatsoever in the planning. From the moment that Avery Bullard had given the order to start work, Jesse Grimm had faced the constant fear that Walling, because he was a graduate architect, would be allowed to intrude. The fact that he had been kept from doing so—that Walling had been held in Pittsburgh until the factory was too far along to permit any change in the plans—was the source of Jesse Grimm's warmest regard for Avery Bullard.

Now, slowing to a stop in the turnout area beyond the corner, Jesse Grimm slid across the seat and looked down on the plant. Directly below him was the black expanse of the white-lined parking lot, deserted now except for a scattering of cars down at the far end, a reminder that Walling was having his test run on the molding press tonight.

Squinting through the haze, he picked out Walling's sand-colored Buick and then, in the moment of its identification, saw the car start to move. Two other cars were backing out. Another was making the turn out of the lot on to Pike Street. It was obvious that the test had failed. If it hadn't, Walling wouldn't be leaving so soon. Jesse Grimm inhaled slowly. The fire in the bowl of his pipe glowed and he drew the warmth within himself, deeper and deeper, indrawn until it finally penetrated the darkest depths of his consciousness. It was there that he had secreted, more hidden than any thought or memory that his mind had ever harbored, his long-standing resentment against Don Walling.

He knew that the way he felt didn't make sense. But the knowing changed nothing. It was like a secret vice that generated shame but not the resolution to forego its practice, a deep festering cancer that was no less virulent because it defied diagnosis.

The closest that Jesse Grimm had ever come to finding an

explanation for the way he felt about Don Walling traced back to those first months in Pittsburgh when Walling had tried to palm himself off as a carbon-copy Bullard. He hadn't let him get away with it . . . he'd cracked down harder than he'd ever cracked down on anyone else, before or after . . . and Walling had taken it, too . . . even thanked him. Walling wasn't the first green kid that had thanked him for something like that, but with Walling it had come too fast. That was Walling . . . always too fast, too quick, too sure, too clever.

There was always that gut-twisting tension when Walling was around . . . knowing that if you couldn't give Bullard the answer he wanted, he'd say, "Well, Don, if this thing has Jesse stumped suppose you take a swing at it" . . . and then that damned Walling luck would go to work! Yes, it *was* luck. Even if Walling was half as good as Bullard thought he was, a part of it was still luck . . . like the way that cockeyed back-pressure idea had worked on the finishing line . . . and those crazy roller-skate pallets . . . and the solvent recovery system. If a thing wasn't good engineering and it wasn't good production practice and it still worked, then it had to be luck. What else could it be?

But it took more than luck to run a factory . . . a hell of a lot more! Avery Bullard would find that out. It wouldn't be long now . . . only four more months.

Jesse Grimm narrowed his eyes, dimming his view of the Pike Street plant, hardening his resolution to support the decision he had made to retire at sixty instead of waiting until he was sixty-five.

The worst part of leaving would be knowing that he'd never see this Pike Street factory again. It was *his* . . . from the bottom of the footings to the top of the dust collectors on the roof . . . every brick, every machine, every inch of every production line . . . the finest furniture factory in the world. Could he leave it?

The bowl of his pipe dropped as his lips softened. Sure he could leave it! Why not? Nobody would miss him. They didn't need a real production man any more . . . just a bunch of

college kids clicking stop watches . . . time and motion studies
. . . industrial engineering . . . research and development . . .
Walling . . . a lot of little Wallings running around with their
stop watches and their clipboards and their slide rules. They'd
change Pike Street . . . tinker and twist, turn and tear, wreck
and rip . . . and then it wouldn't be the finest furniture factory in the world. Could he stand that?

Yes . . . he wouldn't know . . . and what he didn't know
wouldn't hurt him. He'd leave and he'd never come back . . .
waited too long already . . . no more time to lose. Even four
months was too long to wait . . . but he had to do that . . .
wait until he was sixty . . . wouldn't look right if he didn't.
Yes, he had to hang on for these last four months. But no
longer! Nothing could stop him then . . . nothing! Avery
Bullard could argue until he was blue in the face but he
wouldn't change his mind. No, he wouldn't stay on until he was
sixty-five . . . five more years would be too long to wait . . .
everything was ready down in Maryland . . . house all re-
modeled . . . shop almost built. If the carpenters hadn't gone
fishing again this week the windows should be in by now, and
the doors hung. Next week they would start on the workbench
and the tool cabinets.

His hands gripped the steering wheel and his imagination
gave it the feel of oil-rubbed steel. It would be good to have
tools in his hands again. It was strange how a man could be so
blind to what he really wanted . . . work all his life to get
somewhere . . . be somebody . . . and then, in the end, find
out that the only thing that meant anything was what you'd
had to start with . . . a good pair of mechanic's hands and a
shop to use them in. Avery Bullard wouldn't be able to understand that, not the Avery Bullard of today. The old Avery
Bullard might have understood, the Avery Bullard of ten years
ago . . . the Avery Bullard who had stood beside him that
night in the Pittsburgh rain, waiting for the streetcar, and said,
"You're my right arm, Jesse, and I'll never forget it." Then
they'd gone home and Sarah had fixed spareribs and sauerkraut
and they'd sat talking half the night.

Jesse Grimm smiled, pleased that he could. He was learning how to live again. Sometime, just for a joke . . . after it was all over . . . he'd say, "Avery, how about coming down home tonight and letting Sarah fix us a mess of spareribs and sauerkraut?"

His smile broadened as his imagination supplied the look there would be on Avery Bullard's face. Sarah would be even more shocked. "Jesse, have you gone crazy? We don't even have spareribs and sauerkraut ourselves any more."

"But we will as soon as we're settled down there in Maryland," he said to conclude his imaginary conversation with Sarah. "We'll have spareribs and sauerkraut every Monday night, the way we used to when we were first married."

There was a neon-framed clock on a beer joint beside the road . . . two minutes to seven . . . Avery Bullard would be sitting down to have his dinner at that fancy restaurant he always ate at in New York, the one up Park Avenue from the Waldorf-Astoria, the place where the whole menu was in French. What would happen if a man went into a place like that and ordered spareribs and sauerkraut?

Jesse Grimm chuckled at the prospect, letting the sound of laughter come without restraint. There were a lot of funny things in life . . . all a man had to do was relax enough so he could appreciate them.

6.59 P.M. EDT

"You sure that going out Stuart Street won't take you out of your way, Mr. Walling?" Lundeen asked anxiously, his thin fingers rolling the yellow leather case of his slide rule over and over in his hands.

Walling knew that Bill Lundeen's nervousness was traceable, not to his concern over the car's route, but rather to what had happened on the test run, and he decided that it would be a wise kindness to put the young chemist at his ease.

"Don't worry too much about the way things went tonight, Bill. It wasn't your fault. I'm not blaming you."

"Thanks, sir," Lundeen said gratefully. "I know now that I should have stepped up the feed pressure. I thought about it but was afraid to take the gamble that I might back-pressure the whole line and wreck the control instruments."

"I know," Walling said patiently. He couldn't tell young Lundeen that he should have taken the gamble. It wasn't Bill's gamble to take . . . he was a youngster, three years out of college, smart and coming fast, but he couldn't be expected to make management decisions. "Too bad I couldn't have been there myself."

Out of the corner of his eye he saw Lundeen's nod of acceptance. Bill probably thought he had attended a very important meeting, far more important than one little test run in one corner of one of the nine Tredway factories. There was a temptation to tell him what had really happened, just to give the boy a taste of what life was like up there on the twenty-fourth floor of the Tower, but that was something you couldn't do when you were a vice-president. You kept your mouth shut. There weren't many people you could talk to when you got up on top, the higher the fewer, and you didn't talk to the few there were. You thought you would but you never did. You bottled it up, like acid in a jar, and let it eat your heart out. That was one thing you learned when you were a vice-president . . . no matter what happened you held your tongue. Avery Bullard called a meeting . . . you wrecked everything to be there . . . he didn't show up . . . so you picked up your toys like a nice little boy and went home. Had there been one word of criticism from any one of the five of them? Not one damned word! No one had even mentioned Avery Bullard's name.

They were on South Front now and the carillon in the Tower was ringing for the hour, the bell sounds wavering against the south wind coming up the river. Involuntarily, Don Walling glanced up at the lance-point of the white shaft and he saw that Lundeen had done the same thing.

"I didn't think they rang the bell when Mr. Bullard was there," Lundeen said.

He didn't answer. There wasn't anything he could say without saying more than he should.

A weirdly mongrelized dog, fat as an inflated balloon, waddled slowly across the street in front of them, stopping both streams of traffic, and Don Walling chuckled at the dog's ludicrous nonchalance.

Apparently Bill Lundeen had been waiting for a break in the tension, and he quickly took advantage of it. "If you don't mind, sir, Jim and I have an idea that I'd like to talk to you about."

"Sure, go ahead."

"Well, running these tests in the factory the way we're doing wastes an awful lot of time. It'll be two or three weeks now before the production department can give us another break in the schedule."

"I know."

Any agreement was encouragement and Lundeen plunged ahead, his excitement overriding the professional scientist's calm that he usually tried so hard to assume. "Well, Jim and I were rooting around over at Water Street the other day—you know, in that shed behind the dry kiln—and we found an old steam-heated core press that isn't being used. We'd have to reinforce the frame and rig up new controls, but if we'd do it, sir, we could set up a little pilot-plant operation of our own. Then we could run one test after another as fast as we wanted to."

"Sounds like it might work," Don said, evasive, not wanting to take the heart out of the boy by telling him that, a month ago, he had sent a special budget request to the president's office asking for an appropriation to cover the rebuilding of that same press and its installation at Pike Street. For three weeks he had heard nothing. Last week, he had asked Bullard about it and been told that a new system had been set up under which all appropriation requests had to be cleared with Shaw before they could be approved. "This is getting to be a damned big company," Avery Bullard had said. "Can't handle all of these things myself any more—have to delegate responsibility." There had been no possible answering argument . . . Tredway *was* a big corporation and its president did have to delegate authority . . . but couldn't Avery Bullard see what he was doing? Authority wasn't being delegated to the men who should have exercised it. It was simply being transferred to Shaw who was using it to weave a noose of red tape that was choking off the company's growth. That was wrong. Of all men, Avery Bullard should know it. He hadn't built the Tredway Corporation with his hands tied with red tape and a comptroller tripping him at every step . . . why should he now deny to other men the freedom of action that had permitted his own success? Why was he letting Shaw influence him so much? Why had he ever hired Shaw in the first place?

Don Walling's mind suggested an answer, the old memory of Karl Eric Kassel saying, "The bigger a brass hat gets, the more of a sucker he is for some guy that comes along and calls himself an expert. You know why? Because he starts getting scared. The bigger he gets, the more scared he is. When he's on the way up, he's so busy tearing the hell out of things that he never stops to worry about being wrong. Sometimes he gets knocked on his can. Does it bother him? No. He bounces back like a fighting bull. Then what happens? He gets to be a success. Why? Because that's what it takes to be a success. Then what? The first thing you know he's a tin-plated god sitting on a big throne. Now he doesn't like getting knocked on his can. It's not dignified. The stockholders wouldn't like it. He begins to get scared. So what does he do? He turns into a sucker and starts hiring experts. Why? Because they tell him they can keep him from being knocked on his royal can. It's as simple as that."

The answer, for all its aptness, could not be accepted. Don Walling could never believe that Avery Bullard was afraid. To believe that would have meant the destruction of the very foundation upon which he had built his life. He, like all strong men, could submit to a leadership that demanded fear, yet never to a leader that reflected it.

"—and that wouldn't be too expensive," he heard Lundeen say after something that he had missed hearing. "The best estimate Jim and I can make is that the whole thing shouldn't cost more than five or six thousand—providing, of course, that we can get space over at Pike Street so we can tie in with their regular supply lines and save the cost of any supplementary equipment."

"You might put the whole thing in a memo, Bill," he said cautiously. "Don't know what can be worked out but I'll give it some study."

"That's swell, sir—all Jim and I want—just a chance to have you consider it. Maybe it's cockeyed but you can decide that better than we can."

"This your street?"

"Gosh, yes. Got talking so hard I didn't notice." Lundeen got out of the car, awkwardly long-legged. "Good night, sir. Sorry about the way things went."

"That's all right, Bill. Not your fault. Good night."

No, it wasn't Bill's fault . . . and it wasn't his fault either. The fault lay with just one man . . . and that man was Loren Shaw.

He turned at the next corner, not noticing the street sign, surprised a few blocks later when he suddenly realized that he was about to pass the house where he and Mary had lived that first year in Millburgh. It was an old graystone mansion that had been cut up into apartments. Mr. Prescott, the owner, was on his knees in the front yard rose beds and Don Walling slowed as he passed, sounding his horn and waving. The old man stood up, stiff-legged and bent-backed, and his pleasure at the greeting was plainly evident.

The Prescotts were a wonderful couple, Don thought, and then grinned at himself for having fallen an absent-minded victim of the chiché that had been a running joke with Mary all that year. She had said so often that the Prescotts were "wonderful people" that the phrase had become, for some obscure reason, something that made both of them laugh.

The thought of Mary—the first thought of her in several hours—was a key that locked one door and opened another. The opening door flooded his mind with the consciousness that she was waiting for him, and the locked door shut away all the things that had seemed so unforgettable only a moment before.

Don Walling's mind could do that. It was compartmented

into noncommunicating chambers and, with the opening and closing of mental doors, he could shift almost instantly from intense concentration on one subject to equally intense concentration on another. He had created that kind of a mind—and acquired the skill to use it—in the earliest years of his life when he had found that the only way he could do what he wanted to do was to drive himself with a single-minded unity of endeavor that was so intense as to preclude the possibility of any interrupting thoughts. He had discovered at Rubble Hill that he could not lead his class if he allowed himself to break the concentration of his study periods with any thought of his personal plight as an unwanted and deserted child. The same lesson had been relearned at Tech and later with Karl Eric Kassel. By then his ability to compartment his mind and concentrate his thinking had become so effective that he had done some of his best designing for Kassel during periods when, if he had permitted his personal feelings to influence his work, he would have hurled away his pencils and ripped up the paper.

Don Walling was not consciously aware of the mental mechanics involved in the functioning of his mind, but he did realize that it was responsible for the one small deception that he was forced to practice upon his wife. Mary would ask, "Did you think of me today?" and he always had to say, "Yes, of course," but that was usually untrue. Understanding as she was, he knew that he could not make Mary realize that it was only because there were hours when she was not allowed to enter his mind that there were other hours when his mind was hers alone, filled completely with thoughts of her, almost to the exclusion of everything else.

It was of Mary and Mary alone that he thought as he made the turn onto Ridge Road and began the climb that lifted him above the flat lowland of the old city.

In these years since the war, Millburgh had broken through its ancient city limits. All of the new residential developments were on the high lands above the city. Ridge Road, following the cliff edge, was the main artery of the newer Millburgh. Laurel Heights had become for a new generation what North

Front had been for past generations. In the same way that the social value of a North Front Street home had once been measured by its distance from Piccadilly Park, a lot in Laurel Heights was assayed by its distance from the Millburgh Country Club. The house that Loren Shaw had bought—a rambling hybrid of "California Ranchhouse" and "Pennsylvania Farmhouse"—was so close to the club that sliced drives from the second tee frequently landed in his front yard. A few blocks away, safely out of range but with the clubhouse still visible through the trees, stood the Walter Dudley home. It was "Colonial," white-painted brick, green-and-white awnings, and a big flagstone terrace bordered by enormous pots of salmon-pink geraniums supplied by Fowlers, "Millburgh's leading florists for over a century."

The southern boundary of Laurel Heights was Grayrock Road. The north side of the road was "in," the south side was "out." If your home faced Grayrock Road from the south, you could not claim the distinction of living in Laurel Heights. Mary had said, quickly and unequivocally, that the distinction was not worth the two thousand dollars that they saved on the lot. Don's agreement had been equally fast and certain. In addition, the lot they found on the south side was, without argument or consultation, exactly what they both wanted. It was a few perches over two acres, a perfect setting for the house that Don had already sketched—a sweep of lawn that rose gently to the sudden interruption of spectacular outcroppings of quartz-spangled rock, backed by a grove of old oak trees under which the laurel and rhododendron all but covered the ground.

The house had been built of stone quarried just over the hill so that it was a perfect match for the outcroppings and, even in its first-year newness, it had settled into the landscape with a rightness of place that pleased the architect in Don Walling in the same way that it satisfied his lifetime longing for a home.

Swinging wide at the country club entrance to avoid an outgoing golfer's convertible, Don Walling began to look left, waiting for that moment at the crest of the hill where he would catch his first glimpse of the house. He saw it—and then, as a distant pinpoint of fluttering white, he thought he saw Mary standing at the end of the drive. He couldn't be sure, a screen of poplars cut him off, and his impatient desire drove his foot hard on the accelerator. The tires whistled in protest at the sharp turn into Grayrock Road and then he saw that it was Mary. She was waiting beside the mail box, watching for him, and his whole body warmed with anticipation.

Suddenly, more from instinct than definable thought, he sensed her tense alarm. The way she ran toward the stopping car heightened his apprehension. His mind flashed with the terror that something had happened to little Steve.

She was out of breath and the gulp before she spoke was an eternity. Then she said it, the words all together, "Mr. Bullard's dead!"

His alarm for the safety of his son vanished and his mind was left open for the ripping slash of her words. Then—as there is always a moment between the infliction of a terrible wound and the sensation of pain that it causes—he stared at his wife in stunned silence.

"I called Pike Street," she said breathlessly, "but they told me you'd just left. I've tried to reach the others—that's what Mr. Oldham asked me to do—but I haven't been able to locate anyone. I did leave a message with the Shaw's maid but no one answered the phone anywhere else."

"Oldham?" he said blankly, groping.

"Yes. He called from New York. Mr. Bullard collapsed on the street this afternoon and it was only a few minutes ago that he was identified. Mr. Oldham asked that we notify all of the others, so I thought the best thing to do was to—"

A single thought, incongruous and out of context, made him ask, "Did Oldham call us first?"

"He probably tried the others and couldn't reach them either."

Both the question and its answer were washed away in the torrent of realization that was now beginning to flood through his mind. In the roar of a thousand tumbled thoughts, he remembered the way that he had let his anger deface his loyalty to Avery Bullard, and there seemed to be a terrifying connection between the death and his own defection. It was an accusation that reason could not sustain, but in this first moment of grief there was no handhold for reason in the maelstrom of his mind.

He got out of the car and Mary closed the door behind him.

"Don, do you know where any of the others are? We'll have to locate them as soon as we can."

"Walt Dudley's on his way to Chicago. Took the seven o'clock plane. Shaw drove him out. He ought to be back soon."

"Then the maid will tell him. I left the message with her. What about Mr. Alderson and Mr. Grimm?"

"Jesse is on his way down to Maryland. Alderson?" He hesitated, groping for the little memories that were now so deeply buried. "I think Fred said something about going out to dinner tonight. Yes, I'm sure he did."

"It might be the George Smiths' or the Willoughbys'. Shall I try to find him?"

"I suppose so," he said dully.

They were walking up the flagged path, Mary a half step behind him, and he knew that she was watching his face. He turned on the porch, bracing himself against the post. "It seems impossible, doesn't it? I—I can't believe it."

"I know how you feel," she said very softly and her voice was the cooling hand of sympathy.

He avoided her eyes. He had no right to sympathy . . . this afternoon he had . . .

"When did you say he died?" he asked.

"Sometime in the middle of the afternoon."

He closed his eyes and the lash of his remembered anger came back as a cutting backlash of terrifying self-criticism.

"He was a great man," he said slowly, as if he were incanting a prayer for absolution. "He was the greatest man I've ever known."

Mary was murmuring something but it could not be forgiveness . . . there could never be forgiveness. He was guilty of a sin that could never be righted or excused. Avery Bullard was dead. Avery Bullard had been dead when he had hurled his anger against him.

The telephone was ringing and Mary ran ahead of him into the house.

She was back before it seemed possible, holding the door open for him to enter. "It's the newspaper, Don. They've just had a flash from New York."

"You talk to them, Mary. You know all that there is to know, more than I do."

He turned, not waiting for her response, and walked slowly back toward the black oaks where the rock rose from the earth like the walls of the cathedral.

7.12 P.M. EDT

The Aldersons, the Willoughbys, and the George Smiths had eaten together once each month for all of the months there had been in the last fourteen years. There was no particular reason, other than habit, why the custom should have persisted over such a long span of time. Even in the beginning their only bonds had been that they all lived in the same block, all went to the same church, and all carried the common stigma of not being old Millburgh families which excluded them from the social activities that centered around the Federal Club and the Historical Society. The years had broken those bonds. Their homes were now separated, only the Aldersons still attended St. Martin's Episcopal, and both the Federal Club and the Historical Society had long since accepted their memberships. The Friday dinners now owed their existence to the reluctance of all three couples to be the first to break the tradition, a reluctance that was slowly being heightened by the inertia of advancing age and the way that death was beginning to constrict the circle of their other old acquaintances.

"Honestly, the price of things just makes you stop and think," Mildred Willoughby said tonight, talking with the quick little bursts of breath to which she was always limited when she wore her all-in-one foundation. "Jim and I were talking about it the other night when we were going over the bills. Last month alone, our florist bill was almost fifty dollars."

"This month will be worse," Agnes Smith added. "All these June weddings."

"The way it is with us, weddings aren't as bad as funerals."

"No, I guess that's right."

The subject was exhausted and the three women sat in a silence broken only by the blare of the radio from the sun porch where the three men had isolated themselves.

"Jim, honey," Mildred Willoughby called. "Couldn't you turn the radio down just a teeny little bit?"

"Waiting for the ball scores, sweetie," Jim Willoughby called back. "Be on in a minute now. Got a bet on with Fred here and I'm not going to miss taking the old skinflint's money away from him."

He thrust his moon face around the corner so that all of the ladies could see him wink. "Fred's got some big money riding on the Yanks today—a whole dime!"

Everyone laughed. Fred Alderson's penuriousness was a thin-stretched joke, but no thinner than the others that someone else would dutifully remake before the evening was over.

Edith Alderson, watching her husband through the open door, was pleased to see that he smiled. Fred had seemed unusually worn and tired when he had come home tonight, almost as if he were having that old prostate trouble again.

"Oh, Edith?" Agnes called gently.

"Yes?"

"I've been meaning to ask you—"

Whatever she was about to ask was not asked. An imperative command for attention suddenly cut into the radio's music stream.

"We interrupt this program," the voice said dramatically, "to bring you an important news bulletin. We have received a flash from the Associated Press that Avery Bullard died this afternoon in New York. I repeat—we have received a flash that Avery Bullard died this afternoon in New York. That's all we know at this moment. We will bring you additional news as soon as it's received. Keep tuned to this station for the latest developments."

The music cut back in the middle of a phrase. Someone snapped the switch and there was stunned silence in the two rooms.

All eyes were on Frederick Alderson. He stood in the middle of the sun porch floor, his thin body wavering ever so slightly as if to hint that he might faint. Edith hurried to his side.

Mildred Willoughby whispered. "You remember what I was talking about just before it happened—funerals?"

Agnes nodded, awed. "You'd almost think it was presentiment."

"How old was he, Fred?" Jim Willoughby asked, asking the thing that was always asked.

Frederick Alderson moved his lips but there was no sound at first. Then the slow words came. "He was five years younger than I am—only fifty-six."

"We'll have to go," Edith Alderson said in quick decision. "I'm sorry, Mildred, but I'm sure you'll understand."

"Of course. I understand."

"Yes—yes, we'll have to go," Frederick Alderson said.

Jim brought his hat and Edith went back to the living room for her purse.

"If there's anything I can do—" George Smith said and the others repeated the phrase, standing in a stiff little semicircle at the door.

"I'll let you know," Edith Alderson said. Then, her hand on his arm, she guided her husband through the door.

The telephone was ringing and Mildred Willoughby answered it. "Who?—oh, yes, Mrs. Walling—yes, they were here but they just left—yes, we heard it on the radio—yes, they know—not at all, Mrs. Walling. Thank you for calling."

"That was Mrs. Walling to tell Fred and Edith," she explained.

"Looked like it hit Fred pretty hard," George Smith said solemnly.

"Yeh, a thing like that hits you," Willoughby said. "I know

[126]

how it was when Mr. Payne went. Same thing. Heart trouble. Went just like that."

"He'd been mowing the lawn that morning," Agnes broke in. "Mr. Payne always insisted on mowing his own lawn."

"That's why I don't let George mow ours," Mildred puffed. "Or shovel our snow either. Well, if everyone's ready I guess we might as well sit down. I'll just have to leave Fred and Edith's places. The table's all set that way now."

George held his wife's chair and then, still standing, looked across the table. "I've been thinking, Jim—you know what this means for Fred?"

"For Fred?"

"He'll be the president of the company now, won't he?"

"Say, that's right. Guess he will."

"Do you really think so, George?" Agnes asked. "I thought it would be that Mr. Dudley."

"Goodness, isn't he the handsomest man!" Mildred said.

George frowned. "If you want my opinion, I'd say it would be Fred."

"It would be nice for Edith," Agnes said. "Goodness knows she deserves it and I never have cared much for that Dudley woman's ways."

"You can say that again," Mildred said, raising her spoon like a conductor's baton. The spoon plunged into her fruit cup and the dinner was on.

9000 FT. OVER ALTOONA, PENNSYLVANIA
7.22 P.M. EDT

If the advertising manager of Trans National Airlines had been aboard the flight, his professional alertness would have demanded a color photograph of the gentleman in Seat 9. There, beyond the slightest doubt, was the perfect illustration for an advertisement that would convince readers of the mass magazines that TNA was the choice of the nation's most distinguished men. No model agency could possibly have supplied a man who radiated that same aura of true distinction, a man so unquestionably born to the purple, a man whom one and all would instantly accept as a visual representation of the thin top-cut of American aristocracy. No one, even the most discerning, would suspect that the gentleman in Seat 9 was anything but what his appearance credited him with being.

The gentleman in Seat 9 was J. Walter Dudley. The unsuspected truth was that he had been born in a side-road village in Iowa, the son of a down-at-the-heels veterinarian who hated his life. "Doc" Dudley had dreamed of being a famous surgeon but, after failing in an attempt to work his way through medical school, he had made the veterinary profession a reluctant second choice. In a compounding of misfortune, his lack of satisfaction contributed to a bitterness that alienated the farmers and stockmen upon whom he was forced to depend for his livelihood.

Young Walter's mother had done her best to make her husband act in a manner that would make the farmers like him. Her efforts had little or no effect upon "Doc" Dudley, but they had created an atmosphere in which her son learned—as only the young can learn before they know they are being taught—that "getting along with people" was the most important thing in life.

Afterwards, when Walter was old enough to appreciate the extent of his father's failure, he attributed it all to the old man's inexcusable negligence in making people like him. It did not occur to Walter to soften his indictment on the grounds that the castration of pigs, from which his father earned most of what little income he had, was a frustratingly inadequate fulfillment of the dream of being a great surgeon. That did not occur to Walter because he was not, even as a boy, a dreamer.

The nature of young Walter's mind was well adapted to the process of learning and he always made good marks in school. It was easy for him to store away all that he read and heard and, since his carefully ordered memories were never disturbed by imaginative whirlwinds, all that he filed away in his mind was ready and waiting to be recalled when the need for the fact arose. His teachers, particularly those who taught by the transplantation of things to be remembered—and they were in the majority—thought of him as an "excellent student." He graduated as the second-ranking student in a class of twenty-two high school seniors. What minor disappointment he felt in failing to become the valedictorian was more than outweighed by his election as class president and his designation as "Most Popular Senior" in the high school annual.

Walter Dudley's experience with football was in the pattern to which his life had already been shaped. His nature did not incline him toward competitive sports, particularly those involving bodily contact, but in a small school where there were hardly enough boys to fill the required eleven uniforms, his participation was inevitable. He had been large for his age—six feet one and a hundred and ninety pounds—and not playing would have jeopardized his friendship with the entire student body.

He derived little pleasure from the game itself. His body had an essential softness that no amount of training seemed to dissipate, and he was more than usually sensitive to bodily pain. Some of the other boys obviously reveled in the physical satisfaction of a crashing tackle, but to Walter Dudley it was something to be endured as a price that must be paid for the approval of his team mates, the privilege of joining in the rich-tongued banter of the dressing room, and the joy of being included in the circle around the pep-talking coach just before they ran on the field to the welcoming cheers of every person in town.

No one ever knew that Walter was afraid. He did not flinch. He was driven—as the fear-filled sometimes are—to desperately serious effort. In his junior year he was elected captain of the team and, in his senior year, his name appeared in a Des Moines newspaper as an honorable mention tackle on the all state high school team. No one from the school had ever achieved an equivalent honor and a special assembly was called for the presentation of his gold football. What Walt remembered, long after the gold football had revealed itself as tarnished brass, was the entire student body rising to sing, "For He's a Jolly Good Fellow."

Walter Dudley went to college that fall on a scholarship supported by a group of alumni who had selected him as a promising recruit for the football squad. It was evident after the first few weeks of early training that Walter was not of varsity caliber, but he punished himself unmercifully in an attempt to make enough of a showing so that his sponsors would not think badly of him. It was more of a relief than he could admit, even to himself, when he finally cracked a collarbone on a tackling dummy and was barred from active practice. His association with the football team, however, was not broken. His board-and-room job was the care of The Sanctum, a room on the second floor of the field house that was reserved as a clubroom for the lettermen. To all others, none of whom was allowed to cross its threshold, The Sanctum was a place of intriguing glamor. Actually it was a bleak room, gray-brown and eternally musty, furnished only with battered tables and castoff chairs. Before the collarbone incident the lettermen had insisted that Walt acquire some new furniture, a demand that he had rightfully shrugged off as a mild form of hazing. Afterwards, in gratitude for the fact that the lettermen still allowed him to come in and clean up the incriminating evidence which the cigarette smokers left behind, he began to forage in earnest. That was how he met Bernie Sulzman.

Bernie was a man of ideas. He ran a new and second-hand furniture store on College Avenue. When Walt approached him for a donation of furniture Bernie quickly made a counter-proposal. Why not, he suggested, solicit the old lettermen among the alumni for donations to buy the furniture to which Bernie would attach, at no extra charge, a brass plate engraved with the name of the donor? Walt got the list, wrote the letters, and within a month The Sanctum was furnished with twenty-six new chairs, two leather davenports, four table desks, and an icebox. The lettermen awarded Walt Dudley a key to The Sanctum and he became, for the rest of his college career, the only non-letterman ever to have the full privileges of the clubroom.

The story of Walt Dudley's money-raising prowess spread

over the campus and he was appointed to the advertising sales staff of both the newspaper and the annual. In his junior year he was elected not only class president but also business manager of the annual, an unprecedented doubling of honors. His name had become magic on a ballot. Everybody liked Walt Dudley.

In terms of his afterlife, the most important thing that happened during his college years was his continued association with Bernie Sulzman. After his success with The Sanctum project, Bernie offered him a chance to sell furniture to students who were dissatisfied with the sparse furnishings of the fraternity houses and dormitories. Walt's commissions paid for most of his college education and, more to the point, he began to learn the furniture business.

It was Bernie who suggested, after his graduation, that Walt get a job as a wholesale furniture salesman and it was Bernie's recommendation, more than his own diploma or college record, that got him his chance as a junior salesman with A. B. Poindexter, sales agent in the Minneapolis area for the Tredway Furniture Company.

Six years later, Walter Dudley had made enough of a mark so that he was singled out by Avery Bullard, who was then sales manager of Tredway Furniture, and encouraged to establish a sales agency of his own in Kansas City. In 1936, after the Tredway Corporation was formed, he closed his own agency and joined the corporation as a district sales manager. After a number of moves, all of them upward, he had been named Western Sales Manager with headquarters in Chicago. In 1945 he had been brought back to Millburgh and made Vice-President for Sales.

At fifty-three, J. Walter Dudley was probably the best-known man in the entire furniture industry. His memory for names and faces was phenomenal. At one Chicago market, standing at the door of Tredway's display space in the Merchandise Mart, two bystanding salesmen had actually kept a count and heard him greet two hundred and eighteen furniture store owners and buyers by name before he was confronted by an individual whose name he did not know. There were hundreds of furniture merchants who would not have thought a market visit complete without having had the opportunity to shake hands with good old Walt Dudley.

In retrospect, J. Walter Dudley's life seemed to have followed such an unvarying line that fate appeared to have ruled the course with a straightedge. Actually, he had followed no conscious course. In all his years he had wasted a bare handful of hours worrying about his future. He was completely honest when he advised his young salesmen, "Work—that's the answer! Just keep working and don't worry. Don't watch the goal posts—keep your eye on the ball! If you're in there all the time, hitting that old line, you'll score a touchdown sooner or later."

He practiced what he preached. His talent for making friends, coupled with his memory, were important assets but neither ability would have been effective without his never-failing store of energy. When he traveled with salesmen, which he frequently did, he demanded a schedule that started the day with an early-opening store and carried through at a pounding pace until they finally wound up at some neighborhood shop that was open in the evenings. Then there would be a hotel room session until midnight. As he moved across the country, J. Walter Dudley left behind him a trail of worn and astounded salesmen who, when they met afterwards to compare notes, would acknowledge that he was a phenomenon beyond understanding.

If J. Walter Dudley's driving energy was beyond the understanding of his salesmen, it was equally true that it was beyond his own. He himself did not know the source, nor did he waste time in searching for it. His motivation was not—though others often found it hard to believe—the fire of calculated ambition. He was a runner who ran without a goal. Running was his way of life. If you ran hard, and made enough friends, everything would work out all right.

There had been only two people in J. Walter Dudley's life who had ever worried him by seeming, at times, to withhold their total friendship. One was Avery Bullard—the other was his wife Katherine.

Marriage had been no departure from the straight line course of Walter Dudley's life. He met Katherine that first year after college. She was the daughter of a friend of Mr. Poindexter and lived in a near-mansion that fronted on Lake of the Isles. It was in that house that Walter entered the final phase of his education. There he drank his first cocktail, wore his first tuxedo, and learned the amenities of upper-level social life. He was a good student and adapted himself with an ease that confirmed Katherine's estimate that he was the most likely candidate left among the original prospects who had not yet discovered her two shortcomings—first, that her father was considerably less affluent than he appeared to be and second, that she was, if not totally lacking in sexual desire, at least considerably below the expectations of her experienced trial suitors. Walt, fortunately, was a man without experience. They were married the next June.

Afterwards, in the earlier years of their married life, he was occasionally troubled by his wife's failure to respond to him but, before it became of too serious concern, he found that his own desire was waning and, rather than risk embarrassment, his advances were held to a minimum. Every year the minimum had become less and less. There had been no children.

His business relationships with Avery Bullard had actually caused him more concern than his intimate relationships with his wife. There, too, he had suffered from the fault of infrequency. Before the move to Millburgh, he had seen Avery Bullard no oftener than two or three times each year and, since the subject of their meetings was frequently a promotion or a salary raise, he had naturally come to think of Mr. Bullard as a perpetually pleasant man and one of the warmest of his many friends.

After he had moved to Millburgh, almost daily contact with Avery Bullard had brought a frightening revelation. Always before, Walt Dudley had been able to solve all of his problems with the friend-making process that he thought of as "salesmanship." Avery Bullard was shockingly unsusceptible. He was pleasant enough, as a rule, but his questioning was perpetual and he would not accept pleasant generalities as answers. To compound the difficulty, most of Mr. Bullard's demands were for facts about the future. In J. Walter Dudley's dreamless mind, the future was without dimension. He was like a soldier who, having spent his whole career facing only the close-up realities of hand-to-hand combat, is suddenly called upon to return to a headquarters desk and asked to plan the whole strategy of major battles to be fought at some indeterminate time, over an unknown terrain, with weapons not yet invented.

Although Avery Bullard's persistent questioning sometimes seemed to border on persecution, Dudley had not become bitter or resentful. Instead, his respect for the president mounted constantly and he did his best to model himself in the Bullard mold.

There were, inevitably, times of discouragement when he experienced the new sensation of personal inadequacy. It was during one of those times that Loren P. Shaw first came to his rescue. Avery Bullard had recently become imbued with a passion for "long-range planning" and he had demanded an estimate of annual sales, year by year and factory by factory, for the next five years. Dudley had fumbled the task for a week, making one false start after another, until Shaw dropped into his office one afternoon with an offer of assistance. It was only a few months after the comptroller had joined the company and Dudley had no appreciation of Shaw's talent for converting intangibles into neat columns of quotable figures. In a way that he had never been dependent on anyone else, J. Walter Dudley became dependent upon Loren Shaw. The comptroller's figures gave him the answers to Mr. Bullard's more urgent questions. There was nothing that he needed so much.

Over the past four years, dependency had ripened into friendship, both in and out of the office. Although Dudley thought of all of the vice-presidents as his friends, Shaw was unquestionably his best. Every day confirmed it. Today had been no exception. It was Shaw who had driven him out to the airport tonight and Shaw who had called him to his office this afternoon and prepared him to meet a danger that might lay ahead. "Walt, I suspect that you'll find some pressure on prices at the Chicago market. Dealers' stocks are up, they probably won't be too anxious to buy, and some of our competitors will be hungry for business. Prices may break. If you have to move, here's something that will help you."

Then Shaw had given him the folder of charts that he was examining now. There was a chart for each major item and, by simply finding the intersection of two lines, the relative net profit at different price and volume levels could be quickly determined. Fanning through the charts, Walter Dudley felt the comfortable assurance of being able to act in a hurry with no danger that Mr. Bullard could ask embarrassing questions afterward. Loren Shaw was his very good friend.

If there were price trouble, Dudley knew that it would come quickly, as soon as he saw the mail order and chain store men in the morning. He was trying to prepare himself by studying the charts. But there was a night between today and tomorrow, and thoughts of the night persistently wormed themselves into the forefront of his mind.

Resolutely, he put the charts in his saddle-leather portfolio and told himself that the time had come to settle this business of Eva Harding, completely and finally, once and for all. If he weakened tonight, as he had weakened before, and allowed himself to call her again . . . no, there was no need to make that decision again. It was made! He had made it the last time he had left her. It was done . . . over . . . finished! He would never see Eva Harding again. This wasn't like the other times. This time he meant it!

Eva Harding had led J. Walter Dudley into the one side journey from the straight course of his life. There was no argument now about his having been led. Eva had eventually admitted it as freely as she then chided him for his reluctance. Under the intimate circumstances of the confession, he had found the admission as beguiling as the chiding, despite the fact that it made Eva seem, by contrast with Katherine, a rather abnormal woman. His experience had not prepared him for the fact that sexual desire was not an unfeminine characteristic, nor that sexual satisfaction was something other than a favor which was reluctantly granted by a considerate woman to a demanding male.

The face and name of Eva Harding had first been impressed on Walter Dudley's mind at one of the summer markets. She had been introduced to him on the display floor by Mort Finney, a salesman in the Chicago office, and catalogued in his memory along with Mort's whispered footnote that she was "a clever gal who's just opened a decorating shop on North Michigan and is plenty worth keeping an eye on."

At the winter market, J. Walter Dudley's memory performed with its usual efficiency and he was able, without prompting, to call Miss Harding's name and inquire about her shop on North Michigan Boulevard. He repeated the performance the following June and again in January when, recalling her name on a list of customers who had done unusually well with Millway Federal, Tredway's most expensive line of colonial reproductions, he had congratulated her on her success and suggested the possibility that a photograph of her shop might be used in one of Tredway's trade-magazine advertisements. That had led to her invitation to stop by and see her shop, an invitation to which J. Walter Dudley attached no special importance since it was a gesture as commonly made by store owners as their invariable inquiry about the state of business. Afterwards, however, Mort Finney had come to him and said, "Chief, I think it would be swell if you could manage somehow to stop in her place for a minute or two while you're in Chicago. She's really beginning to pick up some volume now on top-end stuff. I've got a hunch that a little personal visit from you would help keep me on the inside track. She's quite a gal—got a lot of tricks up her sleeve. Unless I miss my guess, you'll get a kick out of talking to her."

Mort Finney was never to know how accurately prophetic that last remark had been.

The next Friday, coming down North Michigan Boulevard after a late afternoon meeting at the Drake Hotel, J. Walter

Dudley happened to see Eva Harding's name on the front of her shop and decided that the few remaining minutes of the afternoon could be better spent in calling on her than by returning to the Merchandise Mart.

There was light snow falling and a sharp wind whipping in from the lake. Walking back the long block by which the driver had overshot the mark before he could be stopped, J. Walter Dudley had felt unusually tired. The meeting, which had been held at Avery Bullard's suggestion, had been a complete failure and he faced the prospect of an unpleasant report when he got back to Millburgh. The task immediately ahead of him, calling on Eva Harding, aroused no anticipation of pleasure. He was only fulfilling a promise that he wished he hadn't made.

As a generality—to which, of course, Walter Dudley never gave open expression—he did not like businesswomen, particularly those of the type to which his mind had assigned Eva Harding. He had known many of them and they were all too boldly clever, too hard and brittle, too obviously an incongruous blend of feminine wile and masculine imitation.

There had been nothing in the first few minutes of his visit to Eva Harding's shop that had changed his original estimate of her, although he did find her somewhat easier to talk to than he had expected. She did not feel called upon, as so many of her type did, to display a "personality." Then, too, as she took him on a quick tour of the shop, she showed unusual discrimination in her selection of the merchandising ideas that she picked to call to his attention, by-passing the familiar and reserving her comments for those that were genuinely original.

When they reached the second floor, where the furniture stock was displayed, Walter Dudley's interest sharpened. There was hardly a piece of Tredway furniture to which she had not made some improving modification. A change of brasses on the No. 1604 buffet gave it a distinction that it had not had before. There was a gold Chinese tea paper under the glass of the No. 370B table. Four little brass stars on the doors made a startling change in No. 9181.

She explained that such changes were necessary in order to

escape direct competition from other stores carrying the same items, half apologizing as if she were fearful that he might be offended; obviously pleased when he proved that he wasn't by offering to buy some of her design ideas. She side-stepped the offer. "I'd be flattered to have you use anything you see, Mr. Dudley. You're more than welcome." Then they had talked for more than an hour and he had filled several pages in his notebook.

Time had passed without notice and when he discovered that it was almost seven he felt that the least he could do was to invite her to dinner. He noticed with growing respect that she accepted without hesitation, making no more of it than any male business acquaintances would have done under similar circumstances. At her suggestion they had gone to Jacques Restaurant, which was only a few blocks away, and upon their discovery that the waiting line was impossibly long, she said with the same matter-of-factness, "We'll go to my place. You'll wait no longer for your dinner than you will here, and I'm sure you'll be more comfortable while you're waiting." There had been no chance to refuse, nor any forseeable reason why he should.

When he thought about it afterward—and he thought about it a great deal, so often that the re-creation of the memory finally became almost an obsession—he could never quite understand what there had been about that first evening with Eva Harding that had given him so much happiness. The only explanation that was tenable, even for a moment, was that his pleasure had come from discovering that she was not the same person in her home that she was in business. He had known then that his explanation was incomplete, and later that it was totally inadequate.

The overture to his pleasure had been her apartment. It had offered, the moment he stepped inside the door, an atmosphere of comfort and relaxation which had led to the wish, unexpressed, that Eva Harding had done the interior decoration of his new home in Laurel Heights instead of that famous but strangely offensive man that Katherine had brought down from New York.

"Would you mind making the cocktails, Mr. Dudley?" Eva Harding had asked and then, at her direction, he had found the bottles in one corner of the buffet and the glasses in another and the shaker and the ice in the kitchen and, somehow, when the cocktails were finished they seemed very much better than the ones he made from the carefully laid out silver tray that Katherine always had Violet prepare and place on the sideboard every evening before he arrived home.

Eva had disappeared while he was making the cocktails and she returned in changed clothes, a kitcheny red-checked gingham that was in the sharpest possible contrast to the tailored black suit that she had worn before. "Will it spoil your cocktail if you sit here in the kitchen and watch me start dinner?" she had asked. "Or would you prefer a bit more formality?" The answer was premade and she said, "That's the first guess I made about you and I'm glad I was right."

He had sat watching her, really noticing her as a person for the first time, and it was his opinion then—as it had remained afterward—that she was neither pretty nor homely, but somewhere in the indeterminate middle ground of ordinary appearance. She was by no means as handsomely attractive as Katherine. But there was a radiation of aliveness that came from the quick directness of her every movement, the fast sure reach of her hands, the alertness of her eyes, the instantaneous flashing of her smile that always came without a dulling moment of hesitation before.

They ate in front of the fire that she had asked him to start in the fireplace and, long afterwards, he was bothered because his memory, upon which he could usually rely with complete confidence, would not tell him exactly what he had eaten, but only that it was a delicious dinner. Nor could he remember all that they had talked about, only that what she said, and what she had made him say, somehow transmitted some of her aliveness to him—and that long before there had been enough talk she had said, "Time to do the dishes," and he had laughingly offered to help and she had laughed back and said, "Of course, Mr. Dudley, that's exactly what I expected."

There had been only one thing said in the whole evening

that he could later recall as having carried the slightest hint of what was to come, and that had been a quick exchange at the door when he was leaving. They had shaken hands . . . and that was the first time their hands had touched . . . and she had replied to his thanks with a softly whistled phrase from a popular song and he fortunately remembered the words and paraphrased them in his answer, "It's been so nice to *be* the man around the house" . . . and she had laughed and he had laughed and he had said, "Good night, Miss Harding," and she had said, "Good night, Mr. Dudley" . . . and it had been five minutes after eleven when he had stopped at the desk on the twenty-first floor of the Palmer House to pick up his key and the message to call Avery Bullard at once. He remembered the time because it had been after midnight in Millburgh when he got the call through and Mr. Bullard had said, "Now don't tell me you've been entertaining a customer," and he had replied, "Believe it or not, Mr. Bullard, a customer has been entertaining me."

The next few weeks were the most provocatively mysterious period in Walter Dudley's life. For some totally unaccountable reason, he could not keep the thought of Eva Harding from his mind and, what was even more disturbing, he would awake at night and in the fantasy-breeding darkness she would be lying beside him and his lips would touch hers—and then, frightened, he would get out of bed and go down to the library to smoke a cigarette. If that didn't erase the stain of insane eroticism he would walk through the house to the cold gleaming whiteness of the big kitchen and that always did. Those nights were the only times that he ever went into the kitchen because, as Katherine had warned him, the kitchen was Violet's private preserve and good cooks had to be humored because if you ever lost one it was almost impossible these days to replace her.

In March, he had stopped over in Chicago on his way to the West Coast. He had told himself that he had no intention of seeing Eva Harding and there was not the slightest hint that she had ever expected him to call again when he telephoned her from the airport. Yet, through some force as mysterious as that which had filled his nights with fantasy, when he stepped across the threshold of her apartment they were, without an instant's hesitation, in each other's arms—and the fantasy was no longer a fantasy but something that they had both lived through in the months of their separation.

Until that night, he had accepted the fact that his sexual abilities were waning, that age had almost won the battle against his potency. But Eva Harding had aroused the triumphant discovery of a maleness surpassing anything that he had known even as a young man. Looking up into his face, her eyes gleaming and her hands trembling ecstatically against his cheeks, she had said, "My darling, you're so very, very young!"

That moment he would never forget nor regret—but it all should have ended then as he had promised himself afterward that it would. It hadn't. It might have ended if she had ever made, even once, the slightest demand upon him or exhibited the faintest trace of possessiveness. She hadn't. He would call her at unexpected times and she would always be there. There had never been anything that he asked her to do that had seemed, in any way, to cause her the slightest inconvenience or to interfere, even remotely, with anything else in her life. She asked nothing, not even words of love in moments when the asking would have been a demand impossible to reject, and she let him go with no plea for return. If he had not come back, there would have been no broken promises.

It was only in his returning that a promise was broken—and that was only a promise to himself that had always proved, in the moment of final weighing, to be invalid because it had been made under the false assumption that Eva Harding would destroy his love for Katherine. That had not happened. It would never happen. His life with Eva was something as detached from his life with Katherine as he was now, nine thousand feet in the sky, detached from the earth below.

No, Katherine was not the reason why he must never see Eva Harding again. The true reason was that Eva had become an escape to peace that was all too desirable. Tonight, sitting there in that meeting, waiting, not knowing what was to come, sheltering the fear that always preceded Avery Bullard's arrival, his mind had reached out to Eva Harding. She had become his escape from fear and escape was something that he must never accept. A man had to keep working . . . hitting that old line, even when he was afraid . . . yes, *because* he was afraid! Fear had to be conquered . . . you didn't dare run away . . . you had to stay there and fight it out.

"Mr. Dudley?"

He looked up and the stewardess was smiling at him.

"Would you care for dinner?"

He had not eaten but he said, "No, thank you." If her face had reminded him less of Eva Harding he would have said "Yes."

It didn't matter. He would pick up something to eat after he got down to the Palmer House. There would be plenty of time before he went to bed.

He opened his portfolio again and took out the charts that Loren Shaw had prepared.

MILLBURGH, PENNSYLVANIA
7.28 P.M. EDT

Don Walling stood in the black shadow of a jagged head of rock hidden deep within the oaks behind his home. How long he had been there he did not know, but as he lifted the weight of his slumped body from his hands he saw that his palms were red-laced with the rough pattern of the rock's surface.

The shocking impact of the news of Avery Bullard's death was slowly draining away, but the fading numbness of shock only opened the way to a sharper realization of personal loss. His eyes drifted toward the house and everything he saw reminded him of Avery Bullard's beneficence. All that he had . . . everything . . . had come from Avery Bullard's hands. Even Mary would never have been his if it had not been for Avery Bullard, if he had not met Avery Bullard that night in Chicago, if Avery Bullard had not sent him back to Pittsburgh, if Avery Bullard had not given him the chance to prove that he was worthy of her.

The thought of his wife unconsciously eased the weight of grief. There was a mental link between love and death. He had fallen in love with Mary on the night her father died.

During the first weeks after Avery Bullard had sent him to the Coglan factory in Pittsburgh, Don Walling had tried to find Mike Kovales. There was no telephone listed in his name and the old restaurant out on Schenley Hill had a new proprietor who knew nothing about the former owner. Finally, through a man he met at a Greek-American social club where Mike had once been a member, Don Walling had learned that Mike Kovales was critically ill. He went immediately to the hospital and he was glad afterwards that he had not delayed. That was the last night that visitors were allowed. He had seen Mary in the hospital hall that evening but his mind had been on her father and he had paid her little attention after the first moment of surprise that she could ever have been the gangling child who used to come in the back door of the restaurant and sit in the corner of the kitchen, perpetually reading even while she ate.

A week later, on the night her father died, Mary Kovales had called him as she had promised she would and he had gone out to be with her. It was then—if the moment could ever be marked—when he had fallen in love with her. She was beautiful, with a classic Athenian perfection of features that reminded him of Grecian sculpture, but it was not beauty that attracted him most. It was the inner character she radiated, the strength that allowed her to rise above tragedy without minimizing it, an essential nobility, a femininity that offered all that any woman could offer, yet did not demand the common price of total dependency. There was, he knew, no strength that any man could give that Mary Kovales could not repay in kind.

He needed that strength now and he walked slowly toward the house, conscious that she was waiting for him on the edge of the terrace, yet reluctant to acknowledge her presence by looking directly at her. When he reached her side she took his hand in hers and, for the moment, her silence was wiser than anything she might have said.

"You reach Fred Alderson?" he asked, almost gruffly.

"They were at the Willoughbys' for dinner but were leaving as I called. They'd heard it over the radio."

"I'd better call Fred and see if there's anything I can do."

"He won't be home for a few minutes," she said, carefully calm. "It's quite a drive in from the Willoughbys'. Come eat, Don. It's all ready."

He followed her automatically and as automatically began to eat what she placed in front of him. He sensed that she wanted to talk and he appreciated the understanding that made her wait until his words would come more easily.

Seeing the empty seat where their nine-year-old son usually sat, suggested a side remark to break the silence, "Where's Steve tonight?"

"At the Brewster's—Kenny's birthday party."

He mumbled an acknowledgment of a vague memory that they had talked about it that morning—but now the morning seemed a month past.

"Well—" he said finally, and the word was the plunge. "This is like dumping the world upside down."

"Yes." The sound was only a soft invitation to say more.

"I've thought about a lot of things that might happen—everything but this. It's—well, it's just one of those things that couldn't happen."

"But it has," she said firmly, as if she were demanding his acceptance.

There was a point in her demand. He knew it. Once he had openly accepted the fact of Avery Bullard's death, a door could close in his mind and another door would open. "Yes, he's dead," he said slowly and his voice had the sound of decision.

She pressed the opening. "Don, I know you haven't had time to think about it yet—but you will think about it and when you do, please don't be too worried because someone other than

Avery Bullard will be president of the Tredway Corporation. The company will go on—and so will you."

The earnest intensity of her voice made him realize that she was harboring some secret fear. "What are you worrying about?"

"You."

"Me?"

"Yes."

"Why?"

She hesitated as if she were questioning the propriety of saying more. "Don, I know how much Avery Bullard has meant to you. For you, Avery Bullard has been the company—everything."

He toyed a morsel of food across his plate. "I'll be all right," he said, his voice flat and guarded.

Her fingers walked across the table top, gently touching the back of his hand. "I know you will, Don. Forgive me if I said something that shouldn't have been said."

"Better call Fred now." He pushed back his chair and rose quickly. She glanced away and he knew that he had hurt her. He stepped behind her chair, letting his hands fall lightly on her shoulders. "Sorry. Didn't mean it that way. Little on edge, that's all."

He saw her right hand rise quickly to cover his left, and her head tilt back so that he was looking directly down into the jet pools of her eyes. "I love you, Don, and I don't want you to be hurt—that's all."

His hands gripped her shoulders. "Sure, I know."

"The Alderson's number is there on the pad," she said in quick recovery.

He dialed the number. There was a busy signal. "Maybe I'd better run down, see what I can do."

"Don?"

He turned, silent.

"Will he be the new president?"

"Who?"

"Mr. Alderson."

"What makes you think that?"

"I didn't think it. I merely asked because you mentioned helping him—as if he were the one who would take charge."

It was a question that he had been avoiding asking himself but now, openly asked, the question soared in his mind like a sky-reaching rocket and then burst and reburst into a hundred other questions.

"Well, Fred's the oldest," he said lamely. "Jesse is out of town—Walt, too—no, I haven't any idea who'll be president."

"If Mr. Fitzgerald had lived, there'd be no question about it, would there?"

"I don't suppose so."

"Or if someone else had been elected to take his place?"

"But no one has been."

"I wonder why not," she said speculatively.

His voice picked up her musing tone. "I had an idea that it would happen at the board meeting next Tuesday—no reason particularly—hunch, that's all. Now—" His voice retreated, avoiding the necessity of saying aloud that next Tuesday the board of directors would elect Avery Bullard's successor.

As happened so often, she seemed to have heard his unsaid words. "I suppose I should know this, but I don't. How is a new president elected—by the stockholders or the board?"

"The board. The stockholders elect the board and then the board elects the officers."

He sat down again and she poured coffee. "How many are there on the board?"

"The board? Nine. Well, there were nine before Mr. Fitzgerald died. That leaves eight."

"Seven without Mr. Bullard?" she prompted.

"Oh." His voice caught. "Yes, seven."

Her head went back, counting. "You and Mr. Alderson, Jesse Grimm and Walt Dudley, Loren Shaw and that man from New York."

"George Caswell."

"Yes, that's six. Who's the other one?"

"Julia Tredway Prince."

"Oh, I'd forgotten that she was a director."

"In name, at least. Never comes to a meeting, but she's still a director—officially."

"You'll elect the president—you seven?"

It was another first question, another soaring rocket. "Yes— yes, I suppose we will."

Her glance was a forewarning. "Who will it be, Don? Whom will you elect?"

"Good God, Mary, it's too soon to—" He clipped his voice when he heard its edge, choking back his annoyance at the persistence of her cross-examination.

"I'm sorry," she said quickly. "Forgive me."

His spoon circled the cup, stirring the coffee, and his eyes focused on the vortex of the slow-spinning whirlpool. "You're right," he said finally. "There's no use trying to avoid thinking about it. 'The king is dead, long live the king.'" The spoon stopped moving and the whirlpool spun itself out. "No, I can't see Alderson as president. The job's just too big for him—company's too big. Actually, when you get right down to it, Fred's never been much more than a super-secretary for Avery Bullard. Oh, maybe that isn't quite fair—he is good on financial stuff, damned good—but it will take a lot more than that to fill Avery Bullard's shoes. Fred just doesn't have it."

"Mr. Grimm?" she prompted.

"Jesse? Well, Jesse is a wonderful man—great in a factory, best there is—but—"

A thousand memories floated together in his mind, overlapping, forming one composite image of Jesse Grimm's impassive face . . . the slow puffing of his pipe . . . the taciturnity that made him go for hours without saying a word. No, Jesse would never do what Avery Bullard had done . . . light the flame in a man's heart . . . fire him to do the impossible. "No, I hate to say it because I like Jesse so much, but he couldn't do it—he just couldn't."

[147]

"What about Walt Dudley?"

He started to shake his head before he spoke and then caught himself. Yes, Walt Dudley did have something . . . the words that Jesse didn't have. Men listened when Walt talked. He could sell . . . and he could teach other men to sell. People liked him. Yes, that was Walt's strength, making people like him . . . but it was his weakness, too. Everyone hadn't liked Avery Bullard. There were times when a president had to be hard . . . crack the whip . . . scorch a man's soul. The man might hate you but you didn't dare think about that . . . it was the way you made men . . . it was the way you built a company . . . made it run. Walt Dudley didn't have that inner strength, that hard core, that courage to fight the world without caring what the world thought. His voice dipped into his stream of thought and he said aloud, "No, not Walt Dudley."

"That leaves Loren Shaw."

His rejection was instantaneous. "God no, not Shaw!"

"I hadn't realized that you felt that strongly. I knew that you didn't like him too well personally, but I thought you—"

"Or any other way," he cut in. "The one thing I've never been able to understand about Avery Bullard is why he brought Shaw into the company in the first place."

An almost invisible smile played behind her black eyes, "Perhaps because he's so different from all the rest of you—the leaven for the loaf."

"He'll never be president, I can tell you that!" he said grimly.

"Since you've rejected all the others, apparently you've decided to vote for yourself."

He grimaced at her attempted humor.

There was a quick change in the tone of her voice. "Don, whoever the new president is, he won't be another Avery Bullard. If you're weighing everyone against Avery Bullard, no one else can possibly seem adequate."

He flinched inwardly, freezing the mask of his face to avoid a visible reaction, not because she had probed the secret truth but because she had insisted again on exposing it. It was the one characteristic of Mary's that he disliked, the way that she some-

[148]

times made him feel as if he were a case study in abnormal behavior and she were a teacher announcing her findings to a class.

Yet Mary was right. There couldn't be another Avery Bullard. All that could be done now was to come as close as they could. There were only four choices . . . no, only three . . . Shaw was out. Alderson . . . Grimm . . . Dudley? Alderson . . . Grimm? Alderson. Yes, Fred might carry on. He had been the closest to Avery Bullard . . . knew the most about what was going on in the whole company . . . the things that no one else knew. But Fred was weak. No, maybe it wasn't weakness . . . maybe it was agreement. Yes, that could be true. Maybe that was the reason that Fred never spoke out against Avery Bullard in executive committee meetings . . . because he thought as Mr. Bullard thought . . . as people who are close to one another come to think alike, almost as if they were sharing a common brain . . . as Mary so often knew what he was going to say before he said it.

Mary's voice broke into his consciousness. "Are you sure that Mr. Alderson would want it?"

He blinked, wondering for an instant whether she had actually said it or whether it was only an imagined confirmation of the question that had just come to the edge of his own mind.

"He hasn't been too well lately," Mary went on. "I know that from talking to his wife—and he's not a young man, Don. He must be sixty-one or sixty-two."

He moved abruptly, twisting himself up out of his chair, feeling the urgency of movement, the need for escape from the logic of too simple reason. That's what Mary never realized . . . that everything couldn't be worked out like a little problem in mathematics.

"I'll run down and find out how to get word to Jesse," he said evasively, starting for the door.

She crossed with him. "Don, is there anyone in Mr. Bullard's family who should be notified?"

"There isn't any family," he said, and the words brought a recognition of the barrenness of Avery Bullard's life and a resurgence of his own grief.

[149]

"There's his wife."

"Wife? They were divorced years ago."

"She might still like to know. I think Edith Alderson has her address."

"All right," he said noncommittally, shielding the memory of the bitterness he had felt many years ago when Jesse had told him how Avery Bullard's wife had deserted him when he needed her most. It had been a long time since the thought had entered his mind and, walking toward the car, he wondered at the strangeness of Mary's having remembered that Avery Bullard had once had a wife.

7.38 P.M. EDT

The telephone receiver hung over the edge of the dresser, swinging like a slow pendulum beating against the mechanical drone of the buzzing dial tone.

Erica Martin, prostrate on the bed, heard nothing but the endless repetition of Mr. Shaw's voice saying, "Oh, hadn't you heard, Miss Martin? Mr. Bullard's dead."

It had come, not as a blow but as a cold steel blade, cutting deeper and deeper, severing nerve center after nerve center, spreading a slow paralysis that ended in oblivion.

There had been a time that was lost, and then she had felt the slow return of consciousness creeping back through her body, but not through her brain, distant and remote, as if her body were something detached with its own ability to generate sensation, and the sensation it generated was of the crushing weight of emptiness. It was a dead weight and now that was all there would ever be, never the life weight of a man, never the filling of that never-filled need, never the yielding for which her dreams had so long prepared her. It was not her mind that cried out against her body, but her body that cried out against her mind. It had been her mind that had made her run away when there had been nothing to escape, made her afraid when there had been nothing to fear, robbed her of what might have been but now could never be.

Slowly, like the drifting of a cloud, the ebbing paralysis released her brain. She opened her eyes and saw the telephone receiver hanging where she must have dropped it. She willed her body to move and was strangely surprised when it did move. Standing, she replaced the telephone receiver on its cradle. Then she reheard Mr. Shaw's voice, vaguely distant as if it were a memory of something heard under anesthesia, and he was asking her to come to the office. "I'm afraid I'll need your help tonight, Miss Martin."

The hall door stood open, as it had been open when the telephone had rung, and she walked out through the door, still too numbed to accept the conscious relief of tears.

7.41 P.M. EDT

Edith Alderson stood stiffly erect, staring at the almost closed door. The whiteness of her face was the only whiteness in the murky gloom of the dark hall. Her hands cupped her elbows, making a rectangle of lean arms and thin shoulders that emphasized the sparse angularity of her figure. She was not a happy woman and her body seemed a physical manifestation of her unhappiness.

A few minutes before, driving home from the Willoughbys', she had confirmed what she had fearfully sensed in that moment after the announcement of Mr. Bullard's death—that Fred would be the next president of Tredway. Her own first reaction had been one of enormous relief that she had at last escaped the overpowering domination of Avery Bullard, but that had been before she had seen Fred's face, before he had talked to her on the way home.

She could hear his voice now, talking to that Mr. Oldham in New York about the arrangements for bringing the body to Millburgh, and with every word she could hear Fred's voice becoming stronger and stronger, more and more commanding. In a minute or two the call would be over. Then he would walk out through that door and she would face him. Her whole body tightened in preparation, her muscles taut, her thin lips drawn hard, the cords lining her neck.

These next few minutes would be her last chance to fight back . . . her last chance to save what little there was left of their lives. She wasn't ready . . . it had happened too fast . . . there had been no warning. Even worse, fighting back was a lost habit. There had been too many intervening years since she had given up in her battle against Avery Bullard.

Desperate for time . . . every step would give her another precious second . . . she walked from the dark hall into the almost matching darkness of the living room. The sun outside was still bright but the faint light that filtered in through the dense mask of overgrown shrubbery outside the windows was too weak to dispel the room's eternal gloom.

Edith Alderson's first lost battle had been over this house and, like a warrior imprisoned within the walls of her own defeat, she had been forced to live in it for over twenty years. The house had been built in 1869 by Gustav Krautz, one of the brothers who had taken over the old Mills Iron Foundry and made a fortune supplying gun caissons for the Union Army. On his dollar-made ladder, Gustav Krautz had climbed out of Dutchtown. But he hadn't quite made North Front. He had come as close as a secret meeting in the back room of the Federal Club had allowed, building his house on George Street, where the back of his lot was separated by only a narrow alley from the house that faced North Front Street.

That, Edith Alderson knew, was why Fred had bought the house—because, by the time they had been able to buy, the house across the alley had been the home of Avery Bullard. Nothing that she had said had been of any avail. Her opinion hadn't counted. Fred had countered everything with the, to him, unanswerable argument that "Mr. Bullard thinks it's what we ought to do."

The house, despite everything that she had tried to do with it, had remained as it had been built, the tasteless product of a tasteless mind in a tasteless age. Every room, even the kitchen, was paneled in dark wood so elaborately carved that her one-room attempt to cover it with paint had been a shocking failure. All that she had done was to highlight the fat bellies and rotund behinds of innumerable carved cupids who, like night-flying bats, had been hitherto almost invisible in the all-pervading darkness. No rugs would quiet the perpetual squeaking of the old parquetry floors, no amount of cleaning would keep pace with the up-sifting dust that came out of the cracks, nor would anything banish the pervading odor of mustiness. In the moments of total despair, glancing up, she was faced with sly grins of the fiendish little elves who were caricatured in the stained-glass semi-circles that crowned all of the windows.

But even the house, bad as it was, had not been the worst thing that Avery Bullard had done to her. Put in its simplest terms—and all of the years of loneliness had given Edith Alderson plenty of time to reduce everything to the simplest of terms—Avery Bullard had taken her husband away from her. He had turned her life into the meaningless sham of being married to a man whose first loyalty she could not claim.

What Avery Bullard wanted had always come first. What she had wanted hadn't mattered. It had been that way almost from the beginning, from the second year of their married life. Fred was like a man mesmerized by a demon. When Avery Bullard had snapped his fingers they had left everything and moved to Millburgh. That was when she had made her first mistake. She had been too young and too innocent then to know that there were men in the world like Avery Bullard.

For a while she had blamed Fred and, by the time she came to realize that the fault was all Avery Bullard's, it was too late. By then Fred was completely in the ogre's power. A man couldn't start over again in middle life. What else could Fred do? It was then that she had stopped fighting back. There was only one thing left and that was to wait for Fred's retirement.

Tonight, miraculously, the hope of an earlier escape had burst upon her. Avery Bullard was dead! Then, cruelly, the hope had been torn away by the prospect of Fred being made president. If Fred were to sit in Avery Bullard's chair, he would be eternally condemned as the slave of Bullard's ghost . . . speak with Bullard's voice . . . think with Bullard's brain. Bullard's heart would be his heart and there would be no place for her. All his life, Avery Bullard had defeated her and now he was threatening to continue her defeat even from his grave.

She walked on. Out of the back windows, over the head-high boxwood, she could see the top of the house where Avery Bullard had lived until Florence had left him.

At the time, Edith Alderson had credited Florence's leaving as her first victory over Avery Bullard. She thought that it would bring the man to his senses. It hadn't. After that he was more of a demon than ever. There were many times when Fred would not come home until long after midnight. Red-eyed and drunk with fatigue he would fall asleep beside her without even touching her hand. Later, in the darkness, she would hear the mumbling of his dream-voice mouthing the words of Avery Bullard and then her eyes would burn as the fire of her hatred turned her tears into scalding steam.

"Edith?"

She turned, startled. Her husband was standing in the arch of the living room. His obvious composure was in frightening contrast to her own lack of inner poise.

"Mr. Bullard's cousin," he said precisely. "Unless I'm mistaken we have his address on our Christmas card list. Can you tell me where I might find it?"

She walked toward him and then past him, into the library, carrying in her ear the impersonal formality of his voice.

The list was in the bottom of the drawer where she piled the never-read pamphlets that came each month from the Millburgh Historical Society. She found it. The name was on the first page.

"Thank you." He was leaning over the desk, writing copperplate script with a very sharp pencil.

She had seen another name on the list. "Fred?"

"Yes?"

"You're sending a telegram?"

[154]

"Yes."

"There's someone else we ought to wire."

"Who?"

"Florence."

He straightened and she saw him looking at her, his face softly pink as if he had grown younger in this last hour, the color emphasized by the whiteness of his perfectly combed hair. "I doubt if he'd want us to do that."

"He's dead." The words were too short to register all that she tried to make them say, so she added, "I'll send it myself," and crossed to the cloisonné box in which she kept recent personal letters. There had been one from Florence only last month. She found it and walked back toward the desk lamp so that there would be light enough to read the corner card.

"Give me the address," she heard him say and her heart leaped to the encouragement of this first small victory. "Mrs. Florence Bullard—The Pines Hotel—Packer Beach, Maine."

She had paced her voice to his writing and, when he made the period after "Maine," she spoke his name.

"Yes?" The word was a courtesy sound, not an inquiry. He was starting to write the message.

"Fred, you can't do it!"

The words seemed to explode from her lips. His head came up slowly in poised surprise, the pencil waiting. "Can't do what, my dear?"

"Be president of the company."

"Why?"

Desperation drove her voice. "You're not well, Fred, you know you're not. It—it would kill you. You know what the doctor said—what all the doctors said."

His voice came back, maddeningly calm. "That was before the operation, Edith. I've been very well these last two years."

"But why do you want it—why?"

"Now, Edith, you—"

"There's no reason—no reason on earth. We don't need more money. We have all we'll need. Fred, you're sixty-one. It's only four more years until you can retire. Fred, don't you—can't you—"

Her voice dropped like a lance shattered on the shield of his hard-masked face.

"Edith, you don't understand."

"I do understand! It's still Avery Bullard, it's still—"

"No," he said, sharply enough to interrupt her, but then his voice dropped, not into softness but into the quiet intensity of calculated hatred. "It's Loren Shaw. If I'm not president, then Shaw will be."

"Let him be. What do you care?"

"You don't mean that, Edith."

"I do mean it. You've given your whole life to Avery Bullard. That's enough."

For a moment, seeing the questioning break in the mask of his face, she clutched at the hope that she might still win. He had looked down and was tracing a wavering line on the pad with the sharp edge of his pencil. She held her breath, waiting for the sound of his voice. With the first word of her hope faded.

"No, Edith, I haven't given my life to Avery Bullard. I've given my life to the company—and I'm not going to see it destroyed by a bastard like Shaw."

Bastard! The word struck like a gun shot. She had never heard him use a word like that before. That wasn't Fred . . . no . . . no . . . no . . . that was Bullard . . . that was Avery Bullard talking!

In silent despair she shrank back against the wall. Without looking at her, he finished writing the messages. Then he picked up the telephone and began to dial the number that he had already written on the top edge of the pad.

No, that hadn't been Fred talking . . . Fred wasn't capable of hating . . . that was Avery Bullard . . . only Avery Bullard could harbor a hatred like that.

Then, from the secret recesses of her mind, where that horrid word lay smoldering like a fused bomb, she hurled it back toward the picture of Avery Bullard that hung above her husband's desk.

As Don Walling turned onto Ridge Road he had noticed that the gasoline gauge needle was almost touching the Empty pin and pulled into the filling station that flanked the country club entrance. "Red" Barry, the owner, bounced up from his perch on the grease rack and came toward him, his peaked cap riding jauntily over his indelible grin.

"Hiya there, Mr. Walling. Say, bad news about Mr. Bullard, huh?"

Don Walling held his response to a nod, repulsed by Red's griefless tone and the irreverence of his senseless grin.

A crowded convertible whished by and the sound of young laughter lingered in its wake. More laughter came from the club tennis courts behind the screening trees. The garbled scream of a many-throated cheer floated up from the soft-ball diamonds below the turn of the hill and, still more distantly, there was the honky-tonk music from Joyland Park. The hush of death should have been upon the earth and, because it was not, the aloneness of his grief made it all the more poignant, a feeling that was accentuated by the lurking self-criticism that he himself had been guilty of neglected grief because he had allowed his mind to be occupied with thoughts, not of Avery Bullard, but of who might be his successor.

"Not so old either from what I hear, huh, Mr. Walling?" Red said with the grin that never changed but now seemed hideously ghoulish. "Only fifty-six they tell me. Young man but a hard life, huh, Mr. Walling? I'll stick to pumping gas. That'll be three-ninety-two, Mr. Walling."

He gave him four dollars and drove off in quick escape. But there was no escape from the griefless cacophony of the world. Driving down the hill was like sliding into a cauldron of raucous merriment. Joyland Park was built on the flat floor of an abandoned quarry and the sheer face of cut rock behind it acted as a sounding board that amplified a thousand separate noises and scrambled them into one discordant roar.

Traffic stopped at the bottom of the hill. The roller coaster was just beyond the high board fence and he flinched at the ear-piercing shrieks of exalted delight that accompanied the down-roaring plunge of the cars.

The traffic stream started to move but he had hardly shifted before a policeman's upraised hand halted him again to let a freshet of people storm across the road toward the park entrance, pushing, shoving, driven by the frantic urge to shout and laugh and scream at man-made excitement. He recognized one of the men—a shift foreman in the sanding room at the Water Street factory. The recognition prompted the thought that many of the others must be Tredway people, too, and he recalled Avery Bullard saying, at the directors' meeting where they had approved the company budget for community contributions, that paychecks from the Tredway Corporation directly supported one out of three families in Millburgh, and contributed to the support of at least half of the rest.

Avery Bullard was dead . . . but did it matter to them? So what? they would say . . . who was Avery Bullard? Only a man . . . men died every day . . . just another name in the obituary column . . . not even the name on the bottom of their paychecks. That was the name that counted . . . the name on the paycheck . . . Frederick W. Alderson, Vice-President and Treasurer.

The policeman's hand dropped and Don Walling's mind leaped ahead with the moving car. There was a chance that Mary might be right, that Fred Alderson might not take the presidency. At least he would be reluctant, out of modesty if nothing else. His mind rehearsed what he would say . . . Fred, I know how you feel . . . we all feel the same way . . . no one can take Avery Bullard's place . . . but you've been with him longer than any of the rest of us . . . closer to him . . . know how he thinks . . . all the half-done things that we have to carry on. Carry on . . . yes, that's what we have to do, Fred . . . carry on.

Brakes screeched. He had failed to see a car leaping at him around the sharp back-turn of North Front Street. A twist of the wheel, subconsciously guided, avoided the collision but his heart was still beating overrate when he turned into the Alderson drive.

As he passed the house, turning in the paved area behind it, he caught a fleeting glimpse of Mrs. Alderson's face in the window. She must have hurried to the door because she was opening it as he came up the steps. It was not, as he first thought, a gesture of hospitality because she did not hold the door for his entrance but closed it quickly behind herself and motioned him to the side of the porch.

As he came close enough to see her eyes it was obvious that she had been crying. He was surprised because he had always thought of Mrs. Alderson as a coldly unemotional woman and he had not suspected that she could be so deeply affected by the death of Avery Bullard.

"I know how you feel," he said sympathetically. "We all feel the—"

"Tell me quickly," she broke in, "—before Fred comes. What's this going to mean? It's been so long—so many years— he's given so much of his life—"

His mind leaped to the one conclusion that her words seemed to demand . . . she was pleading that her husband be made president.

"Don't worry, Mrs. Alderson, I'm certain that everything will be all right. I'm only one of the directors, but—"

The door opened. Fred Alderson stepped out on the porch. He stood waiting and then, as Don Walling took the two steps that separated them, he said quietly. "I'm glad you've come." He said it, not as if he were expressing gratitude but as if he were acknowledging something that he had expected.

Behind them, Edith Alderson slipped soundlessly into the house.

Their handshake, under other circumstances, would have been an incongruous gesture but now it had meaning and Alderson's grip was reassuringly hard and firm.

"I'll need your help, Don," he said solemnly. His eyes rose

[159]

to a break in the trees through which, as Don Walling's glance followed his, the white shaft of the Tredway Tower rose distantly against the still more distant blue mist of the river hills.

Their hands were still clasped and the sudden gripping flinch of Alderson's fingers was inseparably timed with his own reaction. They had both seen the same thing at the same instant. A light had flashed on in the office at the northeast corner of the twenty-third floor. That was Shaw's office.

There was an instant of hesitation, but only an instant, and then Alderson said curtly, "Let's roll."

The two words, said as one, reverberated in Don Walling's mind. It was the Bullard battle cry. He had heard it a thousand times. It was said more softly now but they were still the same words and there was a faint but still clear echo of the same tone.

Hurriedly, getting a step ahead, he opened the car door for Frederick W. Alderson.

7.59 P.M. EDT

Luigi Cassoni, operator of the special elevator to the Executive Suite, had two precious possessions. One was the gold watch which had been given to him by Mr. Avery Bullard. The other was the framed certificate which proved that he was a citizen of the United States of America.

He was very proud of being an American citizen but there were times when he was not certain that he was worthy of the honor. Even after twenty-eight years he still could not make himself act, in all ways, as an American man should act. One of his unfortunate tendencies—the habit of using his arms too freely as he talked—had been conquered by learning to keep his hands firmly on the controls of the elevator cab. Unfortunately, he had found no comparable way of guarding himself against the display of tears which his observation had taught him was not an American thing to do.

In the little Italian village where Luigi had been raised, no one had considered it an unnatural thing for a man to cry. His father had cried often—when he was very angry because Pietro

[160]

had stolen the burro—when he was very happy because he had heard Lucia sing "Regnava nel silenzio"—when he was very sad as he had been sad when the Duke had died. On the night of the Duke's death, every man in the village had cried, the men even more than the women. The only man who did not show his tears had been the priest and he, of course, was someone a little different from a man.

The American men were like the priest. Tonight, they had come into the elevator and said words about Mr. Bullard that were like the chanting of the mass, and their faces were like the priest's face, and they did not have tears in their eyes. It was not, Luigi was certain, because they did not mourn the death of Avery Bullard but only because they were Americans.

On the night when the Duke had died a signal fire of cedar branches had been built on the hilltop and everyone had seen it and come to share their mourning in the square of Via Torrenzo. The great bass bell of the cathedral had been tolled, once for each year of the Duke's age and the Duke had been seventy-two.

Luigi lifted his head. From far aloft came the sound of bells, but it was only the carillon and the bass bell tolled only eight times. It was eight o'clock.

The buzzer sounded and he opened the door. It was Erica Martin. For the first time that night, he saw tears. But she was a woman. It was all right in America for a woman to cry. But it was very strange that she should be there. On the night that the Duke had died, the Duchess had been seen by no one in the square of Via Torrenzo.

7

WEST COVE, LONG ISLAND
8.02 P.M. EDT

GEORGE CASWELL had reached the age when the death of a contemporary was not unusual and, had it not been for the events of the day, he would probably not have carried the news of Avery Bullard's death back to the dinner table. He made it a rule not to discuss business with Kitty. He had married her—partially, at least—because she took his mind off stock brokerage. Since she had been admirably successful in the accomplishment of that purpose he had never seen any reason to vary her role. Now, however, walking back to the table after taking the telephone call, his face reflected a concern that he was aware his wife had not missed.

"Will you have dessert, dear, or just coffee?" she asked watching him carefully.

"Only coffee."

"Bad news, dear?"

"I'm afraid so. Avery Bullard is dead."

"Bullard? Oh, he's that man from Pennsylvania, isn't he—the furniture one?"

"Yes, the Tredway Corporation," he said, surprised that she had recognized Bullard's name.

"Isn't that one of your companies, George? Aren't you a director or something?"

"Yes."

"We had Mr. Bullard out to dinner once."

"Did we? I can't recall that."

"When we were in New Rochelle. We had that dinner for all of your important clients."

"Oh, long time ago—perhaps he was." He remembered the dinner well enough but he wanted to side-step the necessity of again explaining why he had never repeated the affair.

"Of course it was Mr. Bullard," she said triumphantly. "He was fascinated by the Baked Alaska and perfectly charming about it . . . and we had Chicken Supreme that night, too."

He glanced up from his plate, surprised again at Kitty's astounding ability to recall the guests and menus of almost every dinner party they had ever had, a feat of memory that always seemed strangely mismatched with her equally astounding ability immediately to forget what she paid for anything she bought.

"He was sort of a shaggy-bear type," she went on. "Growly but sweet—nice. And he's dead? How awful. Does it mean something very bad for your business, George?"

"No, I don't think so," he said uncertainly. "He was a fine man, that's all—one of the finest men I've ever known."

"But darling, I'd never realized that he was a friend of yours! Why haven't we had him out? I'd have loved to—"

"That was Mr. Lindeman who called," he said in a pointedly abrupt change of subject, made so quickly that he didn't realize he was committing himself to going on with the discussion.

"Oh, are they friends of Mr. Bullard's too? Goodness, there was no reason why we couldn't have had the Lindemans with him. They're awfully good at a party, both of them."

"No, Mr. Lindeman was not a friend of Avery Bullard's," he explained patiently. "Mr. Lindeman is the head of an investment fund that holds a rather large block of Tredway stock and

[163]

he was concerned about what effect Bullard's death might have on its market value."

"How horrible," she said distastefully.

"What?"

"He might have waited until the poor man was decently dead. Goodness, don't you men ever think about anything but what effect something is going to have on the market?"

"Frequently."

"I can't believe it."

"Every time I come home to you, my dear." He made it a nice thing to say, nicely said.

She laughed, pleased, and he hoped that the subject had been changed. It hadn't. "You're very sweet, darling, but what did you say to him?"

"To whom?"

"Mr. Lindeman."

"About what?"

She was not to be diverted by diversion. "About what you said, dear—about what would happen to Mr. Bullard's company now that he's dead."

"It's not Mr. Bullard's company, my dear. It's the stock-holders' company. Mr. Bullard was an employee. They had hired him to be president, just as they had hired other men to be—well, truck drivers, or bookkeepers."

"You don't want to talk to me, do you?" she asked innocently.

"Of course I do. I only—"

"Then what did you say to Mr. Lindeman?"

"Darling, why this sudden interest in my business affairs?"

"I just want to know what you said."

Her hidden smile had broken through now, making a joke out of it, and he played along. "Well, I told Mr. Lindeman that he had no reason whatsoever to worry—that any modern business organization that had been as successful as the Tredway Corporation couldn't possibly be a one-man concern—that there were a group of able vice-presidents, any one of whom could succeed Mr. Bullard—that I would be at the board meeting myself next Tuesday and would personally see to it that the very best man was elected—and, as final evidence of my own faith in the Tredway Corporation I had purchased two thousand shares of its common stock this afternoon."

She clapped her hands like a delighted child. "George, you're wonderful! You should tell me things you say more often. It makes you sound so distinguished. Tuesday? Did you say you'd be gone Tuesday?"

"You have it on your calendar. I put it there myself when—" He stopped. "Oh—the funeral. Hadn't thought of that."

"Must you go? They're always so gruesome."

"Yes. Be on Monday, I suppose."

"Down at—wherever it is that he lived?"

"Millburgh."

"Oh, darling, you can't possibly!"

"What?"

"Monday is the yacht club affair and you're the vice-commodore."

It struck him as a particularly silly remark and his mind, rebounding, swung to the opposite extreme. "I'd go to Avery Bullard's funeral," he said solemnly, "if it were halfway around the world and it took the next month to get there."

"Of course you would, dear," she said placatingly. "Would you like to have dinner on the terrace after this?"

"What?"

"The terrace. It's almost July. Don't you remember how nice it was having dinner on the terrace last summer?"

"Yes, very nice," he said, only half hearing, noticing that a subconscious hand had traced "2000" on the tablecloth with the tip of his coffee spoon. He was not surprised. His mind was always full of figures.

"All right, dear?" It was her way of suggesting that dinner was over.

He stood. "I think I'll take a look at the roses, Kitty. Nothing you'd planned for tonight is there?"

"The men were here about them again today. I don't know what they did, but they were here."

"Good." He made it a word without meaning, tossed back as he crossed the terrace and walked out on the lawn. Roses weren't worth what they cost . . . if it wasn't cankers it was black spot, if it wasn't black spot it was beetles . . . you could buy roses cheaper from a florist.

Neil Finch was standing near the low yew hedge that separated their gardens and a greeting was unavoidable. Neither was there any way to avoid telling him about Avery Bullard.

"I knew damned well Pilcher had picked up something!" Finch said triumphantly. "Remember what I told you in the car coming home?"

"But how could Pilcher have known? The news just—Lindeman's son has some kind of a job on the *Wall Street Journal* and he picked the news off the ticker only a few minutes ago." The conviction drained out of his voice as he heard his own words, for he had already told Finch as much detail as Lindeman had given him and now, suddenly, everything had fallen into place.

"You say Bullard collapsed this afternoon about two-thirty?" Finch asked. "Well, Pilcher's selling order came in about two-forty. I remember Wingate saying he'd had only twenty minutes before the bell. Don't you see what that means? Pilcher must have known at the time that Bullard was dead. Where did you say he collapsed?"

"On the street in front of the Chippendale Building."

"That's where Pilcher has his office, isn't it?"

"Yes."

"And Bullard had lunch there with Pilcher?"

George Caswell felt physically ill, as if his swallowed words had become an emetic. "But why wasn't the body identified until tonight?" he managed to ask, knowing that there was no point to the question, that the answer was obvious.

"Because Pilcher didn't want him identified. I never did have a very high regard for Bruce Pilcher but I hadn't realized he was quite that bad!" He flashed a sudden taunting smile. "Nice friends you have, Mr. Caswell."

[166]

"No friend of mine!"

"I thought you'd suggested him to Bullard as an executive vice-president?"

"I did no such thing," Caswell snapped. "He had him on a list of names—possibilities—that's all."

Finch laughed. "Don't take it so hard, George. You aren't the first person that Pilcher has fooled."

"He hasn't fooled me," Caswell said, "—and he won't!"

"He'll pick up a fast buck on that short sale. Bullard's death is sure to break the stock."

"That stock won't break," Caswell said, grimly determined.

Finch's jaw dropped. "Well, I'll be damned! George, you're a clever fox—and I never caught on. With the block you already have—the two thousand shares you got today— pick up any more that might be jarred loose on Monday—hell's bells, boy, I wasn't giving you credit! You'll practically have control of that company, won't you?"

George Caswell's thumbnail clipped a green yew branch. The possibilities of the situation had not occurred to him before. His only thought had been to clear his conscience of anything that he might have said to Avery Bullard in Pilcher's favor but now, rising from an unseen source, as bubbles rise in champagne, the heady vapor of a new ambition rose within his mind.

He was aware that Finch had said something that he hadn't heard. "I beg your pardon, Neil, I—"

"I asked if you, by any chance, were thinking of stepping in and taking the presidency yourself? Hell's bells, you wouldn't want that, would you?"

"I—I don't know. Have to think about it," he said. He had started with a grim expression but finished with something close to a smile, pleased at the way that the taunting grin had vanished from Finch's face.

"Well, George, anything I can do—you know me, fellow, just give me the word."

"Thanks. Well—have quite a few things to do tonight. See you, Neil."

He walked back across the lawn and into the house.

"Roses all right, darling?"

"Roses. Oh—yes. Quite all right. Dear, I've just been thinking—Lindeman is really quite concerned about this Tredway business—who's going to be president, you know. Afraid I'll have to go down to Millburgh tomorrow, get the lay of the land."

"Tomorrow? But, darling, that's impossible. Tomorrow's Nancy Brighton's wedding."

"Oh." He was taken aback. "Well— maybe I'll drive down Sunday. Have to be there Monday, anyway."

He walked on before she could answer, going into the library and closing the door.

He sat on the wide seat-ledge of the bay window, sitting with his torso stiffly erect, as if he were an athlete waiting for a starting signal. He felt that way. This might be the start, the beginning of what he had been waiting for. But it might not be. He had felt this same way before . . . thinking that he'd found it . . . and then letting the hope slip through his fingers . . . never because he couldn't have made any of those dreams come true . . . only because he had not chosen to do so . . . because when he had examined them they hadn't been what he wanted either.

It wasn't anything he *had* to do . . nine-tenths of Wall Street would think he was crazy if he did do it . . . give up Caswell & Co. and start over again in something else at fifty-three. It wouldn't be because of money. He had never had to do anything because of money. His father's estate had taken care of that. He could have been a rich man's son, never done a day's work in his life. He hadn't. He had gone into Caswell & Co. and there was no one who could say that he hadn't made a success of it, even more of a success than his father had made. No, it wasn't money. It was something else. What?

Yes, that was the question. That's where he had always bogged down before, trying to find the answer. It wasn't politics . . . he had thought that through when they had offered him the senatorship, and not with their hands out for a big campaign contribution, either. It wasn't government service . . . those two months on the monetary commission had convinced him of that. It wasn't the presidency of the Stock Exchange . . . the more they'd argued with him the more he'd seen that it would be only more of what he didn't want.

Was it industry? Perhaps. If it wasn't anything else that's what it had to be . . . process of elimination . . . it had to be something. The old senator hadn't been the man he wanted to be . . . nor the chairman of the monetary commission . . . nor the president of the Stock Exchange . . . nor the head of that charitable foundation they had asked him to manage . . . nor the president of that college in Ohio . . . no, none of them had been the man he wanted to be. Avery Bullard? Was he the . . .

There was a gentle but startling knock at the door.

"Yes?"

"You aren't sulking, are you, dear?" Kitty called with a twinkle in her voice.

He smiled and let the smile carry over into his words. "Want something?"

"Um-huh. You."

"Be out in a minute. Something I have to think through."

"Do you know you hurt my feelings?"

"I did?"

"You closed the door."

"Darling, you know I can't think and see you at the same time."

He heard her little-girl laugh and then her fading footsteps. Kitty's wonderful, he said to himself—and then having said it he was forced, as he always was, to go on with the linked thought that it was very strange that marrying Kitty had worked out so well. Actually, it had been a very impulsive and unconsidered thing to do . . . almost the only impulsive and unconsidered thing that he had ever done . . . but it was a good thing that it had been that way. If there had been time to think about it he probably would never have done it.

That was the end of the thought. He never went on from there.

His mind reached back to bridge the interruption. Was that what he wanted to be . . . what Avery Bullard had been? Had Avery Bullard found the answer to what made a man's life worthwhile?

The questions battered down a dam and his mind was flooded with a torrent, swirling to the surface the memory of Avery Bullard saying, "A man can't work for money alone, George. Money is just a way of keeping score—the chips in the poker game—and the chip counter never wins."

George Caswell nodded in belated understanding, knowing now what he should have known before. Yes, that's what he had been all his life . . . a chip counter . . . counting his chips . . . his chips and other people's chips. When the game was over there was nothing left, not even the chips, only numbers on a sheet of paper. A man had to have more . . . something to show for his life . . . something tangible. Yes, that's what Avery Bullard had. He was a builder . . . and the things he built were real . . . things you could see with your eyes and feel with your hands.

Now he understood . . . now he knew what he had always wanted. This was no wild dream . . . this time it made sense. It wasn't as if he were starting something entirely new . . . he had his start. He knew the business . . . he'd been a Tredway director for twelve years. He was no outsider . . . the other directors were his friends . . . he'd have their support . . . Alderson and Grimm . . . Dudley and Shaw and Walling.

The door knock was less startling this time.

"Still thinking, dear?" Kitty called.

He walked over and opened the door. "All through."

"Tell me what you were thinking about?

He shook his head. "Not now, Kitty."

"Please, dear," she demanded. "I want to know what you were thinking and then I can be proud of you."

"I think you will be," he said slowly.

"Tell me!"

"Not now, darling. I want it to be a surprise."

"For me?"

A faint smile warmed his face. "Yes, I think you'll be surprised."

He almost wished that he could tell her . . . but, of course, it wasn't the thing to do. He kissed her instead and she seemed as well satisfied.

NEW YORK CITY
8.13 P.M. EDT

Bruce Pilcher, giving his necktie its final minute adjustment, noticed that the face in the mirror seemed rather pleased with itself. He smiled and the image responded instantaneously. There were many ways in which living with a mirror was pleasanter than living with a wife. At least you could be sure of an occasional smile. That was more than he had ever been able to count on from Barbara. The thought amused him. The mirror appreciated it, too.

Ten minutes before he had established the fact that Avery Bullard's body had been identified by the police. He didn't have a care on his mind. His weekend was free. There wasn't a thing to worry about until Monday at ten when the market opened . . . and nothing to worry about then. His telephone conversations with Scott Lindeman had confirmed his guess that there would undoubtedly be some dumping of Tredway stock. Calling Lindeman had been a very much better idea than calling Caswell.

As he filled his platinum cigarette case, he noticed the slip that had been in his box when he had come into the hotel. It was a request to call Steigel's home number. Poor old Julius was really wetting his pants now . . . trying to get in on the kill . . . it was funny how far some people would go to chisel in on a fast buck . . . and the righteous old coots like Julius were the worst of the lot.

[171]

The face in the mirror winked at him, smiling as long as he smiled, turning away only when he turned away to leave the room.

It was eight-fifteen. He had told this Eloise whatever-her-name-was to meet him at Chambord at eight-thirty. Usually, it wasn't a good idea to get there too early . . . better to make them wait for you . . . kept them in their place. But this Eloise wouldn't need too much of that, not for a month or so. The unsophisticated ones were fun sometimes . . . if they were really on the level . . . but even when they were it never lasted long.

8.17 P.M. EDT

Alex Oldham was not unaccustomed to responsibility—New York was Tredway's largest branch office and he had managed it for nine years—but there had never been anything like this before. Tonight he was the hub of the empire. Shaw's call had been waiting when the police had brought him back after identifying Avery Bullard's body. "Everything is in your hands, Alex, the whole New York end," Shaw had said. "I'm leaving it all up to you to handle."

Actually, after he had called the undertaker whose name Shaw had given him, the rest of the assignment had proved to be disappointingly small. "You may rest assured that there is no detail we'll overlook," the suavely unctuous voice had said. "We're quite accustomed to such situations and there's nothing you need concern yourself about, sir, nothing at all."

As Alex Oldham checked off the few remaining notes that Shaw had given him, his wife said, "Alex, do you suppose this might mean anything for us?"

She was a Millburgh girl—he had met her one year when he had gone down for a sales meeting—and he knew she had always hoped that someday they would move back there to live.

"It might," he said sympathetically, thinking that she'd been a good sport about it, not hounding him all the time the way a lot of wives would have done. "All depends on what happens to Walt Dudley. If he should move up, we might get a break."

"Mr. Shaw will be the new president, won't he?"

"I don't know."

"Well, didn't you think that he was going to be executive vice-president—before this happened?"

"Probably mean that his inviting us up to Maine is off," he said as an indirect agreement.

"Then wouldn't Mr. Dudley be moved up to executive vice-president?"

"Don't start counting any chickens," he said.

"Well, it would be logical, wouldn't it?"

"A lot of logical things never happen. You learn that after you've been with an outfit like this as long as I have."

"Maybe more of them will happen now that Mr. Bullard is dead. If all of the—" She stopped, bewildered by the shocked censure in the sharp glance he gave her. "But Alex, you always said that Mr. Bullard was—"

A snap of his hand stopped her. "I know, I know," he said quickly, impelled by some demanding urge for forgiveness. "Bullard could drive a man nuts sometimes. But it didn't mean anything—nothing! I wish to God he were still alive. I do! No matter what it may mean for us. I wish to God it hadn't happened."

He closed his eyes and saw again, as he knew he would see all the rest of his life, the accusing deathly stillness of the face that had looked up at him when the policeman had turned back the sheet.

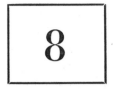

8

MILLBURGH, PENNSYLVANIA
8.28 P.M. EDT

THE TREDWAY TOWER had two lives, one lived by day, the other by night. Its day life was heavily populated, brightly lighted, highly purposeful, and animated by a thousand sounds —men sounds and machine sounds, sighs and shouts, clatter and clack, giggles and groans, door bangs and drawer bumps, whine and whisper, footsteps running, footsteps dragging, the life sounds of business.

The day life ended, except for the final mad rush of outpouring humanity, with the first stroke of the five o'clock carillon, or, if Mr. Bullard was in town and the carillon not rung, with the sweep of the second hand on the master clock that relayed the same moment to repeater clocks on all twenty-four floors.

As the day life flooded out, the night life ebbed in. Gray-faced women shuffled wearily in through the lobby, their eyes down and averted as if they sensed the incongruity of their presence in this great hall of glittering black marble and sculptured bronze. Reaching the back lobby, where marble and bronze gave way to behind-the-scenes gray paint, they clumped into the freight elevator. Finally, after a long and unprotested delay, they would be dispersed to the various floors of the building where, with brush and broom and mop and scrub bucket, they would begin their methodical erasure of the soil that the day life had left.

After the scrubwomen came the men janitors. As befitted their higher level in the social world of the Tower's night life, they claimed the privilege of a momentarily later arrival. After the janitors came the maintenance men who, through such acts of skill as the replacement of light bulbs and the adjustment of flush valves in the washrooms, had raised themselves to the aristocracy of the Tower's night life.

Normally, there was no overlap between the Tredway Tower's day life and its night life. Except for an occasional late-staying day worker—who was called a "hold-up" until eight o'clock and a "sticker" if he remained later—the world of the night life was a world unto itself. It was not as drab as the casual glimpser might suspect. There were coffee percolators bubbling in the slop sink closets, cigarettes and occasionally good cigars in unlocked desks, and the big canvas bags, soft-stuffed with wastepaper, made a pleasantly rustling mattress for an occasional amatory adventure.

Tonight, however, there was neither bubble nor rustle and not a cigar was being smoked. There was at least one "sticker" on every floor of the building. Men had started coming back to their offices just before eight o'clock and now everything was in a turmoil. The head janitors were rushing around from floor to floor trying to reorganize cleaning schedules and placate annoyed scrubwomen. It couldn't have happened on a worse night. Friday was the end of the week, the night when the once-a-week jobs were done.

The explanation that Mr. Bullard had died was widely used by the harried head janitors, but it had little effect upon the women. They all echoed the sentiments of Mrs. O'Toole, who, being the only Tredway scrubwoman of Irish descent, had logically assumed the role of spokeswoman. "If it's a wake they've

[175]

got to be holding, I'm thinking they could have found some place for it that wouldn't be disturbing the work of those that have an honest living to earn."

The only voice that might have registered a dissent was not heard. Anna Schultz, who had cleaned the Executive Suite for the last thirteen years, was sitting stolidly in the darkened back corridor of the twenty-third floor waiting for the meeting in Mr. Shaw's office to break up. Her hopes had been raised several times when someone had come out, but that no sooner happened than someone else went in. Now there were half a dozen men from the lower floor who were waiting around in the hall and, even more discouragingly, Mr. Walling and Mr. Alderson had just come up and gone into Mr. Alderson's office.

Anna accepted her misfortune placidly. The head janitor knew that there were a lot of "stickers" in the Executive Suite so he never argued about the hours of overtime that she got in. Some months, when Mr. Bullard had been in town a great deal, she picked up between twenty-five and thirty dollars extra. Now, filling her wait with lazy speculation, she wondered if the new president would be as good. If it was going to be that Mr. Shaw he was starting out fine. She'd get at least two hours of overtime tonight, maybe three.

8.31 P.M. EDT

Hardly more than a dozen words had been spoken since Don Walling had followed Alderson into his office. Now, watching the older man carefully, he felt an increasing awareness of the diffidence that he had sensed as soon as they had arrived on the twenty-third floor. He had expected Frederick Alderson to enter Shaw's office immediately, an intention that Alderson's first step after he got off the elevator had seemed to confirm, but then he had hesitated, turned, and gone into his own office with a gesture that asked Walling to follow him.

For the last two minutes, Alderson had been occupying himself with his notebook, writing so slowly that he seemed to be drawing the letters of the words.

[176]

Walling finally felt impelled to break the silence. "Shaw seems to have called in most of the major department heads."

The remark touched a nerve-sprung trigger that released a short burst of words from Alderson. "Can't see any point to it, no point at all."

The poised assurance that Alderson had displayed on the way downtown had vanished completely, and Don Walling felt the imperative necessity for its quick return. "If you'll pardon my saying so, Mr. Alderson, I think the point is rather obvious."

"What?"

"Shaw's making a running jump to get into the saddle. He's called in everyone to let them know that the reins are in his hands."

The words had part of the effect that he wanted them to have. Alderson's face did harden with determination but the effort it required seemed more than should have been necessary. He stood up and said, "Let's roll," but the words were more mimicry than command and his stride was hesitant as he walked out of the office and crossed to Shaw's door.

Don Walling, following close behind, saw Loren Shaw look up as Alderson opened the door.

"Oh, Fred! Good. Glad you're here," Shaw said pleasantly. "Oh, Don, too? Fine. Come in. Perhaps you can make a suggestion here."

Van Ormand, the advertising and publicity manager, sat beside Shaw's desk. He was wearing a white dinner jacket, making it clear that he had been called away from the Friday Dance at the country club.

"Van and I have a plan rather well sketched out, I believe, but it's possible that there's something we've missed," Shaw said. "We'll have a major story on the wire within an hour for the New York morning papers—*Times* and *Herald Tribune*. There'll be a special story for the financial papers and a follow-up later for the evening and Sunday papers. The same basic story as the New York release but with a stronger company slant will be sent to all of the morning papers in our factory cities. There'll be a shorter release for all the wire services.

[177]

We'll telephone the business editors of *Time* and *Newsweek*. That pretty much takes care of the first priority stuff. The monthly trade magazines have all closed so we have plenty of time there. *Retailing Daily* doesn't publish tomorrow but we'll have them all set for Monday." Unexpectedly, his eyes flicked toward Alderson. "Anything I've missed, Fred?"

The question followed the rapid-fire recital so closely that Alderson was taken unaware and his only reply was a stumbling negative.

Don Walling, despite his growing apprehension, couldn't help but regard Alderson's bewilderment sympathetically for he, too, had been bowled over by the performance. Shaw had not once glanced at a note nor had he looked at Ormand for cue or confirmation. His tone had implied a thoroughly professional knowledge of the publicist's craft.

Van Ormand gathered up his papers and left on the half gallop with a fervent, "Thank you very much for your help, sir," for Shaw, a quick nod for Alderson, an even quicker one for Walling.

After the door had closed, Alderson said, "I hope Ormand isn't handling this as if it were some publicity story."

Walling winced. It was a pettish remark and made more so by Alderson's manner. Again he could understand the origin because he, too, had been repulsed by Shaw's coldly unemotional approach, but that was no excuse for Alderson's lack of poise.

Shaw had taken a fresh handkerchief from his desk drawer and was pressing it between his slowly rubbed palms. "I'm quite confident that we can rely on Ormand's judgment and good taste, don't you think so, Don?"

The question at the end was another quick thrust. Don Walling hesitated, suspicious that it was an intentional effort on Shaw's part to wedge him away from Frederick Alderson's support. He made his reply as indirect as possible. "I can't see that there's actually much involved except sending out obituaries."

Shaw nodded and added, "—in various lengths with the emphasis shifted to suit the editorial requirements of the different papers and magazines. Quite right. Did you have something other than that in mind, Fred?"

Again the question came unexpectedly, like the cracker on the end of an idly snapped whip. It was the third time that Shaw had done the same thing in the last two minutes and Don Walling was sure now that it was a calculated technique. He would be on his guard from now on.

"The news releases represent more of a task than one might suspect," Shaw said. "I thought it best to reach Ormand and get him down here at once. When it first occurred to me I almost failed to do it, thinking that someone else would certainly have thought of it before I did. Apparently no one did."

The technique had been varied now but the knife thrust was no less sharp. Don Walling hoped that Alderson wouldn't attempt a reply and, fortunately, he didn't.

"I've tied up a few other loose ends," Shaw said, glancing at a sheet of paper that lay in front of him. "None of them of any great moment, but I'll pass them along as a matter of information. The funeral will be Monday at four-thirty. I've asked that—"

Alderson interrupted with a sharply explosive bark. It was not an intelligible word, but no word could have expressed so well the same blend of astonishment and anger that Don Walling felt welling up within himself. It was an audacious presumption for Shaw to have jumped in and set the time of the funeral. He glanced at Alderson and, to his relieved surprise, saw that his jaw was firm and his hand steady.

"The funeral will be at two," Alderson said grimly. The words were a thrown gauntlet, an unmistakable challenge.

Shaw touched the handkerchief to his lips as if he were checking the imperturbability of his expressionless mask. "At St. Martin's?"

"Yes."

"I see," Shaw said, clearing his throat softly. "Perhaps I was misinformed. When I checked the church calendar I found that a wedding had been scheduled for two."

Despite the effort that he had been making to keep from constantly watching Alderson's face, Don Walling could not avoid a side glance. He knew from what had been said coming down in the car that Alderson had not checked with the church, because he had mentioned it as one of the things that remained to be done. He saw now that Alderson had been hit hard and felt the urge to say something that would give him a moment of recovery. The only thing he could think of to say was that the time of the funeral was an unimportant point that was hardly worth arguing, yet he was prevented from saying that because Frederick Alderson had clearly made it a major issue.

"Something can be done about the church," Alderson said finally.

"Perhaps," Shaw conceded graciously. "There was, however, another point that I had in mind. I believe I'm correct in assuming that the highest proportion of the older factory workers—those who might wish to attend the funeral—will be found on the seven to three shift. By having the funeral at four-thirty we'll make it possible for them to be there."

"That makes no difference," Alderson snapped. "The factory will be closed."

"For the day?" Shaw asked blandly.

"Yes, for the day!"

Walling had tried to catch Alderson's eye before his reply but the older man's anger had made him blaze back instantly, too fast to see the trap that he was stepping into. Only a few months before the president of the factory union had died and the vice-president, Max Hartzell, making a quick bid for popularity, had demanded that the day of the funeral be made a paid holiday for all factories. Paid holidays had been one of the most troublesome issues in previous contract negotiations and Avery Bullard, wary of giving more ground, had turned down the request. Hartzell had then carried the issue back to the union membership and, using its emotional content to the limit, had all but caused a walkout. In the end, the strike had been averted but Alderson should have realized, as Shaw obviously did, that a precedent had been established that could not be broken now without the danger of another serious flare-up.

"In view of the union situation—" Walling began, letting his voice drop then, hoping that it would be enough to jog Alderson's memory.

Alderson appeared not to have heard him. He was staring at Shaw, his body immobilized by anger. "I suppose you were thinking of the money it would cost?"

"Not as a first consideration," Shaw explained evenly. "My thinking was largely based on the point that Don just made—the union situation—although you are quite right, Fred, in suggesting that the cost is something that can't be overlooked either. I happened to recall Mr. Bullard's pointing out to the union that a paid holiday would represent a loss to the company of approximately $87,000. That figure, of course, was before the last wage raise. It would be somewhat more at the current rates."

"I thought so," Alderson said pointlessly.

Walling could not avoid a grudging admiration for the way that Shaw kept his face from reflecting, by even the faintest glimmer, any trace of the annoyance that he must be feeling.

"I also recalled," Shaw went on, "Mr. Bullard's argument to the union delegates that a paid holiday could hardly be considered mourning since the crowd at Joyland Park would unquestionably be larger than the crowd at the funeral."

The roller coaster roared again in Walling's mind and he heard the background screams of joy and laughter. Shaw was right. A holiday wouldn't be a day of mourning, it would be a day of celebration. The cost would be a thoroughly unjustified expenditure of a large sum of money. On top of everything else, it would stir up a hornet's nest with the union. What was the matter with Alderson? Couldn't he see that? It was understandable that he had missed thinking about those things before, but now that he had thought about them there was only one possible decision. Shaw had already made it. Alderson had no choice except to confirm it, but it was plain that he wasn't going to do so. He looked as if he were holding his breath and a purplish undertone was spreading slowly over his face.

"There's another consideration," Shaw went on. "It's minor, perhaps, yet it seemed worth taking into account. The four-thirty time would make it more convenient to close the Chicago market display during the funeral period."

Walling clenched his fists. The word "convenient" had been badly chosen and he found himself wishing that Shaw hadn't used it. It made the meaning clear enough but instinct told him that it would only add to the anger that was already fogging Alderson's mind.

"Convenient?" Alderson demanded with an acid bite. "That seems to be your attitude toward everything, Shaw—to make Mr. Bullard's death as *convenient* as possible—for yourself. I think you'll find some other ideas on that subject!"

Alderson's rise and move toward the door was so unexpected and so rapidly made that Walling was caught off guard. He was only starting to stand as Alderson disappeared. His first thought was to follow, but Shaw stepped around from behind the desk and half blocked the way. It was impossible to push past him without obvious discourtesy.

Shaw's voice showed a pronounced change, suddenly presuming an intimacy that had not been there before. "Don, tell me—am I wrong or did the old boy seem a little shaky just then? I know that he hasn't been well but—you know him much better than I do, of course—what do you think?"

"Not too hard to understand. It's only been a couple of hours since we heard of Mr. Bullard's death."

The use of the plural pronoun, grouping himself with Alderson, was only semiconsciously done but Shaw picked it up.

"Am I to take it that you share Fred's disagreement with what I've done?"

"Not exactly."

Shaw evidenced concern. "In what particular don't you agree? Frankly, I saw no alternative to any of the decisions I made. The newspaper releases were obviously necessary and speed was of the essence. Right?"

Walling hesitated. Agreement was strangely disagreeable but disagreement was impossible.

"The time of the funeral and the holiday policy were both dictated by circumstances," Shaw went on. "It's conceivable, of course, that I may have overlooked some pertinent fact. If I have, I'd consider it a great personal favor if you'd call it to my attention. Have I?"

"I'm not arguing with you," Walling heard himself say.

"But I don't have your wholehearted support, do I? That's something I'd hoped I could count on, Don—your support."

It was a bold plea and Shaw, by the barest of margins, overdid it. Up to that point Walling had been battering back his instinctive dislike with the argument that Shaw had been right on every detail, that there was no possible ground on which he could be criticized for any action that he had taken or any statement that he had made. But now, suddenly, he saw what had been going on. The whole scene had been played by Shaw for his benefit. In the beginning he had suspected, but later overlooked, an attempt on Shaw's part to split him away from Alderson. Every part of Shaw's act—the pleasant mask, the resistance to anger, the whip-cracker questions, the invincible logic—all of it had been a calculated attack to show up Alderson in the worst possible light. The empty well from which Don Walling's respect for Alderson had been drained, suddenly filled with sympathy for the old man.

"No suggestions?" Shaw asked. "No criticism?"

Walling paused, arguing with himself that there was neither point nor purpose in saying anything. It wasn't his fight. The battle was between Shaw and Alderson. He was only a bystander. But the compulsion of inner honesty forced him. "Well, since you've asked me, I did have the impression that you were being a little rough on Fred."

"Rough? I can't imagine what made you think that."

"You knew that he was closer to Avery Bullard, personally, than any of the rest of us. It's only natural that he'd be hit a little harder—thrown off balance for a while. You may not appreciate what I'm trying to say, but—"

"Of course I appreciate it," Shaw said hurriedly. "And I did my best to take that into account. I thought that would be evident to you. Surely you saw there was every reason why I might well have been annoyed by Fred's obviously unfriendly attitude toward me—yet I did my best not to show it."

"All right—skip it."

"Wait, Don." Shaw's hand held his arm as he turned to the door. "I wish you wouldn't feel that way—you particularly."

"Why me particularly?"

"Because—well, Don, I've always felt that you and I shared a certain community of interest—unexplored, perhaps, but still something in common. I've been hoping that we might have an opportunity to work more closely together. Perhaps now we shall."

"Perhaps."

"Good."

Shaw seemed overpleased and Walling felt the need to put a sharp limitation on whatever agreement Shaw might think he had been given. "As far as a community of interest is concerned," he said slowly, "—the only interest I share with anyone is the best interest of the company."

"Then we do have that in common. Oh, by the way, I wonder if you'd be good enough to give me a hand with a couple of things here tonight. There are still a number of people waiting to see me and—"

"So I noticed," Walling broke in, making the tone of his voice add a question mark.

"It occurred to me that there were probably a number of matters waiting for Mr. Bullard's early decision," Shaw explained. "Handling them through the executive committee will necessarily slow down action so I thought it might be of some advantage to all of us if I made a fast survey of the situation tonight. That will give us the weekend to get squared away. Then we'll have decks cleared for action on Monday."

Shaw hesitated and then, as if he recognized the need for further justification, went on. "I'm turning up some rather critical situations. Were you aware that our shipments of gumwood from the southern mills are almost four weeks behind schedule? Schaeffer from Purchasing just informed me that Water Street will be out of gum in less than three weeks. Unless something is done immediately, we'll be facing a shutdown. Did you know that?"

Lumber supply was far removed from Don Walling's normal responsibility, but it happened that Jesse Grimm had mentioned the situation at lunch a few days before and now, as a counteraction of Shaw's annoyingly smug voice-of-doom prediction, he got a mild pleasure out of being able to say, "I think you'll find that Jesse has everything set for a switch to beech and birch. A contract has been placed for about a quarter of a million board feet with some of the northeastern mills."

"That's what I thought, too," Shaw said with a sigh that offered a sharing of his own disillusionment. "Unfortunately, the orders were never placed. We have an option—that's true—but the option hasn't been exercised. It was held up by Purchasing, waiting for Jesse Grimm to get Mr. Bullard's approval."

Don Walling felt himself slump.

"Bit more serious than you thought?" Shaw asked with a faint smile. "Fortunately we have until Monday noon on the option so there's still a chance to squirm out. I should talk to Jesse though. I understand he's out of town."

"Yes, down in Maryland," Walling heard himself say, his voice sounding faraway and detached, his mind occupied with the contradiction of Loren Shaw . . . the more you disliked the man, the more right he proved himself to be!

"Would you know, by any chance, how to get in touch with Jesse?"

"I think Fred left a call for him with a message to call back."

A smile rolled Shaw's underlip. "If our good friend Mr. Alderson doesn't object too strenuously, would you mind suggesting that Mr. Grimm talk to me as well?"

"I'll tell him."

It was a natural exit line and he stepped through the door.

"Oh, Don?" Shaw's voice reached after him. "If you do have a few minutes to spare—?"

"Sorry. I'd forgotten. What needs doing?"

[185]

"If you wouldn't mind, hop up and see how Miss Martin is coming along. I've started her sending telegrams to the out-of-town factories and branches. Just look things over, see how it's going. All right, Morrison, come in."

Morrison was one of the men waiting on the bench and Don Walling saw the look of eager subservience on the office manager's face as he bounded to his feet and followed Shaw into his office. The king is dead, long live the king, Walling said to himself, and his mind reacted as if his mouth had been swilled with oil.

He was halfway up the stairs when a twinge of conscience reminded him that Alderson might be waiting for him in his office. Looking back he saw a path of yellow light falling out across the floor from the frosted-glass panel of Alderson's closed door. Sympathy surmounted disappointment and he started down again, but with the first step he heard a sound above his head and looked up. Erica Martin was standing at the head of the staircase. The only light was the side light that came from the open door of her office and, her face and figure etched out of the darkness, made her seem a lost soul standing at the brink of a black abyss.

Quickly, doubling the steps, he was in front of her and, standing a step lower, was looking at her face. She stared past him, her eyes fixed on the door of Shaw's office.

"Are you all right, Miss Martin?"

She reacted as if the sound of his voice had been the first warning of his presence. The flinch of her body started a flashing turn that carried her back into her office.

In the time of the half-dozen steps that it took him to follow her, she regained the veneer of composure and when she turned to face him her eyes were as clear-seeing as the stain of lost tears would let them be.

"Everything's all right," she said, glancing down at her desk to transfer the meaning from herself to the work she had done.

He saw the fan of carbon copies and, quickly reading the top one, realized how many times in these last few minutes she had been forced to repeat, over and over again, the mind-pounding acknowledgment of Avery Bullard's death. His feeling was only the sympathy of transposition, unconsciously putting himself in her place, because there was no prior background of warmth between them, yet what he felt now was strong enough to make him reach out impulsively and place his arm across her shoulder.

Instantly, so fast that her act could only have been as completely impulsive as his own, she threw her body hard against his and her bent head drove itself into the saddle of his shoulder. Then, so close to him that it might have come from his own throat, he heard a shaking sob and a trembling cry of muffled anguish. His arm tightened and his mind flashed the memory of Mary on the night her father had died.

She broke away so quickly that there was only an instant between the beginning and the end, but it was long enough to transmute her blind grief into a frightened awareness of what she had unconsciously done.

"I—I'm terribly sorry, Mr. Walling, I—"

His hand, slipping across her back, found her forearm and he gripped it hard. "Don't be—don't be—I know how you feel —believe me, I do." He felt himself fumbling, feeling that nothing that he could say would have any meaning. Yet there must have been a meaning for her. She looked up at him and he saw gratitude that he had never seen matched in any face other than Mary's. Instinct told him that it was the moment to leave her alone and he did, closing the door softly behind him.

Standing at the head of the staircase he thought again, as he had thought so many times before, how strange it was that most people were so very different from what they seemed . . . and, stranger yet, that the qualities they tried so hard to hide were often more appealing than those they insisted on showing to the world at large.

The yellow path still slanted out from Alderson's door and he hurried down, his mind conditioned to sympathy. His quick excuse to Shaw that Alderson was badly shaken by Avery Bullard's death had gained validity in this last minute, but now it was a sympathy so close to pity that the last spark of hope was quenched. Fred Alderson could never be the president of the Tredway Corporation. That was clearly impossible.

But did Fred realize it . . . or was he still committed to the blind and hopeless course that he had insisted upon following in Shaw's office?

The moment Don Walling opened the door, he knew that Alderson had accepted his defeat. The old man sat at his desk, slumped and starchless. Tension and anger had drained from his face and there was, instead, an expression of apologetic penitence.

"I'm sorry, Don. Made an awful mess of it, didn't I?"

"I wouldn't say that, Fred. You were—"

Alderson cut him off with a raised hand and the hand was trembling. "No, no—you were disappointed in me. Couldn't help but be. I was disappointed in myself. Thought I could do it, but I couldn't."

It was an abject confession and Don Walling squirmed as he always did when he was confronted with weakness. "Fred, I know how you feel about Shaw and—"

"No, it wasn't Shaw—it wasn't Shaw at all. Don't you see that, Don? I was ready for Shaw. I could have handled him. That wasn't it. That's where I made my mistake, thinking I was fighting Shaw. No, that's not who I was fighting. I didn't think you knew."

"Fred, I—"

"No, don't try to stop me. I want you to know. You *have* to know. You can't help me if you don't know. It was Avery Bullard I was fighting. I knew that when we came in downstairs— all the way up in the elevator. That's why I went into my office—trying to convince myself that I could go through with it—but I couldn't. You thought I was afraid of Shaw, didn't you? No, that wasn't it. That would have been easy—it's easy to fight someone you hate. That's the whole trouble—I couldn't fight Avery Bullard. I never could."

It sounded like the emotional gibberish of a second childhood and Don Walling had given up the attempt to find a serious meaning in it when Alderson suddenly went on. "This is what you have to know, Don—Avery Bullard doesn't want me to be president. He doesn't want me to be anything but what I am right now. No, wait—it's true! If it weren't true he would have made me executive vice-president—not just this last time, but the time before—when he gave it to Fitzgerald."

Sympathy demanded a rebuttal. "But that was a part of the merger deal, Fred. Fitzgerald came in because—"

"No, Don, no—it's true. Avery Bullard didn't want me. I've worried about it—no, not because of myself—because he was holding off picking someone else. You see, he didn't want to hurt my feelings, Don—passing me over twice. I was going to talk to him—to tell him that I didn't really care—to go ahead and appoint someone else."

A question forced itself to the front of Don Walling's mind and, despite reluctance, he could not keep himself from asking it. "Fred, if Avery Bullard had appointed some one, who would it have been?"

Alderson clenched his hands. "That's what I was afraid of—why I didn't do it—why I never talked to him."

"Would it have been Shaw?"

Don Walling felt the cruelty of the question yet, once asked, he sensed that it had been the right thing to do.

Alderson, like a child slapped out of an emotional tantrum, stared at him for a moment and then, slowly, his eyes seemed to clear. When he spoke, the overtone of delirium was gone from his voice. "Yes, it might have been—but not if I'd had a chance to tell Avery Bullard what I found out this afternoon." He hesitated as if he were debating an explanation and then, apparently deciding against it, went on. "No matter what, Don, it can't be Shaw. We mustn't let that happen."

Don Walling caught himself nodding in unconscious agreement.

"It has to be Jesse," Alderson said. "That's the only chance we have to stop him now."

"Jesse?"

[189]

Alderson flipped open the notebook in front of him, twisting it so that Walling could read. In his copperplate script, Alderson had set down two opposing columns of names:

GRIMM	SHAW
ALDERSON	DUDLEY
WALLING	CASWELL

"That's the way you think the vote would be, Fred?"

"Yes, I'd support Jesse and I'm assuming that you would, too —at least as against Shaw."

Caution restrained Walling from a complete commitment. "Why do you think Dudley would vote for Shaw?"

"They've been thick as thieves these last few months. Haven't you noticed that? Didn't you see the way Shaw jumped in to take him out to the airport tonight?"

Don Walling nodded an acknowledgment, remembering that he had seen the Shaws in the Dudley's party at the last Federal Club dance.

"And of course George Caswell would vote for Shaw," Alderson went on.

"Why do you think that?"

"Because Shaw is Caswell's man. He came in here on Caswell's recommendation."

"But Shaw came in with Parkington-McConnell when they made our management study. It was because of—"

"It was Caswell who talked Mr. Bullard into taking on that outfit. No, Shaw is Caswell's man. Can't count on anything there."

"What about Julia Tredway Prince?"

"That's what I've been trying to figure out," Alderson said slowly. "I don't know where to put her."

Walling looked at the notebook . . . three votes against three. "The way you have things lined up there, Fred, the deciding vote would be in her hands."

"I know. That's why—well, I thought I might stop in and

see Mrs. Prince on the way home. As a matter of fact, I should do it, anyway. Remember that call I got this afternoon—Miss Martin calling me out of the executive committee meeting?"

"Yes."

"That was from Mrs. Prince. Somebody called her from New York trying to buy some of her Tredway stock. That's what I started to tell you a few minutes ago about Shaw. I don't know for sure but—"

They were both startled at the sudden opening of the door behind them. It was Shaw.

"Good night, gentlemen," Shaw said with forced pleasantry. "Presume I'll see you both in the morning?"

"Good night," Walling heard himself say automatically, and then there was the sound of Alderson's repetition.

The door closed.

Without realizing it, Walling had been holding his breath.

"Do you suppose he was listening?" Alderson whispered after a silence.

"Wouldn't have heard anything if he had. The door was closed."

Alderson nodded but without assurance. "I suppose we might as well go ourselves. No more we can do now."

Outside, waiting for the elevator, Don Walling glanced up the staircase. The light was out in Erica Martin's office.

A scrubwoman came shuffling toward them, dragging her mop.

"Afraid we held you up," Walling said apologetically.

"Coulda been worse," she said amiably. "Anyway you're the last. I had it later than this a lot of nights with him." Her gray hand flicked a gesture up the staircase. "I guess anybody can go to the funeral, huh?"

"Yes, indeed."

"When's it going to be?"

Walling felt his breath catch and then he heard Frederick Alderson say, without hesitation, "Monday at four-thirty. St. Martin's."

"Ought to be a nice funeral, a big man like him," she said,

shuffling off down the dark corridor, her voice fading with her.

The elevator door opened. Luigi avoided their faces, turning his head so that his eyes were shielded. The door closed and the car plummeted down through the shaft.

As they stepped out Alderson glanced up at the clock. It was nine-ten. He turned back. "Luigi, what happened to the carillon at nine? I was listening for it but I didn't hear it."

"Mr. Shaw say to turn it off so it don't ring," Luigi said and closed the door.

Don Walling waited for Alderson's reaction, but none came. They walked together out through the lobby and into the last of the dusk.

"I'd left word for Jesse that I'd be at the office until nine," Alderson said mildly. "That's why I wanted to be sure of the time."

KENT COUNTY, MARYLAND
9.14 P.M. EDT

The last lingering loom of the twilight had faded from the sky as Jesse Grimm crested the hill from which he usually caught his first glimpse of Kinfolk Cove. Now he looked off into blackness and his mind rankled at the delay that had robbed him of the daylight. As he stared the night became translucent and he could see the dim masses of land and water. Memory filled in the detail—the thin line of Kinfolk Creek, the widening cove, the locust-fringed bar that ran out to the wharf. There were three pinpoints of light, one red and flashing, two yellow and steady. The red light was on the nun buoy that marked the channel off the shore. The yellow lights were the windows of the kitchen. One of them seemed to blink and he imagined that it was his wife stepping in front of the window to watch for him. Sarah had gone down in the middle of the week and he had gladly endured the days alone for the pleasure of knowing that she had wanted to go. That was the only thing that had ever worried him about moving to the Eastern Shore

[192]

—whether Sarah would like it—and now she had proved that she did. There had been no way to let her know that he would be late tonight because they were still waiting for the telephone company to run its line down from the highway.

His lateness tempted Jesse Grimm to turn off without stopping at Teel's Store, but he decided that it was worth the minute or two that it would take. Anyway, Sarah might have left word about something that she wanted him to bring down. She did that sometimes. She knew that he always stopped.

Teel's Store was one of the unrecognized reasons that had made Jesse Grimm decide on Kinfolk Cove. He had found, in the nightly gatherings at the back of the store, an easy camaraderie that he had not known since his young machinist days in Pittsburgh, something that he had never found at the Federal Club.

When Jesse Grimm had first started coming to Kinfolk Cove, the Teel-store regulars had fallen silent when he came in, the traditional treatment accorded any stranger, but with the special reticence reserved for visitors who were reputed to have "city money." The change in Jesse Grimm's status from a stranger to an accepted Teel-store regular had come about—although he did not know it—from Jim Bishop's spreading the word that "this Grimm fellow" had fixed the magneto on Tim Culler's boat engine. Anybody could tinker a boat engine, but fixing a magneto was something else again. A magneto's going bad had always meant taking the thing off and sending it to Chestertown, losing a couple or three days of crabbing. It was after Jim Bishop told the story about Jesse Grimm fixing Tim Culler's magneto in no time at all that they started offering Jesse Grimm a coke case to sit on when he came into Teel's Store. Then one night when Matt Teel had been fussing about all the ice cream that had melted because something had gone wrong with the freezing machine on his ice cream cabinet, Jesse had fixed that, too. After the ice cream had started getting hard again Matt had said, "Captain Jesse, it's a mighty good thing you decided to come here." After that everybody had started calling him "Captain Jesse." Being an Eastern Shore "captain" was something like being a Kentucky "colonel," only it meant more. The governor of Maryland couldn't write up any kind of a paper that made the Teel-store regulars call a man "Captain Jesse."

Jesse Grimm stopped his car back of the gas pumps, so Matt Teel wouldn't come running out, and walked up the path. The gritty crunch of the oyster shells under his feet made a good sound in his ears. His nostrils tingled with the spicy scent of salt water and marsh grass that filled the soft sundown breeze.

"Well if it ain't Captain Jesse!" Matt greeted him as soon as he stepped through the door. "Just talking about you—wondering if you were a-coming or if you weren't a-coming."

A voice out of the shadows called, "I knowed he was coming or I'da been fishing all week," and a gale of appreciative laughter went up from the regulars. They had been joking about how Abe had better keep carpentering on Captain Jesse's new shop if he ever wanted to get his wife's washing machine running again.

"Don't tell me that wife of yours has kept you working all week," Jesse said.

Again the laughter rolled. Abe's wife was one of the red-headed Connor girls and everybody knew she could do a lot of hell-raising when her washing machine wasn't working.

"If I hadn'ta done it, she'da made me sleep down to the crab house—sweet as she is on Captain Jesse there," Abe said. You couldn't get ahead of Abe. He could give it back as good as it came.

Jesse's laughter rang out with the rest—and it was laughter that no one in Millburgh had ever heard. Someone shoved a box toward him.

"No, can't stay," Jesse said. "Have to get down home or Sarah'll have me sleeping in the crab house, too. Kind of late tonight. Got held up."

"That's what we figured," somebody said.

There was a lull in the laughter and Matt Teel came up to him with a torn scrap of brown paper. "Telephone call came for you, Captain Jesse. You're to call this man. Said up to nine he'd be at his office. After that you was to call him to home."

The name on the paper was "Fredrik Allerton."

Matt wasn't much on spelling but he ran a good store. There wasn't anything from roofing cement to dill pickles that you couldn't buy at Teel's Store.

Matt was looking at his watch. "Twenty after nine. Guess that means you're to call to his home."

Jesse started for the telephone. He had to pass Abe on the way. "You really been working, Abe?"

"Sure have, Captain Jesse. Got all them windows in, every last one."

"Got the doors hung?"

Abe slapped his bony knee. "I told your wife that's what you'd ask, but she said she was going to have them closet shelves of hers first or you and me was both going to get scalped—so I figured it better be closet shelves."

Jesse led the laughter, pushing past Abe to get to the telephone.

Everyone sat in respectful silence while the operator tried to put the call through but there was no answer at Frederick Alderson's residence in Millburgh.

"Guess it isn't anything that can't wait until morning," Jesse said. "Got to get down home."

Herb Tilligas followed him to the door. "Captain Jesse, you folks like a mess of soft crabs?"

"Sure would, Captain Herb."

"I'll be bringing 'em tomorrow."

Jesse Grimm went out chuckling to himself . . . water pump on Herb's boat must be acting up again.

MILLBURGH, PENNSYLVANIA
9.21 P.M. EDT

Driving out North Front Street, Frederick Alderson had been telling Don Walling about his call from Julia Tredway Prince.

"You say that it was this man Pilcher who was trying to get the stock," Don asked, "and that he's a friend of Shaw's?"

"Don't you remember Shaw talking about him—the time we were discussing that price protection contract for Odessa Stores?"

Don nodded vaguely. "I still don't get the point, Fred."

"Can't you see, Don—Shaw was trying to get his hands on more stock so that he'd have some extra pressure on Avery Bullard?"

"Because he thought he could force himself in as executive vice-president?"

"Of course. It wouldn't have worked—not with Avery Bullard—but Shaw's too much of a fool to realize that."

"But why was he working through Pilcher?"

"That's plain enough—to keep Julia from finding out what was going on. Shaw knows that she's close to Avery Bullard—that she'd never do anything he didn't want her to do. They *were* pretty close, you know—closer than a lot of people realize. I mean—well, I've just been thinking about that—wondering whether I really ought to try and talk to her tonight—so soon. Unless I miss my guess, she's going to be pretty much broken up."

Alderson leaned down to look at his watch in a stray beam of light that fell from the instrument panel. "Sort of late, too—maybe I'd better wait until morning to see her."

They rode for a moment in silence and then Don Walling felt himself impelled to ask. "Do you think there is any chance, Fred, that Mrs. Prince might change her attitude toward the company now that Avery Bullard is dead—that she might sell her stock?"

Alderson hesitated. "I was thinking about the same thing. Yes, I'd better see her tonight. She'll probably appreciate my stopping, anyway. It's right up here in the next block, Don. Just drop me off. I can walk home afterward."

They were already at the corner and Don Walling touched the brakes, pulling in toward the long white wall that guarded

[196]

the old Tredway home from the street, stopping where the wall opened for the driveway.

Alderson started to get out and then, suddenly he was frozen into immobility.

Walling turned in quick alarm. "Fred, what's the—"

Then he saw it. Loren Shaw's car was already parked in the drive.

CHICAGO, ILLINOIS
9.09 P.M. CDT

The trained eyes of the airport porters watched the passengers coming in through Gate 9, expertly calculating their potentialities. Three made an almost simultaneous lunge for the handsome, prematurely gray man who was obviously the pick of the lot. The quickest-footed won and J. Walter Dudley handed over his checks.

Walt Dudley was not unaware of what had happened, nor was he surprised. It was a form of flattery to which he had long been accustomed. He liked it. It was worth that oversized tip that he would be honor-bound to bestow. He knew that it would be several minutes before the bags came in off the plane, so he sauntered toward the newsstand. An overheard crowd voice said, "No, that's Eastern time. It's only nine-fifteen here in Chicago."

Nine-fifteen . . . the whole evening left . . . hotel room . . . alone. No, he would not call Eva Harding! That decision was made. He wasn't even thinking about her. Anyway, the telephone booths were all in use. This time it was different . . . this time he meant it . . . this time he wouldn't give in to himself. Why should he? What did it mean? Where could it lead? Nowhere but trouble. No, that wasn't fair to Eva. She'd never cause him any trouble. It wasn't fair to think things like that . . . made her sound cheap and common. The least he could do was to be fair to her. Eva would never cause trouble . . . no strings . . . no demands . . . nothing. That's why it was so easy to break it off . . . but that's why it was hard, too! But he had made the right decision . . . the only decision . . . never call her again.

The fat woman in the bright blue dress was backing out of the end telephone booth. It was empty . . . waiting . . .

He turned away, snapping his head around, and when his eyes focused he saw a girl who had just rushed into a man's arms. Her lithe young body arched inward, reaching, and there was the mind-feeling of the soft crushing of her breasts and the hard backpress of her thighs. He walked quickly away, his eyes on the baggage counter.

The bags hadn't come in yet and he stood in the long low-ceilinged corridor, looking out through the window at the endless yellow, yellow, yellow of the taxicabs sliding past. It was a good thing he had made his decision. It would be so easy . . . all he had to do was not say, "Palmer House" . . . say, "Thirty-two forty-four north—"

"Your bags, sir. Cab, sir?"

The dollar bill—"Thank you, sir, thank you very much"—and then another voice saying, "Where to, Mac?"

For a moment, he had a hard time answering "Palmer House." It always annoyed J. Walter Dudley to be called "Mac."

All the way down to the Loop he kept telling himself how much easier it was not to think of her than he had imagined it would be.

It was still two minutes before ten when he came into the lobby of the Palmer House . . . two minutes to eleven in Mill-burgh. He would get a good night's sleep . . . store it up. There were two weeks of market ahead. But this market wouldn't be so bad . . . more sleep. Yes, he'd made the right decision . . . no more losing sleep . . . no more of those never-sleeping nights with Eva . . . no more of . . .

"Check your mail, sir?" a bellboy said, eager to please.

"Yes, thank you—J. Walter Dudley."

A sheath of white satin floated up the stairway to the Empire

Room and the body within undulated with the steps . . . that man following her was a fool . . . wasn't going to get a good night's sleep. Eva had never wanted to come to the Empire Room . . . "It's silly, darling, to be anywhere else when we can be here." Silly . . . yes, silly . . . silly to be anywhere else when . . .

"Two telephone messages, sir. Which are your bags, sir?"

He pointed, stripping the little envelopes from the two messages that the bellboy handed him. CALL MR PEARSON AS SOON AS YOU GET IN. Pearson was the manager of the Chicago office. CALL MR SHAW IN MILLBURGH PA IMMEDIATELY

He placed the call to Loren Shaw as soon as he got to his room, without waiting to take off his hat, tipping the bellboy a dollar and acknowledging his salute while the call was going through.

After what seemed like an interminable delay, the operator said, "I'm sorry, sir, we are unable to locate Mr. Shaw. Shall I try again in twenty minutes?"

"Don't wait twenty minutes, keep trying."

Then he called Pearson, and it was from Larry Pearson that he learned of the death of Avery Bullard.

Less than an hour later a keen-eyed redcap in the Union Station spotted a handsome gentleman getting out of a cab, the kind of a gentleman who was usually good for a folding-money tip.

Sitting in Roomette 5, waiting for the train to start, J. Walter Dudley checked back over the fast moves that he made in the pellmell hour since he had talked to Larry Pearson. The meeting was all set . . . Pearson could handle it . . . cancel the appointments for tomorrow afternoon . . . hold the others until the funeral time was set . . . shift the Tuesday meeting to Thursday. Pearson would keep on trying to get Shaw . . . tell him that he was on the train.

The porter passed the open door.

"Porter?"

"Yes, sir?"

"Do we make any stops during the night that would give me time enough to make a telephone call?"

"No, sir. No stops that long, sir."

It was all right. Even if he hadn't talked to Shaw there was no question that getting back to Millburgh was the right thing to do. Too bad there wasn't a plane tonight . . . but getting in at nine-forty-five in the morning wouldn't be too bad. Everything was under control in Chicago . . . Pearson could handle it . . . and Eva would understand why he hadn't called when she read about Avery Bullard's death. She would be sure to see it in the morning paper.

MILLBURGH, PENNSYLVANIA
11.40 P.M. EDT

Mary Walling lay waiting in the darkness, holding her own breath so that she could hear the sound of her husband's breathing. It was soft and even-spaced and she decided that he must be asleep. She was alone now and free to think the thoughts that she had been afraid to think before because of the fear that he might read them in her face.

This had been one of those difficult evenings—the most difficult of all—when she had been forced to balance on the knife edge that separated hindrance from help. One moment Don would ask her opinion, but the next moment he would seem to resent her offering it.

There were times when Mary Walling found her husband a frighteningly mysterious man, when the strange processes by which his mind worked were completely beyond her understanding, yet the fear and the mystery and the lack of understanding in no way diminished her love. They only increased her desire to help him, to be more a part of him, to share his life more completely. That was why, again tonight, she lay awake in the darkness.

At the root of her difficulty was the fact that Don's mind worked in such a different way from her own that she could never reconstruct the pattern of his thinking. Actually, as she often told herself, Don did not *think*—at least not in the sense that she thought of *thinking*. He disliked the orderly setting down of fact against fact, and seemed to instinctively side-step any answer that was dictated by pure logic and reason. He never seemed to study a problem with the intense concentration that she would have applied. Instead, he appeared to skitter about over its surface, snatching up disconnected facts here and there, jumbling them together in a mental tangle that lacked all semblance of order. Yet—and of this fact her intelligence had by now made Mary Walling acutely aware—the end result was often a brilliant flash of pure creative imagination of which her own mind could never have been capable. She had learned that lesson a hundred times. The last time it had been their house.

For years she had clipped house plans and details. They jammed two carefully indexed file drawers. A notebook bulged with meticulously made checklists, corrected and recorrected with every new idea that she had uncovered in her reading. Yet, when they had finally decided to build, it had been almost impossible for her to hold Don's attention long enough to get him to study what she had done. He shuffled clippings so rapidly that she was sure he couldn't have seen them. He turned the pages of her notebook so fast that reading would have been impossible. When he finally settled down to the drawing board, her files were neglected and the notebook was unopened. The fast sketches that he tossed off, one after another, drove her to almost unendurable exasperation. Any sketch that pleased her, any sketch that bore even a faint resemblance to something that she had liked and put in the clipping file, he perversely tore up. The sketches that he saved evidenced neither reason nor logic. She had almost, but not quite, driven herself to the ultimate extremity of suggesting that they retain an architect, when Don had sat down and, in an astoundingly short time, without a single false move, had designed a house totally unlike any house pictured in the clipping file, unlike any house that she had ever seen, and yet by some strange miracle it was exactly the home she had always wanted. When it was built all of those things in her unread notebook were there.

In the earlier years of her married life, Mary Walling had tried to explain the unexplainable by telling herself that Don was the "artistic" type, a conclusion that was supported not only by his art training and obvious ability as a designer, but also by her memory of her psychology courses in which she had been taught that the truly creative mind seldom indulged in purely deductive thinking. Unfortunately, there still remained the unexplainable corollary, recited in the same textbook, that the artistic creative mind was at the opposite pole from the type of mind that could fulfill the requirements demanded of the modern business executive. Don was most certainly successful in business, not only as a designer and inventor—which was explainable in terms of his creative ability—but also in other ways for which there was no ready explanation. Her own judgment of her husband's oddly disparate abilities was admittedly subject to prejudice, but it had been confirmed time after time, most recently and vividly by the suit over the patents on a method of extruding a plastic coating on the steel tubing used for metal furniture. Prior to the suit, she was quite certain that Don had little if any knowledge of patent law. He had dragged home an armful of books and, anxious to assist him, she had volunteered to search out and index pertinent references. He had side-stepped the offer and, much to her concern, had idly leafed through the pages, not making a single note. Yet at the cocktail party at the Federal Club where the court victory had been celebrated, the senior partner of the Wilmington law firm that had handled the case for Tredway had cornered her and said, "Mrs. Walling, that husband of yours missed his calling. He has one of the best legal minds that I've ever encountered in a layman—superior, I might even say, to those of many of my own colleagues at the bar." She had known that it couldn't be completely true—the predominant characteristic of the "legal mind" was its capacity for the exercise of pure logic—yet there was enough truth to deepen the eternal mystery of what actually went on inside her husband's brain.

Tonight, she had expected Don to return home in an extension of the mood in which he had left, fog-minded by the shocking impact of Avery Bullard's death. Awaiting his arrival, she had stocked her mind with the things that she might say to assuage his grief. None of those things had been said. They had talked for over an hour and Avery Bullard's death had not been directly mentioned. She knew that Don's grief was still there but it seemed so deep-buried now that it could not be raised. She was not surprised—there had been other cases before where the same thing had happened—but acceptance did not supply understanding. When something important dropped into the clear quiet pool of her own mind, the surface was rippled for days. When that same heavy stone dropped into Don's mind there was only the quick first splash that a falling rock made in stormy water and then the waves erased the splash. But she knew that the stone still lay heavy on the bottom of the pool.

They had talked tonight about who would be the new president of the Tredway Corporation, not in the orderly and coherent way that she wanted to talk, but in the disconnected way that was demanded by the oddly assorted scraps of his conversation. Pieced together, she had made out that Alderson was out of the race and that Grimm was to be elected, not because of any special qualifications that he possessed, but because he was the one candidate who could defeat Shaw. The votes for Grimm would be votes against Shaw.

How different all of this was, she thought, from the world of big business that she had pictured when she had studied business administration back at the university. In her student days she had thought of the large corporation as a highly organized functioning of economic law, administered by a race of supermen endowed with a combination of the characteristics of the Dean of the School of Business Administration, the Professor of Economics, and the Associate Professor of Statistical Analysis. She could still vividly recall, during the early years of her marriage, the difficulty she had experienced in trying to make what Don told her about the Tredway Corporation fit the pattern that her textbooks had laid out. The bits of evidence that she gleaned from his offhand remarks made the company appear to be a disorganized, fumbling, and decidedly inefficient enterprise. The major executives seemed to be a quite ordinary group of men, disconcertingly human in their limited capacity for high-order thinking and far too given to the man-on-the-street practice of basing decisions on hunch and intuition rather than upon scientifically established fact.

The confusing end point of all that she learned was the seemingly contradictory fact that the Tredway Corporation was undeniably successful. Furthermore, the executives of other corporations, whom she met occasionally, seemed in no way superior to the Tredway officers. Nevertheless, she had felt a certain justification of her opinion when Don had told her one night that Avery Bullard had retained a firm of management consultants to make a study of the corporation's organization structure and management methods. Her vindication had seemed even stronger some months later when Loren Shaw, who had supervised the study, was employed by the company and made a vice-president. The circumstances had given her a predilection for liking Mr. Shaw and, in addition, she found him an interesting man. He was widely informed, had a keen mind, and a marked ability to think in a clear and logical manner. Despite the fact that she had no particular liking for Shaw's wife, Evelyn, she had begun to think of the Shaws as potentially close friends when, to her surprise, she had suddenly been faced with the fact that Don disliked Loren Shaw intensely. She had thought at first that it might be because he disagreed with some of the recommendations that Shaw had made in the management consultant's report, but that had not proved to be the case. Don had been in substantial agreement with most of the suggested changes. His dislike of Shaw was something else, another of those inexplicable things that happened inside that strangely unfathomable mind.

Now, lying in the darkness, she tried again to probe the mystery of Don's feeling toward Loren Shaw. She was driven by no urgency of discovery because she knew that nothing she might conclude would have any effect on Don's attitude. What made her pursue the subject again, after not having thought about it for a long time, was the still lurking fear—largely subconscious—that her husband's dislike of Loren Shaw was a reflection upon herself because she found him an interesting man. She saw him rarely now, except at the larger parties, because they had long since allowed their social relationship with the Shaws to lapse, but, a few weeks before, at one of the Dudley's big dinner parties, she had been seated next to Loren Shaw and had enjoyed the experience. At the very least, Loren Shaw's wide-roving interest and the sharpness of his mind were clearly preferable to Jesse Grimm's clamlike taciturnity, Fred Alderson's piously unbroken preoccupation with the affairs of the company, or Walt Dudley's perpetual desire to be the life of the party.

"Asleep?"

Don's wide-awake whisper seemed as loud as a shout and she felt a moment of unreasonable embarrassment as if her privacy had been rudely invaded.

"No. Can't you sleep, dear?" she asked.

"Not yet."

The breaking of the stillness let the night sounds drift in through the open windows. She heard someone walking up the road whistling, adding incongruous trills and off-key variations to the scarcely recognizable melody of "Some Enchanted Evening." Out of the stillness her ears picked up a sound that it had rejected before, the throbbing of the engine in the pumping station way up on Ridge Road, a distant bark in slow four-four time with a deeper rain-barrel cough on the downbeat.

"I didn't know you were awake," she whispered.

"Lot to think about tonight."

"I know." Reaching out, she found his hand and the hard grip of his fingers was a thrilling reassurance of the intimacy they shared.

"Can't get Fred off my mind," he said impatiently, as if the attempt had built a background of annoyance. "Don't know why I can't stop thinking about him."

"Did you really want him to take the presidency, Don?"

"No, not that," he said with sharp dismissal. "It's just that—you know, it's a pitiful thing to see a man like Fred want something as much as he wanted the presidency, and then sit there and watch him take that horrible beating—punch-drunk—groggy—like an old fighter that just doesn't have it any more."

"Did he ever have it, Don?"

"Sure. If it hadn't been for Fred—" His voice cut off as if he had suddenly discovered that what he had planned to say was either unthinkable or unsayable. "Maybe he didn't. I don't know. It's hard to separate him from Avery Bullard. They were so close you can't figure out for sure what was Fred's and what was Mr. Bullard's. I guess that's what I was thinking about really. You know, it's an awful thing to let anyone come into your life and mean so much to you that when you lose them you lose yourself."

Her flinch came so quickly that she could not prevent the shiver from running down her arm and into her hand.

"What's the matter?" he asked in quick concern.

"Nothing, dear. I—"

"Something bothered you. What?"

"It doesn't matter. I know you didn't mean it that way. I'm just being silly."

"Mean what?"

She made a laugh run ahead of her voice. "That you mustn't let anyone else come into your life and mean so much to you that—"

His lips smothered the words. "Mary, you know I didn't mean—"

Their lips parted just long enough for her to say, "Of course I know, but if I ever lost you—"

"Don't worry, you won't." His voice was roughly male, more caressing than softness could have been.

She pulled back, feeling the warm glow that was spreading through her body. "No—no, Don, no."

"No what?"

"Darling, please—I wasn't tricking you into making love to me."

"Why not?" His hand ran over her and she was trembling and vibrant. She pushed his hand away. "Go to sleep."

"Why?" The word was a throaty bass note.

"No!"

The bass note was in his low laugh. "You're being a very enticing little bitch."

She reacted instantly. "What a horrible thing to—" and then she was struggling against his word-smothering kiss again until the struggle became its own defeat.

He lifted his lips to let her say, "Am I really as bad as that?"

"As what?"

"What you said."

"What did I say?"

"You know."

"Tell me," he teased.

"I couldn't"—but there was something that forced her lips to his ear and made her whisper the word.

"Yes, you are!" he said fiercely, twisting her body and crushing her to him. "Damn it, Mary, I wish there were some way to make you understand, once and for all, that I'll never stop loving you."

"I don't want it to be once and for all," she whispered. "I want you to keep telling me—over and over and over."

She could feel his lips moving silently to the words "I love you" as he kissed her.

"Darling, if there's any time when you don't will you promise to tell me?"

"There never will be."

"Promise me—there are so many times when I'm afraid. Darling, you're such a mystery to me—I want to help you—I want to think the way you think—but when I'm close to you I can't think—all I want is to be a part of you—"

And then she was a part of him through a timeless oblivion and when she could hear the night sounds again the sound that she heard first was his deep-sleep breathing.

She felt as if she were eternally awake, as if she could never sleep again, nor even want to sleep again. She knew now, as she had never known before, that there was nothing more important to him than she was. He had never wanted her as much as he had wanted her tonight . . . tonight of all nights.

11.56 P.M. EDT

Dwight Prince faced the necessity of making a decision, a prospect that he never found pleasant. He stood in the hallway facing the closed door of the bedroom that he usually shared with his wife. He was confronted with two alternative courses of action—he could either open the door or not open the door. If he chose the latter alternative, he would have to sleep alone in the front guest room. If he chose the former, he might find himself an unwelcome intruder. Julia had obviously wanted to be alone when she had gone flying up the stairs the moment that fellow Shaw was out of the house. But that had been an hour ago.

As usual, Dwight Prince let himself be guided by his instinct, which he had found to be more trustworthy than intelligence in all matters where Julia was concerned. He opened the door.

She had been lying on the bed, but the recoil of her body was so swift that she was in a sitting position before the door was half open.

It was his first thought that his decision had been the wrong one, for there was an embarrassed desperation in the way that she tried to stop the flow of her tears.

"I'm sorry, Dwight," she gasped, catching up the fullness of her dressing gown and burying her face in its folds as if she dared not let him see her eyes.

Instinct told him to go to her and he did, sitting beside her, his arm tight around the curve of her thin waist, feeling the sobs that she was now choking into silence. The grief that she had stored since they had heard of Avery Bullard's death, withheld from him and later from Loren Shaw, was still unspent.

"If you'd rather be alone—" he started to whisper.

Her hands dropped and her head flashed back. "Do you hate me, Dwight?"

"No. Why would you think that I did?"

"For feeling this way about Avery Bullard." Her eyes were still avoiding his.

He waited, trying to think and then giving up the attempt. "It's never been a secret that you were once in love with him— you told me that before we were married—so there's no reason now why you should be afraid to let me see your tears."

She turned to him and the tears that she had not been able to stop before had suddenly stopped. She kissed him then, desperately, forcing her strength to overpower his so that it was an act of her own doing.

The hall clock struck twelve but there was no answering sound from the carillon in the Tredway Tower.

Saturday
June 23

*" . . . long live
the king"*

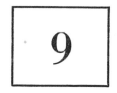

9

MILLBURGH, PENNSYLVANIA
4.47 A.M. EDT

Since midnight Van Ormand had been living at the heady peak of his career. Nothing as exciting as this had happened to him since he had been appointed Director of Advertising and Publicity for the Tredway Corporation. After the releases on Avery Bullard's death had been cleared, he had stopped by the Millburgh *Times* to see how they were coming with the story for the morning edition. To his exhilarated delight, Bill Freisch, the city editor, had grabbed his arm and pushed him into a chair at the rewrite desk. There he had experienced the thrill of coming as close as he would ever get to being a real honest-to-God newspaper editor. He had checked a thousand facts, answered a hundred shouted questions, been the focal point of all of the wonderful hubbub of handling the biggest story that had broken in Millburgh in ten years. Yes sir, that's just what Bill had said—the biggest local story in ten years!

Bill was a swell guy and you could say that again! Bill had even let him write most of the feature story on the company's history, and now here it was in type, word for word, just the way he had written it. The pictures were swell, too.

Bill had forgotten all about the pictures the *Times* had used four years ago when Millburgh had staged its Bicentennial Celebration, but he'd said it was a hell of a good idea . . . that's just what Bill had said . . . and it sure as hell was a good idea! Mr. Shaw would really get a kick out of it! Made a terrific splash . . . the line-up of presidents' pictures across the top of page two . . . old Josiah Tredway dignified as hell . . . good prestige stuff . . . and George Tredway with the big beaver and Oliver with the mutton chops . . . and old Orrin looking like he must have been a nice guy . . . and then a two-column cut of that Underwood & Underwood shot of Mr. Bullard that he always said was the one to use . . . "Doesn't make me look like such a stuffed shirt." Bullard was all right, by God! You could say what you pleased but the old guy had one hell of a lot on the ball!

Out of the corner of his eye, Van Ormand saw Bill Freisch stabbing at the page proof with his pencil and, guiltily, he tried again to concentrate on his own search for errors.

Bill was coming toward him now, flapping a proof in each hand as if they were limp wings. "Catch anything more, Van?"

"Just a few typos, Bill," he said, professionally flippant.

Freisch leaned over his shoulder, checking. "Yah, I got all of those." He spread his own proof before them and his pudgy finger found a query. "What's Walling's first name?"

"Don. You got it right, Bill."

"No abbreviations," Freisch said curtly. "We always use full names. What is it—Donald?"

Van Ormand fumbled. "Well, I think Don is his full name, just Don. That's the way he always signs—" A vague memory floated into his mind and then suddenly crystallized. "Hey, wait. I got it—MacDonald. I remember seeing it one time on his personnel record when I was checking my story about his being made a V.P.—MacDonald Walling."

"M—c?" Bill spelled.

"No, with an 'a,'" he said triumphantly. You sure as hell had to have a memory to be a newspaper man . . . wasn't any time to go horsing around checking things with that old press waiting to roll.

Bill made scrawls on the corners of the page proofs and pushed them toward the old man who had been waiting. Then he glanced at the clock on the wall. "Only twenty one minutes late. The pressroom can pick up most of that. Not too bad, considering."

"I think it was wonderful, Bill, and I sure as hell want to thank you for the way you co-operated—that is, speaking for myself and the company, too."

"Hell, boy, this was news."

"Well, you sure gave it a fine play, Bill, and I just want you to know that."

"Good thing it hit on Saturday," Bill said with a weary grin, looking just the way those big-time newspaper men always looked after the old paper had been put to bed. "We're always light Saturday. If this had smacked me yesterday I don't know what I'd of done for space— all that damn Friday advertising."

"Yah, advertising is a pain in the neck all right," Van Ormand said with a tone of professional comradeship. "A lot of times lately I been thinking of getting the hell out of advertising and back on a good old newspaper."

"Nuts! I bet you're making more dough for yourself than we're paying this whole city room."

"What's dough if you aren't getting any fun out of life?" Van Ormand asked seriously.

Bill laughed. "Why ask me? I don't get any of either. How about going down for a cup of coffee while they get her to bed?"

"Gee, swell, Bill, swell."

"Hey, look—crissake, you really ruined yourself, boy."

Van Ormand glanced down and saw the smudge of grime across the front of his white dinner jacket where he leaned against the composing-room table. "To hell with it!" he laughed, letting a high-pitched giggle slip past his guard. "I'll just put it on the old expense account, that's all I'll do, just put it on the old swindle sheet."

6.05 A.M. EDT

Loren Shaw opened his eyes again and was grateful that the night had finally faded. He had awakened time after time to darkness and each time the return to sleep had been more difficult and more frightening. His dreams had not been flights of fancy—they never were—but simply uncontrolled continuations of his day-thoughts. It was the lack of control that was alarming. That was what had defeated him last night. Another wrong move might destroy everything that he had worked so long to get.

The presidency of the Tredway Corporation had been Loren Shaw's calculated goal since that first evening, four years ago, when he had carefully planted the seed in Avery Bullard's mind that had eventually led to his employment as Vice-President and Comptroller. Actually it went back farther than that, back through all of the companies for which he had directed management studies while he had been employed by Parkington-McConnell. In every study there had been one paramount question, a question that was never asked or answered in his leather-bound final reports but only in the privacy of his own mind—"Is this the company in which I can rise higher than all of the company presidents whose insults I have been forced to endure?"

The insults had been, of course, personal rather than professional. No one had ever dared question Loren Shaw's professional competence—his position as a vice-president and senior analyst for Parkington-McConnell had made him invulnerable on that score—but that had not saved him from the searing injustice of constantly being made to feel that he was the social and educational inferior of the corporation presidents who, ironically, had to pay a stiff fee in order to have him tell them how to run their businesses. "Shaw?" they would ask. "Met a very distinguished gentleman at Bar Harbor last summer— Judge Shaw—a relative of yours by any chance?" Or if it wasn't Bar Harbor it was the *Queen Mary* or Palm Beach or the Riviera. There was nothing he could ever say then except a reluctant, "I'm afraid not, sir." But that wouldn't stop them. "I suppose you're Harvard Business, Mr. Shaw—or perhaps Wharton? Most of you chaps in your line seem to be one or the other." The question would claw at his entrails but again there was nothing that he could do except change the subject as rapidly as possible. His only education beyond high school had been a night coaching-course to prepare him to take the state board examination for a Certified Public Accountant. Loren Shaw's only degree was C.P.A.

Becoming a C.P.A. had been as calculatedly purposeful as had been every other move in Loren Shaw's life. His sharp reading of the newspapers—particularly the accounts of court cases involving famous men and large sums of money—had revealed that rich and socially prominent families offered fat fees and an open door to bright young men who knew every crack and crevice in the income tax regulations. In a very few years Loren Shaw was receiving the fat fees—but the doors did not open. He was not invited, socially, to the homes of his clients and, gradually, he came to see that he never would be. The more successful he became, the more anxious they were to see him only in the guarded privacy of their inner offices.

When Parkington-McConnell had offered him a vice-presidency he had accepted. The vice-presidency in itself was not a great distinction—there were thirty-two of them in order that no client need feel slighted—but Mr. Parkington's promise that he would "live in constant and intimate personal contact with the nation's outstanding industrial leaders" had been a real inducement. Furthermore, as old Mr. Parkington had pointed out, a bright young man ought to find chances to broaden himself. That had been a superfluous observation. Loren Shaw was no fool.

During his second year in his new connection, Loren Shaw had married the kind of a wife that his plan called for. Her father, Harrington Van Tern, was a Parkington-McConnell client so Shaw had access to all the facts about Van Tern's daughter, Evelyn. She was a graduate of Miss Millington's, a member of the Junior League, the great-granddaughter of an ambassador, the granddaughter of a lieutenant-governor, the daughter of a man who could trace his Main Line ancestry to one of William Penn's closest friends, and the sister of the internationally famous Wally Van Tern. As everyone knew, Wally Van Tern's third wife was a French countess, which would automatically make Evelyn's husband the brother-in-law of aristocracy. It was unfortunate—but not unforgivable in the light of her other qualifications—that Evelyn Van Tern was four years older than he was, cadaverously unattractive, somewhat of an alcoholic, and rarely pleasant for more than a few minutes at a time. She gave him what he wanted, and what she did not give him was relatively unimportant.

No one of the Tredway vice-presidents had a social background superior to the one Loren Shaw acquired. That was something that had impressed him early in his study of the Tredway Corporation. Furthermore, the way to the executive vice-presidency was clearly open. A confidential report wheedled out of a bumbling doctor had revealed the fact that Fitzgerald was in bad health. Alderson, whom Bullard had already by-passed for Fitzgerald, was clearly on the downgrade. Grimm was a top-notch manufacturing man but with no experience in any other phase of the business. Dudley, like Grimm, was excellent in his own field but not well-rounded enough to be general management timber.

Fitzgerald's death had confirmed Loren Shaw's faith in his plan. There was, of course, the hazard that Bullard, in one of the moments of impetuous behavior with which he was unfortunately afflicted, might select someone else as executive vice-president. Loren Shaw had not been abnormally worried. The Vice-President and Comptroller was in the winning spot. It was his executive responsibility to run to earth every case of waste, inefficiency, or failure to operate in accordance with the standards of modern business practice—and it was also his responsibility to set the standards. He was playing a game that couldn't be lost because he was both a participant and the referee.

Profit leaks were not hard to find in a rapidly expanding company operating in the biggest boom the furniture industry had ever known. It was regrettable, of course, that the uncovering of every leak inevitably alienated the vice-president who had failed to find and plug it himself, but Loren Shaw did not allow himself to be too concerned. His plan was based on the premise that the only person whose opinion really mattered was Avery Bullard.

In any event, as he often reassured himself, no one could ever say that anything he had done had not been in the best interests of the corporation. No one could argue that he had not been right when he had installed a system of tight budgetary control—nor when he had put complete cost accounting on every factory operation, co-ordinated purchasing with better inventory control on raw materials, established scientific pricing methods and set up sound salary administration. In less than four years the Tredway Corporation's return on invested capital had increased by almost fifty per cent. That was the real answer. No one could fight back against a record like that!

Now, suddenly, Loren Shaw had seen his whole plan blasted to bits—and by the bare margin of a single week. Only a few more days, at the directors' meeting next Tuesday, Bullard would surely have had the board elect him executive vice-president. But now Avery Bullard was dead and Loren Shaw faced the staggering injustice of having his fate determined by the very men whose friendship he had been forced to sacrifice on the altar of his duty to the corporation.

The cigarette that Loren Shaw lighted as he sat on the edge of the bed spread a stale and bitter taste through his mouth. He stumped it out and walked through his dressing room and on into the glass-paneled bathroom. Anger followed him like a clinging vapor. "Damn it!" he said aloud and the curse opened the sluiceway for another torrent of self-criticism. Why had he behaved as he had last night? Because he hadn't had a plan! Yes, that was the reason . . . he had acted on impulse and only fools did that. Yes, he had been a fool . . . worse than a fool . . . a damned senseless idiot! He had handled Alderson in the worst possible way . . . and probably alienated Walling in the bargain. That last thing he had said to Walling at the door had been the worst of all . . begging . . . making himself sound weak and uncertain. Why had he rushed down to the office and called in all of the department heads? Why hadn't he realized that they didn't matter? Department heads didn't elect new presidents . . . there wasn't a vote in the whole twenty of them. Alderson was a vote . . . Walling was a vote. Alderson's vote was probably lost from the start, but there might still have been a chance to get Walling's. Alderson had outwitted him with Walling. Yes, damn it, that's what he should have done . . . what Alderson had been smart enough to do . . . get to Walling! Walling might be the one to cast the deciding vote.

Unconsciously, Loren Shaw lighted another cigarette. The new plan was beginning to take shape in his mind. Alderson's vote was lost. Grimm couldn't be counted on, he'd probably go along with Alderson. Walling and Dudley were question marks . . . but he could get at least one of the two by offering the executive vice-presidency. No . . . there was another way to get Dudley . . . if he had to do it. He could save the executive vice-presidency to pay for Walling's vote. But why hadn't Dudley called him back from Chicago? Maybe the plane had been late . . . he'd call this morning. Yes, he'd get Dudley and Walling. But that was only two votes . . . three votes with his own. He had to have one more. That meant that he had to have either George Caswell or Julia Tredway Prince. Caswell was a possibility . . . Caswell couldn't overlook that profit record . . . but Julia Tredway Prince . . .

A shivering grimace contorted his face as his back-spinning mind recreated the memory of the hour that he had spent with Julia Tredway Prince. At least he had gotten there first . . . beaten Alderson to the punch . . . but he had spoiled everything by letting her throw him off balance so badly when she had asked if he were one of the Shaws of Charleston who had such a lovely place in Jamaica? And why couldn't he have forgotten that she had once been insane and still might be? No, no, no . . . she wasn't the one who was insane . . . he was! If he hadn't been temporarily insane he wouldn't have gone blabbering on to her about profit margins and return on net worth. Julia Tredway Prince hadn't understood a word he had said. All he had succeeded in doing was to make himself look like a groveling, cringing, coal-dusted kid from Wilkes-Barre who was scared to death of the great lady in the big house.

A groaning curse escaped his lips and, braced by his trembling arms as he bent over the lavatory, he fought back the temptation to vomit.

KENT COUNTY, MARYLAND
7.05 A.M. EDT

Jesse Grimm dug his thumbs into the top of his beltless khaki trousers and leaned against the porch post. His gaze followed the cedar-bordered path to the wharf, skipped like a stone across the glass-smooth water of the sheltered cove, and then settled on the distant sweep of Chesapeake Bay. The north wind that had come up overnight had swept the sky until it was as flawlessly blue as a polished jewel. The air was so clear that he could see the patches on the gray sails of an old four-master that was out in the steamer channel beating its slow way to Baltimore with a deckload of lumber. Nearer, a white skipjack trailed the feathered arrow of its wake toward the crab factory, the too-loud single-lunged cough of its engine making it seem closer than it was. Still nearer, gulls screamed in frantic delight over the food-filled tide rush at the inlet and, across the cove from the wharf, a fish hawk plunged down from the top of a dead chestnut and hit the water with an explosive splash.

Contentedly, Jesse Grimm let his eyes swing toward the shop . . . the bright new-wood color so pleasant against the black-green of the cedars that it was almost a shame to think of painting it. He grinned as he thought of the way Abe had kidded him up at Teel's Store last night about not having the doors hung. The doors were all hung and Abe had even made a start on the workbench.

The screen door squeaked behind him and he turned to see Sarah blinking at the brightness of the morning, tucking in a wisp of gray hair that had escaped her hurried arrangement.

"Why didn't you call me, Jesse? I didn't know you were up."

"No hurry," he said amiably. "Nice morning."

"I was hoping it would be," she said as if his pleasure were the only concern in her life—and he knew that wasn't far from the truth.

"Jesse?"

"What now?" That funny little grin on her face told him that there was something she wanted him to do.

"Were you going up to the store to make that call to Fred before breakfast or after breakfast?"

"What did you forget?"

"Syrup—unless you don't want pancakes. I forgot to get any," she said, feigning mock shame at the lapse.

"Sure I want pancakes. Always have pancakes down here on Saturday morning."

He yawned in a deep draught of the clean north-wind air and walked close to her as he passed, doubling a teasing fist at her cheek.

She reached up and took the fist in her hands. "I hope whatever Fred wants you about isn't something that will make you go back early."

"Nothing's going to make me go back early."

"Jesse, you haven't told Mr. Bullard about your retiring yet have you?"

"No. Thinking about it on the way down. Ought to give him as much warning as I can, I guess, so I decided to tell him the first of the week—Monday or Tuesday."

"What's he going to say?"

"Raise hell, I expect."

"You won't let him talk you out of it, will you, Jesse?"

"Not a chance."

She nodded, pleased, calling after him as he walked to the car, "Now, don't get talking to somebody up there at the store and stay all morning."

"Seems to me you're getting kind of bossy lately," he called back.

"Might as well get used to it," she laughed. "First real chance to boss you I've ever had."

"Too bad about you," he chuckled, getting in the car. Funny thing about Sarah . . . up in Millburgh she was always jumping on him because he didn't do enough talking and down here she worried about his doing too much talking.

MILLBURGH, PENNSYLVANIA
7.14 A.M. EDT

Don Walling's awakening was no slow emergence. He was suddenly blasted into consciousness by the explosive impact of a seventy-pound boy landing beside him after a running high jump over the end of the bed.

Steve's young laughter greeted his startled exclamation.

"What kind of a way is that to—say, what are you doing up so early?"

"Fishing," Steve said, and then all in one breath, "Mom said I couldn't go until after breakfast and no breakfast 'til you got up and you had to go to the office so I thought I'd just give you a little nudge."

"Fine nudge," he grumbled affectionately. "You're getting too big for those kid tricks, fellow."

He got up, yawning, pommeling his expanded chest. "Looks like a nice day."

Steve scowled. "Fishing's better when it's cloudy. Say, Pop, tough about Mr. Bullard dying, huh?"

Don Walling blinked, startled that he could have forgotten for even this first minute of his awakening.

"I guess you won't be going to Chicago this afternoon, huh, Pop?"

He was startled again, "No, that's right—I'd forgotten. Have to cancel my reservations."

Steve sat jackknifed on the edge of the bed, his arms wrapping his knees. "Mom didn't think you'd be going. Shall I tell her you'll be ready to eat in about two minutes, huh, Pop?"

He nodded, walking into the bathroom, stripping his pajamas as he heard the outrushing clatter of Steve's dash down the hallway.

The sting of the shower sharpened his nervous response and he made a conscious effort to pick up the strands of thought that the night had broken. Avery Bullard's death seemed like something behind a closed door, near and yet shut away.

Mary had the morning newspaper spread on the table when he stepped out on the porch where they breakfasted in good weather. He saw the black headline from the doorway and then, standing beside her, let his eyes skim down the right-hand column. His name jumped out at him:

> Confirmation of the news flash came from MacDonald Walling, Grayrock Road, vice-president of the company, who had received a call from a Tredway official in the New York office of the corporation. There was

"Where the devil did they get that?" he muttered, his finger indicating his first name.

"It's your name, darling," Mary said lightly.

"It's not. I—" He let his voice fall off into silence. It was one of those unexplainable things that would sound silly if he tried to put it into words.

"I can't see why you object to it, dear. It really sounds quite distinguished—MacDonald Walling of Grayrock Road." She had given her voice a comedy accent and he knew that she was teasing him into starting the day with a smile.

Steve repeated his mother, turning comedy into burlesque with a spoon for a lorgnette.

[224]

"That will be enough of that, young man!"

"Mom said it, too."

"Your mother has very special privileges," he said, and then he looked up, offering the smile that he knew she was waiting for.

Mary gave his shoulder a quick pat and started for the kitchen. "There's more on the inside, Don."

He was turning the page when he heard the telephone ring.

Steve's spoon clattered down into his cereal bowl. "I bet that's for me, I bet. I told Kenny I'd be there at—"

He stopped his son's headlong plunge with an outstretched arm. "Your mother's answering in the kitchen."

Mary came in. "For you, Don." The tone of her voice showed concern. "It's Mr. Alderson."

He started for the kitchen and then, catching himself in mid-stride, changed his mind and went to the hall extension.

The first sound of Alderson's voice justified Mary's concern. Alderson was obviously in a highly nervous state. "Things are bad, Don, bad. I've talked to Jesse—didn't call me last night—couldn't get through—but I just talked to him now and he won't take the presidency. He's going to retire the first of November."

"Retire!"

"That's what he says."

"But he isn't even—how old is he?"

"Sixty in October, but his mind's made up."

"All right, Fred, I'll stop at your place on the way down."

"Would you do that, Don? Well, that's fine. Then we can talk."

He hung up, feeling guilty that he had seemed to offer hope where there was no hope. With Jesse Grimm out of the running, Shaw would be president.

WEST COVE, LONG ISLAND
7.35 A.M. EDT

Going to the Yacht Club on Saturday morning had, for all the summer months of the past five years, been a repetitious part of George Caswell's week. He had bought the thirty-eight-foot cutter, *Moonsweep*, as an escape from his habit-regulated life, only to find that she, too, had now become a habit. In the beginning he had secretly fancied the thought of himself as the swashbuckling skipper of a racing yacht. The first few months had brought the reluctant conclusion that he was not a swashbuckler by nature—which, of course, he had known all along—and he had also discovered that he did not have the sixth sense that made a racing skipper. He had hoped that ocean racing would at least give him a complete break from his weekday world of figure-filled papers but, as things had turned out, his most useful purpose on board was served when he was bent over the figure-filled charts and papers on the navigation table.

The sum of George Caswell's discoveries had not been too disappointing, however, since they had been subconsciously expected, and *Moonsweep* had unquestionably given him a certain amount of pleasure. The crew of sun-bleached youngsters that he had gathered together were admittedly the best in the club and they treated him with a pleasant disregard of the fact that he was a rich man and a Caswell. Ken Case, who was now the boat's real racing master, was particularly likable. There were times when George Caswell thought that winning as often as they did might be considered in questionable taste, but apparently there wasn't too much feeling around the club for he had been elected Vice-Commodore by acclamation. That meant that he would automatically become Commodore next year. His father and his grandfather had both been commodores. It was a pleasant family tradition.

Driving along the shore road this morning, however, George Caswell's thoughts had no association with the yacht club. He had awakened to the rather surprising discovery that what he had been thinking about when he went to sleep was still in his mind. That, in itself, was unusual enough to command his attention. He often had ideas that seemed intriguingly full-bodied at midnight, but they generally proved to be thin ghosts of themselves when examined in the cold light of the next morning. That was not true today. The possibility that he might become the president of the Tredway Corporation was still very much in his mind. The longer he considered it, the more desirable it seemed. His thinking had even gotten to the point where he had actually asked himself what Kitty's reaction might be. His guess was that she would welcome it, even if it did mean leaving New York and Long Island. Kitty wasn't above wanting a bit of excitement now and then, and this would be the most exciting thing that had ever happened to them.

Turning in at the Yacht Club entrance, George Caswell saw that the north end of the anchorage, where the bigger boats lay, was already alive with activity. Squinting against the sun, he could see that his crew had gotten on board ahead of him. They were ranged along the leeward rail now, tying the stops on the big spinnaker.

It was a scene that would, only a day ago, have moved George Caswell to mild excitement. Today there was no such response. Racing for the Whaler's Cup had become remote and inconsequential.

NEW YORK CITY
7.50 A.M. EDT

Bruce Pilcher was awake when the telephone rang and he answered it casually with the preconception that it was the telephone operator giving him his morning call.

But it was a young man's voice, "Mr. Pilcher?"

"Yes," he said guardedly.

"Thank goodness I've finally reached you, sir. This is Bernard Steigel. Grandfather had a stroke last evening and I've been trying to—"

Bruce Pilcher's mind backlashed. No, this was wrong . . . it wasn't Julius Steigel who had suffered a stroke . . . Avery Bullard . . . it was Avery Bullard who was dead!

"—because he seemed rather worked up about something when he came home," Bernard Steigel was going on. "Mother didn't think much of it until she went to call him for dinner. She found him in the—"

[227]

Pilcher shook his head drunkenly. Had he been wrong about its being Bullard? Had it been old Julius who had . . . no, this was all crazy . . . like a bad dream! No, he was awake . . . he wasn't dreaming!

Bernard Steigel's voice faded in again: "—too early to know for sure but the doctors aren't holding out much hope. I'm waiting here at the hospital until we know something definite."

"What—what hospital?" Pilcher groped.

"Mount Sinai, sir."

"I—I'll come up as soon as possible."

"There really isn't much point, sir, unless you care to do it. He's completely unconscious, doesn't know any of us, but if you want to come—"

"Well, in that case," Pilcher broke in, "perhaps you could call me if he becomes conscious. I'll be here at the hotel—or leave word where I can be reached."

"All right, sir. I thought I ought to let you know as soon as possible. I tried to get you last evening but I wasn't able to reach you."

"No—well, I'm glad you did, Bernard."

"Oh, Mr. Pilcher," Bernard said, as if what he was going to say was an afterthought. "When we first found grandfather he tried to tell us something about—well, we couldn't understand it clearly, but it sounded as if he were trying to say something about selling the stores—and he kept repeating someone's name. It sounded like Bullard—or something like that. Perhaps you know what he meant?"

A blue light flashed in Bruce Pilcher's mind, cold steel striking hard flint. "Yes, I know what he meant, Bernard."

"Well, if there's any change, Mr. Pilcher, I'll call you."

"Yes, please do that." His voice was clear and controlled now. "My deepest sympathy to you, Bernard, and I hope you'll extend my feelings to the family. All any of us can do now is to hope for the best."

"I guess that's right, sir," Bernard's voice came back.

The receiver clicked and Bruce Pilcher hurried to the door, opened it, and snatched up the waiting newspaper. His fingers trembled as he fumbled open the tight roll and leafed the first pages. Then the trembling stopped. Avery Bullard's obituary was in the first column.

He opened his hands and let the paper drift to the floor, tramping over it as he walked to the window and looked down into the morning-shadowed gully of Madison Avenue. That blue flash had ignited a cold fire in his mind and the sound of the crackling flame was the sound of Bernard Steigel's voice saying, "—something about selling the stores—Bullard—"

With Avery Bullard dead and Julius Steigel dying, there would be only one person who knew what had happened yesterday afternoon in Julius Steigel's office. He was that person.

10

MILLBURGH, PENNSYLVANIA
8.12 A.M. EDT

Nelson Fowler, Jr., the fifth generation owner of Fowler's —"Millburgh's Leading Florist for Over a Century"—drained the dregs in the last of the paper containers of coffee that had helped keep him awake through the night. Rubbing his red eyes with his knuckles, he arranged the scraps of paper that littered his desk and began to list the orders that he had been able to place with the wholesale florists. The assortment wasn't as well-balanced as he would have liked because June weddings had stripped a lot of the greenhouses, but he'd be able to work things out . . . be a lot of open orders . . . no flowers specified . . . wouldn't be too hard to juggle things around.

The total dozens, when he finally added them up, made a staggering figure but he knew that he wouldn't have a flower too many. This would be the biggest thing in the history of Fowler's. After Monday, his father would have to quit bragging about that wedding back in 1929 when the Pathmore girl had married the governor's son. The Bullard funeral would knock that old record into a cocked hat . . . biggest gross **day** in a hundred years . . . but the hell of it was that it didn't mean anything, just a lot of profit for the government to take away. Still it was fun putting over a big one . . . gave a man a feeling of accomplishment . . . and anyway, it would shut up the old man about that damned Pathmore wedding!

8.18 A.M. EDT

The young priest stood listening in the doorway, impatiently remembering that his breakfast was already on the table and that his eggs were rapidly cooling to an inedible state.

"I understand perfectly," he broke in. "There is no reason to tell me more, Luigi. It will be quite all right for you to attend the funeral services for Mr. Bullard."

"You know it is the Episcopal Church and the mass is not—?"

"I am certain there will be many good Catholics at Mr. Bullard's funeral—perhaps even Father Steiger himself."

"Then it is all right?"

"Quite all right."

"I thank you, father, I thank you very much," Luigi said, bowing to the door that was already closing.

At the bottom of the steps he looked at his watch. He was already late. The last time he had been late was when the first baby had been born and that was so long ago that the baby was now a man. That time he had explained why he was late to Mr. Bullard and Mr. Bullard had said it was all right . . . a man did not have a baby every day . . . but this time it was different. There was no one to whom he could explain.

Hurrying down the street, Luigi remembered with regret that he had not asked the young priest about buying a candle for Mr. Bullard. Maybe it was not necessary to ask—perhaps Father Steiger would say it in the mass tomorrow. Father Steiger was a very good priest and very kind in the confessional. In many ways he was like Mr. Avery Bullard.

A curl of steam wisped across the bubbling water and Erica Martin lifted the pan and poured. Instantly, the powder in the bottom of the cup gave its blackness to the water and the odor of coffee rose with the steam.

She lifted the cup to her lips and drank, not with savor or relish but with the deliberateness of a demanded act. As she raised her eyes she saw, through the window, the white morning-lighted shaft of the Tredway Tower. She saw it now as a monument to a man who was dead, and the seeing was an acceptance of something that would always be, something that could never be changed. Avery Bullard was dead. She would live forever after without him.

Her eyes dropped and, staring into the blackness of the coffee cup, she tried to force herself to think of the future. The cup trembled and she put it down on the edge of the stove. Unconsciously, she crossed her arms, tightening them in a gesture of self-containment and in the instant of feeling the pressure of her arms against her breasts she remembered the moment of lost control last night when she had flung herself into Don Walling's arms. The warm flush of embarrassment started to rise within her, but as quickly as it rose it was as quickly lost in the memory of his understanding. He was, among all the men to whom she talked last night, the only one who had shown her the kindness of sympathy, the only one who had shared her grief.

Don Walling saw Frederick Alderson waiting at the bottom of the stone steps that led up to his house and the expression on his face created an atmosphere quite different from what he had expected. After the telephone call he had been prepared for a trying session with a distraught old man. Now, much to his surprise, Alderson's face reflected eagerness rather than anxiety. His brisk stride as he came toward the stopped car clinched the point that something must have happened to change materially the situation in the last hour.

"Looks better, Don, looks better," Alderson said confidently, coming up to the left side of the car. "It's going to work out all right."

"Jesse change his mind?"

"Jesse? No, nothing like that. Surprised me though, didn't it you—Jesse retiring? Never thought he had an idea like that in his head. Just goes to show that you never know what a man's really thinking about. That's why he's been fixing up this place down in Maryland."

"Then it isn't something that he decided to do because of Mr. Bullard's death?" Walling asked, voicing the question that had been in his mind ever since the telephone call.

Alderson seemed surprised, as if the thought had never occurred to him. "No, he's been planning it for a long time—kept it to himself—but that's the way Jesse always does everything. Doubt if he'd even have told me now if I hadn't brought up the presidency."

"Then you did talk to him about that?"

Alderson nodded and the expression on his face anticipated astonishment. "Know what he said? Fred, he said, I wouldn't take that job for a million a month—after taxes! That's what he said, a million a month after taxes."

"Well, he isn't the only one who turned down the presidency." The words slipped out before he thought and he regretted his carelessness when he saw the flicker of pain that twitched Alderson's face.

"I know, I know," Alderson mumbled, but his recovery was almost immediate. "I guess it seemed a little odd to you last night, the way I—" He shot a quick glance toward the house. "You see, I'd promised Edith that I'd take it a little easier—health hasn't been too good, you know—well, maybe she's right."

"Sure she is, Fred. After all—"

Alderson's voice leaped ahead as if he had cleared an unpleasant barrier. "Anyway, there's nothing to worry about as far as Jesse is concerned. He's with us a hundred per cent—feels the same way about Shaw that we do. That gives us three votes—you and I and Jesse. The whole point is that we need one more."

"But who do we vote for? If Jesse is out, who—"

Alderson by-passed the interruption. "Don't know why I didn't think of this before. Remember how I had the votes lined up—Dudley voting for Shaw?"

"Yes."

A crafty twinkle played about Alderson's eyes. "There's one way to keep him from doing it."

"How?"

"He wouldn't vote for Shaw if he had a chance to vote for himself."

What Alderson was suggesting was so foreign to anything Don Walling had ever considered before that he couldn't believe he had understood correctly. "Do you mean that—Fred, you aren't thinking of Walt as president?"

"Four votes is all it takes. With Dudley, we'll have them."

Walling was so startled that an involuntary movement of his body made his foot slip from the brake pedal and the car started to drift down the drive.

"Wait!" Alderson said sharply, his hand holding fast to the door handle as he walked with the moving car.

Walling's foot found the brake pedal again and the car stopped with a jerk. "Fred, I can't imagine—"

"I know, I know—but think about it for a minute or two and it will make a lot more sense." Alderson walked hurriedly around the car and got in the front seat, raising a restraining hand as Don Walling touched the starter button. "No, wait a minute, boy. Let's talk about this. Anyway, there's no hurry. His train isn't getting in for an hour." He took a deep breath as if he were preparing himself for an effort. "I know how you feel about Walt. I felt the same way myself when I first thought about it, but the longer I thought, the more I could see in his favor. There isn't a man in the furniture business who has more friends than Walt Dudley. You know that as well as I do.

Walt's got a lot of standing. He's been president of the association—on that government committee—all those things—made speeches all over the country. That's important—especially with the company getting as big as it is. What I mean is—well, he makes the right kind of an impression for the company."

"I know that," he muttered to fill Alderson's questioning pause—and from out of nowhere came the memory of Karl Eric Kassel and his red beard.

"And he's a worker," Alderson went on. "You can't argue about that either. Only last month I was talking to Alex Oldham in New York and he said he honestly didn't know how Walt did it—what I mean is, that those boys in the sales department are all pulling for Walt. That's something he has—knowing how to keep people happy and working together—and that's important, awfully important. With Avery Bullard gone—well, that's something the company's going to need."

Don Walling nodded silently. He couldn't argue. The things that Alderson was saying were the same things he had said to Mary last night . . . but still it was wrong! It was like an answer that looked right but wasn't right. He *had* to find a flaw somewhere . . . an error . . . something that would prove the truth!

Alderson's voice droned on, piling words on words, but they were only a meaningless buzz in Don Walling's ear until he heard him say, "Walt has his weaknesses—Jesse and I can both see that—but if it isn't Walt, then it's going to be Shaw and when you get down to making that choice, I'd a lot rather have Walt. I think you would, too."

There was the flaw! His voice leaped at it. "Fred, don't you see that it would still be Shaw? If Walt's elected, he'll make Shaw executive vice-president. Walt will be right under Shaw's thumb and Shaw will be running the company."

"Wait a minute," Alderson smiled. "The president doesn't pick the executive vice-president. He's elected by the board, the same as the president is."

"Oh—" It was the sound of embarrassed deflation.

"I know," Alderson said sympathetically. "With Mr. Bullard

[235]

—well, we've all gotten into the habit of taking the board for granted."

"I suppose so," he mumbled, feeling the finality of his defeat.

Alderson waited for a beat and then quickened the tempo of his voice. "The same votes that elect Walt president will elect you executive vice-president."

The import of what Alderson had said did not strike immediately. It came like a delayed explosion, time-fused until the fire of the pronoun had sputtered its way into his brain. Don Walling's lips parted but he tightened them quickly, holding back the meaningless words that were dropping in his mind like the falling debris after a blast.

"Makes more sense now, doesn't it?" Alderson asked with a thin smile.

There were still no words worth saying.

"Walt's going to need a lot of help," Alderson went on. "That's where you come in. You're strong where Walt is weak. It will be the two of you. What you might call—well, sort of a partnership management."

"I—I don't know what to say, Fred."

"There's nothing you have to say. It's settled. We have our four votes and that's all we need." He extended his arm and picked up Walling's hand from the rim of the steering wheel. "Congratulations, boy."

Don Walling could not bring himself to tighten his fingers in a grip of acknowledgment. It was all too new, too incredible, too totally unbelievable. "Fred, I—Fred, even if you don't want the presidency, you could still be executive vice-president."

There was the break of a long silence while Alderson dropped his hands and slowly spread his fingers over his kneecaps. "I'll admit that I thought about it—but only for a minute or two. It wouldn't be the best thing—not the best thing for the company. The man who goes in now as executive vice-president ought to be the man who'll be the next president of the company. I never would be. I'd retire before long and then the whole thing would be thrown wide open again. God only knows what would happen. There'd be a new board of directors —a new director to take Fitzgerald's place—another one to replace Jesse—someone in my chair, too. Three new directors and there wouldn't be a one of them that was ever close enough to Avery Bullard to know—to understand—"

Alderson's voice suddenly quavered off into silence, choked by the pent-up emotion that had broken through the restraint he had been trying so hard to exercise. It was only partially regained as he went on. "There's only one thing I want for myself—only one thing. I want to be sure that the company will go on being the kind of a company that Avery Bullard wanted it to be. There's only one way to do it and that's to settle it right now—while Jesse and I still have our votes. We'll get you in there with Walt and—you can do it, Don, I know you can! You can keep the company going the way he wanted it to go."

The plea reached into Don Walling's mind and opened again the door that had been so widely opened yesterday, but had been so strangely closed this morning. Once again he felt the full power of the emotional surge and counter-surge that linked his life to Avery Bullard. But now, as if it were a reflected glow, he felt something else, something new, an affection for Frederick Alderson that he had never known before. It was a feeling that rose against odds because, until only minutes ago, he had been thinking of Alderson as a fumbling old man, exposed in all of the weakness that had been so evident when he had crumbled under Shaw's attack last night. Now Frederick Alderson had shown a self-sacrificing loyalty that transcended weakness and actually rose higher because of it.

Words lifted in Don Walling's throat and he let his lips say them. "I'll do the best I can for you, Fred."

"I know you will, I know you will. But it isn't for me—it's for the company." Alderson started to get out of the car.

"Aren't you going down to the office?"

"No, I'll take my own car. I'm meeting Walt's train. He's getting in from Chicago on the nine-forty-five. I'd better get to him before Shaw does."

He remembered that Shaw had mentioned calling Dudley in Chicago. "Fred, unless I miss my guess, Shaw will be meeting that train, too."

"Don't think so," Alderson said with an amused twist to his voice. "Pearson tried to call Shaw last night from Chicago to tell him that Dudley was on his way back. He couldn't reach Shaw so he called me instead. Of course, I promised to tell Shaw —and I will—but not until after nine-forty-five."

Alderson finished with a stiff little salute and turned to walk back toward the old stables that now served as a garage. Watching him, Don Walling had a fleeting feeling of strange disillusionment, as if in this last moment he had seen an unsuspected flaw in his new-made image of Frederick Alderson. But it was gone as fast as it came, washed over by his own wonder at the miracle that had made him executive vice-president of the Tredway Corporation.

ABOARD THE SUSQUEHANNA LIMITED
9.05 A.M. EDT

Four waiters stiffened to attention as J. Walter Dudley entered the dining room. The steward, being a very perceptive man, led him to a table served by a waiter who looked as if he had spent most of his long life in the service of a fine old Southern family.

J. Walter Dudley was no more appreciative of his table assignment than all of the waiters whose suppressed smiles he could not see. Since all of their tips were pooled, they were always glad to have old Henry get a customer who would really shell out for the Uncle Tom act. No one could pull it off like old Henry.

"I'll need a little fast service this morning," Dudley said in brusque command. "Getting off at Millburgh."

"Millburgh? Yassuh! Now don't you worry about that, suh. We gonna get you a mighty fine breakfast that you all is sure 'nough going to enjoy. Yassuh! Now what you sorta hankering for this morning? Maybe a nice piece of the melon I been saving special?"

"Sounds fine," Dudley said, pleased. "Soft scrambled eggs. dry toast and coffee."

"Yassuh!" Henry exclaimed, making the order sound like an inspired triumph. "You know what else I'se going to bring you? I'se going to bring you some real old Southern biscuits like you all don't never get up North. You just read your paper now, suh, and right away I'se going to bring you that melon."

The newspaper was the Pittsburgh *Post-Gazette*. There was a short page-three story on Avery Bullard's death. It contained only one fact that J. Walter Dudley had not known before— that Avery Bullard's collapse had been in front of the Chippendale Building in New York. He asked himself what Bullard might have been doing in the Chippendale Building, but before he could contrive an answer the melon was placed in front of him.

"Now, suh, don't you worry 'bout nothing but enjoying that melon. You all got plenty a time 'fore we get to Millburgh."

The melon was excellent.

MILLBURGH, PENNSYLVANIA
9.12 A.M. EDT

For the last hour, Loren Shaw had been dictating the memorandum that he was preparing for George Caswell. He had listened twice to the playback of every dictated paragraph, the first time to check the figures against the tabulated sheets that covered his desk, the second time to weigh the effect that every word and phrase might have on George Caswell.

He came now to the silence beyond the last word. Every error had been corrected, every mistake had been eliminated. There were no facts that were not completely verified. He was ready. Everything was planned. This time there would be none of the mistakes of impulse that he had made last night.

With a clean handkerchief he wiped away a smudge mark

that his thumb had left on the polished chrome of the microphone. Then he reached over and turned the pointer from LISTEN to DICTATE.

"Center headline—summary. As can be seen from the foregoing outline—comma—the Tredway Corporation offers an unusual opportunity for a marked increase in its net earnings—period. While the writer has made substantial progress in that direction—comma—as is evidenced by the two exhibits which are attached—comma—the fact remains that the management attitude hitherto prevailing has prevented the full application of modern methods and techniques—period. As I have pointed out before—comma—the primary need is for a full recognition by the president that his first responsibility is to the stockholders with whose property he has been entrusted—semicolon—and that the measure of his management success must always be the net earnings which the corporation produces—period."

He turned the pointer, ran back the record, and listened to the repetition of his words.

There was no need for change. No one could argue against those fundamental facts. The truth was the truth.

He took the record from the machine and glanced at his watch. It was still only eight-fifteen in Chicago. Pearson wouldn't be at the office for a half-hour yet. What in the devil had happened to Dudley? Why wasn't he registered at the Palmer House?

9.16 A.M. EDT

Dwight Prince came into the library and Julia looked up from the litter of papers on the desk in front of her. She seemed surprised, as if her husband's existence were something suddenly remembered.

"Did you want to see me?" he asked. "Nina said you were looking for me."

"Nina? Oh, but I was only asking if you'd had your breakfast. She said you had."

"Sorry, darling. If I'd known you were—"

"You must have been up at the crack of dawn."

He shrugged an answer.

"Couldn't you sleep?" she asked.

"One of those nights."

"Something worrying you?"

He added a smile to the shrug.

"What is it, dear?" Her voice had the sound of a patient mother soothing a troubled child.

His hesitance made her put down the pencil that she had kept poised over the paper.

"Nothing new," he said. "Just another attack of the same thing—realizing how damned useless I am."

She was at his side instantly, as a practiced nurse responds to the symptoms of a familiar illness. "Oh, Dwight darling, you know how you always— "

"I mean it, Julia. I feel sometimes that—"

She administered laughter as if it were a prescription. "All right, darling, if you insist on being useful, check these figures for me."

He responded like a bribed child, eagerly seating himself at the desk and picking up the pencil she had dropped. She stood behind him, sober-faced as soon as his eyes were safely averted, almost trapped when he twisted his head unexpectedly and looked back.

"Julia, what is all this?"

"I'm trying to check some of the things Mr. Shaw said last night."

"You didn't like him, did you?"

"It doesn't matter whether I like him or not. He might still be the right man to be president."

"At least there's no doubt he wants it."

"No, there was no doubt about that," she said. "Maybe that's why I'm so suspicious of him."

"I wouldn't be, if I were you. He's the right type."

"What do you mean?"

"He's almost a double for Lynch, the man that took over our company after Dad died. I couldn't help but think of that when

[241]

he was sitting here last night. They're out of the same mold—
even sound alike."

"Yes, Lynch has done a good job with your company," she
said, nodding a grudging acknowledgment.

"At least, he's making me enough money so that I'm no
longer a kept man."

"I don't like your saying that!" she flashed. "You know that
money never—"

"I'm sorry, darling. I didn't mean—"

She stepped away from his reaching hand. "Then you think
Shaw would be the right one?"

"All I know is that he's the type. It takes a man like Dad or
Mr. Bullard to build a big company, but it takes a Shaw or a
Lynch to really squeeze the profit out of it."

She turned, sweeping a nervous arpeggio with her fingernails
across a shelf of books. "I don't know—that's the whole trouble—I don't know. I should know, but I don't. If I'd gone to
the directors' meetings—if I only knew what was going on—

"Couldn't you talk to some of the others?" he asked. "I mean
—well, you could talk to Mr. Alderson or Mr. Grimm. Or if
you want me to, I could—"

Her face came alive with a sudden thought. "Dwight, you've
given me a wonderful idea!"

"I have?"

"Yes, I know now what I want to do."

He waited patiently, watching her eyes as they reflected the
flashing of her mind.

"Dwight, dear, would you do me a favor?"

"Of course."

"Would you mind terribly having lunch today at the Federal
Club?"

He blinked.

She forced a smile. "To be perfectly blunt, I'd like to invite
someone here to lunch and I want to be alone with her."

"Her?"

"Erica Martin."

He looked blank.

"She's Mr. Bullard's secretary."

"Oh—yes, I suppose she would know what's been going on, wouldn't she?"

She gave his cheek a quick kiss. "Now don't ever say that you aren't an enormous help."

He dropped the pencil and, acting on the unworded dismissal in the tone of her voice, moved toward the door. "If you want me, Julia, I'll be out in the studio."

She was already dialing the number. When she had half dialed she cut it off, waiting out a new thought, testing it in her mind, finally nodding her approval. Yes, this way would be better— if it were an invitation to lunch Erica Martin might refuse. This way she would have to come. Lunch could be an afterthought . . . casual . . . or maybe it wouldn't take that long to know. No, it wouldn't! One look would be enough . . . If there had been anything between that Martin woman and Avery Bullard . . .

"Stop it!"

No, that wasn't why she was asking Erica Martin to come. She hadn't thought that . . . it wasn't a thought . . . only the memory of a thought . . . or the memory of a memory.

She dialed again and this time there was no stopping.

"I'd like to speak to Miss Martin," she said and her voice was strong and sure.

9.19 A.M. EDT

Don Walling entered his office, relishing the release from impatience that came to him with the closing of the door. One person after another had blocked his attempt to hurry from the parking lot to his office. They had all wanted to talk about Avery Bullard's death, repeating the time-worn phrases of a litany that had long since been squeezed dry of meaning, demanding the same threadbare replies that came harder to the tongue with every repetition.

A part of the urge that had made him want to hurry to his office had been the hope that this most familiar of all surround-

[243]

ings would restore his ability to think clearly, something that he hadn't been able to do since the moment of his realization that he would be the executive vice-president of the Tredway Corporation.

Glancing about the office he found no fulfillment of his unconscious hope. The room seemed totally strange, something detached from experience, as if he had recently been reborn without memory and was now thinking with a new mind and seeing with new eyes.

The connecting door of Dudley's office stood open and he walked through it, drawn by the pin-marked map of the United States that hung on the wall—yellow-headed pins for the factories, orange for lumber mills and subsidiaries, blue for warehouses, red for district offices, green for distributors and sales agencies. He stared at the pinpoints of color so long that they remained as an afterimage in his eyes when he finally turned to the window and looked down at the city lying below him. Far away on the rise of the hill he saw the wide-spreading expanse of the Pike Street factory. At the foot of the hill were the old buildings that made up the Water Street plant. They were scattered along the river edge, ivy-covered stone at the turn of Front Street, red corrugated metal on the dry-kiln sheds beyond, the lumber storage yard so distant that it was almost lost in the blue river haze. And then, fading in out of the haze, his mind saw what his eyes could not see, and heard what his ears could not hear, and there were the montaged images and sounds of other Tredway factories . . . the steel-mill clatter and clang of the pipe-bending shop in the Pittsburgh factory . . . the fresh-paint newness of Houston . . . the biting saw-whine that came so strangely from under the Connecticut elms . . . the metallic screaming of the cutoff saws . . . the angry drone of the planers . . . the endlessly pulsating hiss of the sanding rooms . . . the air rush of the finishing lines where man-made tornadoes tried to roar down the snorting animal sounds of the spray guns—and there was a man for every sound . . . the man at the saw with the powder of sawdust like yellow frost on his eyebrows . . . the man on the finishing line with a grotesque inhalator mask for a face . . . a man on the lumber crane with eyes that said he could lift the earth itself if he touched the right levers . . . an ancient whose hand stopped trembling only when it touched a carving chisel . . . a youth who spewed unthought curses at the machine that did his work . . . a ladle-man swilling his mouth with salted water in the foundry . . . men, men, men.

On the wide-angle screen of his new mind, he saw not the single images that he had seen in his old mind but the sum of many images . . . two hundred men on a factory floor . . . a hundred men on a finishing line . . . a thousand men pouring in through the gate when a shift changed, another thousand men flowing out with the turn of the tide.

The screen of his mind broadened and there were other thousands of faces . . . now women, too . . . the girl-crowded warrens of the Tredway Tower . . . humanity packed behind a thousand doors on a hundred corridors . . . Offices in All Principal Cities . . . the packed rows of listening faces at the annual sales meeting . . . a salesman stopping a Tredway automobile to drink a coke at a filling station beside an Arkansas road . . . an old woman dusting furniture in the air-conditioned Chicago display room . . . a sweating man scaling lumber at the edge of a steaming Honduras jungle . . .

He let the picture fade until all detail was lost, blackened into the mass silhouette of the whole. This was the Tredway Corporation . . . all of this . . . the factories and the offices, the buildings and the machines, the men and the women . . . yes, most of all, the men and the women.

The whole was a thing of fearsome complexity and awesome involvement, but Don Walling was conscious of neither fear nor awe until his eyes dropped to the rooftops of the city that lay below him. Imagination stripped away the roofs and exposed the honeycombed hive of activity underneath . . . the milling, swarming, cell-living broods. And the cell-center spark of life in every brood was a Tredway pay check . . . a blue scrap of paper that became green bills in a purse . . . and the green bills became the endless inpouring of food for thousands of ever-emptying stomachs . . . clothes to cover a thousand nakednesses and flap from a thousand clotheslines . . . shoes for the feet of ever-running children . . . beer to soften a man's soul on Saturday night and a freehanded buck for the collection plate on Sunday. His wife needed soul-saving too . . . an uplift brassière and an honest-to-god permanent and a pink bottle full of perfumed hope. But their souls could wait for the kids. The kids come first . . . always . . . from that first day when there was no secret cross-mark on the calendar, through all the nights when they whispered the solemn oath that they'd give the kid what they never had. Yes, the kid would have a chance! It would take money but what the hell— money was only a pay check and there was always a new pay check every Saturday night.

Don Walling felt suspended in space, yet tied to the hive of the earth by the awed realization of his new-found responsibility. They were his . . . all of them . . . the uncounted thousands, born and unborn. If he failed them there would be hunger under those roofs . . . there had been hunger before when the man at the top of the Tower had failed them. Then there would be no food . . . and the belongings of the dispossessed would stand in the streets . . . and a man in a black coat would come to take the children to the orphans' home . . .

The free flow of his new mind was suddenly cut off. Where had that memory come from? Or was it a memory? No, it couldn't be . . . he hadn't known Millburgh in those days when Orrin Tredway had closed the factory and stopped the pay checks. Memory was impossible. Was it something that Avery Bullard had told him? No, there were no remembered words.

But there was the memory of Avery Bullard standing where he was standing now, silently looking down over the rooftops. Yes, perhaps there had been words said that had not been remembered because they were then without meaning, as so many things had been without meaning until now.

The image of Avery Bullard moved across the rooftops like the passing of a cloud shadow. Did the people under those roofs know what Avery Bullard had done for them? Did they realize that if it had not been for Avery Bullard there would be no Tredway Corporation . . . that the Pike Street plant would never have been built . . . that the Water Street factory would have rotted and rusted away like the steel mill and the tannery and the wagon works . . . that there would be no Tredway jobs, no Tredway pay checks?

No, they did not know . . . or, if they knew, they would not acknowledge their belief . . . or, if they believed, they were not willing to pay the price of gratitude. Had any man ever thanked Avery Bullard for what he had done? No. He had died in the loneliness of the unthanked.

Don Walling accepted his fate. He would expect no thanks . . . he would live in loneliness . . . but the Tredway Corporation would go on. There would be jobs and pay checks. There would be no hunger. The belongings of the dispossessed would not stand in the streets. No children would be sent to the orphans' home.

He had been unconscious of time and place, and it was a shock when he finally turned and realized that he was in Dudley's office. It was in the instant of that discovery that he saw the error that his imagination had committed. He had somehow tricked himself into thinking that he would be the man at the top of the Tower. He wouldn't! The president of the Tredway Corporation would be J. Walter Dudley.

He saw the empty chair behind the desk and his mind filled it with the image of the man . . . the too soft body in its too smooth chrysalis of too perfect tailoring . . . the too white hair and the too handsome face . . . the too warm smile . . . the too friendly voice. Yes, that was J. Walter Dudley . . . the perpetual beggar of friendship . . . the man who measured his accomplishment by counting smiles and the men who called him by his first name.

But, in the background, like a chanted warning against revulsion, he heard Alderson's voice saying, "—isn't a man in the furniture business who has more friends than Walt Dudley— important—the right kind of an impression—"

He turned to the window again, to the rooftops and the distant factories and the haze beyond and the all-embracing memory of Avery Bullard. No one had ever said of Avery Bullard what Alderson had said of Walt Dudley—*but it was Avery Bullard who had built the Tredway Corporation!*

The thought was a flashing revelation. Now he saw the terrifying error of Alderson's miscalculation, the total opposition of his two completely incompatible objectives. It was impossible to keep the Tredway Corporation what Avery Bullard had wanted and, at the same time, have Walt Dudley as its president.

For a fleeting moment he remembered what Alderson had said about a "partnership management." A partnership with Dudley? His mind gagged on the thought as his throat would have gagged on a rancid morsel. Alderson was a fumbling old fool . . . a weakling resorting to what was always the weakling's last resort . . . compromise. There could be no partnership! That was ridiculous. Couldn't Alderson see that? There was room for only one man at the top of the Tower . . . one man . . . one voice . . . one strong commanding hand!

Then, suddenly, the memory of what Alderson had said broke into his thought stream. "You can do it, Don, I know you can. You can keep the company going the way he wanted it to go."

The voice repeated itself, echoing and re-echoing, building a thunder of reverberation in the great chamber of his new mind and the sound of thunder was the sound of anger. Alderson had tricked him into accepting Dudley as president! He . . . not Dudley . . . was the one who should be president! Alderson had admitted it . . . "You can do it, Don, you can do it" . . . Alderson knew it . . . he'd known it all the time! Yet now, this very minute, the bumbling old fool was ready to destroy the company by offering the presidency to Dudley!

Don Walling's eyes flashed to his watch. There were only minutes left before Dudley's train arrived. Alderson had to be stopped! He threw open the door and ran blindly toward the elevator.

Loren Shaw's call from Pearson in Chicago had finally come through. He was listening now, his face tight with anger, the fingers of his right hand working nervously as they balled the handkerchief into his palm.

"All right, Pearson," he said with crisp finality. "Apparently there was some slip up on Alderson's part in getting the message to me. What train did you say?—nine-forty-five—yes, I understand—no, that's all for now. Let me know how your meeting goes."

Three quick steps carried him to the door, but he stopped abruptly as if touching the cold brass of the doorknob had chilled the impulse to confront Alderson. He stood for a moment, frozen in indecision, reluctant to give ground by going to Alderson's office, yet pushed on by the desperate need to confirm the suspicion that was forming in his mind. He had to know!

Slowly, he opened the door, listening. There was no sound of footsteps or voices. He opened the door wider and stepped through. Then he saw Don Walling standing at the elevator. It was too late to escape. Walling had seen him.

"Oh, good morning, Don," Loren Shaw said with a quick smile, fighting the tremor that threatened his voice. "Just wondering whether Fred was in his office. Do you happen to know whether or not he's coming in?"

"I don't know," Walling said, turning away to make another impatient stab at the elevator button.

Clawing curiosity forced Shaw to ask, "By the way, did you happen to hear anything about Walt's getting in this morning from Chicago?"

Walling pushed the button again, seeming not to have heard.

Loren Shaw was almost ready to repeat the question, when Walling suddenly said, "He's arriving on the nine-forty-five." The words were tossed over his shoulder, cold with what seemed like disdain.

Loren Shaw's hand found the door and, before Walling could turn to see him, he slipped back into his office. His fingers gripped the doorknob to silence the closing. When his hand came away it was wet with the cold dampness of perspiration that was like the meltage of ice.

Walling's manner had confirmed everything. Alderson was meeting Dudley at the train . . . Walling was going somewhere to join them . . . three votes . . . Grimm would make the fourth. Unless something could be done in a hurry, Alderson had the four votes he needed to elect himself president!

His brain was weary, fatigued to desperation by the hours of hard-whipped demands. He had to do something . . . anything . . . it didn't matter what! Dudley . . . Dudley . . . Dudley . . . he had to hold Dudley! Without Dudley all hope was gone.

9.40 A.M. EDT

Don Walling's impatience had risen to the flare-point of anger. Where in hell was that damned elevator! Only five minutes to train time . . . the whole world ready to blow up . . . and all because of a sleepy bastard on the elevator who . . .

The door slid open.

He plunged through. "Where in hell were you, Luigi?"

"We have a—"

"Hurry, damn it, hurry!"

As the door was closing, he caught a flash glimpse of Erica Martin coming quickly down the stairs and he heard her call his name.

Luigi reached out to open the door again.

"No! Damn it, Luigi, I'm in a hurry."

They were dropping through space, the lighted floor numbers flashing on the control panel like the tolled backcounted seconds before a catastrophic explosion.

"We have a meeting, all the operators," Luigi was saying in pleading apology. "We buy flowers for the funeral and I am the one to do it. You understand—it is an election? I cannot help that everybody votes for me to be the one who buys the flowers."

"All right, Luigi, all right," he said in crisp forgiveness. The door was starting to open and he reached out, hurrying it with the full strength of his arm.

Plunging ahead, Don Walling was not aware that Luigi had stepped out of the cab and was watching with the wonder-struck awe of a man who has seen a miracle.

9.42 A.M. EDT

The blaring loudspeaker announced that the train from Chicago was arriving on Track 2 and Frederick Alderson took one last look toward the stairway, giving himself the final assurance that Shaw was not going to put in a surprise appearance at the last moment.

He saw that the waiting crowd had edged forward to watch for the approaching train and he picked a path down the opposite side of the platform to avoid the possibility of being intercepted by someone he knew. He needed this last minute to prepare what he would say to Walt Dudley. There had to be a right way to say it . . . you couldn't just walk up to a man and tell him that he was going to be president of the Tredway Corporation. There had to be a preamble . . . a leading in . . . something about Avery Bullard. Yes, something about Avery Bullard would give him a chance to bring in the business about Walling. That was the part that had be be handled most carefully of all . . . telling Dudley that he had to accept Walling as the executive vice-president. Dudley might not like that . . . might have to argue with him . . . tell him that he and Jesse had decided . . . no, he couldn't bring Jesse into it, not after what Jesse had said on the phone . . . at least not until he'd talked to him again and explained how it had happened. Jesse would be forced to admit that he had done only what had to be done. They had to have Walling's vote. One more minute and Walling would have gone over to Shaw. Yes, that's what Jesse had to realize . . . that Walling had been almost lost . . . that he had caught him in the nick of time.

The train came into view around the jutting cliff beyond Joyland Park, the electric horn moaning like the cry of a wounded beast, the bells at the crossing ringing out a frightening warning.

Frederick Alderson took a deep breath and with the rising of his chest he saw a thread of lint on the almost black suit that Edith had selected for him to wear today. Carefully, he picked off the thread, squared his shoulders, and then stiffened his body against the rush of the train.

J. Walter Dudley was the first man out of the roomette car, nodding to the beaming porter, smiling his acknowledgment of the running arrival of Lester who was the one redcap still on duty at the Millburgh station.

Alderson saw the quick change of Dudley's expression as he recognized him, the fast flipping of masks that traded the smile for funereal sobriety. It was a momentary backstage glimpse of the actor caught unaware and, although he had seen Dudley make the same quick change many times before, it had a strangely disturbing effect now. As Dudley walked toward him, he could not remember what it was that he had intended to say first.

"Fred, I appreciate this more than I can tell you," Dudley said, his voice hushed with a house-of-grief tone.

"Thought I'd meet you," Alderson mumbled.

"I can't believe he's gone, Fred. I just can't believe it."

Lester was waiting with his bags. "Taxi, Mr. Dudley, or you got your car?"

Dudley started to speak but Alderson interrupted. "You'd better have them checked, Walt. We're going over to the club for a few minutes—have a little talk."

There was an instant of hesitation, another flashing mask change, and then Dudley said respectfully, "You bet, Fred, whatever you say. Get that, Lester—check 'em?"

Lester pocketed the dollar bill and hurried ahead of them.

Alderson started to follow but Dudley's arm stopped him. They stood facing each other.

"Fred, I don't know how to say this but—well, I just want you to know that you can count on me—one hundred per cent. But you know that without my saying it, don't you, Fred?"

Alderson felt the embarrassment of letting Dudley think what was obviously in his mind.

"I'm not taking the presidency, Walt."

Dudley was caught between masks. "You're not?"

"No."

"Oh—well, I'm sorry to hear that, Fred, darned sorry. I thought of course that—"

"Let's go over to the club. We can talk there without being disturbed."

As they walked up the stairs there was silence between them and Alderson was conscious of its strangeness. Silence was a mask that he had never before known Walt Dudley to wear.

At the head of the stairs, habitually glancing at the front door as he had done so many times in the minutes before the train arrived, Frederick Alderson saw Don Walling's hurried entrance. He was clearly the anxious pursuer as he stopped, alert and head high, his eyes sweeping the waiting room.

It was only by the barest chance that Dudley missed seeing Walling. In the instant when he might have seen him, Dudley turned toward the bank of checking lockers to pick up the keys from Lester, and then had been stopped by old Dr. Deever from the Seminary.

The flip of Walling's hand toward the men's room was an obvious signal. Alderson, after an anxious backward glance to make certain that Dudley's back was still safely turned, walked hurriedly to the washroom entrance.

Walling was waiting inside the vestibule. "Have you said anything to him yet?"

"No, I'm taking him over to the club to talk—"

"Don't do it. It's off."

"But we—"

"I can't go through with it."

"But you said—"

"No, damn it, no! Get rid of him—stall—anything—but don't say a word, not a word!"

"I'll meet you at the club as soon as I can," Alderson said, automatically, the words completely involuntary, the response of motor centers that, after thirty years, had taught themselves to act on the sound of Avery Bullard's voice even before there was a nerve-sent signal from his own brain.

9.50 A.M. EDT

Luigi opened the door on the twenty-fourth floor.

Erica Martin was waiting for him, but she made no move to enter the cab.

"You took Mr. Walling down a few minutes ago, didn't you, Luigi?"

"Mr. Walling? Yes, I take him down."

"Do you know how soon he's coming back?"

Luigi spread his hands in a broad gesture of negation. "All I know is—very big hurry—very important."

"You don't know where he was going?"

Luigi repeated the gesture.

"When he comes back, Luigi, will you tell him that I want to see him as soon as possible?"

"Sure, Miss Martin, I tell him right away."

"Thank you, Luigi."

"He's fine man—Mr. Walling," Luigi said quickly, stopping the turn that she had started to make.

"Yes, he is. A very fine man."

"How soon he move up?"

"What?"

Luigi used a little smile to tell Miss Martin that it was no use to try to fool him. "I know—after the funeral, then he will move. Before that it would not be right."

She stared at him. "Luigi, he—he didn't tell you anything that—" Of course he hadn't . . . no one knew . . . no one

[254]

could possibly know until the directors' meeting on Tuesday
. . . perhaps not even then.

Luigi used the little smile again. Miss Martin was very surprised that he knew something that he was not supposed to
know. "You don't worry, Miss Martin. I don't tell nobody.
Many years—many things I know I don't tell."

Going down the shaft, Luigi speculated on the strangeness of
Miss Martin's being, in some ways, so very much like Maria. It
always made Maria feel badly to have him guess a secret. Sometimes she would be very angry, so angry that she would sleep
with her back to him the whole night and not even get up to
fix his breakfast.

Regretfully, Luigi acknowledged the fact that he was not a
very smart man. A man who was smart would not let a woman
know that he had guessed a secret. But Miss Martin would forgive him. Miss Martin was a very fine woman. It was nice that
she would not be alone after the funeral. After the Duke had
died the Duchess had lived alone in the castle all the rest of her
life and it was said in the village that there was no night when
she did not cry. That was very bad. It was good that a woman
should cry sometimes because that was her nature . . . and
afterward she was a better woman . . . but it was not good
that a woman should cry every night because she did not have
a man. Every woman should have a man . . . even if he was
not a smart man. That was what he often told Maria and he
knew that Maria knew it was true even if she would not very
often say that it was true. But it was better not to make a
woman say that something was true . . . just as it was better
not to let a woman know that you had guessed her secret.

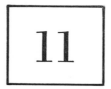

11

LONG ISLAND SOUND
9.52 A.M. EDT

THE SOUND was as flat as a mirror, a dirty mirror, streaked with the scum lines that marked the flow of the tidal currents. Two hours before there had been the promise of a northerly wind but the promise had been broken with the rising sun and now there was not enough air moving to keep *Moonsweep's* mainsail from slatting wildly as the cutter rolled to the wake of a far-passing steamer. The swell moved on toward the shore and George Caswell's eyes followed its passage across the glassy water until it finally broke as a single wave against the Yacht Club dock.

All around them lay the other yachts that were waiting for the start of the race. They squatted as wounded birds, their sails hanging like broken wings. The reflecting surface of the smooth water amplified the sound of a hundred voices and carried them through the still air with amazing clarity, setting up a chatter that sounded more like a cocktail party than a yacht race, an illusion that was enhanced by the floating beer cans that littered the water and, occasionally catching the sun, sparkled like embedded jewels.

For the last half-hour, George Caswell had regretted the habit-made decision that made him come aboard this morning, but now that he was there he could think of no explainably plausible reason for going back ashore. Deserting his crew in the face of a dull drifting match was hardly a sporting thing to do and therefore completely beyond consideration.

Actually, as he had told himself a dozen times, his gnawing inner desire to get to Millburgh at once was also completely insupportable. There was no reason to go. Nothing would happen over the weekend. Everyone would be too stunned by Avery Bullard's death to even start thinking about who the new president might be until after the funeral.

Resigned to patience, he stretched out on the cabin top and stared up at the sky where, as in a mirage, he saw himself in the directors' room of the Tredway Corporation. Admittedly, he would not be able to match Avery Bullard's familiarity with the technical details of furniture manufacture, but that would be no bar to the successful performance of his duties as president. Actually, it might be a help rather than a hindrance . . . he would have the benefit of a more detached attitude. That was a point that A. R. Andrews had made a few weeks ago when they had been talking about Chloro-Chemical . . . managing Tredway would be fairly simple . . . nothing like as difficult as Chloro-Chemical. Andrews was always having some new scientific development come along to upset his applecart. There would be nothing like that at Tredway. Furniture manufacturing was stabilized. Except for a little mechanization coming along now and then, there hadn't been any seriously disturbing changes in the last hundred years. Yes, furniture was a nice stable business . . . the kind of business a man could enjoy.

He brushed away a seagoing housefly that was buzzing around his nose and began to sketch in the first rough outline of his presidential plan, remembering the advice that he had given Ronnie Atkins when he had gone in as president of Rookery Paper, the repetition of advice that he had heard his father give another new corporation president many years before.

Yes, that was the thing to do . . . not try to be another Bullard . . . different approach . . . change of pace. And it would be sound, too . . . more delegation of authority . . . spread the management down the line. Bullard had missed some bets there. With a man like Jesse Grimm as vice-president in charge of manufacturing, there was no reason why the president had to get into that end of it very deeply himself . . . just see that Jesse, in turn, delegated down the line. Same thing with the sales side . . . Dudley was a top-notch man, no question about that, just give him his head. Shaw was an excellent comptroller . . . very thorough, completely reliable. Alderson had the experience background . . . good source of advice . . . use him the way Andrews had used old Mallinson. Walling? Walling was one of those bright young chaps . . . ideas . . . good to have around . . . kept you sparked up. Fine bunch of men . . . hard to beat. With a crowd like that around him, a president didn't have to worry too much about . . .

"See that, sir?"

The voice was above him and he looked up into Ken Case's anxious face. "What?"

Ken was pointing and Caswell rolled his body to let his eyes follow Case's finger to the committee boat at the far end of the starting line. A yellow and blue pennant was flying.

"Another postponement, sir," Ken explained.

Caswell sat up, rubbing a back muscle that had been crushed against the grab rail.

"I've been thinking, sir," Case said, "if you're planning to get back ashore in time for the Brighton wedding—well, sir, it looks now like the race is going to be nothing but a ghoster. It's bound to be a late finish—maybe over the time limit."

He grasped at the straw. "Ken, I do hate to leave you fellows to fight it out alone, but I am afraid you're right about Mrs. Caswell rather counting on me to turn up for that wedding. Sure you wouldn't mind too much?"

"Not at all, sir," Case said, catching himself when he heard his voice sounding a shade too eager. "Of course, it won't be the same without you, sir, but we'll give it the old fight—huh, fellows?"

There was a chatter of agreement from the cockpit and as the boom swung, Caswell saw the other crew members watching him . . . fine bunch of boys. "Well, perhaps it would be best." He walked aft and started down the companionway. "I'm sure you'll do quite as well without me."

The general disagreement was pleasantly reassuring.

"Shall I blow the launch for you, sir?" Ken Case called down.

"Oh, yes, please do."

Case was a nice, clean-cut boy . . . be a good idea to find a spot for him down at Tredway after he finished Harvard Business. There were a few things that Avery Bullard hadn't been entirely right about and one of them was that all the good boys came from the Middle West.

He heard Ken blow the launch signal and by the time he had changed his clothes and come back on deck, the club tender was already lying alongside.

"Sorry about the weather, sir," Ken called down from the rail as Caswell seated himself in the launch. "Next week we'll try to whistle up a real sailing breeze for you."

"Good luck," he called back as the launch started. There was no point in saying that there would be no next week, that he would never step aboard *Moonsweep* again. There would be no spare weekends after he took over the presidency of the Tredway Corporation.

Looking back over the bubbling wake of the launch, George Caswell saw the yacht grow smaller and smaller, farther and farther away. He felt no regret. She was already a part of the past.

The launch landed him on the dinghy float and, because his eyes were down to watch his step as he crossed the plank that joined the float to the wharf, he did not see Bruce Pilcher until they were face to face.

"This must be my lucky day," Pilcher said affably. "I drove out on the chance that I might see you, only to find that you were out on your boat. It was pure luck that I happened to see the launch picking you up. You're not racing?"

It was a direct question and an answer was unavoidable. He made it as short as possible. "No."

"I'd like to talk to you for a few minutes."

George Caswell hesitated. The circumstances under which he was almost certain that Pilcher had made the short sale of Tredway stock had generated a feeling close to disgust, yet his ingrained gentility made open discourtesy difficult. He said, as coldly as he felt he dared, "I'm rather busy this morning."

"Not too busy, I'm sure, to be interested in what I have to tell you," Pilcher said confidently. "It concerns the Tredway Corporation."

"I suspected as much." He was not surprised that there was no humility in Pilcher's approach. He often dealt with men whose prime asset was their ability to run a good bluff when they were in a tight spot.

"I'm assuming, of course, that you know of Bullard's death," Pilcher said.

"Yes." He started to walk up the path, forcing Pilcher to follow him.

"What you may or may not know is that Mr. Bullard had a conference yesterday with Mr. Steigel and myself."

"I know."

"Good," Pilcher said as if an important first point had been made. "What I'm quite certain that you don't know, Mr. Caswell, is what transpired at that meeting."

Caswell held a cautious silence to cover the moment while he considered a question that flashed into his mind. Had Avery Bullard gone so far as to offer Pilcher the executive vice-presidency? It was highly unlikely—yet, knowing Bullard's tendency toward snap judgment and impulsive action, he conceded to himself that there was an outside chance that it might have happened.

"A rather important agreement was negotiated at our meeting," Pilcher went on, "and since it vitally affects the Tredway Corporation—as well as your own interests—I felt justified in coming to you for some counsel as to how I should proceed from this point forward. Of course, if Mr. Bullard's unfortunate death had not intervened—"

"What was the agreement?" Caswell cut in.

"Cigarette?" Pilcher asked, delaying the revelation as if he were savoring its content.

"No, thank you."

They walked a few steps, Caswell determined not to break the silence.

"Perhaps I'm assuming more interest than you have," Pilcher said finally. "I thought you might like to know that we negotiated the sale of Odessa Stores to the Tredway Corporation."

George Caswell's self-control was forced to the limit but he managed to avoid a visible reaction. After the first moment, however, he realized that his silence might be interpreted as acceptance. He stopped, facing Pilcher, his hand on the rail that bordered the walk. "I'm afraid I find that rather surprising."

"Yes, it worked out more rapidly than I expected, too," Pilcher said, his voice bland with assurance.

"What was the basis of the sale?"

"Quite favorable to both parties I should say—three million dollars in cash and ten thousand shares of Tredway common."

Caswell had been prepared to disbelieve anything that Pilcher might say, but a quick mental calculation based on the market value of Tredway common made him see that Bullard might well have jumped at a chance to buy Odessa Stores at what was obviously a bargain price. But logic still failed to counteract his suspicion and he said cautiously, "I'm sure it's unnecessary to remind you, Mr. Pilcher, that any agreement Mr. Bullard might have signed was necessarily contingent upon the confirmation of the Tredway board. I am assuming, of course, that there was a signed agreement?"

"No, unfortunately not," Pilcher said without hesitation. "And to further complicate the problem, Mr. Steigel had a stroke last night. It's the opinion of the doctors that he may never regain consciousness. I'm sure you can see that it's a rather unusual situation."

"Extremely!"

"Exactly—and that's why I felt compelled to seek your advice."

George Caswell hesitated, his anger rising. "My advice would be to forget the whole thing, Pilcher, and as quickly as possible."

"Isn't that a rather hasty judgment?" Bruce Pilcher asked with cool cynicism.

"I can't imagine anyone taking you very seriously. What weight would anyone give to a verbal agreement—"

"—with one of the parties dead," Pilcher picked up, "—the other party completely paralyzed and most unlikely to live through the day—and myself as the only witness. I'm quite willing to admit, as I did before, that it's a highly unusual situation. There is, however, one further fact of some importance. Before he lost consciousness, Julius Steigel told his grandson, Bernard, of our agreement. Since Bernard will be the old man's principal heir, and since he revered his grandfather's judgment, I'm sure he'll be quite willing to complete the deal. There'll be no trouble on that score. From Tredway's standpoint—well, if you're at all familiar with Odessa's statement, I'm sure you can see that it's a bargain price, barely more than current assets. No Tredway director could conceivably vote against confirmation."

"I'm not so certain of that," Caswell said, guarding his voice against an admission of what was undeniably true.

"With further thought, I think you will be," Pilcher smiled. "Now the second point—and I'm sure this will interest you—is that Tredway will undoubtedly float a new stock issue to fund the purchase. Caswell & Co., of course, will handle it. In addition, the security business involved in the settling of the Steigel estate will be considerable. As a rough estimate, I would say that the total profit of Caswell & Co.—properly handled, of course—might approximate a quarter of a million dollars."

The cold chill of anger almost froze George Caswell's voice in his throat. "What's your angle, Pilcher?"

"Angle?" Pilcher asked as if he were surprised at Caswell's use of the word. "Naturally I have an interest."

"Naturally."

Bruce Pilcher snapped his long fingers and flipped his cigarette in a high arc out over the green grass. "All I want for myself is the presidency of the Tredway Corporation."

Caswell knew that he was staring at Pilcher in open astonishment but he was too shocked to make any further attempt to keep from displaying his true feelings.

"You seem surprised," Pilcher said, "—at the modesty of my ambition, no doubt—but that's all I want for myself, Mr. Caswell, only the presidency of Tredway—plus, as you'd expect, the quite normal option to buy a block of Tredway stock at a favorable price. Shall we say ten thousand shares at forty?"

"You're asking me to go along with this?" Caswell asked.

"I think it might be to your interest."

For the first time in his life, George Caswell gave way to total anger. "Pilcher, of all of the rotten bastards that I have ever known, you are unquestionably the worst! You're everything that I despise, everything that—" His voice broke off in trembling rage.

Pilcher's smile froze on his face, but he was a good enough actor to keep his voice almost unchanged. "I must say I find that a rather surprising reaction."

"Shut up, Pilcher! To begin with you're a liar. I know what happened! Yesterday, after you saw Bullard drop dead, you sold Tredway short—two thousand shares."

Pilcher's face blanched. "How did you—?"

"If there were one word of truth in any of the damned lies that you've been telling me, you wouldn't have sold that stock short. God, what a bastard you are!"

Propelled by the force of anger that could no longer be trusted to express itself in words, George Caswell spun on his heel and strode rapidly away.

Behind him he heard Pilcher's muffled shout. "You'll not get away with this, Caswell! No man can call me—damn you, I'll get what I want and you can't stop me!"

There were lost minutes while George Caswell sat in his car waiting for the trembling aftermath of his anger to subside. He was stunned at having experienced an emotional intensity far beyond anything of which he had ever thought himself capable.

With the slow return of clear-headed thinking, he remembered Pilcher's parting threat. One thing was certain . . . Pilcher would stop at nothing to get the presidency of the Tredway Corporation. If Pilcher should talk to Julia Tredway Prince . . .

He stepped hard on the starter and the motor roared. It was an act of decision. He dared not waste a minute in getting to Millburgh.

NEW YORK CITY
10.17 A.M. EDT

"I don't know what to do about going to Chicago tonight," Alex Oldham said uneasily.

"Well, of course you won't go, dear," his wife said astonished at such a ridiculous idea.

"We'll have a devil of a lot of customers out there in Chicago on Monday. I don't know what—" He stopped, embarrassed at the absent-mindedness that had almost made him say that he didn't know what Mr. Bullard would think of a district manager missing the first day of the Chicago market. "I guess you're right, dear," he said submissively. "I ought to go down for the funeral."

"Of course I'm right. Monday's no day not to be in Millburgh."

He knew what she meant . . . things would be happening in Millburgh . . . out of sight, out of mind. She was right.

KENT COUNTY, MARYLAND
10.18 A.M. EDT

"Goodness, Jesse, I don't know what we're going to do with a whole dozen soft crabs."

"Eat 'em. You never really had a soft crab until you ate one just out of the water like that."

Sarah Grimm opened the refrigerator door. "What did he charge you, Jesse?"

"Charge? Nothing. Herb was just being friendly," he said, not thinking it necessary to say that he had spent an hour tinkering Herb's water pump. That was just being friendly, too.

"That's nice, isn't it?" She was moving the milk bottles and the butter jar so that the crabs could be right next to the freezing unit. "Down here it's a lot like it used to be in Pittsburgh, isn't it, Jesse? Remember the time that Mrs. Kerchek brought over that Polish soup when you had the flu?"

He watched her, wondering if she wasn't being a little too cheerful, trying to keep his mind off Avery Bullard's death. "Sarah?"

She turned, wiping her hands.

"Sarah, you sure we're doing the right thing? If you wanted it, you could be the wife of the president of the Tredway Corporation."

Her little smile was as quick as her voice. "I'd rather have free soft-shell crabs and a live husband to eat them."

"Okay, Sarah, I just wanted to be sure."

"You aren't going to regret it, are you, Jesse?"

He looked at her for a long time. "Not if you figure you can stand me around underfoot all day long."

"I guess I'll manage," she said, looking at him sidewise, the way she used to do years ago when she was expecting to be kissed.

NEW YORK CITY
10.21 A.M. EDT

The dress hung in soft scarlet folds over the clerk's arm. "Will this be a charge or will you pay for it?"

"I got the money here," Anne Finnick said. She stepped back into the dressing room and pulled the curtain. It wasn't any of that snooty clerk's business how much money she had. Some of the bills still looked kind of funny from being all soaked the way they were, but she found three twenties that looked all right.

[265]

"But, George darling, you can't!" Kitty Caswell squealed in horror-stricken anguish. "We have to go to Nancy Brighton's wedding this afternoon at six."

She had been put out when he came home to pack a bag and had surprised him as he was leaving a note for her on the front-hall table.

"I'm sorry, Kitty, but I have no choice. Something very important has come up."

"What?"

"It's just business, dear. Don't bother your pretty little head about it."

"I want to know."

"Kitty darling, I—"

"Tell me."

He took a deep breath that barely escaped being a sigh. "A very unscrupulous man is trying to get control of the Tredway Corporation and I have to stop him."

"Who?"

"No one you'd know, dear. Now I do have to hurry or—"

"What's his name?"

He took another deep breath. "His name is Pilcher."

"Pilcher?"

"Now, dear—" He lifted his bag.

"No," she nodded in studied agreement. "We've never had him to dinner. I'm sure of that."

"And we never will!"

He started to plant a farewell kiss, but her voice held his lips away. "Is he really unscrupulous?"

"Very!"

"Maybe we should have him to dinner, George. He sounds interesting. All of the other people we know are so terribly scrupulous."

"Kitty, don't be a fool!" he said too sharply, immediately

softening his voice to wipe the spanked child look from her face. "I'm sorry, dear, but I do have to go."

"All right," she said contritely, tiptoeing up for the kiss.

He said what he hadn't intended to say. "Maybe I can be back in time for the wedding."

She glanced at his bag. "You're just saying that."

"It's only an hour each way and with some luck I might get through in time."

"An hour?"

"I called Ronnie and he's letting me have his plane."

"Oh, George, no! Not in that awful little plane."

"Darling, it's not a little plane—it's his company's DC 3 and they have—"

Unaccountably, she quickly pulled down his face and kissed him again, fervent and crushing, and then quickly broke away. "Hurry, dear, or you won't get back in time."

12

MILLBURGH, PENNSYLVANIA
10.29 A.M. EDT

Don Walling had been at the Federal Club for a full half-hour waiting for Alderson to arrive. How in hell could the old man have taken that much time to get rid of Dudley . . . even if he had driven him all the way home? Talk! Yes, damn it, that was Alderson's trouble . . . talk, talk, talk . . . but they were a pair, Alderson and Dudley . . . probably sitting out there now yapping their heads off.

The long wait had sensitized his nerve ends until every sound was an irritation. From behind the closed doors of the Wagon Room, he heard the crash of a heavy object and jumped up to begin another aimless pacing of the room. Why had Alderson wanted to meet him here in this godforsaken place? The Federal Club was a damned morgue at any time of day . . . all the worse at ten-thirty in the forenoon.

Footsteps sounded in the hall and he wheeled to face the door. It was only an old man shuffling past toward the kitchen. He looked like a flophouse bum, but a glimpse of his face made Don Walling recognize him as one of the old waiters who, after he was attired in his immaculate uniform, would become the social arbiter upon whom Federal Club members would call to verify their own high standing when out-of-town guests were present . . . "Yes sir, old Joe here remembers when my father used to bring me in here when I was only a kid in knickers, don't you, Joe?" . . . and old Joe, or Harry, or George, or whoever it was, would always say, "Yes," because the waiters were a part of the club, too, and as anxious to have an honored past as any of the regular members.

The past! Yes, that was the trouble with the Federal Club crowd . . . and a hell of a lot of other people, too. They thought the past meant something. It didn't! The past was done . . . finished . . . water over the dam. There was nothing you could do about it. Yesterday didn't matter. It was today that counted . . . today and tomorrow and next week and next month. God, but there was a lot to do . . . get that experimental press rigged and no damned makeshift setup, either . . . push that work on the highspeed dry kiln to get rid of that honeycombing . . . and don't try to tell me it can't be done because it can . . . burn the tail off those railroad boys for another siding at Pike Street and keep burning until you get some action because one of these days we're going to need that warehouse and all hell will break loose if . . .

"Oh good morning, Mr. Walling." It was a voice that sounded as if it had been breathed over a lapel carnation. Don Walling turned to recognize the club steward. He had stepped out of the Wagon Room, hastily closing the door as if to guard the room's secret contents.

Walling was surprised that the steward knew his name because, on the infrequent occasions when he came to the club for lunch, the steward always managed to be fully occupied with the window-tables that were secretly reserved for the members whose ancestry traced to an old North Front family.

"Dear, dear," the steward said. "So very sad about Mr. Bullard, isn't it? One of our most valued members. A splendid man, splendid indeed." He spied a stray scrap of paper on the floor and his arm pecked down for it like the long neck of a feeding

[269]

bird. "You must excuse us, Mr. Walling. This time of the morning we're not quite tidied up, you know. It's rare indeed to have one of our good members put in an appearance before noon."

"I'm waiting for Mr. Alderson," Walling said in forced explanation. "He's meeting me here."

"Oh, Mr. Alderson? Yes, indeed! Splendid man, isn't he, splendid, indeed." A thought seemed to strike him and he raised his hand as if he were holding a teacup. "Perhaps while you're waiting—there's Mr. Alderson now."

"I'm sorry it took so long," Alderson said in weary apology. He was breathing hard as if he had been walking rapidly. "I thought the best thing to do was to run him out to his house. Taking him to the office would have meant dumping him into Shaw's lap."

Walling found himself nodding in agreement. Alderson's apologetic manner had already dulled the edge of his annoyance. "Where can we talk?"

"Upstairs in one of the cardrooms?" It was a question, not a statement, and Alderson's voice seemed resignedly apprehensive.

Climbing the stairs, Don Walling thought for the first time of what he might say to Alderson. The preplanning of conversation was something that he seldom did, but he was aware now of the special difficulty he faced. He couldn't come right out and say that he—Don Walling—was the man who should be president of the Tredway Corporation. Of course, Alderson had said practically the same thing out there at his house this morning . . . but he'd have to get Alderson to say it again and then make him see his mistake about Dudley. Yes, that would be the best way to do it . . . but damn it, he couldn't fool around too long humoring the old codger . . . there was work to be done!

The cardroom they entered was one of several cubicles that had been sleeping rooms a hundred years ago when the club had been the Federal Tavern. There was little more space than was needed for a round green-felted table and its circle of chairs. Walling brushed the wall as he edged in and sat down. He saw

Alderson hesitate and for an instant he thought it was a sign of subservience, waiting to be asked to sit, but a glance at his face erased that possibility. Alderson's hesitance was something else and he couldn't be quite sure what it was.

"Well, what happened?" Walling asked crisply, breaking the silence.

Alderson looked surprised, as if he hadn't expected the question. "I told you. I drove him out to his house."

"What did he say?"

"Say? I didn't tell him anything, so there wasn't anything for him to say."

"You must have talked about something."

There was a rack of poker chips in the center of the table and Alderson reached out and picked a blue chip off the top of the stack. "We—he talked about Avery Bullard."

Walling leaned forward, his elbows on the table, softening his voice in an uncalculated effort to ease the tenseness. "Fred, I know you must have thought I was crazy, grabbing you at the station like that, but I had to do it. When I got over to the office and started thinking about what the president of the company had to be—the things he'd have to do—damn it, Fred, can't you see it? Walt Dudley couldn't swing it. There just isn't enough there—not enough strength—not enough anything. He can't do it, that's all!"

Alderson was methodically stacking blue chips. "I thought he might—with you there to help him."

There was the opening! It had come easier than he expected, sooner than he had anticipated. "All that means, Fred, is that I'd have to do the job."

"He'd help you," Alderson said, but without conviction.

"No. That's what I could see after I started to think about it. Walt wouldn't help me. He'd be a hindrance—a millstone around my neck—something that I'd have to push out of the way every time I wanted to get anything done."

He saw Alderson's trembling hand touch the stack of chips and they fell with a slithering clatter. Why didn't Alderson say something? All right, let him keep quiet . . . Alderson didn't matter, anyway! Where had he gotten this crazy idea that it was Alderson who would decide . . . that the presidency was something that Alderson could hand out? Who the hell did Alderson think he was . . . he'd never been anything but a clerk . . . nothing but a . . .

"I'd hoped I wouldn't have to tell you this," Alderson said, his voice so low that Walling had to relisten to the echoed memory of the words before he could be sure that he had heard them.

"Tell me what?"

Alderson restacked the chips. "I didn't want to tell you this because—because there wasn't anything that could be done about it and—well, I didn't want you to get the wrong idea about Jesse."

"Jesse?"

"When I called him this morning—"

He saw Alderson's face slacken, as if the words that had come to his lips were too heavy to speak. What was he going to pull now . . . another one of those cock and bull stories to excuse himself . . . like that business this morning about his wife not wanting him to . . .

Alderson took a deep breath and his rising shoulders lifted his head. "When I talked to Jesse this morning, it was my idea to make *you* the new president—but Jesse wouldn't go along."

The mainspring snapped. "Jesse wouldn't—what do you mean?"

"I've told you that much—suppose I might as well tell you the rest," Alderson said wearily, his forefinger slowly tapping the top of the chip stack. "Jesse said that he'd vote with me—for whoever I decided—as long as it wasn't either Shaw or you."

"Shaw or—Fred, I—I can't believe that—Jesse and I have always been friends—worked together—I can't believe that he feels that way about me."

"Don't ask me why."

"I *am* asking you why."

"I don't know."

"What else did he say?"

"Nothing. I tried to talk to him—but you know how Jesse is."

Alderson looked at him and there was the misery of compassion in his eyes. "That's one thing you learn when you get to be an old man—the thing I said this morning—I was thinking about this then—you never really know what's in any man's mind. You think you do, but you don't. Sometimes you don't even know what's in your own mind until something comes along and forces you into finding out."

"I guess that's right," Don Walling mumbled, staring down at the bull's-eye of a gray ring that someone's highball glass had left on the green felt. "Fred, I owe you an apology. At least—well, I want to thank you for the way you felt about me."

"Don't feel too badly about Jesse. He's a strange man—always has been."

The admonition was a reminder, a catalyst that suddenly transformed disappointment into anger. "It's a damned good thing he is retiring! A two-faced bastard that would—"

"Wait!" Alderson said with unexpected sharpness. "There's no reason to—"

"How would you feel if a man you'd trusted stabbed you in the back?"

"That's happened," Alderson said with disarming mildness.

"I know, but—"

"There's no reason why this has to change anything," Alderson said. "I'm sorry I had to tell you—I knew how you'd feel—but, at least, you realize now that making Dudley president wasn't just an old man's crazy idea. You'll be executive vice-president and that will put you in a spot where—"

"If Jesse wouldn't vote for me for president, why will he vote for me as executive vice-president?"

Alderson picked up the chips and let them click through the cage of his fingers. "Because there isn't anything else that he can do. It has to be either you or Shaw and—well, I think I can make Jesse see that it ought to be you."

The chair fell as Walling stood up, crashing into the silence. He made no move to pick it up. "In that case, Jesse can go to hell and you can tell him so with my compliments."

He kicked the chair out of the way, pushing toward the door.

Another chair fell as Alderson blocked the way. "Don't take it this way, Don. We need you—the company needs you—"

"But I don't need the company," he flashed. He didn't! No! To hell with it! If that was all he was . . . a bad second.choice for Shaw . . .

Blindly, he shoved through the door and started down the hall. Alderson's following footsteps were only the pursuit of something that had to be escaped.

10.50 A.M. EDT

Julia Tredway Prince stepped into the closet, her fingertips playing over the hangers. She was trying to decide what dress she would wear. It was a difficult decision to make because she felt impelled to reject what she liked best. It was important not to be too well dressed. That Martin woman would probably turn up in something dull and secretaryish and there would be barrier enough between them without adding the additional block of making her feel self-conscious about her clothes. She had to put her at ease, get her talking. That was why she had told Nina that they would have lunch in the breakfast room . . . if she decided to have her stay for lunch . . . and the lunch would be nothing but what a secretary would normally eat, consommé and a chicken salad sandwich.

She pulled out an old black crepe and decided that it would do if she took off the rhinestone clips.

10.54 A.M. EDT

The dregs of anger can be either a sedative or a stimulant, depending upon the mind in which they settle. To Don Walling, as he entered the lobby of the Tredway Tower, they were both in alternation. A dozen times in the last five minutes his emo-

[274]

tions had swung the cycle from depression to determination.

He had escaped Alderson with the excuse that he would rather walk than ride, but there was no escape from the memory of Jesse Grimm's treachery. He had coldly and maliciously robbed him of his destiny . . . destroying the whole point and purpose of his existence . . . and there was no way to stop him.

Don Walling slumped again with the listlessness of hopeless despair—but then came the quick counterreaction, the surge of fighting spirit that was so close to the basic urge for self-preservation that it took on the same blindly desperate quality. He wouldn't be licked! He couldn't be!

"Miss Martin—she wants to see you right away," Luigi said as he stepped into the elevator cab.

They were halfway up before the words filtered through to his consciousness.

"You go twenty-four to see Miss Martin?" Luigi was asking.

"All right—twenty-four," he said, not thinking, his voice directed by the habit of responding to a call from Miss Martin as if it were a call from Avery Bullard himself.

There was the hush of death on the twenty-fourth floor and he regretted his decision, but it was too late to turn down the stairs. Erica Martin had heard the elevator door open and was coming out of her office to meet him.

"Oh, thank you for coming, Mr. Walling. I was afraid that I might not have a chance to see you."

The words spilled out as if waiting had accumulated an impelling pressure behind them, making them sound strange to him, and they must have sounded strange to her as well because she added quickly, as if it were a needed explanation, "I had a call this morning from Mrs. Prince. I tried to catch you as you were leaving but I was a second too late."

"A call for me?"

"No, for me. But I wanted your advice. She says there's a box of her personal papers in Mr. Bullard's vault that she wants this morning."

"Do you know anything about it?"

The instant of hesitation made her admission seem reluctant. "Yes, there's a box with her name on it."

"Do you know any reason why she shouldn't have it?"

Again there was that almost imperceptible instant of reluctance.

"No, I don't suppose I do."

This was his chance! He saw it as a boxer sees an opening, a reflex reaction that was faster than thought. A second before he had not known that he wanted to talk to Julia Tredway Prince. Now, instantly, it had become the key maneuver in the first stage of his battle plan. "Suppose you let me take care of it, Miss Martin," he said. "I'll drop it off on my way home."

"Would you?" Her reply was a beat too fast, as her other replies had been a beat too slow. "Are you sure you wouldn't mind?"

"Not at all."

"I'll get it for you."

She crossed her own office and, with only a suggestion of hesitation, opened the door of Avery Bullard's. Don Walling followed her into the cathedral dusk of the big room. The aura of death hung like a heavy vapor. The curtains were drawn and the only light came from the colored shafts that the high sun sent down through the ports between the heavy ceiling beams.

Erica Martin, moving as a shadow in the darkness, went to the wall safe. The door stood open and her hands found the small black-enameled box as if her eyes were unneeded. She gave it to him. "There's something I suppose you should know, Mr. Walling—in case Mrs. Prince mentions it. She asked me to bring this out myself."

"Personally?"

"Yes."

He hesitated, reluctant to lose what he had gained. "Perhaps there are some valuable papers."

"I don't think so. I suspect that it was simply a way to force me to go to her home."

"Why would she want to do that?"

"Because—" She caught herself and he knew that what she

[276]

would say now was not what her first impulse had made her want to say. "I don't know, of course—it's only a suspicion and I may be entirely wrong—but I imagine she wants me to tell her what will happen here. I hardly think that I'm the one who should give information to Mrs. Prince," and then she added pointedly, a question without a question mark, "—even if I knew anything that I could tell her."

He mumbled an evasively wordless sound and tucked the black box under his arm.

Even in the semidarkness, he saw her eyes forecast what she was about to ask. "Mr. Walling, is there anything that you *can* tell me? It may be that you'd prefer not to talk to me—if that's the case I'll understand, of course—but if there's anything you can tell me about what's going to happen—please do it, Mr. Walling."

The last words had been said as a whispered plea, compelling in its earnestness, and he felt that he had to say something. But what? "I suppose you mean who'll be in this office?" he asked slowly, sparring for time.

"You can understand why it's so important to me."

He waited as long as he dared before he spoke, but there was no gain in the waiting. He still had to say the same thing. "I wish there were something that I could tell you, Miss Martin, but I'm afraid there isn't. As I'm sure you can appreciate, it's a rather scrambled situation. If an executive vice-president had been elected before—"

"Yes, I know." She sounded curiously self-critical, almost as if she were personally assuming the blame for an executive vice-president not having been selected.

Suddenly, his caution dimmed by the darkness of the room, he heard himself ask, "Miss Martin, did Mr. Bullard ever give you any indication of whom he was intending to select as executive vice-president?"

Her eyes had been on his face until she caught the import of the question. She turned away for a moment, not long enough to debate an answer, yet long enough to make him acutely conscious of her hesitation. If she did not answer . . .

[277]

But she did answer and there was no undertone of reluctance. "No, he never did. I doubt if he had made a final decision —unless he made up his mind yesterday in New York."

"I didn't know. I—"

"At least there's one person who has it all figured out," she said with a sudden lightness that seemed in strange contrast to all that had gone before.

His mind exploded the thought of Loren Shaw and he braced himself to hear what she would say after the demanded question, "Who's that, Miss Martin?"

"Luigi. He's all ready to move *you* up here."

It came so unexpectedly that he could not avoid a physical reaction and he could see that she had noticed it.

"I'm sorry you were so surprised, Mr. Walling. I'd hoped that you wouldn't be."

The only response that he dared offer was a smile that could only be meaningless to her because it was meaningless to himself.

Her voice, speaking his name, stopped him at the door. "Mr. Walling, if there's anything I can do to help you, I hope you'll call me. If I'm not here, I'll be at home. My number's in the telephone book."

He said, "Thank you, Miss Martin," . . . and back of his secretary he saw the chair behind his desk . . . the red leather bright where it was touched by a blade of sunlight that had knifed in through the drawn curtains.

Luigi smiled when the door opened on the twenty-fourth floor.

LA GUARDIA AIRPORT, LONG ISLAND
11.02 A.M. EDT

Ronnie had said that the pilot would meet him at the Shell office and George Caswell glanced anxiously inside the glass cubicle. Out of the corner of his eye he caught a glimpse of someone waving from a jeep outside and he recognized Hart, the chief pilot of the plane that Rookery Paper Corporation provided for the business use of its president. He remembered Hart from the time last year when he had flown to Canada with Ronnie for a weekend of salmon fishing.

"How are you, sir?" Hart asked genially, using precisely the right blend of respect and informality. Hart was a good pilot. Ronnie had said that there wasn't a corporation president in the country who had a pilot with a record that could match Hart's . . . "an Air Force colonel at twenty-six, more damned medals than there's room for on his chest . . . not an airline in the country that wouldn't give their eyeteeth to get him!"

As they were driven down the field, George Caswell's eyes picked out the plane by the Rookery trademark on the nose. It seemed tiny at first, dwarfed by a near-by Constellation, but when he stepped into the cabin the impression was quickly lost and he felt, momentarily, the waste of all this twin-engine-powered luxury on his own transportation. But there was the quick-covering memory of what Ronnie had said on that trip to Canada. "Sure, what the hell, it's cockeyed economically. It doesn't make sense, but the damned income tax doesn't make sense either! A big corporation can't pay its president enough after taxes to mean anything any more, so they have to give me something besides money to keep me happy. Damned good incentive plan, too. If I don't keep those earnings climbing the boys on the board will take away my plaything."

Caswell reflected as he sat down that Ronnie must have been doing all right with his earnings lately. The plane's interior had been completely done over and redecorated since the Canadian trip.

Hart stopped beside him to ask, "Everything all right, sir?"
"Perfect."

Hart answered with a friendly half-salute and followed the co-pilot forward.

George Caswell surveyed the new furniture with a critical eye. It was nice enough in its way . . . quite all right . . . but hardly up to what the boys down at Tredway could do for him. Give that chap Walling a chance and he'd design an interior that would be something quite special . . . perhaps on the order of the cabin of the ketch that Dan had brought over from Sweden. No, that was the wrong way . . . leave it to Walling . . . delegate the authority . . . that was the way to handle it.

The first motor coughed and then roared into full-throated vigor. Then the second. George Caswell settled into the downy cushion and looked ahead through the porthole. His new life was beginning. He was closer to happiness than he had ever been before. Millburgh was only an hour away.

Far back in his consciousness, at the very fringe of recognizable thought, was the faint awareness that his handling of Pilcher had hardly been in the Caswell tradition of gentlemanly conduct . . . his father most certainly would not have approved . . . but his father had never been a truly happy man.

MILLBURGH, PENNSYLVANIA
11.14 A.M. EDT

As Don Walling drove out North Front Street, there was no longer any vacillation of his inner mind between hope and despair. That had been the preamble, the process of genesis, the creation of fact. Now it was true. He would be the president of the Tredway Corporation.

He knew that he still faced the task of forcing acceptance, but that was neither strange nor unusual. It had happened before. There had been many times in the past when he had known the truth long before he had been able to make others see it. He had known from the beginning that the back-pressure system would work on the finishing ovens, but it had taken six months to get Jesse Grimm to realize it. He had known that the Millway Federal Line would be a success long before Walt Dudley had stopped worrying . . . that the patent suit would be won . . . that Pittsburgh should drop the paint finish and concentrate on chrome . . . that Pearson was the right man for Chicago manager . . . that the union was really after company-wide bargaining . . . yes, he had known all of those things but still there had always been the nerve-rasping delay while he had been forced to wait for slower minds to overtake his own . . . but, damn it, this time it was different . . . there was no reason to wait! They should know . . . all of them!

An oddly errant thought, almost amusing enough to make him smile, made him remember that it was Luigi who had been the first to know . . . first Luigi and then Erica Martin. Now it had to be the others . . . and the first of the others was Julia Tredway Prince.

Don Walling's decision to go to Julia Tredway Prince had been almost totally impulsive, a subconsciously grasped opportunity to counteract Jesse Grimm's treachery by substituting her vote for his. Now, even though it was difficult to think of the election as anything but a meaningless ritual that would confirm what he already knew, the realization flashed that he didn't have Dudley's support. He had forgotten, momentarily, that the presidency had been the price of Walt Dudley's vote.

Had Alderson really been crazy enough to do that . . . to toss away the presidency for one vote? The old coot must have been insane! Julia Tredway Prince's vote was not enough . . . he had to have Dudley's vote, too. What was the matter with Alderson . . . why had he fumbled around and let Dudley slip through his fingers? Yes, damn it, it was Alderson's fault and now it was up to Alderson to do something about it!

Impatiently, annoyed at the delay that would keep him from settling things with Julia Tredway Prince in a hurry, Don Walling turned off North Front Street and headed for Alderson's home. He'd put a burr under Fred's tail . . . get him out there to square away Dudley. The old boy probably wouldn't like it but he might as well learn once and for always that the president of the Tredway Corporation was too damned busy to sit around and wait for a lot of fumbling vice-presidents to catch up with him.

Good God, even Luigi knew!

11.21 A.M. EDT

Frederick Alderson stared at the carved window frame but he saw neither the fat-buttocked cupids nor the bunches of grapes that were the always unattainable objects of their endlessly upward flight. He fervently wished that he had not, in a moment of lost control, started to talk to Edith about Don Walling. As much as he had needed to talk to someone, he should have remembered that Edith could never recognize . . . particularly when she was knitting . . . the end point of any conversation, the point beyond which there was nothing more that could be said.

"But, Fred, if Mr. Walling can't be elected president, why does he think that he can be?" It was a questionless question, aimlessly said in a stitch-counting voice.

"I don't know, dear," he said repetitiously, saying the same words that he had said, spoken and unspoken, a hundred times in this last half-hour.

"Doesn't he see that it's impossible?" She was talking only for the sake of the sound, as a happier woman might have hummed while she worked. "If Jesse won't vote for him and if Mr. Dudley votes for Mr. Shaw—now where did I put that blue—oh, there it is. Doesn't he see that it's impossible, Fred?"

"I don't know, dear."

Her voice was fading but it was a long time before he realized that the fading was not a self-protective blocking of his ears, but that he had unknowingly walked the length of the hall and was standing now in the library. The voice that faded back into his consciousness was not Edith's voice but the voice of the man in the picture frame that hung above his desk.

"I know you think it's impossible," Avery Bullard said, "but damn it, Fred, we're going to do it anyway!"

Impossible . . . yes, that's what everyone had said . . . impossible to save the old Tredway Furniture Company from bankruptcy . . . impossible to pull off the merger . . . impossible to buy Coglan without a cent of cash . . . impossible to float that 1937 debenture issue . . . impossible, impossible, impossible . . . "Fred, don't you understand that by the time every slow-witted fool can see that a thing's possible, then it's too damned late?"

That was what you learned about Avery Bullard . . . not to

argue with him . . . not to try to tell him that anything was impossible . . . not to be a slow-witted fool. You couldn't fight back against Avery Bullard because you never knew what you were fighting against. Before you could speak there was something else in his mind . . . the old thought fading as fast as the new one flashed . . . the anger of one moment lost in the next . . . "To hell with Jesse Grimm! I don't need him. I can . . ."

Frederick Alderson blinked away the blankness of his stare. That last voice had been another voice, deceptively alike but still perceptibly different. It wasn't Bullard's voice . . . it was Walling's. He tried to erase the difference, to force the acceptance of resurrection, to believe that death would become life, that the man who was dead would become the man who was alive.

He waited out the last slow heartbeat of a lost hope. It could never be. He should have known. He had been fooled by that intuitive feeling this morning that it would be Don Walling who would take Avery Bullard's place. He shouldn't have let himself be fooled. He should have remembered that he could never trust his intuition. He had none. It had been true all his life . . . was still true . . . he should have known.

His slumping body found a chair and he sat heavily, pressed down by the weight of his old man's knowledge that he was terrifyingly alone in this world in which he so strangely still lived. Avery Bullard was dead. The picture on the wall was only a photograph. The eyes did not see . . . the lips did not move . . . there was no command . . . no instruction . . . only the unbreakable silence of death.

A shudder ran through Frederick Alderson's thin body as he acknowledged the terrifying enormity of the error that he had committed. It was he who had given Walling the hope that he could be president. It was his fault that Walling would tear out his heart in the fighting of a battle that could never be won.

Edith's voice was in his ears now, old words twice repeated before he could believe that they were not a memory. "Fred, are you all right?"

"Yes, I'm all right."

"Mr. Walling is here to see you."

"Walling—here?" Hope leaped. Walling had realized it, too! He had come around to see things straight . . . that half a loaf was better than none . . . that Walt Dudley wouldn't make such a bad president after all . . . that it was all for the best.

A warm glow of satisfaction welled up within him as he turned to meet Don Walling, prepared to brush aside the apology that he expected to hear.

But there was no apology in Don Walling's crackling voice, not even an introductory greeting. "You took Walt home, didn't you?"

"Yes, I—"

"And you said nothing to him about voting for me?"

"Voting for—?"

"Damn it, Fred, didn't you realize that I need his vote. I want to get this thing settled in a hurry! Why let it drag on with a lot of pointless argument? If he and Shaw get together there'll be time wasted. We have to get the election out of the way. You know that as well as I do. Million things that need to be done. Get out there and talk to him, Fred—line him up—tell him what the score is!"

Halfway through the tornado of words, Frederick Alderson's bewilderment changed to a reassuring recognition. A lifetime of living with Avery Bullard had taught him that there was a calm center in every storm, and that it was his duty to drive through and find it . . . yes, that was his job. It wouldn't be easy . . . it never had been . . . but, afterwards it would be appreciated.

"Now just a minute," he said, drawing out each word in the exaggerated tone that had always been so effective in slowing down Avery Bullard's word-storms.

"Fred, damn it, I can't—"

"Wait, now!" He gave his voice the sharp change of pace that he had learned to use at this point. "If you'll tell me *what* you want me to do, and exactly *how* you want me to do it—"

"Why should I have to tell you *how* to do it!" the storm

[284]

howled. "I want it done, damn it, and I don't care how you do it!"

Frederick Alderson felt a pleasant strengthening of his assurance. Everything was going according to the pattern, almost word for word. The worst was over. The storm was about to blow itself out.

Walling exhaled in a full-chested blast that seemed to collapse his ribs. "Fred, I need your help. If you can get Dudley squared away, and I can line up Julia Tredway Prince, then we can wrap up this whole thing in a hurry and get going."

There was a temptation to ask Walling how he proposed to get Julia Tredway Prince's vote, but Frederick Alderson knew better than to make that mistake. He had long since learned that he must always clean his own hands before he picked up a new subject. "I'm sorry you don't feel that I handled Dudley in the right way, but I can't see—" Alderson paused in a skillfully executed invitation to interrupt.

Walling came in on the beat. "I didn't say you hadn't handled him in the right way, Fred. All I meant was—well, forget it—just get out there and find some way to line him up. I'm counting on you, Fred. I need your help."

"Well, perhaps I can manage it," Alderson said, saying the thing that always proved to be the right thing to say at this stage. But now he was baffled as to what his next move should be. He knew that he couldn't mention the difficulty of his assignment without launching another full-scale storm, yet it was obvious that there had to be some inducement to draw Dudley from Shaw's camp. What about offering him the executive vice-presidency? At least that would match what Shaw would do for him. Yes, that was an idea . . . but, as always, it would be a better idea if it weren't his own. "Well, let's see, now—if Shaw were to be president, he'd probably offer Dudley—"

"Shaw isn't going to be president! Can't you understand that?"

"No, no, of course not," Alderson said quickly, backtracking. He shouldn't have given him that opening. "I was only thinking that if we could offer Walt something tangible—"

"Why do we have to offer him anything?" Walling demanded belligerently.

"Well—"

"All right, do whatever you have to do," Walling said with sudden impatience. "I don't have time to argue. I have to see Mrs. Prince."

Walling had been standing all through the conversation and the start of his exit meant only a turn and a step. The performance of duty forced Frederick Alderson to stop him and a quick command made Walling's head snap around impatiently.

"What?"

Frederick Alderson dampened his lips. This was the turning point, the crucial moment when he had to force the acknowledgment of his helpfulness.

"How well do you know Mrs. Prince?" he asked quietly, carefully voicing the question so that it was also an unmistakable warning.

"What do you mean?"

He saw that he had won. "Sit down a minute. If you're going to talk to Julia Tredway Prince there are some things you ought to know about her."

Walling half obeyed, sitting on the edge of the desk. "What about her?"

"Well, as you realize, I was quite close to Mr. Bullard—close enough to know a lot of things—" The words stopped as he raised his head. Behind Walling, over his shoulder, he saw that Avery Bullard was watching him through the picture frame with cold unblinking eyes.

"Well?" Walling demanded.

Alderson moved, shifting his position, trying to escape the eyes, but they seemed to follow him, enforcing a prohibition against saying anything about the personal relationship that there had been between Avery Bullard and Julia Tredway Prince. "She—well, everything she has she owes to Mr. Bullard. If it hadn't been for what he did for her—well, she wouldn't have anything—the stock she inherited from her father wouldn't be worth a penny."

"She knows that, doesn't she?" Walling demanded impatiently.

"Yes, I suppose she does—in a way. But she's like a lot of people with money. After they have it, they forget where it came from. They think it gives them a right to—well, what I'm trying to say is that she doesn't have the same attitude toward the company that the rest of us have—that you and I have. The only thing that matters to her is her dividends. There've been times when she—well, times when she caused Mr. Bullard a great deal of difficulty."

Walling's face told him that he was losing ground, fumbling, making a bad job of it, and the undertone of impatient annoyance in his voice confirmed it as he said, "What's the matter—isn't she satisfied with a two-dollar dividend?"

"No—no, it hasn't been so bad these last few years—not since we raised the dividend," Alderson said weakly, feeling his hold slipping.

Walling moved toward the door. "You'll go out and see Walt right away, won't you?"

"Anything you want me to do," he promised hurriedly, forcing his voice in a last desperate demand for understanding.

It came in the last instant of hope—Walling's hand reaching back to touch his shoulder, the quick grin, the strong voice. "Thanks, Fred. I won't forget this. Don't know what I'd do without you."

And then he was gone. But his voice remained—urgent—commanding—the sound of life.

"Fred, where are you going?"

It was Edith's voice. Somehow, without knowing it, he had found his hat and the front door had already opened to his hand.

"Something I have to do for Mr. Walling."

Whatever it was that she called after him was lost, fading away as he hurried down the steps.

As he approached the white wall that surrounded the old Tredway mansion, Don Walling found himself unable to throw off the warning about Julia Tredway Prince that Alderson had voiced. Actually, he had said nothing definite—his ambiguity had been more of a warning than his words—but it had stirred up vague memories and odd bits of circumstantial evidence that supported the need for caution.

He had heard, long ago, some behind-the-hand gossip about Avery Bullard and Julia Tredway Prince, but now the memory was only of the hearing and not of the content. What had not been washed away by disbelief had long since been faded by the passage of time.

There were other more recent memories, however, and one of them was seemingly more pertinent because of its linkage to Alderson. It was of an evening when he had given Alderson a ride home. Passing the Tredway mansion they had seen Bullard's car parked in the driveway and Alderson had said, "Nobody appreciates what a man has to go through these days to be the president of a big company."

In the recreation of the mental picture of Bullard's car standing in Julia Tredway Prince's drive, Don Walling found a delayed explanation of the shock he had felt last night when he had seen Shaw's car in the same place—but the realization was quickly passed over. The only thing that mattered now was the urgent necessity of solving the mystery of what he would have to do to take over where Avery Bullard had left off in his relationship with Julia Tredway Prince.

His difficulty—as he was now acutely aware—was that he had never taken an interest in Julia Tredway Prince as a person, nor had he ever thought of her as having any important connection with the company's operations. He had accepted her as a strangely living holdover from the past, paying no more attention to the cocktail party gossip about her than he had to the too-often-repeated tales of her father's eccentricities. He knew, from the occasions when he had seen her across the room at some large party, and the even rarer times when she had spoken to him, that she was actually a living person, but his impressions of her had been filed in the same subterranean chamber of his consciousness that held an image of Orrin Tredway as a bronze bust in the lobby of the Tower, and of Oliver Tredway as an oil-painted face that scowled down upon every meeting in the directors' room. Now he wished that he had given Alderson more encouragement to tell him all that needed to be known about Julia Tredway Prince.

He was a half-dozen strides away from the car before he remembered the black box and went back to get it.

As he rang the doorbell, he was startled at the matching memory of pressing the elevator button in New York that first time he had gone to see Karl Eric Kassel, startled because it was so rarely that his mind ever dredged up a memory as old as that . . . particularly such a meaningless one.

He was startled again when the door opened. He had expected a servant, a maid or even a butler, but the man who stood in front of him was unmistakably Dwight Prince. He had seen him so rarely, and now not for so long, that his face was hardly familiar but his clothes made the identification positive. There was no one else in Millburgh who would have worn that sport coat.

He knew that it should not have been unexpected that Dwight Prince would fail to recognize him, but he found the necessity of introducing himself unpleasant.

"Oh—Walling? Yes, you're one of the men at the office, aren't you?" Dwight Prince said in vague confirmation, gesturing him through the door but not offering his hand.

"I've brought something for Mrs. Prince."

The black box was under his arm—he thought inconspicuously—but Dwight Prince's eyes found it and a look of faint amusement flickered on and off his soft face.

"Is Mrs. Prince at home?" Walling demanded, trying to block the possibility of Dwight Prince taking the box himself.

Prince looked at him as if he were debating a decision.

"I believe she's dressing. If you'd care to—"

"I'll wait."

Dwight Prince went slowly up the winding staircase that dominated the great center hall of the house, looking back once with that same flickering grin.

The coldly formal atmosphere of the hall did nothing to dispel the foreboding with which he anticipated the appearance of Julia Tredway Prince. There was a long lapse before there was any sound to break the silence and then it was Dwight Prince's voice, muffled and distant, somewhere in one of the back rooms of the big house, his presence there making it plain that he pointedly used a back staircase to avoid a reappearance.

There had been no confirmation that Julia Tredway Prince would come down to see him and, goaded by impatience that had risen close to anger, his apprehension heightened by Alderson's warning, Don Walling was completely unprepared for the warmth of the low feminine voice that unexpectedly spoke to his back.

Wheeling around, he saw her standing a few steps above the floor, her lithe black-dressed figure blending gracefully into the curve of the winding rail.

"How very nice of you to come, Mr. Walling," she said fervently, extending her hand as she came down the last steps, all but two, standing now with her eyes on the same level as his. "I had just called Miss Martin, offering to send a car for her, and she told me that you were coming. I'm very pleased and very flattered and so sorry that I was forced to keep you waiting."

She took the last two steps and he saw that she was smaller than he had expected, almost childlike, less beautiful at close range than he had thought of her as being in that first glimpse on the staircase, but still a pleasant contrast to the person that his apprehensive imagination had set up as its target.

She took the black box from his hands without comment and he noticed that the casual way she left it on a table as she crossed the wide hall confirmed Erica Martin's suspicion that its delivery had been a ruse.

"Let's go in the library," she said, opening a door, and he knew that he was over the first hurdle. At least there would be no trouble about getting her to talk to him.

The room they entered was not at all the kind of a room that the formal entrance hall forecasted as the Tredway mansion's "library." For the second time Don Walling was startled by the intrusion of an old memory—the wonderfully pleasant headmaster's office at Rubble Hill. Books over-jammed the ceiling-high shelves, spilling out into floor stacks and a heaped scattering that spread across the wide ledge of the huge bay window that all but filled the far wall. There were enormous chairs, several almost sofa size, upholstered in dark green leather that looked as soft as doeskin, and a surpassingly beautiful desk that demanded his second glance.

"I'm glad you like it," she said perceptively. "It was my grandfather Oliver's. He made it himself in a shop that he had out in the coach house. This is one of his pieces, too!" She indicated a grandfather clock, the case of which had seemed, as he saw it in the shadowed corner, to be made of some exquisitely grained wood, but as he stepped closer he saw that what he had mistaken for graining was actually a montage of carved figures done in very low relief, a difficult art that required superb craftsmanship.

"I had no idea that your grandfather was the kind of a man who—" He fumbled into an impasse, unable to credit the beautiful workmanship of the clock case to the hands of the stern-visaged man whose portrait could have been used as a stock illustration for the cold-eyed nineteenth-century captain of industry.

Again her perception was evident. "He was a very different man than his pictures make him seem."

"You knew him?"

"Only through his diary. He died before I was born."

"He kept a diary?"

"Yes, almost his entire life—from the seventeenth birthday until the year before he died." She had walked to a small bookcase, separated from the shelves, and he saw that the gesture of her hand was almost a caress as her fingertips ran over a row of oddly assorted volumes.

"His diary must be very interesting," he said, a remark made only to fill the silence.

"Yes, it is," she said thoughtfully, "but confusing, too. I know the kind of a man he must have been to do the things he did—strong, powerful, the master of his fate. Yet when you read his diary, you find so many cases where he was so—so lost. He never seemed to know what he would do next. He'd fill a whole page with all the reasons why something couldn't be done—all his doubts and fears—and then when you turn the page you find that he went ahead and did it, anyway. I've always thought of him as a great man—and he *was* a great man—as being someone with an unusual ability to think clearly—to know just what he wanted to do and how he was going to do it—yet the most important things that Oliver Tredway did were things that he could never explain."

His mind was full of thoughts of Avery Bullard and his lips were parted to say how much, in so many ways, he had been that same kind of a man, but she interrupted before he could phrase what he wanted to say.

"I'm sorry, Mr. Walling," she said, her voice suddenly lightened. "I hadn't intended to give you a lecture on family history. Do sit down. Since I have you here I intend to make the most of it."

He was conscious of the fact that she pre-empted a chair with her back to the window so that her own face would be in shadow while his would be in full light, but he brushed aside the suspicion that it had been purposeful. She seemed too guileless for that.

"I'm sorry this is the first time you've been in my home, Mr. Walling. I'm sure you won't believe this because it's one of those pat things that people always say on occasions like this, but I've often thought of asking you and Mrs. Walling to come to dinner some evening. I know that you're interested in the arts and I thought you and Dwight might find something in common."

Before he could force through a reply she went on, "Your wife is very beautiful, isn't she? I saw her at the flower show a few weeks ago. She was wearing a dress that was the color of the green verdigris on old bronze—a topaz brooch and some wonderful thing in her hair—and I thought she was quite the most handsome woman I'd ever seen."

The accuracy of her description surprised him, erasing the first-thought possibility that he was being subjected to blatant flattery.

"Yes, Mary's beautiful," he said. The words felt immodest to his tongue as if he were guilty of self-praise.

"She's Grecian, isn't she?"

Again he was surprised. "Yes, her mother and father were both born in Greece."

"Dwight and I spent a winter in Athens. They're wonderfully strong—the Grecian women—but still without sacrifice of femininity. Perhaps that's why I admired Mrs. Walling so much—as we all admire the person we'd like to be but never can be. Or is that only a feminine characteristic? No, I'm sure it's not."

Answering her own question had given him no hand-hold for a reply and he groped for something to say that would turn the conversation in the direction that he wanted it to take.

Suddenly, as if she were signaling the end of a pointless preliminary, her hands made an impatient darting gesture, "We're both being rather silly, aren't we—avoiding talking about him?"

The thought of Loren Shaw's having sat in this same room last evening had been close to the surface of his mind and his throat constricted.

"Avery Bullard is dead," she said as if she were forcing the admission of a fact.

He nodded, annoyed with himself for his lack of perception, for having let a thought of Shaw intrude.

She had twisted her legs up under her and was sitting far

back in the corner of the huge chair. "I want to talk about him, Mr. Walling. Do you mind?"

"Of course not."

"I should say that I *need* to talk about him—and to someone who knew him very well. I'm sure you did."

"Yes, I think so."

"Dwight knew him hardly at all, of course, so most of his impressions were erroneous—and there's no point in arguing about Avery Bullard. It's like believing in God—you either do or you don't." She cut herself off as if startled by what she had said, and then added quickly. "That was a bad simile, wasn't it? You'll think me blasphemous."

"I believe I know what you mean, Mrs. Prince," he said, not certain that she thought the simile as badly chosen as she pretended. "It's true that you had to know Mr. Bullard to understand him—and a great many people never did, even people who imagined they were close to him. I thought of that a moment ago when you were talking about your grandfather. In some ways they must have been a good deal alike—Avery Bullard and Oliver Tredway."

She gave him a startled glance and he thought at first that she, too, must have had the same secret thought, but what she said seemed to deny it. "I don't think you're right, Mr. Walling. You said that you could only understand Avery Bullard when you knew him well. I don't think you could ever understand him. He wouldn't let you. When you came close to understanding, he did something to throw you off the track—like a magician who was afraid that you might discover how he did his tricks."

He had been listening with only half an ear, and a moment passed before he realized how aptly she had characterized Avery Bullard.

"Still a bad simile?" she had asked.

"No, a very good one. I was just thinking about it."

That wasn't quite true. What he had actually been thinking about were the implications of that curious tone of faint rancor that had underlaid her voice. Could it be that there had once been something between her and Avery Bullard . . . a relationship that Bullard had broken when she had tried to draw him too close? Yet she had said that believing Avery Bullard was like believing in God . . . and the unadorned black dress was obviously mourning.

She picked a cigarette out of the heavy bronze jar at her elbow and he moved quickly to light it for her. She gestured him back. "Thank you but please don't bother, Mr. Walling. I chain smoke when I'm nervous."

It was the first cigarette that he had seen her smoke but he saw the opening that her remark gave him and his impatience goaded him to take advantage of it. "Why should you be nervous, Mrs. Prince? I hope not about the future of the company?"

"The company? No, I wasn't thinking about the company— or perhaps I was, in a roundabout way," she said, preoccupied. Then suddenly she flicked her eyes toward him, "Mr. Walling, do you mind if I ask you some questions about the company?"

"Not at all."

For a fleeting moment there was a return of her earlier lightness. "It's my own fault, of course, that I'm forced to ask you these questions. If I hadn't been such a negligent director I'd know the answers."

Matching her lightness, he said, "That's not so inexcusable, Mrs. Prince. Directors' meetings haven't meant too much usually."

"That answers my first question," she said with a faintly victorious smile. "I wanted to ask you if it were true that Avery Bullard was something of a dictator. That was pretty much the way the company was run, wasn't it, Mr. Walling?"

Both the phrasing of the question and the tone of its delivery brought back the memory of the hours he had spent on the witness stand in the patent suit on the extrusion process. He had learned then that an honest answer to an apparently innocent question could sometimes be grossly misconstrued, and that apparently innocent questions were often less innocent than they seemed. Julia Tredway Prince was not so guileless as he had first thought.

"I'm not certain that I know what you mean, Mrs. Prince. If you're suggesting that Mr. Bullard played a very strong part in the management of the company— yes, that's true."

"Apparently you don't think that was a bad thing for the company—or do you?"

"The record pretty much speaks for itself."

"Then you think there's nothing wrong with a dictator management?"

"I wouldn't go quite that far, Mrs. Prince. There's something wrong with everything. I suppose—and I'm still not certain that I know what you mean by dictator management."

"Have you resented it, Mr. Walling? Men of your type usually do resent buckling under to a dictator, don't they? That's why dictatorships usually fail, isn't it—when the good men underneath can no longer stand the subjection?"

He felt the first vapor of resentment rising within him but he fanned it away. "Let's get one thing clear, Mrs. Prince, I have nothing but admiration for Avery Bullard. He was a great man and I'll never be out of his debt. Everything I have came from Avery Bullard."

"I know how you feel, Mr. Walling," she said—and for an instant he thought he had scored—but then she went on. "But that isn't precisely true, is it? What you have came from the *Tredway Corporation*—not personally from the man who happened to be its president."

"He *was* the company! If it hadn't been for Avery Bullard there wouldn't be a Tredway Corporation."

"Isn't that a little like saying that if it hadn't been for Franklin D. Roosevelt there wouldn't be a United States of America? Admittedly, the country was in rather bad shape when he became president—but there had been a George Washington before him—and a Jefferson and a Lincoln and—"

"Yes, of course," he said hurriedly, trying to escape the consequences of his quick tongue . . . he'd been an idiot to say what he had, knowing how she felt about her grandfather!

"That wasn't an original thought of mine," she said, smiling almost as if it were an apology. "It was something that Dwight said to me once after I'd made much the same remark about Avery Bullard that you just did. He reminded me that a company is much larger than one man—any man—and that many people contributed to its building. Even my father, whom I'd come to regard as a failure, actually made a great many important contributions to the company. Even building the Tower doesn't seem so foolish now, does it?"

He felt a twinge of annoyance at the way she persisted in taking advantage of his too quickly made remark. "You're quite right, of course, Mrs. Prince—a company is much more than one president."

"Much more than any president," she persisted, "—and particularly so today with the company as large as it is. I had a very interesting discussion of that subject last evening."

Shaw! Now it began to make sense . . . all of the things she had said were tying together . . . yes, now she was even sounding like Shaw . . . the same pat phrases.

Her words faded back into his consciousness. "—that a pronounced change should be made in the whole management concept of the Tredway Corporation. He made the point that the dictator was an outmoded form of industrial government, just as it's an outmoded form of political government."

He choked back the impulse to argue. There was nothing to be gained. He had to get to the point . . . get it out in the open. "I presume the man you talked to was Mr. Shaw."

Surprise lifted her face. "Yes, it was Mr. Shaw."

"I thought so."

"Why?"

"I recognized his point of view."

"It isn't yours?"

"Hardly."

"Just what is your point of view, Mr. Walling?"

He hesitated, momentarily silent. It was plain that those old

[297]

rumors about her sanity were only malicious gossip. She was a clever woman . . . damned clever! He had to watch his every word.

She took advantage of his hesitance and said, "Perhaps you'd prefer not to answer that question."

"No, no," be countered, side-stepping what was clearly a trap. "That's a big assignment, Mrs. Prince, asking me to give you my point of view. I was trying to think how to state it briefly."

"Then let me simplify it. A few minutes ago you said that you felt Avery Bullard was very much like my grandfather. Did you mean that Mr. Bullard has been running the corporation in the same way—in the 1890 concept that the boss was a god-on-a-hill—supreme—unquestioned—the absolute dictator?"

Anger had risen to become a barrier to his voice, not anger at Julia Tredway Prince but at Loren Shaw. It was Shaw who was to blame . . . she was repeating Shaw's words . . . it was Shaw who had planted the "dictatorship" notion in her head. He had to fight back! But how? There were only two courses and there was a deadfall ahead on both paths. If he defended Avery Bullard he would be defending "dictatorship" and all that Shaw had made it mean . . . everything that was wrong with the company. Yes, there *were* things wrong . . . plenty of things . . . and he'd do something about them as soon as he could! But any admission now would mean walking into the trap that Shaw had set for him.

"It's hardly possible to compare your grandfather's management of the old Tredway Furniture Company with Avery Bullard's management of the Tredway Corporation. In your grandfather's day—"

The flip of her hand signaled an interruption. "That's the point, Mr. Walling—the phrase you just used—*Avery Bullard's* management of the Tredway Corporation."

"That was only a figure of speech, Mrs. Prince."

"Was it really? Isn't it true that Avery Bullard has been managing the corporation almost singlehandedly, making all of the decisions himself?"

"No, that isn't true—it couldn't be true. The corporation is much too large for that to be possible. There are literally thousands of decisions made every day. With factories all over the—"

"I meant the important decisions, the top-level ones, the decisions that really count."

"If it's a decision that involves a major policy then, of course, it becomes a matter for the board of directors to decide."

"But, Mr. Walling, I thought you said a minute or two ago that the directors' meetings never meant very much."

He flinched inwardly, feeling himself unfairly trapped, forcing a smile to help him keep from losing his temper. "We seem to be going around in a circle."

"Yes, don't we."

"May I turn the tables and ask you a question, Mrs. Prince?"

"Of course."

"You seem concerned about Mr. Bullard's management of the company. Why? Don't you feel that it's been successful?"

She answered so quickly that she must have anticipated the question. "I'm much more concerned with the future than I am with the past, Mr. Walling—but don't you agree that it's reasonable to ask whether or not there should be perpetuation of Mr. Bullard's kind of a management attitude?"

"I'm not certain that I know what you mean."

"I hesitate to use the word again because I know that you dislike it."

"You're still thinking of him as a dictator?"

"Wasn't he?" Her faint smile did nothing to weaken the dogged persistence of her attack.

He locked his fingers, gripping so hard that the knuckles showed white. "Mrs. Prince, there always has to be one man at the top. It can't be any other way. That's true whether it's an industrial corporation—an army—a nation—any organization of any kind. No matter how you set things up, there has to be that man at the top. In the end, he has to take total responsibility. There's no other way. In that sense—"

"You speak of responsibility, Mr. Walling. To whom?"

"To the company."

"Not to the stockholders?"

"Yes—partially."

"Partially? Don't you believe that the stockholders *own* the company, Mr. Walling—that it's their *property*—that the only purpose of a company is to make a profit for the benefit of its stockholders?"

He had fought hard to fan away the rising vapor of anger but now the hot vapor suffused his brain. In the smoking haze there was no longer any visible demarcation that separated Julia Tredway Prince from Loren Shaw. The words were Shaw's but the voice was hers. She could not escape the responsibility for having said them.

What right did she have to put him through this inquisition . . . to make him crawl to her on his belly? Because she was a stockholder . . . because she had a few scraps of paper that let her live like a honey-sucking parasite on the work of other men? Alderson had been right . . . dividends were all that mattered to Julia Tredway Prince . . . money . . . money to support that worthless husband who had never done a useful thing in his life . . . "she caused Mr. Bullard a great deal of difficulty" . . . no wonder! Was she so money-depraved that she could feel no human gratitude . . . so self-blinded that she could not see that she was a rich woman only because of Avery Bullard . . . that her precious stock wouldn't be worth a cent if it had not been for him? It was Avery Bullard who had given her everything she had . . . the food she ate, the dress she wore, even that cigarette she was snuffing out in the ashtray . . . and now she had turned against him, stabbing the corpse that could not fight back.

There was no barrier of caution now. He was beyond the last compromise, the last evasion, the last half-lie. Words came out of nowhere, unpremeditated, fresh-spoken. "You asked for my point of view, Mrs. Prince, and I'll give it to you. Avery Bullard was a great man and he built a great company. Yes, *he* built it! And he did it because he was strong and because he wasn't afraid! He wasn't afraid of weaker men who called him a dictator, or a god-on-a-hill, or anything else. He didn't care. It didn't matter. Nothing mattered to Avery Bullard but one thing—the company! I say, thank God he lived, thank God there was an Avery Bullard, and you should say the same thing, Julia Tredway—you above anyone else!"

The force of his words had propelled him to his feet and he wheeled to the door, but she had bolted toward him and her arms fought to hold him.

"No, no," she cried in a total abandonment of restraint. "You're wrong, wrong, terribly wrong! You don't think I loved him, but I did! As much as you loved him—more! Please believe me—please!"

He stared down at her, unbelieving, the vapor of anger drifting away.

"I can't let you think what you are thinking—don't—please don't," she pleaded. "You said, 'you above anyone else!' Yes, that's true! You have no idea how true. Do you know where I'd be today if it weren't for Avery Bullard? I'd be in an asylum for the incurably insane. It's true. He saved me. The doctors will tell you it's true. He brought my mind back—he gave me my life. You think you owe him a lot? I owe him a thousand times more. Can't you see now that I didn't turn against him as you thought I did? I couldn't. I never could. It would be impossible. I was only—"

She had driven her voice to exhaustion and she took quick sobbing breaths, as fast as heartbeats. "You think I'm still insane?"

He shook his head. "But I don't see why you were—"

"Because I knew he was dead! Because Mr. Shaw said there could never be another Avery Bullard—"

He felt her exhaustion become his own, the draining away to emptiness, the weakness of convalescence after anger. "No, there can never be another Avery Bullard."

"—but there can be a MacDonald Walling," she whispered, a whisper so intense that it had the timbre of a shout. "I didn't know that before, but I know it now! You'll be the president of the Tredway Corporation—you—MacDonald Walling."

It was a strange victory, as victories are often strange after the warrior has forgotten why he fought.

She was anxiously watching his face. "You will do it?"

He managed a smile.

The victory had been no stranger than the cold sense of reality that had now swept through his mind. "It will take more than the two of us, Mrs. Prince. There'll have to be four."

"Four?"

"It takes four votes to elect a president."

"Oh. Will that be hard to manage?"

"I don't know."

"Of course Mr. Shaw wants it for himself. He made that plain enough when he was here last night."

"I know."

"And Mr. Alderson, too. I gathered from what Mr. Shaw said that he regarded Mr. Alderson as his principal competitor." Her eyes twinkled. "Mr. Shaw will be very surprised when he finds out who it's really going to be."

He passed her last remark. "I think I can count on Alderson's vote. I'm sure I can. There's a possibility that I might have Walt Dudley's vote too. Alderson was going out to see him."

"When will you know?"

He thought for a moment. "Could I use your telephone?"

"Yes, do!" The excitement of impatience was in her voice and her eyes followed him eagerly as he crossed to the desk.

12.12 P.M. EDT

Erica Martin dialed 9 for an outside line and even the moment that it took before the dial tone sounded seemed like an eternity. She dialed the number. The busy signal roared back at her ears. Her finger ran down the column: *Prince, Dwight R 800 N. Front . . . 2-4342.*

Yes, the number had been right.

She dialed again. It was ringing! She stiffened herself against the sound of that woman's voice.

It was Don Walling's voice!

"Mr. Walling, this is Erica Martin. I've just had a call from Mr. Caswell. He's flown down from New York and is out at the airport now. I have my car and I'm going out to get him. I thought you'd want to see him—so—yes—no, he wanted to talk to me and I told him I'd meet him."

She waited as he had asked her to wait, closing her eyes like doubling her fists. Why should she feel this way just because he was talking to that woman . . . why, why, why?

There was his voice again. "Yes, Mr. Walling?—yes, I can bring him there if—if that's what you want me to do."

She closed her eyes again . . . fighting something that shouldn't need to be fought again . . . but now it was starting all over. It was her own fault . . . she should never have let Don Walling take that box out there. But Julia Tredway Prince wouldn't win . . . not this time. When Mr. Caswell went in that house she would go with him.

She started for her hat, forgetting that it was on her head, that she had been ready to leave when the telephone had rung.

12.15 P.M. EDT

"If we can get George Caswell's vote that's all you'd need?" Julia Tredway Prince asked.

"Yes, that's all," Don Walling said.

"Then I don't think we have anything to worry about. Fortunately, I know Mr. Caswell. As a matter of fact I was talking to him on the telephone yesterday—about someone who was trying to buy some Tredway stock. I think you can safely leave Mr. Caswell in my hands."

"Do you think it might be better if I weren't here?"

"Perhaps. Where can I call you—at home?"

He nodded. "I'll make a stop at Alderson's—see if he's there yet—and then I'll go home."

12.19 P.M. EDT

Until Frederick Alderson glanced at the speedometer, the screaming siren had been only another of the wild sounds that coursed through his mind. He saw then that the needle was wavering just about sixty-five and his quick side glance caught the thumb jerk of a state trooper who was motioning him toward the edge of the road.

There was a terrifying wait after he had stopped the car. Frederick Alderson had never before been guilty of the violation of a traffic law.

The trooper's face finally appeared in the window. His voice had the diabolical pleasantness of calculated doom. "May I see your operator's license, please?"

Somehow, thick-fingered, he managed to separate the orange card from the pack in the wallet. "I'm sorry, officer, I have to get down to Maryland in a hurry and—well, I hadn't realized how fast I was going."

"You the Alderson that's with the company?" the trooper asked, marking him as a Millburgh man. Everyone in Millburgh always referred to the Tredway Corporation as "the company."

"Why, yes—yes, officer. I—"

"My old man's been with the company all his life. John Sweitzer. Up at Pike Street now."

"Well, of course!" Alderson said, able to take his first full breath since the siren had wrapped a steel band about his lungs. "One of Mr. Grimm's men. That's where I'm going now—to see Mr. Grimm. It's—"

"Too bad about Mr. Bullard, huh?"

"Yes."

"Not so old either—only fifty-six the paper said."

"That's right."

The orange card came back through the window. "Take it a little easy from here on down, Mr. Alderson. We don't want to be burying you, too."

12.21 P.M. EDT

"No, I haven't any idea what happened to him, Mr. Walling," Edith Alderson said unhappily. "He went out right after you left and I haven't heard anything from him since."

It had been something of a shock for George Caswell to discover, as he stepped out of the telephone booth at the Millburgh Airport, that Loren Shaw and J. Walter Dudley were waiting for him.

They had already gone through the ritual of saying the things that had to be said about Avery Bullard's death and now Shaw explained, "Something came up rather unexpectedly this morning, George. I wanted your advice so I called your home. Mrs. Caswell said that you were flying down so Walt and I slipped out to pick you up."

"Wonderful to have you here at a time like this," Dudley added in a bishop's voice. "Glad you could come, George, glad you could make it."

"More than I could have hoped for," Shaw said.

George Caswell left himself warming to their gratitude. They were good boys, both of them . . . appreciative and considerate . . . right attitude.

"I didn't know whether there was anything I could do or not —probably not—but the plane was available so I thought I'd come over on the chance that there might be."

What was it that Shaw had meant about something coming up unexpectedly this morning . . . had Pilcher called him? Yes, that was possible . . . Pilcher knew Shaw . . . but now was not the time to bring up anything like that.

"Suppose we slip down to the club and have a bite of lunch," Dudley said, easing his voice out from under the unctuous mantle of grief.

"I wish that were possible," Caswell said uncertainly, "but I've already called Miss Martin and she's on her way out to pick me up. I wasn't certain who I'd be able to reach so I thought it best to call her first—and there are two or three little things that I want her to check for me."

"Well, now, that's simple enough," Dudley said. "We'll just take her along down to the club. Nothing wrong with three men taking a secretary out to lunch."

The remark seemed suspiciously like an attempt at levity, which George Caswell found in slightly questionable taste, but it actually wasn't a bad idea. He had taken his secretary in New York out to lunch once and, as he explained to Kitty, it had proved highly beneficial. A secretary was very important to the head of any business—in many ways almost as important as a vice-president—and it was essential that she be thoroughly conversant with his point of view.

"All right with you, Loren?" Dudley asked.

"Yes, of course," Shaw said, but without enthusiasm.

"She'll appreciate it, too," Dudley said. "Yes sir, you bet she will. This has probably hit her mighty hard—she and Mr. Bullard must have been pretty close—couldn't help but be after all these years. Be a nice thing to take her out and buy her a good lunch. She's probably never been in the club before in her life."

George Caswell winced inwardly and he noticed with some satisfaction that Shaw apparently shared his own discomfort at Dudley's garrulousness. Of course that was something you had to accept . . . went with the sales type . . . but it was good to know that Shaw was a man of some discrimination.

They had walked out on the little paved area in front of the airport building and, as they watched, a gray-green Ford coupé turned in from the pike and came up the road, braking to a gravel-spattering stop in front of the steel fence.

"That's her," Dudley said, walking out to greet her as she stepped out of the car. "Well, my dear, it isn't every day that this happens—three handsome gentlemen waiting to take you out to lunch!"

From the shocked look on her face, George Caswell was pleased to see that Erica Martin, too, was a person of discrimination. That was a quality that he always insisted on having in his secretary.

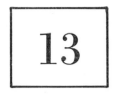

13

MILLBURGH, PENNSYLVANIA
12.40 P.M. EDT

Mary Walling was waiting—and conscious, as she was so often conscious, that waiting was so much of her life. It seemed to her that she was always waiting . . . waiting for Don to call . . . waiting for him to come . . . waiting for him to talk to her . . . to tell her the things she needed to know if she were to share his life.

The sharing was important . . . the point, the purpose, the very essence of her love . . . but was it of his? She could never be sure. There were so many times when he seemed to want to live within himself . . . when sharing was a favor so reluctantly given that it was hardly sharing at all.

Why couldn't Don realize that she could help him if he would let her . . . help him do what he couldn't do without her? No, not for his gratitude, not for his thanks . . . there was something even more satisfying about helping him without his knowing that he had been helped. Then it was a pure gift of love. Yes, that was love . . . the giving . . . but the gift had to be wanted.

I think too much, she thought—and then went on thinking. Her fingers automatically lifted his socks out of the basket, pairing them, rolling them into soft-wound balls that she put across the top drawer of his dresser, placing them in three ruler-straight rows . . . gray, blue, black . . . neat, orderly . . . not like Don at all. But he *could* be like that if he would only let her help him! She could do so much for him . . . separate his confused thoughts . . . put them in straight rows . . . let him think without that awful turmoil . . . without the confusion . . . without the doubts and fears. But that was when he always insisted on shutting her away the most completely . . . when he needed her the worst . . . like this morning when they had talked about Avery Bullard and who his successor might be.

She had gone farther than she had ever gone before to force him to talk to her, yet even then he hadn't been willing to open his mind and share the fear that she had known was there. If he had only given her the smallest opening . . . the barest chance! She could have told him that there was no cause to be afraid . . . he wasn't dependent on Avery Bullard . . . he had his own strength . . . so much more strength than he ever seemed to realize. He didn't need Avery Bullard! All that he needed from anyone was what it would be so easy for her to give him.

Mary Walling was closing the drawer when she heard the squeal of tires on the turn into the drive. It was a sound as characteristic as the sound of his footsteps, and she hurried toward the front door. His arm went around her shoulder. Something had happened this morning! She could feel it in the tingling tenseness of his muscles, in the aura of confidence that surrounded him.

"Mrs. Prince call yet?" he asked crisply, his voice suddenly denying the intimacy that the moment before had promised.

"Mrs. Prince?"

"She's wrapping it up with Caswell. Going to call me as soon as she does."

He had spoken as if she should know what he meant. It was another case where he had forgotten that she couldn't know what he hadn't let her know. "Don, what's happened?"

"Happened?" he asked, his voice edged with surprise, then suddenly flat. "Oh—I'm taking over the presidency."

"The presidency! Don, not really! I—I can't believe it! I—" His eyes seemed to twist the words in her mouth.

"Why are you so surprised?" he asked, almost as if it were an accusation.

"Oh, Don, Don, how can I help it. I never imagined that—" She cut off her voice, knowing now that she had said the wrong thing again, that somehow he was interpreting her surprise as a lack of faith. She threw up her arms, cupping his head in her doubled palms. "Darling, you must let me be a little excited—just because I'm so proud of you. It is what you want —isn't it?"

"It's what I have to do," he said, so tonelessly that she couldn't be sure what he meant. "I'm hungry."

While she put on the coffee and made the sandwich that he insisted was all he wanted, she chipped out scraps of information about what had happened during the morning, risking his annoyance by asking questions that had to be answered before she could fit the bits and pieces together into anything like a connected pattern. After she had gone as far as she dared there were still things that she didn't know, but she had explored deeply enough to be able to ask finally, "Then it all depends on Mr. Caswell?"

"Julia will take care of him."

"Julia?"

"Mrs. Prince," he said impatiently.

"What's she like, Don?"

"Like? Clever woman—damned clever—mind like a man's."

She lifted the coffee pot. Mind like a man's . . . was that what he wanted?

"Don't know when I've enjoyed talking to anyone so much," he went on, the first time that he had said more than she had demanded. "Stepped right into this thing—feet on the ground—never had any idea she was that kind of a woman. I owe her a lot for the way she's backing me up—watch out!"

The coffee she was pouring had splashed over the edge of his cup and she snatched at a tea towel, dabbing up the spreading brown stain until there was time enough to tell herself that she was being a fool . . . that she wasn't the kind of a silly wife who did silly things. Then she could say, calm and sure, "You don't owe anything to anyone, Don. You'll be president because it's *you*—because you're wonderful and brilliant and four times a genius and—" In the moment that her voice hung suspended she felt a clawing urge to tear down the curtain that seemed to hang between them, to re-establish their intimacy. "—and because it's going to be something very special to go to bed every night with a real live president."

She waited—laughter poised on her lips ready to join his—and then came the terrifying realization that he wasn't even going to smile.

1.20 P.M. EDT

The coin that Erica Martin dropped in the telephone had been warming in her palm for the last half-hour. It had not been until the waiter had come to take the dessert orders that she had found a chance to break away from the table.

Dialing, she hoped that it would again be Mr. Walling's voice that answered, It wasn't . . . but at least it wasn't *hers!*

"May I speak to Mr. Walling?" she asked.

"I'm sorry but Mr. Walling is not here. Mr. Walling left—oh, one moment please."

And now it *was* her voice. "Miss Martin?"

"Yes."

"This is Mrs. Prince. Have you had trouble?"

"No, I—"

"I'd understood that you were bringing Mr. Caswell here. I've been imagining that you must have had some difficulty with your car."

[310]

There was no way to avoid telling her what had happened. "Mr. Shaw and Mr. Dudley were at the airport when I got there. We're at the Federal Club now, having lunch. I wanted to get in touch with Mr. Walling to tell him—" She felt her voice suddenly blocked by an unanswerable question . . . why should she be telling Don Walling . . . what was her reason . . . her excuse?

"Thank you, Miss Martin, I'll get word to Mr. Walling immediately. By the way, Miss Martin, I do want to see Mr. Caswell myself. How long do you suppose he'll be there at the club?"

The receiver felt heavy in her hand . . . heavy and hard . . . like a weapon to be hurled. "I'm sorry, Mrs. Prince, but they'll be leaving for the office almost immediately."

1.22 P.M. EDT

Mary Walling saw her husband glance at his watch again, squinting to make certain that it was still running.

"Don't know why the devil she hasn't called," he mumbled impatiently, gulping the last swallow of coffee. "Been an hour— over an hour."

She waited. There was nothing that needed to be said . . . he hadn't been talking to her . . . only to himself . . . not expecting her to answer . . . only to wait . . . to wait and to wait and to wait. For what? Was this what the rest of her life would be . . . waiting . . . silently waiting while she watched him turn, irretrievably, into the man that these last few minutes had hinted that he might become . . . not the man that he really was, not the man that she had married, but only another Avery Bullard?

Her terror fanned the belief that it was possible. There *was* something alike about them . . . yes, she had recognized that for a long time . . . but she had always thought that it was only the unconscious imitation that grew out of his admiration for Avery Bullard . . . something that he would lose in the end . . . a tie that would break . . . that she had been hoping would be broken by death. Now she saw the mind-stunning possibility that it could be something more . . . that there might be, within those unfathomable depths of Don's mind, that same capacity for fanatical devotion to the company . . . that same blind zealot's drive that had made Avery Bullard forget everything else in life . . . destroyed his marriage . . . turned him into a bloodless effigy of a man . . . cold . . . driven by an insane urge to build and build and build . . . bigger and bigger and bigger . . . as if he had been afflicted with some aberration that had made him believe his soul would be measured on a balance sheet where there was no credit for love.

The telephone rang and the way her husband's arm shot out was a frightening confirmation of everything that Mary Walling was struggling so hard not to believe.

She turned away, not wanting to see his face. The sound of his voice made her turn back.

"Yes— yes, I understand—yes—yes, of course."

The words themselves were meaningless but every shade and intonation of his voice was a language that the years of marriage had taught her to understand. She knew that something highly disappointing had happened. Unexpectedly, he glanced up at her and then said to the telephone, "All right—yes, right away, Mrs. Prince."

The telephone receiver dropped from his hand. She waited again, determined not to speak until he did, trying not to feel the sympathy that his eyes asked for, afraid that anything she might say or do would let him know that she was hoping that whatever had happened would keep him from becoming the president of the Tredway Corporation.

"Shaw and Dudley got hold of Caswell first," he said, the words coming hard, forced against reluctance. "Met him at the airport—took him to the club. They've been down there having lunch—Miss Martin, too."

Did she dare speak . . . even to ask him what it meant? No. Wait . . . wait . . . wait.

"Mrs. Prince has managed some way to get them out to her place. She wants us to come, too."

"Us?"

"Yes—and I wish you would," he said slowly.

He was looking at her strangely, his eyes telling her that he saw something that he hadn't seen before, but she was afraid to ask him what it was. It was enough to know that she would be with him . . . that there would be a sharing . . . that she would be a party to whatever happened.

"I'll change," she said quickly, starting down the hall to their bedroom, conscious of the excited anticipation that was growing within her.

1.40 P.M. EDT

"Suppose I ride out with Miss Martin," George Caswell said. "That is if—"

"No point to that," Shaw broke in quickly. "No need to take two cars. I'll drop you here on the way back, Miss Martin." The torture of curiosity had driven him to the point where the thought of anything being said out of hearing was almost unendurable.

"I really would like to have my car with me," Erica Martin countered.

"Then I'll go with you," Caswell said. "Where are you parked, Miss Martin?"

"In the lot. Mind walking?"

"Not at all," Caswell said, calling back over his shoulder as they walked off together, "see you in a few minutes."

Shaw's eyes followed them, their every footstep adding another question to the thousands that already writhed tortuously through every furrow of his brain. Why did Caswell want to talk to her . . . why was she so anxious to talk to him . . . what would they say?

"Well, I'll run along, too," Dwight Prince's voice said.

Shaw had forgotten that Prince and Dudley were still standing beside him.

"Yes sir, Dwight, you bet. See you in just a minute," Dudley said heartily.

[313]

"Yes—see you," Dwight Prince said, walking away.

"Not such a bad guy when you get to know him—I mean for that type," Dudley said after Prince was beyond the range of his voice. "Say, you don't think Julia's got any idea of getting Dwight into the company, do you? Hear that crack he made about how he'd always been interested in furniture?"

Shaw grimaced, trying to block his ears. There were too many questions already and for every one that was asked, his brain spawned a dozen more. Why were they going out to her house . . . what would happen . . . did it mean anything that there were four of them . . . four votes? Did it mean that he had convinced her last night . . . that she had decided to support him? Would she have invited him if she weren't . . . invited Dudley and Caswell, too? Why had she insisted on Miss Martin's coming . . . or was that only Dwight Prince being polite? Could it possibly mean . . .

Walt Dudley's voice smashed through to his consciousness. "You think it means anything, Loren—George Caswell coming down here today?"

Shaw stiffened. Questions . . . questions . . . questions! Was Dudley trying to drive him insane by re-asking the same questions that he had asked himself so many times before? "Why should it mean anything?" he demanded curtly. "There's nothing unusual about it. He was a friend of Mr. Bullard's—he had a plane available—he flew over. That's all there is to it. What makes you think anything else?"

He wished that he hadn't asked that last question. Why open himself to any more torture? He had weighed every word that George Caswell had said during lunch and there hadn't been the slightest indication that there was any purpose whatsoever behind his surprise visit.

"Just a hunch, that's all," Dudley said.

Uncontrollable curiosity forced Shaw to say, "What's your hunch?"

"You understand this is probably cockeyed, but in the selling game a man learns to pay attention to hunches."

"Well?"

Dudley's voice dropped to a heavy whisper. "You don't suppose, do you, that George might be thinking of stepping into the company himself?"

It was such a totally ridiculous thought that he dismissed it with a snort, not bothering with words. There were enough serious questions without adding any of Dudley's crazy hunches.

He let Dudley pay the attendant and noticed that he took no change from the dollar bill. No wonder his expense accounts were so high! Dudley was a fool . . . all right as a sales manager but he'd never do in top management. Thank God, he hadn't lost his head and offered him the executive vice-presidency! He'd need that to get Walling's vote. But he had to hold Dudley, too. There hadn't been time to get a commitment from him at the office . . . too many other questions to answer . . . still to answer. Had Dudley told him the truth . . . the whole truth? Would Alderson have gone so far as he had —holding back that call from Pearson so that he could meet Dudley alone—if he didn't want the presidency? Of course he wanted it! Had he pulled the wool over Dudley's eyes . . . or was Dudley lying? Could it be that Dudley was a stooge for Alderson and Walling . . . that they had sent him to . . .

Once again, like a man fingering a frightening weapon, he thought how easy it would be to guarantee Dudley's vote. All he would have to do would be to speak two words . . . a name . . . the name on a Chicago apartment-house mailbox . . . and Walt Dudley would be in his power. Could he do it? If things got down to the point where everything depended on Dudley's vote, would he be able to admit to anyone, even aloud to himself, that his terrifying curiosity had driven him to the despicable end of following Dudley that night in Chicago . . . that he had hidden in a dark doorway across the street and watched those shadows on the drawn blinds?

Loren Shaw shuddered, shaking the thought from his brain, knowing now that he could never do it. Facing the temptation had destroyed it. Inexplicably, the thought of George Caswell flashed into his mind and, once there, it became the touchstone of an enormously satisfying victory. George Caswell was a gentleman . . . the Caswells of Long Island . . . but no more of a gentleman than Loren Shaw.

1.47 P.M. EDT

George Caswell was finding Erica Martin a pleasantly forthright person and he decided that there was no harm to be done by asking her the question that was in the forefront of his mind. "By the way, Miss Martin, would you happen to know if anyone here had a call this morning from a Mr. Pilcher in New York?"

"I know of no such call," she said promptly, "but that doesn't mean there might not have been one. If you'd care to have me do so, I could have the switchboard log checked. A record is kept of all long-distance calls."

"Oh, that isn't necessary—" he started to say, and then suddenly reversed himself. "Would it be a great deal of trouble, Miss Martin?"

"No indeed. All I'd have to do is make a telephone call. Would you like to know immediately?"

He hesitated. "I dislike troubling you, but it would be helpful if I knew before I arrived at Mrs. Prince's."

"The filling station up at the corner probably has a phone," she said, working the car across to the right lane for a stop. "You said the name was Pilcher?"

"Yes, Bruce Pilcher."

He watched her through the window, experiencing an unaccustomed feeling of dramatic suspense as he saw her place the call and then wait for the information.

"There were no calls this morning from a Mr. Pilcher in New York," she said when she came back to the car. "Nor were there any New York calls that were unidentified as to source, except one to the order department. I'm assuming it wouldn't be that one."

"No, it would have been a call to one of the officers of the company—possibly Mr. Shaw or perhaps Mr. Alderson."

"No such call came through the office board."

"Thank you very much, Miss Martin."

[316]

"You're quite welcome, Mr. Caswell."

As they drove up the street, he became increasingly aware of a sense of deflation, the growing feeling that he had embarked on a fool's errand. He should have known before he started that Pilcher, as soon as his anger cooled, would realize that he couldn't get away with it. It had been no more than one of the empty threats that so many men make in the heat of a big deal. Afterwards, they forgot them. Pilcher probably had. Still it might not be a bad idea to mention the incident out here this afternoon . . . not all the details, of course, just enough to be certain that Pilcher would be blocked if he were enough of a fool to try some kind of a move. At least doing that would give some purpose to the trip. It was obvious that he could accomplish no more today. It had been evident at the luncheon table that neither Shaw nor Dudley had gotten around to thinking about a new president yet. Their minds were still too full of Avery Bullard . . . all those stories about him that Walt Dudley had told.

Erica Martin's surprised voice broke the silence. "There's Mr. Walling!"

They were stopping behind another parked car and, looking up as she spoke, he saw the Wallings walk through the gate in the white wall.

The oddly exultant note of discovery that he had heard in Erica Martin's voice made him glance back at her. Her eyes seemed to be looking through the wall.

"Miss Martin?"

She was startled out of her preoccupation. "Yes?"

"There's something I'd like to ask you before we go in. It's a question that may seem inappropriate at the moment— so soon after Mr. Bullard's death—but I'm certain you'll understand that my asking it reflects no lack of either grief or respect. It may well be that I won't have another opportunity to talk to you for the next several days."

"Of course, Mr. Caswell."

The interest that flashed in her eyes was reassuring and he went on. "As both of us know—I'm sure you were quite as familiar with Mr. Bullard's affairs as my own secretary is with mine—Mr. Bullard was concerned over the selection of the right man to be his executive vice-president."

"Yes, I know. I'd been hoping that he would make up his mind before the board meeting on Tuesday so that it could be included in the semiannual report."

He nodded, telling himself that he had been right in imagining that Miss Martin knew the whole story, inside and out. "As you know, Mr. Bullard had been considering a number of men outside the company. However, when he left my office yesterday noon I was convinced that his choice would inevitably be one of his own men. I imagine—knowing him as well as you did— that you'd probably known that from the beginning?"

"I'd never thought that Mr. Bullard would bring in an outside man," she said slowly.

"Miss Martin, which one of the vice-presidents would he have selected?"

The long pause before she spoke made him realize how difficult it was for her to think of anything beyond Avery Bullard. "I don't know, Mr. Caswell. He had never made a definite decision."

"But you knew the man that was in his mind." It was a statement rather than a question.

"I could only guess."

"Will you tell me your guess, Miss Martin?"

He saw her hand start to tremble but before his sympathy made him withdraw the question her fingers had tightened around the steering wheel.

"It would have been Mr. Walling."

Walling? Perhaps she was right. He had been thinking of Shaw as his executive vice-president, but it might well be that Walling was the right choice. Yes, Walling's abilities would be a better complement to his own. Walling knew the design and manufacturing side and had a good understanding of sales, too . . . where he would most need help.

"Thank you, Miss Martin. I can't tell you how much I appreciate your—well, your helpfulness."

She avoided his eyes but, under the circumstances, there was nothing strange about that. It was thoroughly understandable. She had been Avery Bullard's secretary for many years . . . close to him . . . yes, even closer than he had realized before. Miss Martin would be a great help . . . a very great help . . . as soon as she could accept the fact that Avery Bullard was dead.

He held the door for her as she got out of the car. It was, beyond an innate gesture of gentlemanly courtesy, an expression of genuine respect.

KENT COUNTY, MARYLAND
1.57 P.M. EDT

"I beg your pardon," Frederick Alderson called for the second time.

The long legs of the man on the porch of Teel's Store unwound slowly. He opened only one eye, saving the other from the bright sun, and a prodigious yawn created a startling cavern in his gray-stubbled face.

"Sorry to disturb you," Alderson said, "but I'm afraid that I'm lost. Would you happen to know where Mr. Jesse Grimm lives?"

A slow grin puckered the man's face. "Well, mister, you ain't so lost as some I've seen. Tell you what now—you see this here road right along to the side of the store? You just take that road and you keep on a-going till you can't go no more and that there's Captain Jesse's place. You can't miss it on account it's got a fresh painted house and he's a-building a new shop. No sir, mister, you ain't so lost as you thought you were. Tain't more'n a mile down there to Captain Jesse's."

"Thank you very much," Frederick Alderson said.

Only a mile. Then he would be talking to Jesse. That would be his last chance. He had failed once . . . Dudley had gotten into Shaw's office before he could catch him. He dared not fail again!

MILLBURGH, PENNSYLVANIA
2.05 P.M. EDT

Mary Walling was acutely conscious of the atmosphere of
hair-trigger apprehension that hung over the stiffly seated group
in the library of the old Tredway mansion. The conversation
that had filled these first few minutes was forced and aimless,
without point or purpose. There had been, of course, no open
acknowledgment by anyone of what would be decided here this
afternoon—and she sensed that there would be no such acknowledgment, even after the decision was made—yet she was
sure that all of the others secretly shared her awareness that,
before they left his room, the new president of the Tredway
Corporation would be selected.

There had been no lessening of Mary Walling's earlier fear
that her own happiness would be jeopardized if her husband
moved up to the presidency, but that threat had been overbal-
anced by the later-rising and even more terrifying fear of what
the effect on Don might be if he were to lose what he now
so clearly regarded as the fulfillment of his own destiny. She
knew that he could never be happy now without it—and his
happiness was a prerequisite of her own.

The moment she and Don had entered the room, Mary Walling's apprehension had been aroused by the way that Loren Shaw had already pre-empted a seat beside the desk, as close to Julia Tredway Prince as it was possible for anyone to be. When, a moment later, George Caswell had come in with Erica Martin, Shaw had adroitly maneuvered Caswell into a chair between his own and Dudley's. Thus—partly by accident and partly, she was sure, by Shaw's design—Don now sat alone facing the shoulder-to-shoulder solidarity of Shaw, Caswell and Dudley. She knew that the three had lunched together and it was only too clear that the addition of Julia Tredway Prince's vote was all they needed to make Loren Shaw president. Don had said he was sure of Mrs. Prince's support, but Mary Walling found it difficult to share her husband's certainty. There had been nothing beyond simple courtesy in the way that Mrs. Prince had greeted Don when they arrived and, during these past few minutes, Loren Shaw had been making the most of his strategic position at Julia Tredway Prince's side.

Feeling herself an outsider—almost an observer with no right of participation—Mary Walling had slipped back into the corner behind her husband. She realized too late that his face was hidden from her view—by then Erica Martin had already taken the chair in the opposite corner—but there was the compensating advantage of being able to watch the room from his viewpoint and to see every glance that was sent in his direction by any of the others.

Of one thing she was now certain—Loren Shaw wasn't thinking of Don as his competitor in the battle for the presidency. The way that Shaw's eyes stabbed toward her husband when Alderson's name had been mentioned by George Caswell made it clear that Shaw regarded Don as only the lieutenant of his real adversary.

"I, too, am sorry that Mr. Alderson isn't here," Julia Tredway Prince said. "You weren't able to locate him, were you, Mr. Walling?"

Don shook his head in silence and Mary Walling wished that she could see his eyes, wondering whether he was aware as she was that Julia Tredway Prince's remark had been the first admission, even by indirection, that there was a purpose behind the invitation that had brought them together—and aware, too, of the implications of Shaw's glance.

If Julia Tredway Prince's remark had really been purposeful, the purpose was quickly abandoned. She turned to George Caswell and again asked a question that seemingly had no point except to force conversation. "I understand that you flew over, Mr. Caswell?"

"Yes—and quite luxuriously. A friend of mine was good enough to give me the use of his company's plane for the day."

"You know that's getting to be quite a thing," Dudley burst out as if he had withstood the restraint of silence as long as possible, "—all these presidents of big companies having their own private planes. I was on this NAM committee last year—had a meeting down at New Orleans—and three of the big boys came down in their own planes. Man, that would really be the life, having your own plane!"

Shaw cleared his throat. "I should think it might be an extravagance that would be a little difficult to justify to the stockholders."

"Oh, I don't know," Caswell said in mild rebuttal. "There has to be some way to compensate a corporation president adequately these days. It's hardly possible to do it with salary alone, income taxes being what they are."

Julia Tredway Prince looked up at her husband who was lounging against the doorframe. "Dwight and I met a man in Jamaica last winter who had flown down in his own plane. He was the president of some steel company—remember, Dwight?"

Dwight Prince's long face contorted in a forced grin. "Yes, he'd traded a duodenal ulcer for a DC 3—which hardly makes me think he'd gotten the best of it. As a matter of fact—" he hesitated as if he were enjoying the attention he was receiving,"—it's a little difficult for me to understand why any man would want to be the president of a large corporation these days. As far as I'm concerned it's one of the least rewarding forms of suicide."

Mary Walling was not surprised to see Shaw's head snap up

and her husband's shoulders square, but she was puzzled by George Caswell's squinting frown.

"Oh, hardly as bad as that," Caswell said, his poise quickly recovered. "In a properly organized corporation, with adequate delegation of authority, there's no reason why the right man should be under too great a strain."

"The right man," Shaw repeated as if it were a point to be driven home. "And it does take the right man these days—a very different type of man than was required in the past."

There was a warning in Shaw's purposeful tone and Mary Walling glanced anxiously at the back of her husband's head. His shoulders were hunched and he seemed to have no interest in anything except his clasped hands.

"I'm not certain that I understand you, Mr. Shaw," Julia Tredway Prince said.

Shaw seemed surprised. "It's the point that I made last evening."

There was something close to shock in Caswell's quick side glance, but Shaw was looking at Mrs. Prince and didn't see it.

"Oh, yes," Mrs. Prince said. "It's quite an interesting theory. You see—well, suppose you explain it to the others, Mr. Shaw."

There was the stillness of tense expectancy and Mary Walling saw Loren Shaw shake out a fresh handkerchief. It was the second time that she had seen him do the same thing during the bare five minutes they had been in the room.

"Well, it's a bit more than a theory," Shaw said. "The point I was making was that—well, there was a time, of course, when most of our company presidents came up on the manufacturing side of the business. In those days that was excellent preparation for general executive responsibility, because most of the problems that came to the president's desk were concerned with manufacturing. Later, as distribution problems became more important, we sometimes saw a president rise from the sales organization—and again that was quite appropriate. Today, however, we have a very different situation. The problems that come to the president's office are predominantly *financial* in character. Matters concerning manufacturing and distribution

[323]

are largely handled at lower levels in the organization. The president—who we must always remember is the agent of the stockholders—must now concern himself largely with the primary interest of the stockholders."

"And the typical stockholder isn't interested in anything but dividends?" Julia Tredway Prince asked, more as a prompt than a question.

"Exactly," Shaw said. "Of course you're an exception, Mrs. Prince. You still have what we might call a sense of *ownership*. The average stockholder doesn't think of his stockholdings as ownership—any more than he thinks of himself as the part owner of the bank where he has a savings account—or the part owner of the government because he has some Defense bonds. When he buys Tredway stock he makes an *investment*. The only reason he makes it is to get a return. Thus, at the top level, the corporation must now be governed to be what its owners want it to be—a *financial institution* in which they can invest their money and receive a safe return with the emphasis on *safety*. As a matter of fact—well, you know this, Mr. Caswell —there isn't one stockholder out of ten who could even name the cities where we have our principal factories."

"You're absolutely right," George Caswell said—and the strength of the support that he offered Shaw made Mary Walling feel the hard clutch of despair. "There's no doubt that the emphasis in corporation management has gone over on the financial side. I'm sure that's why it has become so common during these last few years for men to step from investment or banking into corporation management."

Loren Shaw hesitated as if his caution had been aroused, but then quickly went ahead. "Yes, there have been cases like that —where a corporation was so unfortunate as to find itself without a major executive who was trained in financial control and modern management methods. More typically, of course, there's such a man available right within the organization."

It was a direct bid, a challenge, a throwing down of the gauntlet, and Mary Walling's heart sank as she saw that her husband wasn't going to respond. She leaned far forward attempting to see the expression on his face and, looking up, her eyes met Julia Tredway Prince's.

"Oh, Mrs. Walling, you aren't very comfortable there, are you?" Mrs. Prince said quickly. "Won't you come up here?"

It was an invitation that could not be denied and as Mary Walling moved forward Julia Tredway Prince rose from the chair behind the desk and she sat down beside her on the sofa in front of the window.

"I don't know that I get you completely, Loren," Walt Dudley said in a petulant grumble. "I can see that we have to keep the stockholders happy—got to earn a profit—but I don't see how you can say that selling isn't important—or manufacturing either."

"Of course they're important," Shaw said, his voice tinged with the forbearance of a teacher for a not-so-bright pupil. "But don't you see, Walt, they're not ends in themselves, only the means to the end. Then, too, it's a matter of management levels. As I said a moment ago, by the time you get to the presidential level, the emphasis must be predominantly financial. Take income tax as only one example. To a far greater degree than most people realize, income tax has become a primary governing factor in corporation management. In our own case—well, over the past year I've devoted a substantial amount of time to the development of a new relationship between the parent company and some of our wholly owned subsidiaries in order to give us a more favorable tax situation. Here's the point—that one piece of work, all purely financial in character, will contribute more to our net earnings than the total profit we'll make from one of our smaller factories.

"Take another example—one that I'm sure will interest Mr. Walling. Don and his associates have done a very capable job of reducing cost on our finishing operation at Water Street—producing some very nice savings—but, unfortunately, it will add little to our net earnings, less than a quarter as much as we will gain from a new accounting procedure that I was fortunate enough to get the government to approve in connection with the depreciation of the assets of our lumber company. Do you

[325]

see what I mean, Walt—that top management has to be largely financial these days?"

Dudley said something and Shaw went on talking, but Mary Walling's ears were blocked with the realization that Don's hopes were blasted. What Shaw said was true. The world was changing. The Bullards were defeated and the Shaws were inheriting the earth. The accountants and the calculators had risen to power. The slide rule had become the scepter. The world was being overrun with the ever-spawning swarm of figure-jugglers who were fly-specking the earth with their decimal points, proving over and over again that nothing mattered except what could be proved true by a clerk with a Comptometer.

Julia Tredway Prince cleared her throat. "Are you suggesting, Mr. Shaw, that there's no place any more for corporation presidents of Mr. Bullard's type?"

It was the first mention of Avery Bullard's name and it came like an unexpected clap of thunder. Every eye in the room was on Loren Shaw. Even Don Walling, as Mary noticed gratefully, was watching him sharply.

Shaw was balling his handkerchief in the palm of his right hand but his voice, when he spoke after a moment's hesitation, carried no trace of the nervous tension that his fingers betrayed. "I was speaking in general terms, of course—not specifically about the Tredway Corporation."

"I'd still be interested in having your viewpoint," Julia Tredway Prince said pleasantly. "I'm sure the others would, too."

The handkerchief was a hard ball, tight-clutched in Shaw's hand, but his voice was still carefully casual. "No one can deny that men of Mr. Bullard's type played a great part in our industrial past. They belonged to an important phase of our commercial history. I would be the first to acknowledge the great debt that we owe Mr. Bullard for his leadership in the initial formation and early development of the Tredway Corporation."

The way in which Shaw had relegated Avery Bullard to the distant past was so purposeful that Mary Walling was certain that Don couldn't have missed it. She glanced at him and caught the fading of an odd half-smile that seemed to recall some memory in her mind, yet despite the quick, frantic racking of her brain she could not remember when she had seen it before, nor what special meaning it had in the lexicon of their intimacy. Then, suddenly, she forgot everything else in the realization that Don was about to speak, that he was going to fight back. Hopeless or not, he would make the try! She knew that the effort might make his defeat all the more bitter, but that realization could not dim the elation that made her heart pound wildly as she waited for his first words.

"As I get your point, Loren," Don said, "you're maintaining that Avery Bullard was the right man to build the company, but now that the company has been built we need a different type of management in order to make the company produce the maximum amount of profit for the stockholders."

Mary Walling watched her husband intently, surprised at his composure. She had been expecting the flare of half-anger but his voice was cleanly dispassionate.

Shaw, too, seemed surprised, his hesitance betraying his search for a hidden trap. "I don't know that I'd express it in exactly those terms—but, yes, that's substantially what I mean."

An expectant hush had fallen over the room and George Caswell broke it by saying nervously, an undertone of near-embarrassment shading his voice. "I don't know that this is anything we have to thresh out here today—too soon for any of us to see the situation clearly. After all—" He had glanced at his wrist watch and suddenly stiffened, his eyes fixed and staring, and there was a long pause before he said in a low voice. "Coincidence, of course—happened to look at my watch —exactly two-thirty."

Mary saw other blank looks that matched her own.

"Just twenty-four hours," Caswell said in whispered explanation. "He died yesterday at two-thirty."

Mary Walling's heart sank—afraid that Don had lost his chance, afraid that the cloud of grief that now shadowed the room could not be broken. Then she heard Julia Tredway

Prince say, "Avery Bullard is dead. Nothing can change that, no matter how long we wait to talk about it."

There was strength in her voice but when she turned Mary saw, in puzzling contrast, that there was a mist of tears in her eyes. She knew what Julia had done—that she had purposefully saved the situation for Don—and she felt the warmth of a gratitude that was chilled only by the sensing of her own failure in not having been able to do for her husband what another woman had done.

But one thing was now clear. Don had been right about Julia Tredway Prince's support. With her vote and Alderson's, he needed only one more. Where would it come from? Her eyes polled the faces of the three men who sat facing him . . . Shaw, Caswell, and Dudley . . . close-shouldered and resolute. What could Don possibly do to break through the barrier of their tight-woven opposition.

Unexpectedly, it was Dwight Prince who spoke. "I've often wondered about men like Mr. Bullard. He was a great deal like my father, you know—willing to give his whole life to a company—lay everything on the altar like a sacrifice to the god of business. I've often asked myself what drives them to do it—whether they ever stop to ask themselves if what they get is worth the price. I don't suppose they do."

"It's accomplishment that keeps a man going," Dudley said in his sales-meeting voice. "That's what I always tell my boys—it isn't the money that counts, it's that old feeling of accomplishment."

An enigmatic smile narrowed Don Walling's eyes as he looked intently at Loren Shaw. "Going back to this question of the kind of a management that you think the company ought to have from here on out, Loren—the kind of a management that measures its accomplishment entirely in terms of return to the stockholders. We'd need a strong man to head up that kind of a management, wouldn't we?"

A faint flush warmed Loren Shaw's neck. "Of course."

"And it would be a big job, even for an able man? He'd have

to throw himself into it—make a good many personal sacrifices in order to do a job?"

Shaw hesitated, wary and unblinking. "If he were the right man there'd be no worry on that score."

"What incentive would he have?" Don Walling demanded, and for the first time there was the sharp crackle of attack in his voice. "You will grant that there'd have to be an incentive?"

Loren Shaw forced a cold smile. "I'd say that sixty thousand a year might be considered something of an incentive."

"You would?" Don Walling's voice was whiplashed with astonishment. "Do you really think a man of that caliber would be willing to sell his life for money—for what would be left out of sixty thousand a year after taxes?"

Dwight Prince's tongue-in-cheek voice cut in unexpectedly. "You could always give him his own plane as a bonus."

The flush on Shaw's neck spread like a seeping stain. "Of course there's more than money involved."

"What?" Don Walling demanded. "What Walt just called a sense of accomplishment? Would that satisfy you, Loren? Just suppose that you were the man—that you were the president of the Tredway Corporation."

Mary Walling's heart stood still as her body stiffened to the shock wave of what Don had said. She had not expected this . . . that it would be brought out in the open . . . and the taut silence made it plain that the others hadn't expected it either.

Don Walling leaned forward. "Suppose that you were to spend the next twenty years—all the rest of your working life —in doing what you say needs to be done. Would you be satisfied to measure your life's work by how much you had raised the dividend? Would you regard your life as a success if you'd managed to get the dividend up to three dollars—or four—or five or six or seven? Is that what you want engraved on your tombstone when you die—the dividend record of the Tredway Corporation?"

The blood-color had crept out over the mask of Shaw's face,

but Mary Walling saw that it was not the flush of an embarrassment that acknowledged defeat, but the stain of an anger born out of desperation.

Like a fighter at bay, Shaw tried to escape the attack with a diversion. "That's all very well, Mr. Walling—to take the high-minded attitude that money isn't important—but how far do you think you'd get next month if you offered the union negotiators a sense of accomplishment instead of the six cents an hour they're demanding?"

George Caswell grimaced, shifting uneasily in his chair. Mary Walling could sense his disappointment at Shaw's weak evasion of the issue. Had Don seen it, too? Did he realize that Caswell might be split away from Shaw—that Caswell might give him the one vote that was all he needed?

Don Walling's eyes were still on Shaw. "What sense of accomplishment would you offer them—the wonderful hope that if they passed up a raise and sweated their guts out to make that production line run a little faster, that we might be able to raise the dividend from two dollars to two dollars and ten cents?"

There had been a smile in his voice, dulling the edge of his sarcasm, but now as his eyes left Shaw and fanned the whole room his words were soberly measured. "I don't want to be facetious about this—it's too serious for that. Loren's right when he says that we have an obligation to our stockholders—but it's a bigger obligation than just paying dividends. We have to keep this company *alive*. That's the important thing—and a company is like a man. No man can work for money alone. It isn't enough. You starve his soul when you try it—and you can starve a company to death in the same way. Yes, I know—sometimes our men in the factories give us the impression that all they want is another raise in wages—and then another and another and another. They make us think that getting more money is all that matters to them. But can we blame them for that? God knows, we've done our best to try to make them believe that money is the only measure of accomplishment that matters to us.

"Look at what we did this last year with what we called a

[330]

'communications program.' We put out a movie that analyzed our financial report and had meetings in all the plants. The men weren't much interested in our financial report—we knew that to begin with, it was the premise we started from—so what did we do? We tried to *force* them into being interested. We disguised the dollars as cartoons—little cartoon dollars that jumped into workers' pocketbooks—other little cartoon dollars that dragged in piles of lumber and built factories—and a big fat dollar that took a trip to Washington and was gobbled up by Uncle Sam. Oh, it was all very clever—even won some kind of an award as an outstanding example of how to promote industrial understanding. Understanding? Do you know what it forced our men to understand? Only one thing—the terrible, soul-killing fact that dollars were all that mattered to the management of this company—dollars—dollars and nothing else."

"But that program was Mr. Bullard's own idea," Shaw cut in like a quick knife thrust.

Mary Walling had been so completely swept along that her guard had dropped and Shaw's interruption came as a shocking surprise. Her eyes flashed to her husband. Had he been caught off guard, too?

"No, I don't think we can call that Mr. Bullard's idea alone," Don Walling said. "It's something that's in the air today—the groping of a lot of men at the top of industry who know they've lost something, but aren't quite sure what it is—nor exactly how they happened to lose it. Mr. Bullard was one of those men. He'd been so busy building a great production machine that he'd lost sight of why he was building it—if he ever really knew. Perhaps he didn't."

Julia Tredway Prince's voice, so close to Mary Walling's ears that even a whisper seemed like an explosion in the silence, asked, "Do *you* know, Mr. Walling?"

Mary Walling held her breath through the moment of silence. Could he answer that question? A smile flickered on his face . . . that same tantalizingly familiar smile that she hadn't been able to identify before. Now suddenly, she remembered when she had seen it before . . . that night when he had finally designed their house . . . when, after all of his groping and fumbling had frightened her almost to the point of losing faith in him, he had suddenly made everything come right and clear.

"Yes, I think I do," he said. "You see, to Mr. Bullard, business was a game—a very serious game, but still a game—the way war is a game to a soldier. He was never much concerned about money for its own sake. I remember his saying once that dollars were just a way of keeping score. I don't think he was too much concerned about personal power, either—just power for power's sake. I know that's the easy way to explain the drive that any great man has—the lust for power—but I don't think that was true of Avery Bullard. The thing that kept him going was his terrific pride in himself—the driving urge to do things that no other man on earth could do. He saved the company when everyone else had given up. He built a big corporation in an industry where everyone said that only small companies could succeed. He was only happy when he was doing the impossible—and he did that only to satisfy his own pride. He never asked for applause and appreciation—or even for understanding. He was a lonely man but I don't think his loneliness ever bothered him very much. He was the man at the top of the tower—figuratively as well as literally. That's what he wanted. That's what it took to satisfy his pride. That was his strength—but of course that was his weakness, too."

Mary Walling listened in amazement. Where were those words coming from . . . those words that he could never have said before but were now falling so easily from his lips? Was that actually Don who was talking . . . the same man who had never been able to answer those dark-of-night questions before?

She watched him as he rose from his chair and in the act of standing he seemed a giant breaking shackles that had held him to the earth . . . shaking loose the ties that had bound him to the blind worship of Avery Bullard. He stood alone now . . . free.

"There was one thing that Avery Bullard never understood," Don Walling went on. "He never realized that other men had to be proud, too—that the force behind a great company had to

[332]

be more than the pride of one man—that it had to be the pride of thousands of men. A company is like an army—it fights on its pride. You can't win wars with paychecks. In all the history of the world there's never been a great army of mercenaries. You can't pay a man enough to make him lay down his life. He wants more than money. Maybe Avery Bullard knew that once —maybe he'd just forgotten it—but that's where he made his mistake. He was a little lost these last few years. He'd won his fight to build a great company. The building was over—at least for the time being. There had to be something else to satisfy his pride—bigger sales—more profit—something. That's when we started doing things like making the sixteen-hundred series."

He turned and confronted Dudley. "Are your boys proud when they sell the sixteen-hundred series—when they know that the finish is going to crack and the veneer split off and the legs come loose?"

"But that's price merchandise," Dudley said in fumbling defense. "There's a need for it. We're not cheating anyone. At that price the customers know that they can't get—"

"How do you suppose the men in the factory feel when they make it?" Don Walling demanded. His eyes shifted from Dudley to Shaw. "What do you imagine they think of a management that's willing to stoop to selling that kind of junk in order to add a penny a year to the dividend? Do you know that there are men at Pike Street who have refused to work on the sixteen-hundred line—that there are men who have taken a cut of four cents an hour to get transferred to something else?"

"No, I wasn't aware of that," Shaw said—and the weakness of his voice signaled the first thin crack in his armor. "I don't suppose it would hurt too much if we dropped that line. After all, it's a small part of our business."

A voice in Mary Walling's mind wanted to shout out at her husband, urging him to drive in for the kill that would clinch his victory. Couldn't he see that Shaw was defeated . . . that Caswell was nodding his approval . . . that Walt Dudley was waiting only to be commanded?

But Don Walling turned, looking out of the window, and his

voice seemed faraway as if it were coming from the top of the distant white shaft of the Tredway Tower. "Yes, we'll drop that line. We'll never again ask a man to do anything that will poison his pride in himself. We'll have a new line of low-priced furniture someday—a different kind of furniture—as different from anything we're making now as a modern automobile is different from an old Mills wagon. When we get it, then we'll really start to grow."

His voice came back into the room. "We talk about Tredway being a big company now. It isn't. We're kidding ourselves. Yes, we're one of the biggest furniture manufacturers but what does it mean? Nothing! Furniture is close to a two-billion-dollar industry but it's all split up among thirty-six hundred manufacturers. We have about three per cent of the total—that's all, just three per cent. Look at other industries—the percentage that the top manufacturer has. What if General Motors had sat back and stopped growing when it had three per cent of the automobile industry? We haven't even started to grow! Suppose we get fifteen per cent of the total—and why not, it's been done in a dozen industries? Fifteen per cent and the Tredway Corporation will be five times as big as it is today. All right, I know it hasn't been done before in the furniture business, but does that mean we can't do it? No—because that's exactly what we *are* going to do!"

His voice had built to a crescendo, to the moment that demanded the shout of an answering chorus—and then in the instant before the sound could have broken through the shock of silence, Mary Walling saw a tension-breaking smile on her husband's face. In the split second that it took her eyes to sweep the room, she saw that the smile was mirrored in all the faces that looked up at him . . . even in the face of Loren Shaw.

She had sensed, a few minutes before, that Shaw was defeated, but she had expected a last struggle, a final flare of resistance. It had not come. Instinctively, she understood what had happened. In that last moment, Loren Shaw had suddenly become aware that his brain had been set aflame by a spark from Don Walling's mind—a spark that he himself could never have supplied. Now he was fired to accomplishments that had been far beyond the limits of his imagination. Mary Walling understood the faintly bewildered quality of Shaw's smile, because she, too—long ago—had found it mysteriously strange that Don's mind was so unlike her own.

George Caswell was standing, extending his hand. "We're all behind you, Don. I can promise you that."

"Yes sir, Don, you bet we are!" Walt Dudley boomed.

Shaw shook hands silently but it was a gesture that needed no words to make it a pledge of loyalty.

And now Julia Tredway Prince was standing, too. "I think the occasion calls for a toast. Dwight, would you mind—yes, Nina, what is it?"

Nina was standing in the doorway. "There's a telephone call for Mr. Walling. The gentleman says it's very urgent."

Dwight Prince stepped forward. "There's an extension in the back hall. Come and I'll show you."

Mary saw that Julia was about to speak to her but George Caswell stepped up as an interruption.

"I'm afraid I'll have to run along. The plane's waiting and I—well, I have to be back in New York for a wedding at six. I'll be down on Monday, of course."

"And you'll stay over for the board meeting on Tuesday," Julia said.

"As far as I'm concerned, it's all settled now," George Caswell said. "But you're quite right—we do need the formal action of the board."

Mary realized that at some missed moment Julia's hand had found her own and that the world had become an out-of-focus haze filled with drifting faces and floating words . . . Shaw . . . Dudley . . . Erica Martin . . . all saying the same unsaid thing in a different way . . . and then, slowly, the consciousness dawned that there was another voice saying something else and the voice seemed to come from the warm, tight-holding grip that held her hand. She was alone with Julia Tredway Prince.

"You should be very proud, Mary."

"I am—but frightened, too."

"Because you don't understand him?"

She felt her mind go blank with amazement. How could Julia Tredway Prince know . . . how could anyone know?

"Don't worry about it, my dear," Julia said. "You'll never understand him completely. Don't try. You'll be happier if you don't. He'll be happier, too. Not understanding will make you very lonely sometimes, Mary—when he shuts you away behind a closed door—when you think he's forgotten you—but then the door will open and he'll come back and you'll know how fortunate you were to have been his wife."

"I know, I know," she murmured, making no move to wipe away the tears in her own eyes because she saw that there were untouched tears in the eyes of Julia Tredway Prince. It was only after her memory echoed what Julia had said that she realized those last words had been in the past tense. Was it possible that Julia had . . . ?

There was the interruption of a sound like distant wind chimes.

Nina stood before them, uncertainly, holding a tray filled with glasses and an opened bottle of champagne. "Mr. Prince said to bring eight glasses, but—"

"Thank you, Nina." Julia took the tray from her hands and put it gently on the desk.

As her hand touched the offered glass, Mary Walling understood, for one fleeting instant, the miracle of her husband's mind. Now it had happened to her! She knew without knowing why she knew . . . and as if it were something done in a dream she was raising her glass and saying, "To Avery Bullard."

There was a long moment, a moment that could not be filled with old tears or old wine, but only with the silence of two women who shared a secret that bridged the ending of one world and the beginning of another.

"Thank you," Julia said.

When Don Walling came back into the room they were standing at the window that looked out on the Tredway

Tower. It had been a long time since there had been a word between them. There had been no need for words.

They turned together.

"Sorry it took so long," he said. "There was some trouble about the connection. The others go?"

Julia nodded. "Is Dwight coming back?"

"I believe he's still talking to Walt Dudley. I heard their voices in the garden. Loren Shaw is driving George Caswell out to the airport."

"That was Fred Alderson on the phone," Don Walling said. "You know, he did the darndest thing—drove all the way down to Maryland to see Jesse Grimm. Good thing he did—cleared up a misunderstanding—but I can't imagine why he'd go to all of that trouble for me."

Julia's eyes twinkled with taunting amusement. "Of course it's possible that he didn't do it for you—he might have done it for the company."

His face slowly softened into a boyish grin and, even without understanding, Mary Walling's heart raced exultantly when she heard him laugh and say, "All right, I'll learn. Just give me a little time."

He hadn't changed! He would never change . . . she must never think that he would. Julia was right . . . don't try to understand him . . . yes, that had always been her trouble. It was only when she had tried to understand him that she had been afraid. She would never be afraid again . . . never!

3.20 P.M. EDT

Slowly, the on-edge platter of the earth fell back to a sensible horizontal and George Caswell eased back into his seat. The plane, he reasoned, had taken a long climbing turn into the southwest wind and now they were passing over Millburgh again, heading east. They were only a few hundred feet above the earth—perhaps as much as a thousand now—but the city had taken on a very different look, dwarfed to inconsequence

[337]

by the widening rim of the horizon. The Tredway Tower, which his eyes sought out as the center point of orientation, had become startlingly insignificant. In truth, as he now saw, it was not a tower at all.

The brown band of the muddy river slipped past the edge of the porthole and the earth, rising to the high land beyond the cliff edge, lifted the airport into the sharp focus of his eyes. The plane that he had noticed beside the runway before their take-off was now a yellow insect feeding on the green earth . . . and the black bug that crawled toward the thin gray line of the highway was Loren Shaw's car.

A smile began to form on George Caswell's face, wavering and indeterminate, undecided between amusement and compassion. There was, as always, the temptation to smile at these very earnest young men like Loren Shaw who took life so seriously, yet you couldn't help feeling a little sorry for them, too. There were so many things they didn't understand . . . why Don was so different . . . different because of something that you couldn't reason into credibility . . . something that was beyond explaining with words . . . as a Beethoven Symphony was beyond explaining with the rules of harmony, or a Cézanne painting with a recital of the theory of composition.

It was discouraging, of course, when you were young and ambitious to be forced to recognize that you were not one of those chosen few . . . but when you were older and wiser it was a great comfort to know that there were still men like that being born, that the cult of mediocrity had not yet sterilized the womb of the earth . . . that it never would . . . that there would always be men like Avery Bullard and Don Walling and all the others who were the builders of great companies and great institutions and great nations. No, all of the men who sat at the tops of all of the towers were not men of that stripe . . . there weren't enough to go around . . . so there were the fakirs and the charlatans, too . . . the hangers-on, the jackals and the vultures . . . the Bruce Pilchers.

George Caswell's smile hardened with grim satisfaction as he thought of how shocked Shaw had been when he had told him about what Pilcher had done. He had been right to tell him . . . yes, that was a part of Shaw's education . . . learning that there were men like that . . . the money-mad and the greed-crazed . . . not as many as the public thought there were, but still enough so that a man had to be taught to be on his guard . . . not, of course, that Shaw needed that kind of teaching but still it was a lesson that it didn't hurt anyone to learn.

Yes, Shaw was a good man . . . but a little naive, too . . . worrying that Walling might have gotten the wrong impression because he had pushed so hard for recognition of the impor- tance of financial management. No need to worry . . . a presi- dent expected his vice-presidents to push their specialties . . . and Shaw had been right . . . the financial side of the business was important . . . required a lot of attention. They would never be able to finance those ideas of Walling's out of earnings alone. There would have to be a lot of securities sold . . . a debenture issue this fall . . . probably another next year . . . common as soon as the market looked right for it.

Unconsciously, George Caswell's habit-trained fingers had reached for his notebook and slipped out the little gold pencil that was tucked in its pin-seal cover. He flipped a page and the blank paper suggested a note. He wrote it—a reminder to speak to Kitty about inviting the Wallings to come over for a week- end . . . sometime soon . . . but not this next weekend or the one after . . . wait until the Whaler's Cup races were out of the way.

3.32 P.M. EDT

Stealthily, like an invader in his own home, J. Walter Dudley tiptoed across the dining room and opened the kitchen door, opening it only wide enough at first to make certain that he was alone. Then, assured, he stood and stared into the coldly gleam- ing room, waiting for its reflected whiteness to burn the black shadows out of his mind.

[339]

His heart slowed its beat. He could breathe again. Resolutely, he walked to the far wall and opened the little white-enameled door. His closed hand reached in, the fingers opened and a crumpled wad of yellow paper fell down the black shaft. Almost instantly, there was the quick light of a distant flame as the incinerator consumed the telegram.

With the flash of the flame there was the flash of regret that he had not read it once more. But there was no need of that. He could remember. He would always remember. He could read it any time he wanted to read it. It would always be in his mind.

MR J WALTER DUDLEY

TREDWAY CORPORATION MILLBURGH PA

MY DEEPEST SYMPATHY FOR THE LOSS THAT THE ENTIRE INDUS-
TRY HAS SUSTAINED IN THE DEATH OF A GREAT MAN

EVA HARDING

MILLBURGH, PENNSYLVANIA
3.43 P.M. EDT

Erica Martin's hand burrowed into the drawer, her ringless fingers sliding smoothly down through the slickness of crepe and satin and the woolly warmth of cashmere until, at last, her fingertips found the hard coolness of the glass and the yielding softness of the leather frame.

Gently, she lifted it from hiding. Avery Bullard had never known that she had kept this picture. It was a print that he had rejected from several that a New York photographer had made. He had studied it the longest of all but in the end he had tossed it across the desk and said, "Better get rid of that one, Miss Martin. Makes me look too damned human. Don't dare give people the wrong idea, you know." Then he had laughed and she had laughed and there had been so few times when they had ever laughed together that she remembered all of them, but this time more than the others . . . remembering it too often and

[340]

too vividly when the picture had been on the mantel. That was why she had hidden it away months ago.

Her arms lifted the picture and her inner voice, clearer than her lips could have spoken said, "Don't be angry with me, Avery, because I guessed that it would be Don Walling. I knew you never wanted me to guess what was in your mind—I don't know why you wanted it that way but I know you did—but this time I *had* to admit that I knew. There was no other way. Don't you see that? And I was right, wasn't I?"

He understood. He was human. Why had he been so afraid to admit it? Why had they both been so afraid?

NEW YORK CITY
3.50 P.M. EDT

The crotchety old man in the florist shop looked at the twenty-dollar bill doubtfully, rubbing the water stain with the ball of his thumb, finally deciding that he would take a chance. "That'll be twelve-sixty all together for everything—the flowers and sending them to this place in Pennsylvania. You want to put in a card, miss, you'll find one over there at the desk."

Anne Finnick looked at all the cards. There was an awful pretty one that was just right . . . a picture of one of those big boats and seagulls flying and everybody waving like they were saying goodbye . . . and the printing said BON VOYAGE TO A WONDERFUL FRIEND. *Bon Voyage* was French. It meant like when somebody was going away. That's what he was doing, wasn't it? He'd like it being French. All of those rich people were crazy about French.

3.55 P.M. EDT

Luigi Cassoni knew that he was a fortunate man. Not only was he blessed by having most of his prayers answered, but also he was lucky. When a man was not very bright it was a great comfort to know that he was lucky. There seemed to be a connection. If he had been bright it would not have taken him so long to count the money that he had collected for Mr. Bullard's flowers and to write all of the names on a piece of paper. But if he had been able to do it quickly, he would not have been there to take Mr. Walling and his wife to the twenty-fourth floor. That had been a very important thing to do. When the old Duke had died without a son to take his place, the men who sat by the fountain in the Via Torrenzo had shaken their heads and said that it would be bad. They had been right. That spring the olives had been only half as heavy on the trees as they had been when there was a Duke in the castle—and that was the year when not one of Pietro's ewes had twin lambs—and when Angelino ran away to marry a Sicilian, and Maria's burro fell from the cliff and was killed on the rocks at the sea. There was not a man in the village who had lived long enough to remember when there had been so many misfortunes in a single spring.

Yes, Luigi decided, he was a very lucky man to live in a country where there was always a new duke for the castle.

A shadow crossed Luigi's mind, fast-moving like the earth shadow of a sea cloud crossing the Via Torrenzo, when the wind was from the Mediterranean. It was too bad that the carillon could not ring but that was one of the things that was not understood in America . . . that the bells could sound both grief and joy at the same time.

3.56 P.M. EDT

In those first few moments after they had entered the office that had been Avery Bullard's, Mary Walling felt that there was something almost improper in their presence, that they were guilty of irreverence in thus entering the precincts of death. She knew that Don had felt it, too, because he had said obliquely, "I don't actually move up until Tuesday, of course."

"I'm glad you brought me," she said. "Now I'll be able to imagine you here."

"Probably take a lot of imagining," he said in a tone that

asked for denial. "You never thought that anything like this would happen, did you?"

She said, "No"—because she thought it was what he wanted her to say—and then, "You were wonderful out at Julia's. I'll always remember every word that you said."

"Will you?" His arm found the curve of her waist and, looking up at him, she saw his boyish grin of confession. "You know, all the way down here I've been trying to remember what the devil I did say. I didn't make any crazy promises, did I?"

"Only a whole new world," she laughed, breathless with the hope that this moment would last, this wonderful sharing, this moment when his mind was hers, when she could completely understand.

But the door was closing. His face sobered. "God, but there's a lot to do! I suppose I should have talked to him out there at Julia's—gotten him started on some things for Monday morning."

"Who, dear?"

"Loren Shaw. He'll be executive vice-president, of course."

"He'll be——?" She stopped in astonishment.

"What's the matter?"

"Nothing. I—well, I never thought you liked him, that's all."

The door was tight-closed now. "Where did you ever get that idea? Damned capable man—Shaw. Not too much imagination, perhaps—but sometimes that's an asset. It's possible to have too much imagination around the place. I'll need somebody to help me keep my feet on the ground."

"I know," she whispered.

"Well, let's get out of here," he said, tensely impatient. "Oh —better leave a note for Miss Martin."

He found a piece of paper and a black pencil and she watched as he wrote:

Call executive committee meeting nine o'clock Monday morning.

MacDonald Walling

She heard Julia's voice . . . you'll never understand him completely . . . don't try . . . you'll be happier if you don't . . . he'll be happier, too.

Julia was right.

"Ready?" he asked.

"Ready," she said—and they walked together out into the dark corridor.

THE END